The feather felt like a wisp of silk between his fingertips, hot as a Flower's underthings and just as full of promise.

Siyon teased it out, wrapping it in a length of actual silk before tucking it away in his satchel.

He was so focused on it that he barely heard the whistle from above. Not like a bravi signal, no human sound at all; more like the sigh of air ripped through a grate. The sound of an angel's wings scything through excuses.

But he did hear it, and his body was already moving before his mind caught up, hurling him sideways a moment before the broadsword came slamming down right where he'd been crouching.

The force of it buried the edge in the rocks as though they were cheese. Flames licked blue-bright along the length of the blade. Light washed dazzling over Siyon—not from the sword, but the one who wielded it, looming above him resplendent in armour even whiter than the sand. The brutal white of perfect virtue, the unflinching white of implacable justice.

The shattering white of an angel.

Her face was a smudge in the searing light; Siyon just got an impression of a wild halo of fire around diamond eyes and hawk beak.

That beak opened and she *screamed*, like a raptor diving upon its prey.

NOTORIOUS SORCERER

The Burnished City: Book One

DAVINIA EVANS

orbit

orbitbooks.net

Copyright © 2022 by Davinia Evans
Excerpt from *The Undertaking of Hart and Mercy* copyright © 2022 by Megan Bannen

Cover design by Lisa Marie Pompilio
Cover illustrations by Shutterstock
Silhouette illustrations by Andrew Broyzna
Cover copyright © 2022 by Hachette Book Group, Inc.
Map by Sámhlaoch Swords
Author photograph by Gray Tham

Orbit
Hachette Book Group
1290 Avenue of the Americas
New York, NY 10104
orbitbooks.net

First Edition: September 2022
Simultaneously published in Great Britain by Orbit

Orbit is an imprint of Hachette Book Group.
The Orbit name and logo are trademarks of Little, Brown Book Group Limited.

The publisher is not responsible for websites (or their content) that are not owned by the publisher.

The Hachette Speakers Bureau provides a wide range of authors for speaking events. To find out more, go to www.hachettespeakersbureau.com or call (866) 376-6591.

Library of Congress Cataloging-in-Publication Data
Title: Notorious sorcerer / Davinia Evans.
Description: First edition. | New York, NY : Orbit, 2022. | Series: The burnished city
Identifiers: LCCN 2022006898 | ISBN 9780316398039 (trade paperback) | ISBN 9780316398138 (ebook)
Subjects: LCGFT: Novels. | Fantasy fiction.
Classification: LCC PR9619.4.E956 N68 2022 | DDC 823/.92—dc23/eng/20220310
LC record available at https://lccn.loc.gov/2022006898

ISBNs: 9780316398039 (trade paperback), 9780316398138 (ebook)

Printed in the United States of America

LSC-C

Printing 1, 2022

For airgiodslv (again, thirteen years later)

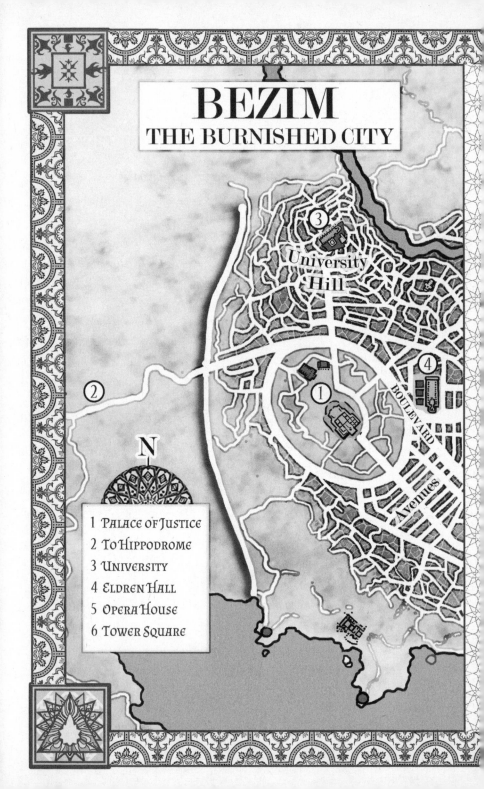

BEZIM
THE BURNISHED CITY

University Hill

BOULEVARD

Avenues

N

1 PALACE OF JUSTICE
2 TO HIPPODROME
3 UNIVERSITY
4 ELDREN HALL
5 OPERA HOUSE
6 TOWER SQUARE

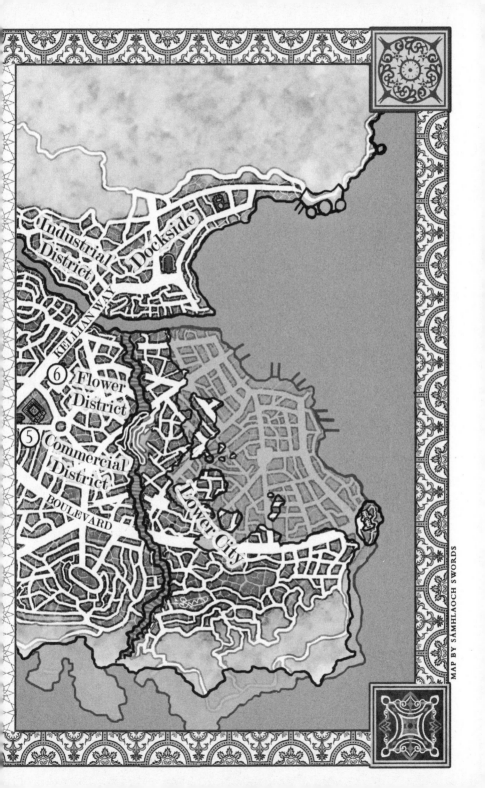

Industrial District

Dockside

KELLAIN WAY

⑥ Flower District

⑤ Commercial District

BOULEVARD

Lower City

MAP BY SÁMHLAOCH SWORDS

CHAPTER 1

Siyon couldn't get the damn square to line up, and the hangover definitely wasn't helping.

He squinted at the ash lines on the floor. The tiles tessellated in a not-quite-repeating pattern of swirls and spirals that could probably cause headaches all by itself. It was left over from before this place was taken over as the Little Bracken bravi safe house, when it had been a...temple? Church? Whatever. They called it the Chapel now, so probably one of those. Siyon didn't know much about all that religious stuff. He'd been born and bred here in Bezim, where they preferred the certainty of alchemy instead.

The building was nice; tidy brickwork, tall pitched roof, narrow windows of coloured glass. From the pale hair and impressive beards on the figures, Siyon thought the stories probably drew from the cults and myths of the North, not the remnants of the Lyraec Empire he was more familiar with.

The Chapel was quiet right now, with the morning sun cutting through the dust motes dancing around the lofty beams. The bravi were denizens of the night—the feet that rattled fleet as a passing rain shower over your roof tiles, the midnight laughter that promised mayhem and crossed blades and adventure. Last night they'd been all of that, the stuff of the dreams of children and poets, and now they were sleeping it off. So the tall, vaulted space—which might otherwise be cluttered with the scrape of a sharpening sabre, the clatter and call of training duels, the bicker and bellow of arguments over style—was all at Siyon's disposal.

He still couldn't get his delving portal square.

Siyon's tea had gone cold on a pushed-aside pew. He lifted the tin-banded glass, high and higher, until the light through the stained-glass windows both made him wince and turned the remaining liquid a fiery golden orange. A colour burning with righteousness. An *Empyreal* sort of colour.

Siyon *reached* through that connection and snapped his fingers.

And then nearly dropped the suddenly scalding glass.

Allegedly Kolah Negedi—the long-dead father of alchemical practice—had strong views about casual use of the Art. Something about the essence of another plane not being a dog to fetch your slippers. Poetic, but frankly, the great Kolah Negedi didn't seem all that applicable to the life of Siyon Velo. Let the fancy azatani alchemists, with their mahogany workbenches and expensive bespoke glass beakers, debate his wisdom. All Siyon did was fetch and carry for them. And that's all he'd ever do, unless he could scrape together enough hard cash to pay for lessons. Today's work would barely add to his stash, but one day, maybe…

In the meantime, at least he could have hot tea.

Siyon blew gently across the surface of the liquid, took a careful sip, and sighed as the blissful heat smoothed out the jagged edges of his hangover.

"Sorry," someone said. "I can come back later if you're enjoying your alone time."

Not just any someone; that was the tight, pointed accent that went with leafy avenues and elegant townhouses and lace gloves. That was an azatani voice. Siyon cracked one eye open, and looked sidelong toward the doorway.

The young woman wouldn't have come up to his chin, but she stood straight and tall, barely a trace of a girl's uncertainty in the way her weight shifted from one foot to the other. She was clad head to toe in bravi leathers—sturdy trousers, tight vest, bracers laced up to her elbows. They creaked with newness, and the sabre at her hip gleamed with oil and polish. The tricorn balanced atop her tied-back ebony curls had an orange cockade pinned on with a Little Bracken badge.

They'd probably run the tiles together, two fish in the great flickering school of the Little Bracken, but Siyon never paid too much attention to the azatani recruits. They joined, they had their youthful adventures, they left to take up their serious adult responsibilities. None of his business.

But here she was, getting in his business. "What are you doing here, za?" he demanded, though he had a bad feeling he knew the answer.

"I was sent by the Diviner Prince to…" Her words petered out, uncertainty conquering the assurance she was born into. "Er. Assist you? Hold something?"

Siyon snorted. "I need an anchor, not a little bird. Go back and tell Daruj—"

"No," she interrupted, her chin coming up in a belligerent jut. "I can do it. I'm bravi. Same as you."

Siyon sauntered out into the aisle, where she could in turn get a good look at him. At the fraying of his shirtsleeves and the scuffs on his boots, at the battered hilt of his own sabre, at the lean length of his limbs and the freckles and even the glint of red in his brown hair that said *foreign blood*. That confirmed he was a mongrel brat.

She could probably trace her family back a few hundred years to the end of the Lyraec Empire. They'd probably helped overthrow the Last Duke and claim the city for *the people*. People like them, anyway. They'd renamed the city *Bezim*—in Old Lyraec, that meant *ours*.

"Yeah," he drawled, stretching the Dockside twang. "We're peas in a fucking pod. How old are you, anyway?"

"How old are you?" she demanded right back. There was a flush of colour in her warm brown cheeks, but she wasn't backing down. Was it even bravery when you hadn't heard the word *no* more than a dozen times in your life?

"Twenty-three," Siyon said. "Or near enough. And I've been on my own since I was fourteen, delving the planes since seventeen. That six years of crossing the divide between this plane and the others tells me I'm not trusting you"—he jabbed a finger at her, in her new leathers with her boots that probably got that shine from the hands of a servant—"to hold the only thing tying me back to the Mundane. No offense, princess."

She hesitated in the doorway, but then her chin came up again. "Fuck you," she stated primly. "I can do it. And I'm all you've got, anyway. Daruj went down to the square; Awl Quarter have called public challenge." There was a twist to her mouth. It stung, to be sent to do this, rather than being included in the party to bare blades against another bravi tribe, even in a small morning skirmish.

Siyon knew what that felt like. He drained his tea and set the glass down on the pew next to him. "You're well out of it. It'll be dead boring. Lots of posturing, barely three blades getting to kiss daylight. No audience in the morning, see? So no pressing need to fight."

She really did look like a doll playing dress-up, but she hadn't fled. And if Daruj was off playing *Diviner Prince* (Siyon never found his friend's bladename less ridiculous, whatever its proud history), then she probably was the best Siyon was likely to get until later this afternoon. Which would be cutting it fine to make his deliveries.

He sighed. "What's your name again?"

She grinned, sudden and bright and blindingly pretty. She was going to carve her way through society when she set aside the blade to take up a ball gown. "Zagiri Savani. And I'm eighteen. If it matters."

Siyon shrugged. "Not to me. Come on."

His ash square still looked a little skewed at one corner, but he wasn't redoing it again. "How much did Daruj tell you about what's involved?"

Zagiri stayed well back from the lines of ash, so at least she was sensible. "You're going to raid one of the other planes. For alchemical ingredients."

Basically right, but she'd need more than basics. "I tear a hole between the planes," Siyon elaborated. "Which is what the square is for. Keeps the breach contained. There's no risk—not to you, not to the city." The inquisitors might feel differently, but they weren't here, and what did they know anyway? "That also cuts me off from the Mundane, so to get back, I need a tether."

She nodded. "Which I hold."

"Which you hold." Siyon watched her for a moment. Clearly a little nervous, but she had a strong grip on herself. That irritating azatani arrogance might be good for something after all.

He unhooked his sabre from his belt and set it down on a pew, picked up a coil of rope instead. It was rough stuff, thick hemp and tarred ends, liberated from docks duty. As mundane—as *Mundane*—as rope could get, heavy with work and sweat and dirty, fishy business. "One end ties around me," Siyon said, looping it around his waist, under his shirt and the weight of his cross-slung satchel. "And you hold the other. You hold it no matter what you see, or what you hear, or how much it jerks around. You hold on to this."

She wrinkled her delicate little nose as she set a hand just above the thick knot tied in the end. She'd probably never put her pampered hands on anything this coarse in her life. "What happens if I don't?" Not a challenge, more curiosity.

Siyon smiled, tight and brittle. "I get stuck in there. Since I'm delving Empyreal today, that means I'm trapped in unforgiving heat with the angels on my back until either I can find a way out or you"—he prodded at her shoulder—"scarper off and find someone to summon me back. I recommend Auntie Geryss, you can find her through the tea shop near the fountain in the fruit market. If, y'know, you fuck up completely."

Zagiri swallowed hard, wrapped the rope around her fist, and braced her heels against the tiled floor. At least she was taking this seriously. "All right."

"Don't worry." Siyon grinned, the thrill of what he was about to do starting to tug at him as surely as a tether. It never got old. "I'll be right here. Well. Right here, and on the other side of reality at the same time."

She didn't look reassured.

Siyon stepped into the ashen square and vanished into heat haze.

Between the planes was the void, and the void was perfect; it flashed by in a fraction of a blink, and Siyon was through.

It was like stepping into an open oven, snatched up in the Empyreal plane's hot, dry fist. Siyon staggered, dizzy and dazzled, as the universe tilted around him. It always took a moment to get his balance, like he'd jumped from a moving cart.

Doing this with a hangover had been an awful idea.

Sand skewed beneath his boots, and whipped up on a keening wind. Or at least, it looked and felt like sand, abrading his skin and gritty between his teeth. Not actually sand, not here. Tiny grains of duty, or conscience, or something equally uncomfortable and insistent. Stung like a bitch, making his eyes water, and Siyon pulled a thin scarf over his face. Easier to see through it than with his eyes scrunched closed against the blast.

Dunes undulated away in all directions, toward shimmering horizons. The not-sand was white—scalding white, pale as purity, clean as righteousness—and the sky was seething fire that sizzled in sheets of orange and yellow and incandescent blue. It was dangerously beautiful; easy to overlook the tiny black specks within the burning gyre.

First rule of delving: The longer you gawk, the less time you have to harvest. Get in, load up, get out.

Siyon lowered his head again, and concentrated on slithering down the side of the dune without falling. This not-sand was so fine, it ran like water. You could drown in it, if you didn't look lively.

In the gully between dunes, there was a little shelter from the sandstorm. Siyon could crouch without fear of being buried, and shovel aside the fine, flyaway grains at the surface. Deeper down, the sand took on a molten glow, clinging to his fingers like an itch. Siyon scooped up a stinging handful, funnelling it hurriedly into a flask. He shook the excess off with a wince and wiped his hand against the rope around his waist; the roughness of the hemp was great for stripping away the last little bits, or maybe it was the sheer Mundanity that did the trick.

He got one more vial of firesand using the other hand, and tucked them both away safely inside his satchel. Trying to get any more would be asking for burns or—worse—recurring attacks of guilt back in the Mundane.

Standing, he laid a hand on the rope around his waist again. The tether leading back to the Mundane wasn't visible, but Siyon could *feel* it, tugging at him when he moved. The pull wasn't too much right now, so Zagiri didn't seem to be getting impatient. It was always difficult to tell how much time had passed while he was here. Tears were nudging at the corner of his vision, but Siyon could blink them away. The breath still came easily—though harsh and burning—to his lungs, and he wasn't experiencing any strange urges toward crusades, justice, or self-improvement.

Perhaps he could try for a little more.

He shouldn't. Get in, load up, get out, remember? The vials of firesand were what he'd been commissioned to deliver.

So if he could find something extra, it could be bonus cash. If he could find something *good*, he might be able to get his hands on a book—a real one, a proper alchemic tome. One that might *teach* him something. Make him more than just an interplanar errand boy.

Hey, a guy could dream.

Siyon flipped his satchel open again, running a finger blind along the dozens of little loops and pockets sewn into the lining. He needed to move fast; he needed something that might lead him to something powerful and lucrative.

Ah. Perfect.

He pulled out a feather—small, plain, grey, notched at one end. Just a pigeon feather. But like called to like, and in this place there were far more interesting—more powerful—things than pigeons on the wing.

Siyon lifted the feather and let the breeze pluck it out of his grip.

It zipped away, moving fast, and Siyon had to scramble after it. Up the dune and down, crosswise along the next, hauling himself up a rocky outcrop that surely hadn't been here a moment ago. The pigeon feather danced up and over the lip, smudgy against the fire-bright sky, and Siyon dragged himself after it. The rocks scraped against his ribs like pious privation, but he pushed onward. If he lost the feather, it would all be a waste.

Just over the lip of rock, atop the outcrop, the feather snagged on the sharp black edge of a nest. Siyon could've whooped in victory, if he'd had the breath for it.

The nest wasn't built of sticks, but of slabs and shards of obsidian, razor-keen and gleaming. It wasn't big, barely wider than the length of Siyon's arm, and there were only two eggs within, nestled among smouldering embers. When Siyon peeled back his scarf to peek over the edge of the nest, the heat nearly took his eyebrows off.

He didn't want an egg, though. What the hell would he do with a phoenix chick? (Answer: Set fire to his bunk in the Chapel and be left in the ashes for the inqs to pick up at their leisure.) Instead, Siyon edged carefully around the nest, peering into the nooks and serrated crannies, until he spotted the butter-bright gleam of a trapped feather. Extracting it was like sticking his hand into a shark's mouth, sliding careful fingers between knife-like obsidian and the roaring heat of the nest itself. The feather felt like a wisp of silk between his fingertips, hot as a Flower's underthings and just as full of promise. Siyon teased it out, wrapping it in a length of actual silk before tucking it away in his satchel.

He was so focused on it that he barely heard the whistle from above. Not like a bravi signal, no human sound at all; more like the sigh of air ripped through a grate. The sound of an angel's wings scything through excuses.

But he did hear it, and his body was already moving before his mind caught up, hurling him sideways a moment before the broadsword came slamming down right where he'd been crouching.

The force of it buried the edge in the rocks as though they were cheese. Flames licked blue-bright along the length of the blade. Light washed dazzling over Siyon—not from the sword, but the one who wielded it, looming above him resplendent in armour even whiter than the sand. The brutal white of perfect virtue, the unflinching white of implacable justice.

The shattering white of an angel.

Her face was a smudge in the searing light; Siyon just got an impression of a wild halo of fire around diamond eyes and hawk beak.

That beak opened and she *screamed*, like a raptor diving upon its prey.

"Zagiri!" Siyon shouted. "Pull m—"

The angel backhanded him, slamming the words from his mouth and the sense from his head. Air spun wild around him; he bounced against the rocky outcrop once, twice, before plummeting to the sand.

This wasn't his physical body, Siyon reminded himself, trying to drag breath back into his lungs. Not real, not him.

Still hurt like a motherfucker.

Sand sucked at him as Siyon heaved up to hands and knees. His satchel pulled him off balance; at least he still had it. Tears crawled down his cheeks, actually cool against the heat around him.

"Pull me out," he said, but the words were barely a scrape in his throat. No power to them at all.

The world shook as the angel landed in the sand next to Siyon. Her arm wrapped around him, binding as a solemn promise, and she hauled him effortlessly up. His legs dangled, ribs creaking beneath her grip. "*Thief,*" she snarled in his ear. It wasn't speaking so much as a stone-chiseled statement of immutable fact. "*You must earn what you would steal.*"

Siyon had no idea what that meant. But her fingers—or talons, by the sharp sting of them—dug into him as she closed her fist around the rope at his waist. It grew warm against his skin, and something shimmered into being in front of him; a twist of connection, spiralling away into the air like a faint and billowing umbilical.

Siyon gaped. He'd never seen his tether in the planes before. It was sort of beautiful.

The angel lifted her sword.

Siyon thrashed against her grip, but she only clutched him tighter, and his ribs cracked and his lungs spasmed and no sound at all came from his throat.

The sword flashed in its descent, bright with blue-hot flames.

Her grip around him tightened, impossibly, and then yanked. No, wait, it was the rope itself, and Siyon popped fish-slippery from the angel's hold, whipping into half a moment of dizzying blackness—

—and then there was stone under his feet, and his knees giving way as he crashed into another body and they both went down.

A whistle in Siyon's ears—no, in reality. "Look out," he gasped, and shoved hard as he rolled in the other direction.

Something slammed down where he had been with a screech of ironwork and a frustrated hiss, and then there was silence.

Siyon sat up too fast, and paused for the whirling sparks to dance away from his vision. Zagiri was backed against the end of the pew, knees drawn up to her chest and eyes wide. Between their bodies, the ash square was nothing but a smear across the floor.

Except the tilework—and the stones beneath—were sliced through in a deep gash the length of Siyon's arm.

Zagiri's dark eyes were wide. "It just—it was—"

"Angelic broadsword," Siyon croaked. His throat still felt scorched. His cheeks were stiff with dried tears. He reached out to the wound in the floor, but stopped short; the heat was still rising from it, with a smell like midday-baked stone paving. "Thanks," he said. "You did well."

She made a noise somewhere between a squeak and a sigh, and lifted her fist. The rope was still wrapped around it, but there was barely an arm's-length left before it ended, abrupt and fire-blackened.

The end was still smouldering.

Siyon scrambled over and pried it carefully from her trembling grip. He held it gently, moved it slowly, to avoid killing the flame or dislodging ash. There could be good use—good *money*—in angel ash. How much more in a still-burning fire?

Never mind the phoenix feather, what could this earn him? More books? Equipment? *Lessons*? Proper ones from a Summer Club alchemist, not just occasional tips from Auntie Geryss.

Zagiri wiped her hands on her trousers. Her fingers were still shaking, but only a little. More backbone to her than many Siyon had seen tangle with the fringes of alchemy. "We're done now, right?" she asked, evenly enough.

"Change of plans," Siyon said, eyes still on the smoking rope. "Delivery time. This is too important to wait."

CHAPTER 2

This was not how Zagiri Savani thought her day would go.

And that was *before* the flaming broadsword appeared from thin air and buried itself in the damn *floor* a bare handspan from her knee. She'd stared at the thickness of the blade and the intricate patterns etched in the steel that were somehow still visible through the blue-hot fire, and the only thing she could think was how long it must be, and could she even *lift* something like that?

"Zagiri," Siyon said—from the sharpness, not for the first time. "Come on, let's get going."

Now he just wanted her to pick up the still-smouldering remainder and carry it around. In a *fishbowl*, of all things. Amazing, the random rubbish the bravi picked up on party raids.

"I just—" She hesitated. "Are you sure it's safe?"

Stupid question, of course. *He* was holding it in his bare hands.

Then again, he was Siyon Velo. Bravi gossip had a lot to say about the petty alchemist of the Little Bracken. Zagiri should have known most of it would be tripe, given the number of wild tales *she'd* embroidered. But in her experience, alchemists were a bit more serious than an unshaven lout drawing with ash on the floor.

A bit less serious than a screaming angel blade, though.

Siyon gave her a flat look. "You carry a sabre and run around on rooftops, and you're worried about safe?"

He was right. He was wrong. That was different.

Zagiri wrapped the burlap carefully around the damn fishbowl, keeping it between her skin and the glass. Not what she'd been expecting at all, when Daruj whistled her over. She could've been carrying a challenge, or even delivering a prize to his secret lady-love. (Everyone knew he must have one, an opera singer or an inappropriate azata or even the sister of a baron.)

Instead, Zagiri was playing delivery girl for a petty alchemist whose coat, when he shrugged it on, was wearing thin at the elbows.

"Look," Siyon said, failing to tug his collar straight. "If you're going to start screaming about angels or anything, do it now, and not when we're out in public where any inq keen to poison sorcerers can hear you."

"Piss off," Zagiri stated, scorn rising quick. "Takes more than a close shave to rattle me."

Though admittedly, every time her eyes fell on the gouge in the floor, a shudder went down her spine. It was the way it swept, sheer and deep, across two paving stones. It was the fact it was carved into *stone*, without any apparent effort beyond what Zagiri's sister might use to apportion a pastry at afternoon tea.

Wanting to get well away from *that* didn't mean she was rattled. It was just sensible.

"Are you sure it's safe?" Siyon mimicked, in a voice far higher than hers.

"I'm just *asking*," Zagiri retorted, "whether I'm going to cause another Sundering if I drop this." Tipping half the city into the ocean *again* wasn't the sort of fame Zagiri had in mind.

Siyon hauled the leather strap of his battered satchel over his shoulder and shrugged. "Probably not?" That blithely cheerful face was not made more reassuring by his bloodshot eyes or the ash dusting his reddish stubble. "Here's an idea: Don't drop it."

"Great," Zagiri muttered, and hugged the bowl tighter against her stomach.

They slipped out the side door, and Siyon checked the square before he beckoned her out of the alleyway. It was late morning and everything was quiet, everyone either sleeping off last night, or busy about today's business. The sea breeze was just starting to pick up, and the whiff of solder and sawdust from the factories across the river chasm was welcome compared to the memory of stone dust sizzling in angelfire. From the square outside the Chapel, there was a lovely view out over the bay, ships bobbing at moorage, with the messy business of Dockside hidden away by the sharp slope down to the water.

Siyon turned his back on it and started uphill toward the university, leading a zigzag path through the tangle of little streets. Half of them turned into staircases where it got steep, but it was still easy going compared to running roof tiles, and the fishbowl wasn't heavy, just bulky. What it was, though, was *boring*.

"Where are we even going?" Zagiri grumbled.

"To someone who'll hopefully pay me extravagantly for what you're carrying," Siyon replied.

Zagiri glanced down at the burlap. "What's extravagantly?"

Siyon considered that as they climbed another staircase. "Not sure, really. I've never struck something this big. Thirty rivna? Forty?"

About what they'd spend on Zagiri's dress for her presentation, but she wasn't going to say *that*. "You should've gotten the buyer to come to you. More than one. Had an auction."

"Like I was a Flower?" Siyon laughed. "Yeah, because your lot would come at *my* beck and call. Then they'd have to risk lugging the thing across the city."

Zagiri snorted. "Instead, I get to. Wait, risk? I thought you said this was safe."

"I did *not* say that," Siyon pointed out merrily, but after a glance at her, he sobered. "No, really, don't lick it or anything. But otherwise, the prime danger is how it'd earn us a whirlwind visit to a horrified magistrate and a fatal cocktail of poison and sanctimonious moralising. Well, me at least." He lifted an eyebrow at her. "No long-term trouble for the little azata led astray."

"Get bent." She spat the words. "I've done time in the cells."

He snorted. "In the holding cells. For disturbing the peace. With half of the rest of the tribe, released by morning, no charges pressed."

"*And* trespass." Zagiri knew she sounded sulky, and couldn't help it. It wasn't that she was *proud* of having been swept up on an evening of bravi tribe business, but...well, everyone at the Palokani garden party had been very impressed.

Siyon was not impressed. Siyon was laughing openly. "Regular little crime baron, aren't you?"

She might have punched him, if she hadn't been holding *angelfire*.

He steered them under the moss-lined gate of the university grounds, winding upward through the tangle of residences. The commons beyond was, as always, littered with idle students, lying on their shed robes, studying, chatting, playing handball. Zagiri shrugged down beneath the wide brim of her plumed hat and hoped none of them knew her. This was hardly the glamour of the bravi life.

But Siyon looked around like a girl on her first visit to the dressmaker's, if one who knew that her mother had a very tight budget. His gaze lingered on the bronze-domed bulk of the library, and if there was longing in his eyes, there was also a bitter twist to his mouth.

Thirty rivna was extravagant, he'd said. And Zagiri hadn't paid any attention to university fees—had never seriously considered attending, not when she'd rather be on a rooftop than reading a book—but she was pretty sure thirty rivna might cover tuition for a season. Maybe.

Zagiri hurried after Siyon—and his stupidly long legs—through the law school cloister, down a winding stair that curved around a bastion. "Do they even teach alchemy here anymore?" She tried to make it casual; from the quick stab of Siyon's attention, she hadn't managed it. "I'm just saying, it's kinda illegal."

"Kinda." Siyon snorted. "It's *entirely* illegal, though the magistrates won't prosecute if you aren't a danger to Bezim. Which means you're fine, as long as you're *respectable*." He sneered the word, cutting a glance at her again.

Yeah, Zagiri knew what that meant. Respectable like *her*.

"They do teach chemistry," Siyon continued. "Basically the same, you just only use things from the Mundane plane. Which means no power. Because the material of other planes is alchemical power." And as the stairs widened out, spilling down toward the Boulevard, he turned to point at the bundle in her arms.

Oh. Material of other planes. Zagiri thought again of the blinding flash of the sword—the *scream* of it—and swallowed hard. "I'm guessing this is a lot of power."

"You're holding part of an angel," Siyon said, like that wasn't a *terrifying idea*. "A higher-order sentient being. Still burning with the righteous fire of her wrath. That's serious power."

Zagiri frowned. "Are you sure we should be selling this to just anyone?"

"You sound like an inq." Siyon smirked sidelong at her umbrage. "But Joddani's hardly *just anyone*."

Oh shit. "*Nihath* Joddani?" Maybe it wasn't. Maybe he had a cousin who dabbled as well, and she'd never heard of him because, well, Zagiri tried not to talk to him at all, honestly.

Siyon gave her a weird look, and Zagiri realised he might not actually be on a first-name basis with azatani clients who commissioned him like any other errand boy to fetch and carry. That'd be just like bloody Nihath.

Zagiri sighed. "We're acquainted." That was putting it mildly, but frankly all she wanted to admit to a fellow bravi. She nodded across the wide, paved expanse of the Boulevard, starting to grow thick with people, at the distant fuzz of green trees and close-ranked tile roofs. The Avenues, where the azatani lived, her among them. "He won't be at home at this hour, you realise."

"You know where he will be?" Siyon stepped aside with a fancy bow—which he messed up, leading with the wrong foot and twisting his back arm around.

Zagiri took them along the Boulevard, hefting her bundle of angelfire. "What I meant," she said, "was why not just keep this yourself? I mean, yeah, money, but you nearly *died*—*I* nearly died!—and you could use the power for something actually interesting." Nihath, the few times she'd been forced to overhear him chatting with his equally boring friends, had gone on about things like *ascertaining the sublimation potential of aligned matter*, whatever that meant. Siyon could—could— "Ooh! Could you make our sabres do that fire thing like the angel blade did? Imagine that, if Bracken showed up to an all-blades and our first six were just *on fire*, it'd be so—"

"I can't do that," he interrupted, scowling. "That's serious alchemy, working with angelfire. Or demonscale, or djinnfrost. Firesand is basic, it just gives you a bit of a zing. But something that big, you need experience, and proper training, and a solid grounding in theory from a whole library of books and a proper workshop with all the right equipment. Otherwise it could—y'know..." He waved a hand off toward the sea.

Toward the sea, except two neighbourhoods from here, you hit the Scarp, where a jagged cliff rent the city asunder on this side of the river. The lower part had been sunk to its knees, wallowing in the encroaching sea, struck down more than a century ago now during the calamity known as the Sundering.

Bezim didn't need proof of the dangers of alchemy. They lived in it.

"Y'know what?" Zagiri said. "Let's ditch this damn thing and go have a drink."

Siyon laughed, but this time he was laughing with her.

The buildings around them grew taller and more respectable, with elegant shop windows interspersed with discreet doors marked with brass plaques announcing offices, businesses, private apartments. It was even more likely they'd see someone Zagiri knew here, so she hurried them along, looking for the polished sign that said merely SUMMER. "Here."

Siyon caught her elbow before she'd taken more than one of the steps that led to the front door. "We can't go in this way. Not even you."

"What?" Zagiri frowned at him, and then down at her bravi leathers. "Oh, you mean dressed like this?"

He laughed, and looked both ways up the street. "You could be naked as a Flower or done up to the nines. Front door is for members and their guests only. Come on."

He led this time; they had to go halfway around the block to find the alleyway that cut down past the back courtyard of the Summer Club, and if Zagiri had no idea where they were going, now Siyon seemed far more at home.

There was a footman taking his break in the courtyard of the Summer Club, pipe between his teeth, smoke haze coiling around his head, a pale glass of tea on the step beside him. "No deliveries 'cept by arrangement," he stated.

"We've something for Azatan Joddani," Siyon said, kicking the gate closed behind Zagiri. As the footman opened his mouth to repeat himself, Siyon added, "You all know me, don't pretend I'm a time-waster."

The footman jerked his chin at Zagiri. He still hadn't taken the pipestem from his mouth. "Who's she?"

Zagiri opened her mouth; Siyon got in first. "My assistant."

The footman shrugged and stood up, but he took his sweet time knocking out his pipe, dousing the embers with the remainder of his tea, and sauntering back inside. The door closed—heavy and forbidding—behind him.

"Rude," Zagiri huffed.

"What?" Siyon asked. "You think he should have invited us in and given us tea while we wait?"

That was almost exactly what she'd been thinking, and now that he pointed it out, it was a completely ludicrous idea. She wasn't used to being on this side of things.

Time slipped past, one grain at a time. Siyon took the footman's spot sitting on the steps. There was room for Zagiri, but she took a look at the step and remained standing. "So you aren't a member," she said, looking up at the building. "Because you aren't a real alchemist?"

That turned Siyon's smirk sour. "Yeah, that's the sum of it. You have to satisfy a panel of members that you can harness the planes and turn them to your purpose. Doing it like Kolah Negedi said." Siyon sighed and dragged a hand through his hair, making it even more of a ruffled mess. The sun caught red glints in it. "You're supposed to do it through an apprenticeship. Know the right people. Otherwise, you need books, and glassware, and practice. Proper teaching. Time." He looked at the bowl Zagiri was carrying.

She could translate that. He needed money. He needed money like *this* was worth. He needed money like Zagiri's family spent on a dress.

Zagiri cleared her throat. "I hear a lot about this Negedi bloke. Sounds like he'd be boring at parties."

Siyon laughed. "Kolah Negedi has been dead for a few hundred years, so yeah, probably. He was the first true practitioner of the art of alchemy. Separated fact from wild stories, figured it out from first principles, wrote it all down in his notebooks. They taught his structures at university, once upon."

Before the Sundering. Before the Scarp.

"So what," Zagiri said, squinting at him. "You gotta do things his way or you're not allowed in the club?"

Siyon shook his head. "There is no other way. He didn't make rules, he...discovered how the universe works."

That didn't seem right. Zagiri frowned and opened her mouth, always ready to pick a fight with anyone who said *You must do it this way*—

But the door behind Siyon opened, and a figure stepped into the doorway. Not azatani, not with that strawberry-blond hair curling gently around his pale and elegant neck. He was a slender wisp, draped in linen and lace and flyaway ribbons. His eyes were the same blue as the sky, and he was delicate as porcelain, and all the words soured in Zagiri's mouth to see him.

In a breathy voice that was nearly a whisper, the new arrival said, "Goodness, what rats have washed up upon my shores?"

Zagiri should have realised he'd be here as well, if Nihath was.

Siyon frowned up from his seat on the step, hanging on to the doorframe like he was worried he'd fall over. "Who the hell are you?" he demanded.

"Tehroun." He spoke in that annoying way he had, soft and gentle as a summer breeze. "You have something for my master?"

"Ugh," Zagiri said, and Tehroun's blue gaze drifted languidly over her, lingering rather more pointedly on the bundle she held. More attention than he'd ever given her before.

Siyon scrambled down from the steps with a little sway. "We have material that will be of extreme interest to Azatan Joddani."

Tehroun finally looked away from the shrouded fishbowl. "Yes. My master. I rather think you are right." He wafted back from the door. "Do follow me."

Siyon glanced at Zagiri, and frowned. "Are you all right?"

No. Yes. She just hated the idea of having to tell Anahid about this. She didn't want to talk about any of that. So she scowled, and said, "Let's just get this over with."

A hush enfolded them in the main hall of the Summer Club, insulated from the city by wood panelling, heavy green drapes, carpeting thick and even as snowfall. A wide marble staircase coiled around the walls, and in the lofty central space loomed the massive spire of an alchemical clock. It hissed and clicked and seethed with the slow trickle of sand and other mysteries. Other sounds fell from above, disembodied and embalmed—snatches of murmured conversation, the tap of a footstep, the shuffle and thud of a book.

Everything about the Summer Club declared that it was respectable, decorous, upstanding. There was nothing here that could be, to use the crass word of the law, a *danger to the city*.

Everything about the Summer Club clawed bitter jealousy through Siyon's veins, and made him want to break the respectable, decorous, upstanding silence. Just because.

A brass sign on a heavy stand guarded the staircase, the physical equivalent of a discreet cough as it informed visitors that the upper floors were for members only. Tehroun drifted straight past it, a wisp of cloud on a summer breeze. Zagiri followed without hesitation, so Siyon did as well.

He tried not to gawk as the upper corridor unfurled in both directions. He'd never been up here, nor had any other alchemical supplier he knew. They got to make their deliveries in the back courtyard, or the servants' hall if the weather were inclement.

Now he passed open doorways like glimpses into another world.

Book-lined rooms with lamplit desks; storerooms crammed full of carefully labelled drawers and boxes; parlours with elegant furniture in sombre colours. Siyon loitered, craning his neck to see more. He was dying to explore every corner, and yet had no idea what he'd do if he were invited in. Wouldn't know where to start. Couldn't participate in any of the conversations he caught in snatches: gossip, small talk, exclamations about astronomy. He didn't belong here. Wouldn't fit in.

Not yet. And his ticket to one-day-maybe was nearly at the end of the corridor. Siyon caught up as Tehroun held open one half of a wide double door. Siyon stepped through on Zagiri's heels—

Into a cavern of wonders. *Books*, so many books, lining the walls, soaring up to the ceiling, marching away on either side in soldier-straight rows. Ahead, a balcony railing, and beyond a view down to the lower floor, where there was more. Shelf upon shelf of yet more books, scrolls slotted away like wine bottles, and giant carved tablets from the ancient days of the Khanate mounted in glass-topped tables.

Siyon was so dazzled by the sheer volume of knowledge that it took him long moments to even hear the voices.

The group argued over a table scattered with books and loose pages and empty glasses of tea and wine. It looked much like the tail end of a long night of running the tiles, a bravi tribe gathered around their plundered spoil and comparing notes on who drew fastest or parried most flamboyantly.

A different sort of tribe, this. Siyon recognised every person at the table by reputation, if not personally.

Across the table, the Kalyrii twins, with their dark red hair pulled back like the sailors they weren't quite, lounging identically though one sketched in a notebook while the other lifted a hand, declaring, "The Lioness is far too close to the Oasis at this time of year, of course a crosswise working cannot be attempted without risking Empyreal blowback."

On this side of the table was Master Yvok, tall and long and pale as an icicle, his face lined by northern winters. He scoffed. "Stars are Mundane."

"You are mundane," the other Kalyrii twin stated, not looking up from his sketch.

On *that* side of the table, Auntie Geryss leaned back in her chair, amusement creasing her dark face. Her quick eyes caught on Siyon; she tilted her head in its bright blue turban, seeming entirely unsurprised and possibly even pleased to see him here. It was embarrassingly reassuring.

Beside her, the Margravine Othissa leaned forward. "This is all rather far afield from the central question. Can we not agree that the planes are out of balance?"

The sketching twin tossed his notebook down. "They have never been *in* balance!"

Othissa shrugged one well-rounded shoulder, bared by the sleeveless cut of the sort of gown they favoured in the New Republic. She was all dimples in honey, and sweet conciliation. "More out of balance, then. Even you cannot deny that."

The Kalyrii frowned as one.

And the last person, sitting with his back to the new arrivals, said, "That is precisely my point." Joddani was everything an azatan of Bezim should be—dark hair oiled in curls, shoulders broad in a well-cut brocade longvest, wisdom evident to the finest and brightest alchemical practitioners of the city. "The margin for error on all workings—even the most commonplace—is now far beyond that described by Negedi. All planar accessions must factor in modifications for the unctuous nature of the planes, or else they will slip away from the grasp."

Siyon wasn't sure what half those words meant, but he was startled to get the gist. Of course you had to connect carefully to the other planes. They were slippery, they moved unpredictably. That was part of the fun. Just what the planes were *like*.

Wasn't it?

Joddani was still declaiming: "It is quite simply obvious that this will have repercussions for the entire Art. As the current foremost practitioners of the city, we must consider that some manner of redress may be necessary."

"Redress?" Yvok frowned like a blond cliff-face. "You cannot be meaning this nonsense about a Power of the Mundane."

A strange noise came from beside Siyon, a strangled sort of sigh. He'd almost forgotten Tehroun was even there, in the wonder of this room, of these occupants.

But as soon as Siyon looked sidelong, his gaze snagged on the pale young man. That feeling that he'd had outside, that Tehroun was something known. Something that itched at him. Nothing so simple as familiarity. This was more—

Tehroun turned to look back at Siyon. Some strange trick of the light in here made his eyes almost lavender, weirdly pale.

"Sorry," Siyon murmured, under the noise of both Kalyrii twins shouting about how the Power of the Mundane—the Alchemist—was naught but a fairy tale. Might as well say he rides a dragon. Might as well worry about the Demon Queen invading the Mundane. "Sorry, have we met before?"

Tehroun frowned, the faintest crease between his alabaster-pale brows. "Of course we have." He sounded faintly affronted that Siyon had forgotten.

"Enough." Auntie Geryss slapped her hand down—it was the same colour as the tabletop, though rather less polished. "Lads, you are rowdy, and this is a library. Don't get me started with you." She pointed a finger at Othissa, leaving no space for that lady's gasp before she continued, "Nihath, you won't convince them today, and besides, you have visitors."

Joddani glanced over his shoulder, then rose unhurriedly, tugging his longvest straight. "I am right," he stated, and turned from the table. He'd only taken a step away from it when Tehroun was at his shoulder—*draped* against his shoulder, more precisely—and brushing fingertips through the curls just behind Joddani's ear. Joddani barely seemed to notice, fixing a stern gaze on Siyon and saying in the same curt tone: "You are early. I am not conducting business at present. Come as we arranged."

"Things have changed." Siyon spoke quickly, even as Joddani was turning away again.

He paused, lifted an unimpressed eyebrow. Siyon considered just walking away, selling the angelfire to someone else, letting Azatan bloody superior Joddani know later what he'd missed out on. It was a happy little fancy.

But the whole time he was finding another buyer, he'd be lugging around something that the inquisitors would love to arrest him over. So Siyon whipped out a thin smile and said, "You'll want to have first crack at what I've got." He tilted his head significantly toward Zagiri—where *was* Zagiri?

She'd backed up, barely in the door, and her face twisted as they all turned to look at her.

Joddani said, voice sharp, "What are *you* doing here?"

"Yeah." Zagiri winced. "Can we *not* tell my sister about this?"

"Your sister?" Siyon repeated.

"My wife," Joddani said.

Siyon blinked at him. He hadn't known Joddani was married—hadn't seen any sign of a lady in the house he delivered commissions to. Then again, it wasn't like he was invited in for tea. And if Tehroun was still clinging to Joddani's arm like a pennant on a string, well, it was absolutely no business of Siyon's how anyone else arranged their lives, especially the azatani.

Tehroun sighed, like this was all tremendously boring. "You want to see what they have brought," he whispered.

That was all the confirmation Joddani needed, apparently. "Fine."

They found the nearest unoccupied parlour—all sea-foam upholstery and pale wood. Tehroun cast himself down on a chaise like a discarded silk scarf. Joddani closed the door firmly behind them. "Let's see it."

Zagiri set her bundle down on the low table and scuttled away behind a sofa as if that might offer protection. The burlap sack was incongruous against the lacquered wood, but that hardly mattered once Siyon flipped it aside to show the glass bowl—and its contents.

He was relieved to see that the rope-end inside was still smouldering, just a few pinpricks of glowering orange appearing all the brighter for the low light in the parlour. "Angelfire," he stated.

"You cannot be serious." Joddani crouched to peer at the rope. He called an Empyreal spark to his snapped fingers, and watched the flame tilt toward its more powerful cousin, even through the glass.

Siyon leaned smugly against the mantel of the cold fireplace. This was going to be worth a lot. He might even be able to—

Joddani straightened and whirled about. "You blithe and irresponsible *idiot.*"

Siyon blinked. "What?"

"To bring such potential power into the plane with matters so— why, I've just been remonstrating with my colleagues for a little more *moderation*, and you—" Words, apparently, were insufficient; Joddani flourished a hand in the direction of the glass bowl.

Siyon shrugged. "What, are the inqs getting prissy again? We got here safe, and no one's going to arrest *you.*" Not a first-tier azatan like this one.

Joddani made a cramped little noise, dismissing the inquisitors like a speck of dust on his well-tailored trousers. "I mean the planar imbalance, Velo. The intrinsic relationship of the planes within the universe, the very way in which we relate to each other, surely even *you*—" He paused, gaze sweeping Siyon from head to toe. "Well, perhaps you have not the wherewithal to feel, let alone understand, the matter."

That stung, like he'd swallowed firesand. "No, I just skip between planes twice a week, what would I know about anything?" Siyon snapped.

Joddani had turned away already, frowning at the fishbowl and its burning contents. "How did you even get this?"

Siyon cleared his throat. "Angel sliced my tether. I was already back."

"You see?" Joddani jabbed a finger toward Siyon. "Accidental transference of intrinsic matter. That shouldn't be possible, I'm sure Negedi says so, if you consider all the mentions in the other related works. Something has shifted. In the circumstances, I cannot permit this power to be sold to some other practitioner who may use it without regard for the damage he—or she—is causing." He glowered back toward the library. "I will give you fifty rivna. For this and the firesand I commissioned."

Siyon laughed. "Fuck off."

Behind her couch, Zagiri gave a little huff that might have been laughter. Joddani sniffed. "That is all the ready funds I can draw."

"Trade's fine," Siyon pointed out, doing his best to seem nonchalant. Negotiation was all about not letting the other bastard see how much you genuinely wanted. "Let's say...teach me a lesser working. Your choice."

Joddani sniffed. "I have far better things to be doing with my time. I'll trade you a dozen lesser imbued gemstones." He shot a glance at the rope-end and added, "And half a dozen vials each of stardust, heavy lightning, and moonbeam liquor."

That gave Siyon pause. He had trouble raiding the Aethyr—had never been able to open a gate to that plane, no matter how he tried. So getting hold of Aethyreal ingredients would expand the range he could provide to other clients. Would that be worth *more*, in the long run?

And yet, he had a sure thing here. Joddani sneaked another look at the angelfire, and Siyon countered, "Keep the vials. I want access to your library."

Joddani glowered at him; Siyon grinned back. "There are books in my personal collection that would be quite dangerous in the hands of an untutored—"

"So teach me," Siyon interrupted.

Joddani barked a harsh and dismissive laugh. "You may come, once a week, for the duration of a season, and read from certain books that *I* will select."

"Two seasons," Siyon countered. "Until the Salt Festival."

Joddani sniffed. "Very well. But ten gemstones only."

"Done." Siyon didn't bother containing his grin. He felt *ebullient*. Two seasons of reading! Even if Joddani only stuck to the basic primers, it was far more than Siyon had thought he'd be able to get hold of in two *years*. With that, and fifty rivna..."Oh yeah, I'll take the money now, if it's all the same."

Joddani would never be so ill-bred as to roll his eyes, but he did sigh. "Yes, yes, wait a moment, will you? Out in the hall. And don't *touch* anything."

So they waited while Joddani went to extract the money from wherever it was stashed; stuffed down his trousers for all Siyon knew or cared. Siyon leant against the banister overlooking the alchemical clock. It looked like a whole apparatus of glassware tied up in knots, varied pieces of equipment, little of which he could afford, even with fifty rivna in his pocket.

Don't think about it like that. Fifty rivna *would* buy him a good few lessons with Auntie Geryss, the sort that she crammed in around other work, as long as he paid for the materials he used—or, more often, wasted—and cleaned up afterward (which sometimes took twice as long as the lesson itself had). With that, he could put into practice the theory he'd learn from Joddani's books, and then—

And then *what*, Siyon? Somehow scrape together a half-arsed version of one of the Summer Club entrance tests? A tenuous path to a difficult goal.

Zagiri was right; it was past time for a drink.

Siyon turned his back on the clock and considered her instead. She was slouched against the wall, the heel of one polished boot balanced against the toe of the other. At his sudden attention, she frowned. "What?"

"You all right?" Siyon asked.

"I can roll you in feathers," she suggested caustically, "if you want to be a mother hen."

He laughed—the sound was far too loud in these muted corridors, but it felt good. "Fine, see if I worry about you anymore." He jerked his chin back toward the parlour where they'd left Joddani. "Any more surprising connections you'd like to tell me about? Your mother run a Flowerhouse? You best friends with the niece of a crime baron?"

Zagiri snickered. "My mother likes to pretend the whole Flower district doesn't exist. And don't the barons steer clear of azatani? Aren't we too much trouble?"

Siyon made a *they-have-a-point* face, and she made a cheerfully rude gesture.

Though a moment later, she was frowning thoughtfully at the parlour door. "Is what he said a thing? Like, the planes being imbalanced or whatever?"

Siyon shrugged. "Hardly matters, right? Fuck all I can do about it."

"But you…" She gestured with one hand, an arc from here to there and back again. "Surely that can't help."

Standing here, of all places, that seemed bitterly hilarious to Siyon. "You have any idea the sort of thing alchemists like your brother-in-law can do? Harness luck, bottle lust. They can charm a shirt so it turns a blade—you've seen 'em, Haruspex had them at the last all-blades. They can boil metal and freeze sunlight." The jealousy was so thick on Siyon's tongue that he wanted to spit, but he didn't want to get kicked out before he got paid. "If something's askew with the universe, it's none of my doing. None of my business either."

"You." The voice was new, brusque rather than azatani-crisp. Siyon whirled around to face the speaker, and nearly groaned. Jaleh Kurit might be carrying a pile of books that nearly reached her sharp-pointed chin, but she could still glare at him like he'd clambered through her bedroom window.

He'd done that, once or twice. She hadn't looked at him like that then. But that had been before she apprenticed to Othissa and decided she was above sleeping with a lowly supplier.

Now she was wearing a kerchief wrapped around the near-black curls he'd run his fingers through—not quite an azata's headscarf, but making a pretense. Siyon didn't want to kiss her even half as much as he wanted to demand she tell him everything she'd learned in the half-year since last they'd spoke.

From the hard slant of her mouth, neither was likely. "You are unaccompanied and you are certainly not a member. Begone, before I summon the stewards."

"We're not here to see *you*," Siyon shot back. "Scurry off back to your mistress."

She gave him a blatant once-over, mouth pursed and eyes hard, and Siyon felt scaldingly aware of his stained shirt, scuffed boots, smudged face. Had he shaved this morning? Had he shaved *yesterday*?

Jaleh—dressed simply but well, carrying an armful of knowledge Siyon wildly coveted, walking these halls as one who belonged—simply sniffed and turned away into another parlour.

As the door shut, Zagiri said, "Bad break-up?" Her voice ran with laughter over an undercurrent of sympathy.

At the height of their final argument, Jaleh had called Siyon a pathetic futureless gutter grubber, and he'd called her a jumped-up talentless clerk, and she'd thrown a pestle at his head and screamed for her brothers, who'd chased Siyon halfway across the city. (Awl Quarter bravi, both of them, and unaware until that moment of the affair. It had nearly caused an incident.)

Siyon said, "About average."

Zagiri snorted, but before she could make any more smart remarks, Joddani came out. "Here." He tossed a small sack to Siyon—small, but gratifyingly heavy when it clanked into his palms. "You," Joddani added, pointing at Zagiri. "A word."

She looked beseechingly at Siyon, and she *had* saved him this morning. "Actually, we should really get going—"

"It will be but a moment." Joddani didn't even look at him. "Come along."

Zagiri pulled a face, but she slouched after him into the parlour.

Silence settled back on the corridor; the alchemical clock sighed, and scraped, and chuckled liquidly. Footsteps climbed the stairs, and Siyon turned to watch a young man ascend—a shining head of oiled curls with a faint bronze sheen, an ornate purple-and-silver brocade longvest over immaculate shirtsleeves, boots just as perfect as Zagiri's.

This day was riddled with azatani like weevils in flour.

Siyon knew just enough about the fashion of the Avenues to recognise a follower—or perhaps a setter—of trends. All in the details: the lace cuffs that fell over his long-fingered hand on the banister, the cut of his longvest that made him look slender and supple as a sapling, the length and tousle to his burnished hair that meant he had to toss it out of his eyes as he crested the staircase.

Under the consideration of those clear brown eyes, Siyon embraced the burning awareness of his scruffy appearance. If they were going to look and judge, then so be it: He'd be the vicious gutter brat they all saw.

"Goodness," the azatan murmured, sardonic laid over languid laid over scandalised like the gossamer robes of a Flower. That gaze slid down Siyon and up again, less lazy than measuring, and it set Siyon's teeth on edge even before the azatan said, "Are *you* a practitioner?"

"Are you?" Siyon jerked his chin back down the stairs. "Sign down there says members only."

One perfect eyebrow rose just a fraction. "So you *are* a practitioner."

Of course. Signs applied to other people. Everything this guy wanted no doubt dropped into his hand with a grateful sigh for being allowed the opportunity.

It was a nice-looking hand. Long, tapered fingers, narrow palms, no doubt smooth as a fishmonger's lies.

Siyon grinned, or at least he bared his teeth. "Sure. I'm the best practitioner you've never heard of. I make angels dance and harpies weep. I make the others look staid, boring, uninspired." He leaned forward; it was a feral relief to vent a little bile. "I could make all your wildest dreams come true."

The azatan tilted his head in a careful and practised gesture, but there was a glint in his eye. Like the spark of light off a drawn sabre, like the thrill of leaping from one gutter to the next, like the flash of nothing between the planes. "You don't know what I dream about."

"Don't care either. I don't do love potions or petty poisons or—" Siyon darted a glance over the azatan. "Performance aids."

Both eyebrows went up now, and Siyon found himself wondering how much more reaction he could wring out of this mahogany-carved statue of azatan perfection.

Probably just as well that the door opened, and Zagiri came storming out. "I don't care!" she snarled over her shoulder. "Velo, come the fuck on, we're—oh." She stopped dead at the sight of the azatan, clapped a hand belatedly over her mouth.

He merely gave a little bow, showing no sign of bother at her dress, her language, her presence. "Miss Savani. Regards from my family to yours."

"Miss?" Siyon repeated. "Isn't she an azata?"

Behind her hand, Zagiri mumbled, "Not until I'm out. I have to sponsor a—y'know what, can we talk about this, oh, never?"

Siyon grinned; she took the hand away from her face to make that rude gesture again, and then turned a placid smile upon the bemused azatan. "Thank you, Azatan Hisarani, and returned in due measure." Even her voice had changed, smoothed out like silk. "I beg you excuse us."

She shot Siyon a fierce glance, and hurried off down the stairs.

Siyon shrugged, and followed her, but the azatan—Hisarani, apparently—stepped sidelong to block him with one arm, fingertips resting lightly against the banister.

Something skittered down Siyon's spine—the thrill of a challenge, the outrageously expensive scent of Hisarani's cologne, or perhaps just the knowledge that this young man (this *brat*) could probably have him arrested with a snap of those long fingers. Siyon didn't step back. "Darling," he snarled, "not here."

Hisarani watched him without blinking. "Then where?" Siyon just stared at him for a moment, not following at all. "I have need of an alchemist and get no satisfaction from the regular practitioners," Hisarani stated, his Avenue accent carefully snipping off each word. "I am willing to consider an irregular one. So where can I find you, sir?"

Siyon still had no idea what he was talking about, but he hadn't spent years among the bravi just to back down when he could bluff through instead. "*Sir*, you can't." He pushed Hisarani's arm out of the way, brushed close on his way past to murmur, "You can't afford me."

Zagiri was waiting at the bottom of the stairs, nearly dancing from foot to foot in her impatience. "Drink," she demanded.

"Drink," Siyon agreed, just as vehement.

They went out the front door, Zagiri breezing past the disapproving clerk.

When Siyon glanced back, Hisarani was still watching them from the top of the stairs.

CHAPTER 3

The early afternoon sun hit Tower Square like a hammer on an anvil. The customers of the teahouses clustered beneath umbrellas colour-coded for their loyalties. Here the Bower's Scythe bravi lounged in pale pink shade, dripping lace and trading half-hearted couplets. Over there, beneath awnings plain and brown as the hopeful sparrows, students from the university complained and panicked over their study notes. The blue-striped canopies beyond them shadowed less crowded tables; the Awl Quarter bravi were probably still wallowing in their riverside boathouses in the lower city. They'd be up before sundown, ready for the real business of the bravi—raids and tile runs and all manner of midnight mayhem.

Siyon followed Zagiri between the yellow-umbrella'd shade of the favoured coffeehouse of foreign merchant consortia, and the forest-green of Haruspex, whose bravi sat quiet and shadowed. The Harus-pex sergeant—a woman as long, thin, and weathered as a whip, known only as Slender—was haggling with two alchemical suppliers Siyon knew well; he raised a hand in greeting, and earned a hiss from the nearest knot of black-clad Haruspex bravi.

Siyon grabbed at Zagiri's arm as she went for her sabre. "It's fine. They just don't like me."

Zagiri let him drag her away from the fight. "They don't have a monopoly on street alchemy," she grumbled.

"But they'd like to." Siyon gave Zagiri a final push in the small of her back, out into the clear centre of the square.

The sun lifted shimmering heat haze from the unsheltered cobblestones around the fountain. Above the splashing water loomed the statue of the Last Duke, massive and majestic on horseback, kitted out in his Lyraec armour, like the relic he'd been. Someone had draped a Flower's veil over his head and jammed an ostentatiously plumed hat over his horse's ears. A typical display of respect. Bezim had scant use for nobility these days.

As they skirted past a wedge of blood-red umbrellas, two young men in duelling leathers and gilt-edged sashes leapt out. "Halt!" one cried. "Who goes there?" His hands were empty, held bracingly wide; the other wielded a straw-bound bottle of rakia and half a well-chewed apple.

Siyon let his hand fall away from his own sabre as Zagiri laughed. "Assholes!" she declared, warm and fond, and stepped forward to embrace each lout in turn, touching cheek to cheek. She nodded to the bottle. "Starting already?"

Other azatani, Siyon diagnosed, from the jewelry that adorned them and the quality of the lace that frothed beneath their leather duelling vests. All of the Bleeding Dawn bravi were flashy bastards, full of drama and dash, but this pair had more genuine quality than fake glitter in their finery.

And they were drinking the good stuff, even at this hour.

Zagiri nudged his side. "You still need me?"

Siyon had wanted to keep an eye on her, in case the morning's work had left scars, but her laughter was reassuring. A little frivolous nonsense might be just what she needed, and these Bleeders seemed born to frivol. "Just don't share any tribe secrets, yeah?"

Her level look said she heard what he really meant: Don't go blabbing about what they'd been up to. She set a finger to the brim of her hat, tipping it just enough that the sun glinted off the Bracken badge.

Siyon took her message in turn: She was one of them, and if tonight's rampages meant drawing blade against these two, she'd probably do it with glee. He grinned. "Don't do anything I wouldn't."

She grinned right back, and slung an arm around each of the Bleeders. The three of them clattered away across the square, heading for the clock tower.

Siyon kept his own course. Onward, past the rest of the Bleeding Dawn (three of them were standing on their chairs, shouting ever more unlikely boasts at each other like the posing wankers they all were) until he reached the sunset-orange umbrellas of Café Regal, the chosen public headquarters of the Little Bracken bravi.

At the point of the wedge of tables, three figures lounged in their chairs, duelling leathers adorned with ribbons and flourishes in browns and golds, like autumn trees looking for trouble. Across the table—covered with half-empty glasses of tea and a little plate of pastries—a woman in the sashed dress and headscarf of an azata gestured while she talked. No doubt describing what she had in mind for the party she was here to hire Little Bracken to guard—or perhaps to raid as entertainment for her guests. None of Siyon's business, until his sergeant told him where to be and what to do.

That sergeant sipped at her tea as she listened to the azata's plans. Voski Tolan was short and sharp as a knife to the kidney, and her leathers were almost as battered as Siyon's own, but it would be a stupid man who underestimated her. Fortunately, the city held many such; Voski hated, above all, to be bored.

Beside her, Tein Geras—the stocky and thorough quartermaster of the tribe—looked up from the discussion to mark Siyon's arrival. He reached around behind the sergeant to prod at the third figure's shoulder.

Daruj, the Diviner Prince, one of the most celebrated blades of the Little Bracken bravi, excused himself from the table and came bounding out to sweep Siyon up in an embrace. "Brother!" he cried, his grin wide and white across his dark and merry face. "It's about fucking time."

The beads of his many braids clicked together, and a heavy pearl dangling from his ear caught the light. Siyon flicked it with a fingernail. "New bauble. Successful morning?"

Daruj tilted his head, preening like a cat. "The Awl Quarter should shut up if they don't have the blades to match their boasts." He said it loud enough to carry; the nearby tables of bravi, Bracken and neighbouring Bleeders both, laughed and cheered and lifted glasses in toast.

Which gave Daruj plenty of cover to lean closer and lower his voice. "And you?"

Siyon let his smile turn smug. "I've won my own prizes. I'll wait for the boss." He tilted his head toward where Voski and Tein were touching palms with the azata in agreement. "Much more business to go?"

"The Bowerboys sent a message." Daruj flicked a finger toward where a pair of bravi in the fluttering pink ribbons of the Bower's Scythe were playing cards—looked like carrick—with three Bracken. "Voski might summon you first to let 'em wait longer on her pleasure, but we're all keen to know the proposal." It could be anything; an allied raid on another tribe, a public bout to raise both their profiles, a declaration of challenge to get their names on everyone's lips.

What use was a bladename, after all, if half the city wasn't repeating it?

Daruj prodded a finger in Siyon's side, and Siyon jabbed at his ribs in turn. As they scuffled, Daruj said, "And Savani? How did she go?"

"Not bad, for an azatani," Siyon allowed. He wrapped a hand around Daruj's wrist and felt a wild surge of triumph—he'd not managed that in years—before his friend's boot tangled between Siyon's ankles, and Daruj nearly flung him into the nearest Bleeding Dawn table. The Bleeders hooted and hollered, clutching their glasses, as Daruj swung Siyon around in a mad dance instead.

"Oi!" It was Voski, beckoning them over. "Honestly, you pair, trouble from the moment I took you on." But one corner of her mouth quirked upward—rapturous joy, from Voski Tolan—as Siyon took the azata's vacated seat. "What's the word?"

The payment from Joddani clanked very satisfyingly when Siyon set it on the table; satisfaction that doubled when Tein Geras weighed the little sack in a plate-sized palm, and his eyebrows twitched upward. "You can keep something back for yourself," he rumbled.

"Oh, I did." Siyon slouched happily in his chair, and patted his satchel. His cut of the money *and* the phoenix feather that he'd near forgotten in the subsequent excitement. An excellent morning's work, indeed. "I'm owed ten gems as well, but they'll be better off on hilts than anything else I might do with them."

Voski twitched a finger at Tein, who deftly tipped half the coins in the sack into his palm and pushed the sack back across the table. Siyon glanced uncertain at his sergeant; Voski gave a nod. "We appreciate your contribution to the tribe, Velo. Your benefit is our benefit."

As close as she'd come to saying, *Go and become a better alchemist*. At least sitting in the middle of Tower Square. The bravi were too beloved of the city for the inqs to round them up as nuisances to order—and too ostensibly harmless, fighting only among themselves and with those individuals who chose to take up the sabre, and only occasionally mounting token raids on high-profile entertainments whose organisers had neglected to engage a bravi guard. But alchemy was technically illegal, and too much dabbling might get the bravi labelled as *dangerous to the city* as well. Haruspex regularly danced the blade's edge on what they could get away with, but why should they have all the fun?

Daruj, teetering two-legged on his chair as he watched Tein counting the money, smirked. "You do better without me."

"How did Savani do?" Voski asked. Her gaze flitted around the café tables, and a faint frown creased down between her brows. "You didn't break her, did you?"

Siyon waved a vague hand toward the sun-hammered square. "She went off with a pair of Bleeders. She did fine. Got solid nerves."

"Those Bleeders?" Daruj asked, pointing across the square, and up, up, up.

Siyon tilted to look out from beneath the umbrella. At the top of the tower, the sun shone golden and glaring off the open face of the clock, burnished hands ticking ponderously over the bared cogs. Mechanical clockwork, not alchemical, and all the more fascinating for it.

"Are they out on the clock face?" That was the wild and heedless Bleeding Dawn for you.

Voski grunted. "If they bollocks up the workings, the Bleeders can answer to the prefect for it. Listen—" She tapped a blunt finger on the table. "This is all above board, yeah? Anyone going to come knocking?" Not disapproving, just curious. She could defend better against the strikes she saw coming.

"All good," Siyon said. "It—well, it's a long story." But Voski leaned back with her tea—and beckoned a waiter for more, including a glass for Siyon—so he settled in and told it, all the strange happenings of the morning.

Interrupted, just as he was skipping over Jaleh (no need to let Daruj say *I told you so* again) and getting to the part with the haughty young azatan, by Daruj gasping. "Bloody hell. Those fools are actually out on the clock hands. Are they *duelling*?"

That got Voski's attention—her tribe crossing blades was her business. But after a moment squinting in the sun, she stepped back under the umbrella again. "Just dancing. *Balance*, you said." She pointed at Siyon. "What does that mean?"

Siyon shrugged. "Some theory about how the planes fit together. Lean on each other? Spin like a top? I don't know. Mostly I think they use it as an excuse for why alchemy doesn't work outside Bezim, or why someone else shouldn't do something, or just why their complicated workings fuck up. Not sure I believe it. The planes just are. It'd be like a mountain being out of balance."

Tein grunted. "Heard of volcanoes?"

Siyon blinked, but before he could really think about that, a scream rang out across the square, bright as a bell.

He was on his feet a moment later. Only as he launched into a sprint did Siyon consciously realise what had him in motion.

He recognised that scream. He'd heard it once already today.

The figure up above, dangling kicking from the end of the clock's hand, was Zagiri.

A crowd gathered beneath the clock tower as people stopped to point and gawk at the dangling figure. Siyon skidded into their midst, shouldering aside objections.

Behind him, Daruj bellowed, "Out of the fucking way!"

He'd come with Siyon, half a step behind him when usually it was the other way. Voski was there too, giving orders: "You and you, get up the damn tower. You three, sort this lot out."

It would all take too long. Four storeys up the tower, a narrow and winding staircase. Siyon had been up too, in his youth. Everyone did it. You went up, looked down at the city, felt like you owned it because you were young and invincible.

Zagiri wasn't invincible. Not even an eighteen-year-old azata could fly.

The crowd thinned and skittered aside, shoved by bravi in their leathers and Bracken badges. They formed an avid ring, hands over mouths, no one looking away.

Siyon shielded his eyes from the glare of the sun. His throat was dry, the cobblestones tilting beneath his heels. Someone jostled his elbow, a dark shadow at the edge of his vision. "What do you need?" Daruj muttered.

A miracle. The impossible. A single solitary idea of how he could fix this.

He had to do *something*. She'd saved his life this morning, hauled him out of an angel's vengeful grip. He couldn't stand by and let gravity kill her.

"Just keep them back." Siyon hauled his satchel open without looking away from Zagiri's distant, swinging feet. His fingers ran over the little pockets that lined the satchel, bristling with vials and knotted bags and the prickle of dried herbs. Literally his stock in trade, and he knew it all by heart.

What did he have? What could it achieve? Everything seemed so paltry, set against this problem. But this was all he had, and here and now *he* was all *Zagiri* had.

Siyon pulled out a slim vial. Even through the smoked glass, the contents glimmered and sparkled like a Flower's veil. Stardust, the alchemists called it, though it was neither dust nor from stars, but rather the very base matter of the Aethyreal plane itself, the not-quite-air through which the djinn moved.

Most alchemists would just consider it a starting point, the water you added to your soup. But when it was all you had available to you, you learned to wring the most out of it.

Siyon thumbed the cork out of the vial, and let the stardust unfurl. It was barely visible in full sun, just a wink and a shimmer in the air, but he hooked his fingers through it anyway, coiled the stuff around his hand—a little slippery, a little cool, a little whispery against his skin—and then *reached*—

Up toward Zagiri. And through the stardust, across the planes, hooking just a little of the strangeness of the Aethyreal back into the Mundane. His head spun with sudden vertigo, like he was high on a mast in heaving seas, but Siyon had even less patience than usual for the skittishness of the planes. He blinked hard, and tightened his grip, and pushed through.

Here was an irony: Siyon couldn't delve the Aethyreal plane— drew the portal, but it never opened—but Aethyreal matter always responded to his workings, easily and readily, happy to bend to his vaguely formed plans. Siyon barely had to think to conjure a breeze or blast or noise on the wind.

He could certainly twist the air between himself and Zagiri to his will, make it carry sound and meaning. "There," he grunted.

Above him, Zagiri's feet kicked wildly. "Siyon?"

The spark of satisfaction was nearly drowned by a bitter tide. If he could do this, then why couldn't he make it solid, why couldn't he wrap her up in air and lift her down?

Why wasn't he a *proper* alchemist?

That sort of thinking wouldn't get him anywhere. He *had* to be enough. He was the only one here. "Down in the square," he confirmed. "Don't look! What the hell is going on?"

She swung from the clock hand. "Accident. I slipped. We were climbing the gears, daring each other to—" She swallowed the specific lunacies of combining the Bleeding Dawn and rakia. "I can't get back in." Her voice was very small, very far away, even through the Aethyr.

"It's going to be fine." Siyon had no idea how. "Can you swing back to the face?"

Above him, one shadowed limb stretched toward the clock. It was too far; at a swing, her toe barely brushed against the exposed workings. Zagiri whimpered. "Fuck, my hands are getting tired."

"Gullshit," Siyon declared. "You can duel all night, you can swing from the gutters until dawn, you can hold on a little longer." He twisted the Aethyr connection around one hand as he rummaged in his satchel again. What could he *do*? "Are the others still there? Can one of them throw you a rope?"

"The clockwork has shifted." Zagiri sounded strained, which was hardly surprising. "They might be able to reach me again in another five minutes."

That was a long time, dangling over a drop like this. Siyon couldn't help thinking of this morning, when he'd been knocked off a rocky outcrop nearly as high as the clock tower, and no real damage done, but that had been in the Empyreal plane and—

Oh.

Siyon's mind raced. Could he? Would it work? (Did he have any other ideas?) He pulled a jar from the bottom of his satchel, the lid smudged with dirty fingerprints. Just ash, entirely Mundane, but you didn't need power to mark a portal. Like called to like, and intention did the rest.

"I have an idea," he said.

"Oh good." Zagiri giggled, a touch shrill. "I'm all ears."

Except he couldn't get the bloody jar open while holding the Aethyreal tether with one hand. Someone grabbed it, twisting the lid; Siyon gave Daruj a grateful smile, and said through the Aethyr, "I'm going to draw a portal. You'll fall through it, into the Empyreal."

"I'll what?" Zagiri sounded even more agitated now. "Back with the motherfuckers with flaming broadswords? I won't have—like you did, with the rope. I won't have a tether."

"You also won't be dead," Siyon snapped. He crouched, set the open jar down on the cobbles, and dipped two fingers in the ash. "I will come after you. I will get you back. I promise I will save you, Zagiri. Someone get me a rope," he added, over his shoulder to Daruj, who dashed away.

The ash tingled against his fingers. Weird, it didn't usually do that. Then again, he wasn't usually holding an active working while he did this. Siyon started drawing a line of ash across the cobbles.

Silence from above—just the wind whistling around the clock— and then Zagiri said, "Hurry."

Siyon hurried, but not too much. The line still needed to be straight, the angles exact, not to mention the portal placed correctly and large enough that there was no question she'd land inside it. The crowd seethed around him, shifting bodies and breathless speculation—*What's he doing?* and *Is that sorcery?*

How long did Siyon have before someone brought the inquisitors running? He had to concentrate; there was no time for screwing up. He drew one side, long enough to be certain, counting out the steps as Bracken bravi shouted and shoved the crowd out of the way. He turned the corner, drew the next side, same number of steps. Now he was very close to the base of the tower, its shadow starting to nip his heels.

He started on the third side, then stopped at a whirring, mechanical sound. Not down here, through the Aethyr. Zagiri said, "Oh shit, it's going to—"

A thunk through the Aethyr—barely a faint click in the hushed and regular air of the square—as the hand of the clock ticked down one notch. Zagiri's dark silhouette against the bright blue sky jerked with the movement. Legs flailed, grip jolted, hands scrabbled...

She fell.

No. *No.* Siyon's heart clenched, panic clawing at his throat. The portal wasn't finished, couldn't be finished, she was falling *now.* The crowd screamed, and Siyon reached up with his ash-smeared hand like he could do something, like he could catch her. The sun's glare seared his eyes, and desperation scoured his throat.

"Please." The word was a whisper, and yet it was also a scream; it tore out of him like it had fiery wings, like it was *reaching*—

Another scream ricocheted around the square like a flung blade. It was fierce and piercing, the shriek of a hunting animal, the screech of tortured armour, the sound of dreams torn asunder. It rattled Siyon's senses, took them over, like a sudden smell thick enough to coat his tongue with sand, with ash, with rage.

—and something crashed into Siyon's hands, his arms, his chest. A building, an elephant, the world. The square slammed against his back. Dazzle danced in his eyes, and his ribs creaked as Siyon tried and failed to draw breath.

He blinked, and a face danced in after-image behind his eyelids. Just visible against searing light—hawk-sharp nose, diamond-bright eyes, a wild halo of tightly curled hair—and then it was gone.

"Fuck," someone said, the word more felt through Siyon's chest than heard by still-ringing ears.

He knew that voice. Had just been hearing it through Aethyr and alchemy. "Zagiri?" Siyon croaked, trying to shift arms that felt turned to rubber and bruise.

There was hair across his face, dark and glossy and smelling—as the stench of blackened feathers cleared from his nose—of expensive perfumes. There was weight across his chest, not an elephant at all, but a slim body in new, creaking leathers.

Siyon struggled to sitting, difficult as though he were trussed up in bolts of linen. Zagiri slumped against him, but when he turned her over, she winced and coughed, tangling her fingers in the front of Siyon's shirt.

Here. Unbroken. Alive.

What the fuck had just happened?

The cacophony of the crowd veered around Siyon like the whole world was drunk. Babble of voices, clatter of boots, crash of a table overturning. Overhead, an umbrella of open sky, edges blurred by gawping faces. Odd details leapt out at him—freckled face beneath a headscarf; thick brows over narrow black eyes; shouting mouth and pointing finger; a tangle of dark blonde curls like a wild halo, grey eyes hard as diamonds over a nose stark as a hawk's beak—

He turned so fast he nearly tipped Zagiri off his lap. That face—*that face*, the one he'd seen in a dazzle of sun and impossibility—it had been here, in the crowd.

But no, surely not. That had just been a flashback to the angel, screaming sword held aloft. There was no one like that now amid the shock and curiosity.

Daruj flourished a bared blade. "Back, vultures!" His voice boomed, honed for street theatre and calling challenge. He paced around Siyon and Zagiri, sprawled on the cobbles, and other bravi enforced the distance, making a wall of their bodies.

Voski crouched, setting a hand on his shoulder. "Velo." Not the first time she'd said it, from the urgency.

Siyon's head felt stuffed with linen and stardust. He clutched Zagiri tighter to his chest. He'd seen her fall, and now here she was. "I don't know—" He stopped. Couldn't even find the words to encompass all the things he didn't understand right now.

"No kidding." Voski snorted. "But it won't stop the inqs asking. They're on their way, you can bet your blade on it."

The inquisitors would arrest him just for the little twist of Aethyr he'd used to speak with Zagiri, let alone . . . whatever the rest had been. He'd broken the laws of physics. He'd fractured a little of reality.

Laughter bubbled up in his throat, choking and bitter as vomit. He might die for this, and he had no idea what he'd done, or how.

"Velo!" Voski snapped her fingers in front of his face. "Get up, get out of here. We'll figure it out later."

Zagiri was breathing, apparently uninjured, but unconscious and limp. Siyon tried to pick her up, but could barely make it to his knees; in the end, Daruj had to hoist the girl over his shoulder, while Siyon staggered upright by himself.

Tein shouldered through the cordon of Little Bracken bravi. "Inqs incoming on the Boulevard."

"Right." Voski clapped her hands, summoning attention. "Knots of three, diversionary scatter. Move fast, be seen, but *no* mayhem. Regroup at the Chapel in half a bell." She whistled—a short blast of air—and the assembled Little Bracken bravi echoed it in brief chorus, before they fragmented like a shattered cup.

"Go," Voski ordered, shoving Siyon toward Daruj. Siyon's boot caught at the edge of a cobblestone, and by the time he'd righted from his stumble, she was gone, along with the others. The crowd milled and seethed in their wake, reluctant for the show to be over.

Daruj led the way, with Zagiri flopping against his back like a landed fish. Siyon followed them through the thinning crowd into the arcade beneath the clock tower. There were raised voices coming from the staircase winding up inside, but Siyon ignored them and kept moving. Time enough later to reassure her erstwhile companions that Zagiri was all right. Once they'd got away. Once Siyon had made sure that she was, in fact, all right.

Out the back of the clock tower, down a laneway, and Siyon stumbled against Daruj when he stopped suddenly, ducking close to the brick wall. "Dammit," he muttered.

On the cross street ahead, bodies rushed past. Coloured coats, brown student robes, and the grey tunics of inquisitors, marching in their midst. No escape that way, not carrying an unconscious body.

Daruj squinted speculatively upward. "Lower city style, like that time with the dancing girl?"

The memory, as always, made Siyon wince. "Inqs aren't the same as a baron's bruisers, and this lane's too wide, and the cobbles too hard." Not to mention he didn't think he was up to climbing a building, let alone helping with Daruj's burden. The world still spun around him, though he no longer felt like every footfall might skid away beneath him.

Siyon looked around for other options among the nondescript back doors of the shops that—ah, yes. He grabbed Daruj's shirt and tugged him back down the laneway. He found the right door by the delicate scent of lavender and resin, and he held it open for Daruj, who lifted a hand to steady Zagiri as she brushed against bundles of sweet-smelling herbs. Siyon had to duck, slipping quickly through the storeroom and nearly running into someone at the door into the shop proper.

The woman squeaked, and he clapped a hand over her mouth, then yelped as she bit him—not hard, but he pulled his hand away and shook it.

"Do you mind?" she snapped. "Should've guessed this mess had your name to it, Velo."

"Sorry." Siyon tried to flash her a smile, the sort of devil-may-care his clients expected from the plane-skipping bravi who sold them tidbits for their wares—expensive cosmetics, in this case. He hoped he looked less sick than he felt. "Is it clear out there?"

"Not even slightly." She flipped a hand toward the shopfront windows. "There's some inquisitor out there giving orders."

Siyon slunk forward to one of the thick panes of blue-tinted glass. The inquisitor was in front of the next shop along. Difficult to tell his rank without a good look at the badge on his tunic. He didn't have a captain's cloak, but he gave orders with a fiery expectation of unhesitating compliance. No azatani arrogance to him, though. His hair was shorn to dark fuzz on his scalp, and he was solid with muscle—not quite a Dockside brawler, but certainly not the elegance of the Avenues.

Daruj edged up beside Siyon, running an eye over the streetscape. "Lot of grey for bravi mayhem," he muttered.

"Sorcery mayhem," Siyon corrected in a whisper.

"Was it even sorcery, though?" Daruj sounded more conversational than concerned, like there was nothing unusual in skulking in a shop, carrying an unconscious girl, hiding from the law. "You were using *ash*, that's barely alchemy, right? And then you did—what?"

Siyon didn't *know*. It harried at his temper. "I'll just step out and ask that guy what he thinks about the technicalities, shall I?"

The hefty inquisitor whirled about, shouting after someone, and they both ducked down. There'd been a glint in his eye; perhaps a true believer, joined to rid the city of the scourge of alchemy, or perhaps he just had something to prove.

Either was an edge that could flay Siyon if he wasn't careful.

"Hey," the shopkeeper said, just behind them, and Daruj stifled a yelp. She gave him an unimpressed look, but turned back to Siyon. "Can I get more Abyssal brine? I'm nearly out."

Siyon stared at her. "Is this really the time?"

She shrugged. "If you're going into hiding, it's get it now, or talk to someone else. Is Corbinus still down behind the university?" She smiled at him blandly.

Siyon grumbled, but he was hardly going anywhere, so he found a couple of vials in his satchel. He handed them over; she laid a couple of coins in his palm in exchange; he looked at them, and then at her.

She blinked, all innocence. "I figured, in the circumstances, there'd be a discount, right?

Outside, the inquisitor shouted, "I want every single one of them in custody!"

Daruj was laughing silently but gleefully. "She's got you there, brother."

Siyon glared but let it slide, and a few moments later the inquisitors were stalking away down the street. With a cheery little wave from the shopkeeper, he and Daruj slipped out of the shop and scurried across the road, into another laneway.

Siyon was happy to run until they were out of breath, but after everything that had happened—and Daruj's burden—that barely took them four blocks into the deep tangle of tenements.

They stopped at a corner fountain, where Daruj propped Zagiri against the edge of the water basin. Daruj rolled his shoulder with a grimace, beaded hair shifting. "I'm getting too old for this."

"You've been saying that since we were seventeen." Siyon hunched over Zagiri, finding her pulse in her throat—steady enough—and gently lifting one of her eyelids.

She grumbled and shoved at his wrist; Siyon nearly fell over with relief. But she didn't wake up, just slumped a little more into the corner between fountain and wisteria-wound trellis.

Siyon sat back on his heels. "We need to get to the Chapel." But Daruj winced, and Siyon realised. "We can't. The inqs will come knocking."

"Plenty of witnesses to see our badges." Daruj pinged a fingernail against his own, pinned to the front of his shirt. "Voski won't give you up—you know that—but she can't keep them out and if they find you…"

There was naught they could do. Siyon nodded numbly. "Of course. I guess I head for the lower city." The inqs rarely went below the Scarp; lower city folk kept their own sort of peace, and didn't care for the official kind. But he could hardly take Zagiri there—couldn't think how to get her down the Scarp unconscious, for starters—and he couldn't just abandon her up here. Not when her condition was his fault.

He shifted, his satchel knocking against his hip, and that was enough to remind him of the morning's work. Or rather, of their visit to the Summer Club. To Joddani. "She has family."

Daruj snorted. "You're not taking her back to the Savani town-house like *this*. They'll call the inqs on you."

Siyon shook his head. "Her sister's married to a practitioner. I know where *he* lives."

Daruj considered that, nodding slowly. "The inqs aren't likely to toss the Avenues. Long way between here and there, though."

Nothing but the truth. "Hate to ask it," Siyon said, "but do you think Voski would be willing to run a little more distraction?"

From his grin, *Daruj* certainly was. "We'll cover you, brother. Are you going to be all right with her alone?"

Siyon shrugged. "I'll figure something out."

Hopefully something a little less dramatic this time.

CHAPTER 4

Sitting beneath the vine-shaded pergola of Azata Parsola's garden, Anahid Joddani heard the clock tower bell, and thought of her sister.

Mostly, she thought of how Zagiri would have found this luncheon even more tedious than Anahid herself did. She'd likely not have lasted past the second course—fiddly little bird legs in a delicate sauce—before committing some outrage. Anahid wondered if she'd ever manage half as much heedlessness as Zagiri could encompass in an afternoon.

Laughter shimmered down the table. The vine-dappled sun glinted on the beadwork on headscarves and sparkled on ringed fingers. All very discreet displays of wealth, power, and respectability.

Across the table was Azata Malkasani, the committee chair of the Harbour Master's Ball, who had held the social lives of new azatas in her net-gloved hand for a dozen years now. A few seats down was Azata Prishtani, who had taken the family finances in hand when both her brothers died in the storms of the Dragon's Summer twenty years ago. At the end of the table was Azata Filosani, who had served in the Palace as clerk and secretary and magistrate, and would surely be contending for prefect when Syrah Danelani's term ended in two years' time.

Nearly every woman at this table was at least a decade older than Anahid, with power social, mercantile, or political to her name. Anahid had served no clerkships, sat on no committees, sailed on no trade voyages. So she was here to be assessed, or to be delightful, or both.

If she could manage *delightful*, it might not have taken Anahid three seasons to marry. Zagiri might well have been the better choice for this invitation. At least she always left an impression.

The best Anahid could do was *respectable*. She could give the right responses, wield her cutlery expertly, defer perfectly. She could have managed the proper etiquette to turn down the invitation, but it would have been more trouble—cards to send, inquiries to manage— than simply sitting through the event. And of course, she had to come if she wanted to be invited again.

Anahid should *want* to spend time in this company. She should want to impress them. This was her life, and she should make the most of it. She had cast off on this voyage. It was no one's fault but her own if she now found herself lost at sea.

Nurturi Parsola, their hostess, wasn't azatani, but she'd brought such an extraordinary amount of wealth with her when she left the Khanate that most of society was quite willing to allow her to borrow the title, and to be hosted by her at her grand and sprawling house. It was far too close to the Scarp for a proper azata to be comfortable living here, but being out of the cramped Avenues did mean space for beautiful, bee-humming, sun-nodding gardens.

"Anahid, darling." Azata Malkasani spoke with the easy familiarity she'd earned guiding Anahid through all those pre-marriage balls, as Anahid grew desperate and gossip grew biting. "We were all hoping when you married Joddani that we would be seeing you both out and about a little more."

"Quite so," interjected her neighbour, an elderly azata in a bright orange headscarf. Malkasani straightened her cutlery on her plate; she'd always had the habit of fiddling when what she wanted to adjust was behaviour around her, but perhaps her neighbour didn't notice, too busy saying, "What's it been now, half a year? Haven't seen you once at the opera."

"Only five months," Anahid corrected, her smile fixed. Not even half a year for all her dreams to collapse.

The lady at Anahid's left—who had been conversing on her other side so far—broke suddenly into the exchange. "Did someone say opera? I've been twice, just since we got back." She laughed merrily, in a flash of white teeth. "Nearly two years is far too long to go without hearing Gayane Saliu sing."

"Seva is there every week, even in low season," Azata Malkasani said, with the serenity that often hid a sly remark. "With her glasses trained firmly on the crowd."

Her neighbour—Seva, presumably—gave a disgruntled huff and turned pointedly the other way.

Malkasani waved her fingers—diamonds sparking on her knuckles—across the table. "Anahid, were you properly introduced to Tahera Danelani? Tahera, my duckling, this is Anahid Joddani, who would have been Savani before you went away to the New Republic."

Anahid needed none of her rigorous drilling on the azatani families to recognise the importance of her neighbour's name—not when the prefect herself shared it. She even thought she remembered attending the wedding procession, six years ago or more now, of the younger brother Demian, marrying one of the first-tier Kurlani daughters.

Tahera was the one other at the table close to Anahid's age—probably only a handful of years older, rather than ten or more. Her dress blended the wide-cut neckline of southern Republic fashion with the long sleeves and wide waist-sash of Bezim, and the whole thing made the most of her long neck and plump curves.

As always, Anahid felt too tall, too gawkish, too angular. But Tahera smiled at her; she had generous features that carried her delight handsomely. "Oh yes! I heard you slapped Avarair Hisarani at the Fortune Regatta, and I was *so* sorry not to have a chance to make your acquaintance before we left."

Anahid's cheeks threatened to heat with the remembered shame of it—both the attention to her actions and the words that had snapped her restraint. Two years and not long enough ago. "Gracious," she said mildly. "I had quite forgotten about that."

"Can't think why," Tahera chirped, bright as a little bird. "If *I'd* had the chance to slap that irritating prig, I'd burnish the memory daily. At least he's not as bad as my nephew, yes?"

She appealed across the table, and Anahid had to stifle a laugh in her napkin as Malkasani aligned her finger bowl with precision. Though all she said about Enkin Danelani was: "He is a terribly handsome lad who will one day make a fine azatan, I'm quite sure of it."

"He is terrible, at least, on that we can agree." For all Tahera's blithe mirth, she kept her voice down. He was still the son of the prefect of the city. "And one day he will make a disaster even his mother can't smooth over."

Malkasani sniffed. "Or perhaps he will meet the right partner, who will change his ways." She shot a pointed look at Anahid.

Who hardly wished to be anyone's example of marital reform. "You have been in the New Republic?" Anahid asked quickly, turning to Tahera. This was a far safer topic, and one much more comfortably not about *her*. She sifted through her memories of news and gossip. "Of course, your husband was the prefect's special cultural envoy."

Tahera laughed and reached for her glass of sparkling pink djinn-wine. "Demy did not want to come home!"

"And you?" Anahid prompted.

Her glass emptied, Tahera handed it to a servant and accepted a tall glass of rose tea in exchange. It was nearly the end of the meal. "Oh, I had plenty to do. So many opportunities!"

Opportunities for trade, she meant. Trade, or investment, or another way to turn a profit and increase an azatani family's reach and capacity to generate *more* opportunities. Bezim, it was said, could grow nothing in its rocky hinterland, and thus plowed the sea, sowing and reaping a mercantile harvest.

"But it's good to be home," Tahera sighed. "There are so many things one doesn't even think of until one has to go without them for a year and more."

At the near end of the table, their hostess set down her empty teaglass and said, "Will you join me at tiles, ladies?" A question without need of an answer, as the cases were already being brought out.

Anahid swallowed hard against the urge to groan. The last thing she wanted was to be trapped in a game of tiles, with all its infinite iterations of blind luck and long spates between turns. The game was usually just an excuse to idle and gossip.

But at the other end of the table, one azata was asking another after her newly arrived grandchild, and Anahid found that actually, the *very* last thing she wanted was to have anyone turning their eyes upon *her* and asking questions about children.

Beside her, Tahera set her napkin upon her plate and said, "I would dearly love to take a little stroll in the gardens. I've missed our wonderful climate so. Azata Joddani, may I press you to join me?"

Merry eyes and a wide smile suggested Tahera Danelani knew just how little Anahid wished to remain at this table.

They walked along the terrace, and then down a few steps into a lush rose garden. As the conversation from the table fell away behind them, Tahera said brightly, "Oh, thank goodness. If I were forced into playing tiles, I might have done something uncouth."

It was just the two of them, Tahera's face turned up beaming into the sunshine, so Anahid allowed herself to say, "We can go back, if you like. I shouldn't be the only one who's slapped someone in public."

Tahera laughed out loud—far too loud—and skipped a few merry steps on the grass. "Oh, slapping that old bat Palokani might be just as satisfying as a Hisarani. Chair of the Committee for Moral Reform for six years now, you know, and she still cheats at tiles. Brazenly, and if you say anything about it, she makes out that you're unreasonable and carping." She reached out and touched the vibrantly red petals of a rose. "And in the Republic all they play is lottery. I have been absolutely dying for a game of carrick, but they think cards are for divination and alchemy. As though it works over there." She looked over her shoulder. "I don't suppose you play?"

Anahid shook her head, trailing after more slowly and circumspectly. Habit kept her hands folded over the sash around her waist. "The only card games I know are the society ones. Triumph, or tapers."

Tahera's face was just as expressive with dismissive disgust. "Simple enough that everyone can spend more time on their gossip than their cards."

It was so true that Anahid couldn't help laughing.

"You can find carrick in society as well," Tahera said, offhand as she squinted into the sunny garden. "If you know where to look. Would you be interested in learning?"

Yes. The vehemence of her answer, clenched tight inside her, surprised Anahid. She did want to learn. Wanted like she could learn a little of Tahera's easy confidence along with the rules. Wanted it so strongly she couldn't quite shape her mouth around the word.

Was saved from trying by a voice calling from the terrace. "Azata Joddani!"

It was one of Azata Parsola's footmen. He gave a little bow. "There's been a runner. You are needed at home, most urgently. Some matter involving your sister."

Fancy that. Zagiri wasn't even here, and she'd still done something outrageous.

◆

Zagiri was cast up on the rocks after a storm, aching in every part of her body.

No, she was strapped to the spina of the hippodrome, hooves whirling thunder in the baking sand.

No, she was stumbling through back alleys, arm wrenched over someone's too-tall shoulders, toes catching at the edges of cobblestones, ribs gouged by a sabre hilt. She staggered, she tilted, her head dropped back. High above, framed in the chasm between buildings, she saw the sun.

A swoop, a plummet, a wrench of vicious righteousness.

She screamed.

They stumbled; she slipped. Someone yelped, "Fuck!" A hand clapped over her mouth—it smelt of copper and sweat and, strangely, of lavender.

Zagiri spiralled into darkness again.

She swayed in the arms of the sea, standing lookout watch in the prow of a trading voyage—but wait, she had decided against going into trade. She couldn't be here.

She jostled in a palanquin—but no, she could *run*, free and strong and her own mistress. She shoved aside the cushions and draperies, and the palanquin dissolved around her.

Her boots hit paving stones. Zagiri staggered, and someone gripped her arms. A voice—that voice, she knew that voice—muttered, "If I'd known this was going to be so much trouble..."

"Siyon!" Yes, that's who it was. Zagiri blinked, and blinked again, keeping her head down. The paving crawled with djinnsparks in her vision, but the squares were grey and even and laid in familiar patterns. They were in the Avenues.

Zagiri grabbed at Siyon's shoulder, found the strap of his satchel. "You can't take me home." She couldn't remember what was wrong; she didn't *feel* drunk, not quite. But if she went home like *this*, she'd never hear the end of it from Mother. "No. No. Chapel." It was barely a mumble.

"We can't. Not with the inqs out for us."

The inqs? She looked up at him—too fast.

This time the darkness was velvet-deep. She wallowed in it, not wanting to get up and face the morning. She was safe; Siyon had caught her; stop prodding her and let her *sleep*.

Far away, Siyon snapped: "Well, can you send for her? This is her sister."

He couldn't be talking about Zagiri; Anahid would never see someone like Siyon. She got that pained look about Zagiri's bravi leathers, and hers were infinitely more presentable than Siyon's battered clothes. *Propriety is our armour, Giri*, she said.

Zagiri heard just that voice, her sister's precise and whiplash voice, saying, "What have you done to her?"

Was Anahid *shouting*? Curiosity roused her; Zagiri opened her eyes, the ceiling swimming out of heat haze and into focus. Not as tall a ceiling as she was used to; was she understairs? A face bent over her—fox-canny, hair pulled back severely, vaguely familiar. Of course, it was Nura, her sister's new housekeeper. The one she'd got when the old one refused to cede to the house's new-married mistress. But what was Nura doing here?

Nura said, "Mistress, she's—"

Interrupted by Anahid, definitely shouting this time. "If this is some alchemical attempt to extort—"

"I didn't do anything!" That was Siyon. "Well, I did, but—"

"He saved me." Zagiri meant to say it firmly. It came out as a croak.

It was enough. Suddenly Anahid was there, though Zagiri barely recognised her sister. Who knew Anahid could look that worried, that relieved, that *anything*.

Zagiri shifted—on the couch in Nura's office, she realised—and winced as even that small movement strummed a chord of pain across her body. "Fuck, I feel trampled."

Her sister's face slid into cool composure, with a grace note of exasperation. *Now* she looked like Anahid. "Language, Giri. What did you *do*?"

"Something stupid." Zagiri wanted to grin, but it felt more a weak smile. "Like always." She blinked at Anahid; at her headscarf, whose gold beading matched the detail work around the neck of her gown. "You were out. Sorry. I'll just—" She tried to sit up, and nearly blacked out again.

"Don't you move." Anahid laid a hand on Zagiri's forehead, and it was cool and gentle. Zagiri missed it when her sister shifted instead to her shoulder.

"A doctor?" Nura asked.

Siyon said, "Uh, that might not be the best idea."

Anahid turned to look at him; Zagiri lolled her head and found Siyon standing by the door of the office, looking even more of a mess than he had this morning. Her sister had always been oddly perceptive—certainly seen more of what Zagiri was up to than had ever been comfortable—but what could Anahid see here but an out-and-out ruffian?

Anahid said, "Nura tells me you have dealings with my husband."

Siyon nodded. "I supply certain necessaries for his work."

"I presume that what ails my sister is not entirely Mundane in origin." It wasn't really a question; Anahid sighed, and rubbed at her forehead. For someone who'd married an alchemist, she didn't seem to like alchemy very much. "The runner who fetched me from lunch mentioned a great deal of inquisitor activity around Tower Square. 'Buzzing like a hive of kicked bees,' I believe was his precise expression. Would that have anything to do with this?"

"Probably." Siyon winced.

Not with the inqs out for us, Zagiri remembered suddenly, from what must have been the long, staggering journey here. Of course they'd have shown up. Siyon had—done what? Zagiri remembered the sickening lurch of the clock hand, the cold panic of her lost grip, the awful pull of gravity. Then—

Blast of sunlight, screech of an eagle, something gripping her entire body as though in a scalding fist.

Then nothing.

Anahid stood, breaking Zagiri's moment of dizziness. "Nura, ask the footmen to convey my sister to her usual guest chamber. Master Velo, thank you for bringing her to me. If you wait here, my housekeeper will ensure you are properly rewarded."

Things seemed to move very fast. Zagiri felt dizzier than ever. There were two of her sister's footmen lifting her, Siyon dancing aside from the door, and wait. "Wait!" she croaked, and caught at the doorframe.

The footman banged his elbow against the door and hissed, but Zagiri ignored him. Anahid snapped, "Honestly, Giri, can't you just—"

"He saved me," she repeated. It was hard to find words—she had to chase them through the maze of her mind—but she hung on grimly and tracked them down. "With sorcery. They'll want to catch him."

Anahid frowned as though she didn't understand why Zagiri was pointing out the obvious. "You've somewhere safe to go, Master Velo?" She turned to him expectantly.

But he didn't, Zagiri was sure of it. Couldn't go to the Bracken safe house, not while the inqs were after him. Anywhere else he had to go wouldn't be close by. She remembered the state of his coat. Not an upper city coat.

Siyon said, "Um."

Which was all Anahid needed. "Then you'll stay here, of course. Nura will see to a guest chamber. And perhaps a bath as well." She turned away with a faint sniff, and fixed a stern eye on Zagiri. "Now stop impeding my servants in the execution of their duties."

Zagiri glanced at Siyon—who seemed utterly shocked by this turn of events—and let go of the doorframe. The swaying sensation of being in the footman's arms felt familiar; Siyon had carried her part of the way here, she realised.

As they started to climb the stairs, she heard Siyon say, "I'm not sure your husband will be very pleased to have me here."

And she heard Anahid reply primly, "I don't particularly care what my husband likes."

Siyon woke gasping in panic, clawing for the surface of the dark, still water. He struggled and kicked, and the strange scents of cedar and rosewater lifted away the shroud of nightmare.

He wasn't drowning. He was—somehow, impossibly—in the guest bedroom of an azatani townhouse.

As his heart slowed, Siyon shoved fine linen away from his face. The curtains were so thick, they could turn day to gloaming; Siyon had no idea what time it was. Furnishings lurked in the shadows—a hulking wooden clothespress, a washstand, a table with a covered tray, two chairs— Wait.

Siyon's stomach growled as he fought his way out of the sheets he'd tangled in his flailing. The bed was reluctant to let him go; it was far softer than anything Siyon had ever slept in before.

It was day outside, and the tray was breakfast—coffee and bread, with a pale, piquant cheese and fresh apricots that burst with flavour. Siyon was ravenous; it was only with his mouth crammed with bread and cheese that he noticed garments slung over one of the chairs, along with his satchel. *His* garments, Siyon realised after a moment of suspicious staring. He barely recognised the shirt without the stain on the shoulder it had had since last summer. And the thin patch at the elbow had been darned.

Nice life for some. Siyon could get used to all this, though he assumed he had about a day before he was back on the street, with Azata Joddani's polite, stern, but now spent thanks. It was fine. Zagiri was safe, and Siyon needed to get to the Scarp, get *down* the Scarp, bury himself in the lower city like a crab in sand.

It would all be easier if he were well rested and well fed. So he ate as much as he could and tucked two apricots away in his satchel, before he dressed and stepped out of the room.

And nearly ran into someone—a slender someone, draped in linen and lace, with pale straight hair and a faint fragrance like the city after a storm. Siyon staggered, fighting a moment of wild vertigo. (Frantic bubbles clouding his face, which way was *up*?)

The someone jumped back. "Don't *do* that!" he gasped, more air than voice in the words.

It was the young man from the Summer Club, the one who had taken Siyon and Zagiri up to see Joddani. Today he was in periwinkle blue with cloud-grey lace, his feet in ridiculous house slippers the bright yellow of a child's drawn sun, and he still made something itch in Siyon's mind.

"Wait," Siyon said, looking down at those slippers. "You *live* here?" In the same house as Nihath's wife?

Tehroun frowned, like he didn't understand the question at all, and Siyon reminded himself that how the rich and powerful wanted to live their lives was none of his business.

Maybe it was just that *he* wouldn't want to cross Anahid Joddani. He couldn't have denied her likeness to her sister, but the older was hard and sharp everywhere the younger was pert and girlish. Not that he'd met that many azatas. Maybe they all had that faint edge of anger barely contained when they spoke about their husbands.

It was a relief when a new voice said, "Ah, Master Velo, you are risen. Good." The housekeeper, Nura, crested the stairs. She seemed young for the role, and determined to make up for it in pinch-mouthed severity. Her brisk once-over left Siyon feeling scrubbed raw. "There is a visitor. Come."

"For me?" Siyon followed her by perplexed reflex. When he paused to look back, Tehroun was gone and the corridor empty.

Nura directed Siyon into a study on the next floor down. It was crowded with heavy furniture and lined with books. Nothing compared to the glories Siyon had glimpsed at the Summer Club, but a dizzying number when Siyon realised this was the library from which Joddani would select the books *he* was allowed to read.

Then he forgot about books in the relief of seeing the woman perched on one corner of the large desk. Her turban was a deep, rich purple today, but the glint of humour in her eyes was the same as ever. "Auntie." Siyon hurried forward to clasp her hand and press a cheek to hers in respectful greeting. It had taken him nearly a year to realise that the term was one of respect and affection, and that she wasn't Daruj's actual aunt. By the time she invited Siyon to address her so as well, she'd already taught him to reach across the planes, to delve for ingredients, to yearn for more.

Far more encouragement than Siyon's actual aunts had ever given him.

Geryss chuckled in his ear. "Boy, what *have* you been up to?"

"Rather my question as well."

Siyon startled—he hadn't even realised Joddani was here, though it made sense for a man to be in his own study. He turned and gave a little bow. It didn't really cost him anything. "Sorry, za, I didn't see you there. Thank you for your hospitality, I won't trouble you further. Is Zagi—"

Joddani slammed a book down atop a pile of others. "*Now* you think of trouble? After turning my house into a circus and doing—" He waved a hand. "Whatever that was in the square. Without a care for the proper counterbalancing of forces unleashed, and leaving all sorts of who-knows-what *flying* around—"

"You're a force unleashed," Geryss interrupted, leaning back and kicking her heels in their worn and mud-spattered boots. "Carrying on like a trained parrot. You been down there, Nihath? You walked the cobblestones and tasted the sunlight?"

Joddani glared at her; Geryss just looked more amused. "I don't need to engage in such fanciful nonsense. The most cursory consideration of the incident makes it quite clear that a significant outlay of energy must have been required, and I very much doubt Velo bothered to construct any sort of baffles or absorption."

They both looked at him. Siyon tried to look like he had any idea what they were talking about. "There wasn't a lot of time."

"And yet," Geryss pointed out, "there *isn't* any additional imbalance in the square. No, shut up, Nihath." He closed his mouth again, though he looked mutinous. "I don't care what Negedic theory insists must be so. Yes, I felt the lurch when he did it. But today—here, right now!" She stabbed a finger at him. "You tell me the planes are not steadier than you've felt them in a season."

Joddani glowered like a simmering kettle. "Variability is part of the problem, I've always said that. The periods of stability do not negate the severity of the overall problem."

"But it's just as normal!" Geryss pounced, satisfied as a hunting cat. "You know I'm with you, Nihath. The planes *are* out of alignment, and only slipping more so. I've felt it shift since I came to the city, even if the young ones like him"—she waved a hand in Siyon's direction—"have never known any different. They think you always had to hold the planes steady just to step across."

Siyon blinked. "You didn't?"

Both of them ignored him. "What I'm saying, Nihath, is that whatever Siyon did yesterday is not part of the problem."

Joddani chewed that over. He sounded almost sulky when he said, "That is not possible."

Geryss shrugged. "You and your dead pal Negedi are the experts in what's possible. I just know what I see with my own two eyes." She got a wicked glint in her eye. "You could ask him, you know. He's right there."

Joddani heaved a sigh. "What did you do, Velo?"

Siyon shoved away the whole question of planar balance—still not *his* concern—and grinned at him. "Absolutely no idea."

"What?" Joddani's frown deepened.

But Geryss cackled. She was the only practitioner in the whole city who'd ever had any time for him, and her amusement felt a lot like support. Very welcome support, given Siyon was cut off from near everything else in his life right now.

So when she cocked her head like she was listening, if he wanted to share, he did. "I had a plan to open a portal and let Zagiri fall through it—"

"You *what*?" Joddani demanded, awful close to a yelp for azatani dignity.

Siyon continued regardless. "But she fell before I was finished and I just—" Words evaporated. What *had* he done? "She was falling, and the sun was in my eyes, and I needed to catch her, and then...I did. Is she all right, by the way?"

"What?" Joddani batted away the question. "Yes, fine. What do you mean you *needed* to? How is that—" Words failed his incredulity. He picked up a pair of eyeglasses and set them vengefully on his nose, all the better to glare over the top. "If you're not going to take this seriously, I fail to see why I should continue this conversation at all."

"You won't object if I take him off to the club, then." Geryss hopped down from the corner of the desk.

"Yes, yes." Joddani waved a grand and dismissive hand. "Take him away and—wait. I hardly think this nonsense merits admittance."

He looked sour; Geryss looked serene. "Your opinion is noted. I'll canvas the others. Come along, Velo."

Admittance? To the *club*? But even with that possibility shimmering, Siyon paused in the doorway to ask: "*Is* Zagiri all right?" He couldn't really believe it. Not after...that.

Joddani frowned at him. "I told you, she's fine. Quite restored by sleep and food, already gone off back to her own home. *Whatever* you did, it seems to have caused no lingering imbalance to her either."

The relief of it unknotted something inside Siyon. He jogged down the expensive hall runner to Geryss at the top of the staircase, grin growing with every step. "Are you serious?" he asked. "About—I mean, I can't go to the Summer Club."

She cocked her head at him. "Why not?"

"He's right, I'm nowhere near membership." Siyon could be honest about this with Geryss; she wasn't judging him. "I'd like to, obviously. I have the money to take you up on those lessons, once—y'know." He waved a hand down the grand and sweeping staircase, at the front door and the world beyond. "Once the inqs aren't combing the streets for me."

Geryss just hummed. "What makes you say you ain't ready now?"

Siyon huffed a laugh. "You've seen me try to set up an alembic. I can't even do that. And whatever I did in the square....I don't know what it was, but it wasn't alchemy."

"Then what was it?" Geryss didn't wait for an answer before she leaned in. "Alchemy's just a word. Just a box so they can say inside-yes and outside-no. You know what people called the Art, before they started dressing up fancy with their longvests and glassware?" Her smile curved wicked and keen as a blade. "*Magic.*"

Siyon slumped against the banister, rubbing at his face. "Auntie. Are you saying I did magic?"

"You did something." Her eyebrows lifted. "What's the matter, Velo? Haven't you wanted to join the Club as long as I've known you? Hustling and scrimping and bartering for lessons to edge toward the entry criteria...Boy, why jump through their hoops when you just leapt over the moon?"

Because that was how it was done. That series of impossible hoops was what he'd been focused on for years, the fixed if-only stars in his sky. He'd clutched so tight to the faint chance of getting into the Summer Club, getting access to it all. Their books, their workshops, their storerooms.

"I can't go out there," Siyon said, and it felt flimsy even in his own mouth. "The inqs are looking for me."

"The inqs," Geryss corrected, "are looking for some Bracken that no one can describe accurately. One fish in the ocean."

In a city that ate so much fish, that was less than totally reassuring, but Siyon could be just as slippery. "Do you really think I have a chance?" he asked.

She grinned so wide he could see the glint of gold from a back tooth. "Only one way to find out. Let's go."

CHAPTER 5

The Summer Club was even more grand from the front door, with the full majesty of the alchemical clock framed by the mahogany and alabaster fittings of the entry hall.

The effect was somewhat spoiled by the confusion of the footman who popped up to take a hat that Siyon didn't have. "Your, er, satchel, sir?" he asked instead.

"Don't you dare," Siyon told him.

The guy behind the counter was better dressed than Siyon, in snowy linen and a plain black longvest. He pushed a leather-bound ledger across the counter. "Please sign in your guest, Mistress Hanlun." She took up the slim pen; the guy flicked his gaze quickly over Siyon. "I must remind you that your guest may have the freedom of the lower levels, but cannot enter the workshops on the upper floor save in your immediate presence."

"Yeah yeah," Geryss said, up on tiptoes to flourish a signature. "Come on, Velo."

The general parlour simmered in a mid-afternoon miasma of heat and gossip and the lingering scents of luncheon; raffia-work sails fanned from the corners of the vaulted ceiling, stirring the soupy air. Little groups dotted sofas and armchairs, worrying over food, or arguments, or business arrangements. Footmen in plain black livery dodged potted palms, carrying snifters of rakia, thimbles of coffee, tall jugs of tea, little dishes of olives or fried cheese or rosewater delight.

Siyon tried to take in all the details. Daruj would want to know later.

Over the cold fireplace at the end of the room, an enormous painting showed half a dozen figures in armour sticking long spears into a massive scaled beast. Allegorical, of course. The dragon was superstition and so-called magic; the men represented reason and rationality, the fathers of modern alchemy.

Siyon's eye snagged on how the dragon threw back its serpentine neck, flared leathery bat-wings, clawed at the ground with massive talons. Sadness plucked at him, seeing something so fearsomely magnificent brought low.

"Hey." Auntie Geryss dug an elbow into his ribs. "Glass of rakia, while he's going?"

Siyon blinked at the lofty footman with his tray. "Um. Sure."

The footman wafted away, and Auntie Geryss gestured around the room with her rakia. "Ridiculous, isn't it? They're not all terrible. You know that lot, right?" A knot of soberly suited men and women, nearly smothered under a blanket of pipe smoke. Industrial alchemists, who plied their trade in the factories and workshops across the river, preserving and enhancing and applying all sorts of practical alchemical effects. Siyon traded ingredients to at least half of them regularly, and best of all, they all paid promptly.

As though that had opened his eyes, he picked out more familiar faces around the room; Joddani was far from his only azatani client, and he'd acquired bits and pieces for a lot of the foreign and mercantile practitioners as well.

That had been trade, though. Today, more of them met his gaze than Siyon would have expected. A couple even nodded, or lifted a glass.

Auntie Geryss let out a low whistle. "Well, aren't you flavour of the month? All to the good; I'll see if I can rustle up a membership panel, shall I? Have a wander. Chat with some folk. I'll be back in two flicks of a swordfish's tail."

That sent a thrill down Siyon's spine—a panel to adjudicate on his entry to the club's list of members. Just like that.

All it took was a public feat of impossibility.

Of course, not *everyone* looked pleased to see him, or even intrigued. Over in one corner, beneath the improbably snarling taxidermy head of a lion, Jaleh Kurit was glaring like she'd swallowed something noxious she was too polite to spit out. Siyon lifted his rakia to her in a silent and mocking toast, and she twisted away into the crowd.

"Hey." An elbow nudged into his side, and Siyon turned to face a stern, hatchet-faced woman. Melis looked like someone's bony spinster sister, her face permanently pulled into a frown, and her grey-streaked hair pulled back into a tight bun, practical for the timber yard she worked at. An amused light glimmered in her eye, as she waved the stem of her pipe to the other industrial alchemists. "Come take your ease for a moment before the wolves pounce."

Gladly.

"So it's true?" asked Ingermann, with the pale yellow beard of a Northerner and the myriad burn scars of a smith. "That was you in the square?"

Siyon nodded.

Next to him, Talyar of the textile mills sniffed disapprovingly. "Flashy work."

But that seemed to be the entirety of their commentary upon it. Endlessly cheerful Josinda, who had a standing order with Siyon for Abyssal goods for her paper mill, returned to complaining about metal corrosion by extraplanar materials. Siyon perched on the arm of Melis's chair and let the discussion distract him from the rest of the room's ogling.

Wooden tools weren't much hardier; stone implements turned brittle. Josinda had been experimenting with shell and coral; Melis raised the benefits and problems of obsidian. Talyar shook his head over the idea of making the tools themselves from extraplanar material.

"Unpredictable results," he said shortly. "No good for factory work."

They all nodded in sympathy, and Siyon thought of the conversation Joddani and Auntie Geryss had been having. "Are planar effects getting more unpredictable in general?" he asked.

Ingermann laughed in a puff of smoke. "You sound like them." He waved a hand at the rest of the room. "Theory this, hypothesis that. Nice for their delicate little workshops, yes? On the factory floor..." He shrugged.

"They are, though," Melis interjected. "As an apprentice, I sharpened the saws first thing in the morning only. Now I'm stopping the line once a shift, and we still get snags some days."

"We can't do anything about that, though," Josinda pointed out. "Might as well complain that some days are windy. That's the way it is, so we deal with it."

Siyon opened his mouth to wonder aloud—*what if something could be done about it?*—but a waft of firelily scent engulfed him, and a new voice purred, *"Darlings."*

He looked up—though not very far—at the dimpled little cushion of the Margravine Othissa. Dark beads woven through her honeyed hair glinted rosy pink, matching the rustling mass of skirts that flared out from her waist. She was smiling—always smiling, he'd never seen her otherwise.

Just behind her shoulder, her apprentice Jaleh Kurit was definitely *not* smiling.

"I simply *must* introduce myself to the mysterious saviour of Tower Square," Othissa declared, and held out a hand glittering with rings that nearly eclipsed the little scars of the burns and nicks no practitioner could avoid. "I am the Margravine Lyralina-Othissa de Ivrique Kortay the Third, but please do call me Othissa."

Siyon took her hand; it seemed only polite. "Siyon Velo. Though, ah, we've actually met before. I acquired Abyssal ichor for you last winter."

Jaleh's glare sharpened; Siyon could, but didn't, remind her new mistress of Jaleh's role in that acquisition.

"Did you? How *thrilling*. You must let me borrow you, there are so many people simply *dying* to meet you." Othissa tucked her fingers into the hook of Siyon's elbow without waiting for a reply—from either him or anyone else—and pulled him firmly away.

It was like being manhandled by a scented pillow; she was soft and sweet and gave the impression that struggling would just be embarrassing. "My goodness," she declared, steering them between a marble-topped table and a towering cactus. Jaleh trailed behind like a thundercloud. "There has been positively nothing to talk about but you all morning, which makes a delightful change from everyone going on about their tincture of this and titration of that— *Darlings!* Look who I've found."

She dragged Siyon into the midst of a circle of well-dressed figures. He recognised the Northerner, Master Yvok, and there was a lady dressed expensively but without the headscarf of an azata who was declared to be *Miss Plumm, of course*. Othissa rattled off the names of the three azatani gentlemen so fast that Siyon missed them, but one had definitely traded from Siyon before, and paid only a fraction of what was owed. From his bland smile, he didn't remember it at all.

"Well?" Yvok glared expectantly. "How did you do it?"

The azatan who'd stiffed Siyon tittered. "You can't just *ask* a fellow that, Yvok."

"Quite," his neighbour agreed. "It's not like you go about just telling people how you achieve your philtre of clarity."

The third azatan squinted at Siyon. "Velo, was it? Siyon Velo? How *exotic*. Where do you come from?"

Miss Plumm picked at a dish of sugared almonds. "Velo is a clan of fisherfolk in Dockside." She eyed Siyon, cracking a nut between her teeth. "I rather thought they tended to insist all menfolk take up the trade."

Siyon smiled like a flinch, his collar suddenly as tight as though a heavy hand had gripped and twisted at the back of his neck. He looked around the circle, but there was no easy reprieve; the azatani were exclaiming over his low origins, the foreigners laughing at them. Miss Plumm watched him steadily. Siyon cleared his throat. "I declined."

"Declined," she repeated blandly.

He *wasn't* getting into this with some nosy stranger. Especially not with Jaleh watching closely over Othissa's shoulder. He'd not told her about his family. He'd not even told Daruj all of it. It didn't matter. It was in the past.

So Siyon stared at Miss Plumm, and she stared at him, until Yvok turned around and barked, "Joining then, are you?"

"That's the idea." Geryss slid into the group on Siyon's other side. She grinned at them all. "So who'd like to be on his panel?"

"Happy to stand examiner," Yvok stated.

It made the azatani chortle. "Think you'll get to learn his secrets that way?" one teased.

"What a lark!" Othissa seemed likely to clap her hands with glee. "Can I be invigilator, oh can I? You'll be standing sponsor, of course, won't you, Geryss?"

"Grand," Geryss declared, and took a swig of her rakia. "I've checked the roster for witnesses, so we can—look lively, here comes trouble."

Siyon had barely registered her last hurried words when a new voice sliced across the group. "Othissa, you sweet morsel, what *have* you got hold of now?"

Othissa dropped a dainty curtsy, and Siyon turned to witness possibly the *most* azatani azatan he'd ever seen, from the tight near-black curls that just kissed his stiff lace collar to the knee-high boots so chased and tooled and polished that it verged on the ludicrous. He carried a gold-bound cane in one heavy-ringed hand, and he looked Siyon up and down like he might buy him.

He probably could. Even Siyon recognised this young gentleman. The prefect of Bezim—Syrah Danelani, may the wisdom of the council guide her—had only one son, after all.

Thick black eyebrows twitched together; Siyon realised he hadn't bowed, and decided it was too late now. Enkin Danelani sniffed. "I heard you summoned a guardian angel that swooped down like a sunbeam and caught the falling fool. Is that what happened?"

No one told *him* he couldn't ask that. No one spoke up at all. Nearby conversations had ceased, all eyes turned their way. Siyon shrugged. "Something like that."

He certainly wasn't going to admit he had no idea. Not when they might be about to let him into the club.

"Come with me." Danelani marched away without checking if Siyon followed.

Siyon did, of course. He wasn't *that* stupid. Othissa's hand fell away from his arm. Geryss tipped him a little nod, as though she thought he could manage this just fine. Jaleh watched him wide-eyed, scandalised or irate or possibly something else altogether.

Two other azatani gentlemen fell in behind him, lesser shadows that Siyon hadn't even noticed behind the dazzle of their sun in splendour. They marked a sort of protective distance, taking up guard as Danelani stepped into a window embrasure, crooking a peremptory finger. It was a large window, but Siyon could have done with more space.

"What you did took an enormous amount of power." Enkin Danelani spoke to his own rings, adjusting their weight and balance on his fingers, rather than to Siyon. "Everyone says it. Everyone also says that you have hitherto been involved in the trade of alchemical ingredients and you are well known for your precision and your discretion."

There was a pause, so Siyon assumed he was supposed to say, "Yeah, that's me."

Danelani wrapped his hands around the gold head of his cane. "I require some ingredient or reagent that will provide significant power."

That was almost a relief; Siyon had been worried he was going to ask for some feat of alchemy, some strange and potent working that was beyond the ability of the huge array of alchemical talent he already had at his beck and call in this club. But ingredients? *That* Siyon could manage. And the prefect's son could afford to pay prettily. "Sure. What's your fancy? Infernal kelp's a good one for your base urgency, but if you'd prefer moonshine I'll need to go through—"

"No." Danelani spoke quietly, but with a keen urgency. "I need *significant* power. And I need it *now*."

What for? Siyon didn't ask. However keen his curiosity, no azatani had ever deigned to explain a thing to him. "I don't carry around that sort of thing." Who would? Just wander blithely about with something like kraken ink, or sphinx mane, or— "Oh."

Or a phoenix feather.

Siyon laid a hand on his satchel, and watched Danelani's attention pounce like a cat on prey. "Might just be your lucky day. But, za, what you're asking isn't a cheap thing."

"Let's see it." Danelani beckoned imperiously. "I'm not paying you a copper knuckle for promises."

For a breathless moment, reaching into his satchel, Siyon couldn't find the little bundle, but then his questing fingers snagged a corner and drew it forth. Even in the well-lit room, the phoenix feather glowed within the silk wrapping.

An echoing light kindled in Danelani's eyes. "Name your price." He snapped his fingers at one of his followers. "Prishtani! How much money do you have on you?" The hapless azatan produced a leather purse; Danelani didn't look away from the silk-wrapped feather as he thrust it at Siyon. "Enough?"

The purse weighed as much as the sack Joddani had given him yesterday, near as Siyon could tell. Just the notion of that much money was distracting, his mind slipping sideways into speculations of what he could buy, but Siyon needed to focus. Danelani snapped his fingers at his other follower. "No, wait," Siyon said, and caught a flicker of relief on the other azatan's face. "Enough money. I want surety. Protection. Your name and influence, something I can call on if the inqs get their hands on me."

That was worth more, right now. It might be worth his life.

Danelani rolled his eyes. "Is that all? Look." He pulled a ring off his finger, a heavy square thing embossed with a trident on its golden face. "Here. My family sigil given into my hand by my mother at my first Harbour Master's Ball. It's yours. Now give me the bloody thing."

Siyon juggled the ring and purse as Danelani grabbed the feather, tucking it carefully away into the inner pocket of his longvest. He laid a hand over it, almost cradling. "What do you even want it for?" Siyon asked.

Danelani's eyes flashed back to him, quick as a bravi sabre. "None of your business," he hissed.

And stormed away, across the general parlour of the Summer Club, his two followers hurrying in his wake.

Siyon barely had a moment to shove the ring and purse into his satchel before people started to move his way, like gaudily dressed pigeons closing in on the pastry crumbs left on a teahouse table. He scanned the avid faces, didn't recognise a single one of them.

A gong slashed through the hubbub, shimmering away into silence. In the open doorway, a steward in black livery declared: "The entrance examination of Master Siyon Velo will now convene in the peacock parlour."

At his elbow, a bright voiced chirped, "*There* you are!"

As the Margravine Othissa hauled him undeniably toward the door, Siyon managed to find his voice. "*Now?*"

Geryss bobbed up at his other elbow like a turbaned cork. "Little point messing about," she stated.

"And a practitioner must always stand ready to be called upon by the Planes," Othissa carolled.

They swept up the grand staircase. The alchemical clock hissed and whirred ineluctably. Siyon felt caught in a far less tangible machine. This was what he wanted, he reminded himself. This was his chance. He just wished he had any idea what was going to happen.

"Wait here," Othissa sang as she bustled through a vibrant purple door and closed it firmly behind her.

"Chin up, *darling*," Geryss said, rolling the word just like Othissa did in her lavish New Republic accent. "You'll do fine."

"I don't know a thing," Siyon pointed out. He felt trapped in a dream. The prefect's son, of all people to approach him. A membership panel, for him. And the conversation with the industrial alchemists…He frowned. "This planar balance business. Should I be worried?"

"Were you worried yesterday?" Geryss asked, and Siyon wasn't sure whether she meant *Did it matter for catching Zagiri?* or *Don't worry about what you don't know and can't change.* She waved a dismissive hand. "What do we really know about the planes anyway? What Negedi said? How did *he* know?"

Siyon blinked at her. He'd thought her jokes about Kolah Negedi were just irreverence. Daruj was like that too, always making light of things he actually took very seriously. But this wasn't a joke. She was looking him straight in the eye, and asking: *How can we be sure that the father of alchemy knew what he was talking about?*

"But we're only here because of him," Siyon said. The thing they all knew to be true.

Geryss nodded. "We are here. And the planes are falling out of balance. If you don't like the catch, do you keep fishing in the same place?"

Before Siyon could really think about it, the purple door opened again, and Othissa was effusing, "Come in, come *in*, we're all ready now!" She straightened Siyon's collar with one hand as she pulled him inside. "Oh, it's so exciting!"

The peacock parlour was decorated in shimmering blues and greens, though the feathers clustered in tall Khanate vases were ostrich. Siyon had expected—well, something like the Palace of Justice. Serious people with paperwork facing him down over a counter while he steeped in his temerity in daring to address them.

Instead, they sat around on couches like they were about to take tea.

Othissa plopped down beside Siyon. "Shall we begin?" she asked, and barely paused for breath. "Now *I* am going to be the invigilator, isn't that delightful? And here's Yvok, he'll be asking the questions, and Miss Plumm and Master Unja here will be our witnesses to method and materials."

The one Siyon didn't recognise—Master Unja, presumably— tucked his watch back into his longvest pocket. "Do let's get on, I have an appointment at the next bell."

Othissa waved a blithe hand. "Shall we skip the familiarity criteria? There can hardly be any doubt that—"

"You can't just *skip* parts," Yvok interrupted, his moustache bristling. "The proper forms have been established!"

Othissa rolled her eyes. *"Don't* start going on about the legal and moral standing of the club again."

"And yet they must be considered," Miss Plumm countered. Siyon got the distinct impression she didn't approve of something, but he wasn't sure whether it was Othissa, or him, or this whole process. All of them together, perhaps. "The club threads its loophole precisely because our criteria establish that a practitioner will not present an unintentional threat to the safety of Bezim."

"Velo's familiarity with planar material can hardly be questioned," Othissa declared. *"I've* traded with him, *you've* traded with him, we've *all* traded with him."

Unja coughed. "We can't let in every supplier and petty street alchemist; there are *standards*—"

Othissa ploughed over him. "And we're only *here* because Velo achieved something yesterday that can only be explained alchemically—"

"Can it?" Miss Plumm asked.

Othissa blinked at her. "Can it what, darling?"

Miss Plumm leaned forward a little. "Can the happenings in Tower Square yesterday be *explained* at all, alchemically or otherwise?"

She looked at Siyon, but Auntie Geryss answered. "Velo owes us no secrets of his own practice. It's clear in the club charter; a practitioner's methods are his own to teach on his own terms or not at all."

Siyon was grateful to her for paving that road for him, but it seemed a tenuous and clifftop one.

And Miss Plumm looked even more disapproving. "We cannot base a candidate's eligibility on an unverified and unrepeatable working."

"Fine!" Othissa pouted, ostentatiously. Siyon wondered, not for the first time, how on earth brisk and bold Jaleh could possibly bear to work with the woman, even if she *was* a very accomplished alchemist. "Then we get him to do another one. Off the standard list, if we're being boring; does anyone remember it off the top of their heads?"

"Sublimation of base planar matter." Yvok ticked items off on his thick, pink fingers. "Distillation to stable essence. Application of core attribute. Or I suppose saturation of prepared medium is still on the list, but no one's bothered with that in years. What's your fancy, Velo?"

Siyon tried his best to look like he had any idea what they were talking about, but dread was stretching his stomach like taffy. Did it matter which he picked, when he didn't even know what equipment he'd need for any of them? Distillation was the one that used an alembic, right?

"This is missing the point entirely." Auntie Geryss slouched nonchalantly on her couch. "Velo's not here because he's a *standard* alchemist."

Master Unja frowned. "What are you suggesting, that we let him do another inexplicable and unverifiable working? That's hardly in keeping with Negedic principles."

Geryss smirked, a sharp and amused little twist of her mouth. "And if he could do something that's been verified impossible?"

"Ooh!" Othissa's eyes lit up. "Oh Geryss, I know just what you mean. Miss Plumm, darling, would you mind popping out and asking a steward if Azatan Hisarani is here?"

That name seemed familiar to Siyon, but the past two days had been a parade of bloody azatani. As Yvok started blustering about this being entirely unorthodox, and Othissa batted at his words like a kitten in a knitting box, Siyon made eye contact with Auntie Geryss. *What?* he mouthed.

She just grinned at him. Thanks.

"I see no reason," Master Unja stated, adjudicating between the other two, "why you'd want to do this. Azatan Hisarani's commission has been attempted and failed by four members that I know of, and declared impossible by at least three others."

"But won't it be fun!" Othissa actually kicked her slippered heels in a froth of skirts. "I'm so glad I'm a part of this."

The parlour door opened, and Miss Plumm escorted an elegant young azatan into the room.

Siyon recognised him. Fashionable lace and a well-cut longvest and just-too-long burnished curls that Azatan Hisarani tossed back. A light of recognition kindled in those clear brown eyes as well.

They'd met at the top of the stairs, the last time Siyon was at the Summer Club. *You don't know what I dream about*, Hisarani had said.

You can't afford me, Siyon had bluffed, grandiosely.

Well, this was a bit embarrassing.

Siyon stood and held out a hand. "Siyon Velo."

The azatan hesitated, something that might have been a smirk loitering in the corner of his mouth. Then he slipped his languid hand into Siyon's to shake. "Izmirlian Hisarani."

"Iz, *darling*." Othissa insinuated herself against Siyon's side. "Velo here is going to do your little thing as his entrance examination to the club; isn't it just *too* delicious?"

"Let the man assess the commission before he agrees," Yvok insisted.

It hardly made a difference, did it? Siyon could have laughed in despair. Choose between failing at this impossible thing, or failing at something they all thought entirely ordinary. He didn't have a chance, did he?

There was a knowing and smug arch to Hisarani's perfect eyebrow, and part of Siyon wanted to tell him to stick it. Another part was curious; what *was* this commission? Siyon opened his mouth—to say yes, to say no, to ask for more details; he hardly knew himself.

He never found out, for the world lurched and rattled like dice in a cup.

Siyon staggered. Othissa dragged at his arm, nearly tipping them both onto the couch; Siyon clutched at the back of it. Miss Plumm's grip on the door handle tightened; Unja braced himself on his seat; Yvok planted his feet and shouted, "What the very devil?"

Hisarani stood just as he had, staring at them all with mouth agape. "Is everyone quite all right?"

Other shouts drifted along the corridor, doors banging open and feet thundering. Siyon blinked, shaking his head carefully.

"What happened?" Geryss croaked, pushing gingerly up from the couch.

Another shudder then, like the universe had an itch between its shoulders. All of them flinched, but it rolled over them and subsided. Hisarani didn't so much as twitch.

"It came from that way." Yvok pointed, and Plumm was first out into the corridor, the rest of them hot on her heels.

Siyon skidded on the carpet, and Hisarani caught his elbow, hauling him upright. He smelt new and differently expensive today, all fragrant wood and orange blossom. Siyon shook him off and hurried after the others.

They caught up as Yvok lifted a heavy boot and kicked open a recalcitrant door. Behind it, an azatan crouched on the sumptuous carpet.

Siyon recognised him. His purse was tucked into Siyon's satchel.

"Help!" shouted Azatan Prishtani, Enkin Danelani's meek follower. He clutched at his lace collar, tangled a hand in his own brown curls. His voice crackled and snapped. "Oh help us. He's gone, he's *gone.*"

"What?" Yvok demanded. "Who's gone?"

Siyon had a terrible feeling that he knew just who; he shoved past Othissa having hysterics on Unja's arm, and through the door.

The air in the room was so thick it felt like drowning. Panic clawed at Siyon for the moment it took him to drag in a frantic lungful. An illusion, an overreaction. The room merely *felt* brackish, close and hot and thick with sweat, the sense of the Abyss nearly overwhelming. Siyon hung on to the back of a couch until the stars cleared from his vision.

Prishtani sobbed behind him. "Danelani! He's *gone*, she *took him.*"

The furniture had been pushed back and the carpet rolled up. A triangle was marked on the bare floorboards, large enough for a man to stand inside. Not drawn, as Siyon would have done to delve, but a solid space where the wood had aged and splintered and become crusted with salt. As though, impossibly, it had been left out to weather storm after storm, sea-soaked and sun-baked.

Inside the triangle, a wisp of black tar smeared across the floor, in the unmistakable shape of a feather.

A hand caught at Siyon's elbow; he batted at it, but he still felt dizzy and weak, and Hisarani had little trouble dragging him out of the room. The others were all shouting at each other and paid them no attention.

Hisarani's face was serious, his eyes ablaze. "You have to get out of here."

"What?" Siyon said. How did *Hisarani* know this was Siyon's fault?

Hisarani's mouth thinned. "The inquisitors will be all over this place in short order. Membership is largely azatani, so it will go all the harder on those like you." When Siyon just stared, Hisarani actually rolled his eyes. "You are apparently my only chance at achieving my goal, I don't want to see you vanish again. Come *on*."

The shove was enough to get Siyon going; he ran down the hall, dodging around those coming up the stairs. The entrance hall was a turmoil of shoving people. A door slammed; someone shouted, "Greycloaks in the street!"

And then it was mayhem, a surge of humanity toward the back as everyone sought the servants' entrance Siyon had been heading for himself. He skidded to a halt halfway down the stairs.

Hisarani ran into his back, steadied them both. His breath came fast against Siyon's neck for a moment, until he straightened and pulled them both against the railing, grip tight on Siyon's elbow. "Do you carry anything suspicious?" he demanded.

"What?" Siyon asked again. He wasn't used to being the one left behind, but Hisarani wasn't the languid azatan he'd seemed. And clearly wasn't dealing with the world having tilted under him.

"The inquisitors will have ways of finding the non-Mundane, yes?" Hisarani waved a hand. "Whatever ways those are."

A chill coiled down Siyon's spine. "A dowsing rod. Yes. They probably will." He set a hand on his satchel, unthinking.

But Hisarani's sharp eyes followed the movement. "Give it to me," he said, and hooked a finger beneath the strap on Siyon's shoulder. Siyon knocked his hand away by reflex, and Hisarani made a *tsk* sound. "They will not search me, not with the same fervour, and if they *do*, they will allow whatever plausible tale I can spin."

Siyon's fingers curled around the buckle of his satchel. It was the finest thing he owned, well made and warded besides to keep its influence inside, charmed to have space and depth and to keep everything where it should be. If the inquisitors waved a dowsing rod over him, they would get no sign of the satchel's exotic contents.

But that wasn't all they would do, was it? Not to *him*, not to Siyon Velo, gutter rat, Dockside brat, out of place. He would have to open it, let them search it, let them find out all his secrets.

Azatan Hisarani, damn his bright and pretty eyes, was entirely correct.

Siyon pulled the strap up and over his head. Hisarani wrapped a hand around it, but Siyon held on a moment longer. "If you try to open this, it will sting your fingers. If you persist, I will do worse."

Hisarani nodded. "I understand. And you have my word."

Siyon gritted his teeth, but he let go. Let Hisarani sling the satchel across his own body.

There came a hammering at the door of the Summer Club, heavy as justice. "Open up for the inquisitors!"

Not even the snooty clerks of the Summer Club could deny entry to the inquisitors, and once the black door was open, they came streaming in like regimented rats, determined to leave no corner of the premises uninspected.

Izmirlian Hisarani stepped back—leaving Velo alone at the curved railing—and let them do it.

Velo went quietly, which Izmirlian hadn't been expecting. He'd not seemed short on pithy commentary previously. But he made nary a peep as the first inquisitors up the stairs enthusiastically twisted his arm up behind his back and marched him back down.

An inquisitor looked from Izmirlian's curls to his equally polished boots and said very respectfully, "Za, at your convenience, please step into the downstairs parlour, where the commander will make a note of your details."

"The commander," Izmirlian repeated. "I am glad there's someone appropriate in charge of all this."

Shouting from upstairs, amid hammering on doors, and thundering feet muted by expensive carpeting. Shouting in the entry hall, as the desk clerk argued about the charter rights and responsibilities of the Summer Club, and whether it was legal for the club register to be released.

But in the general parlour, the mumble and hum of conversation was barely louder than usual. There were perhaps two dozen azatani practitioners and guests in here already, milling around beneath the gilt-framed *Triumph of Reason* by Uzbeto. (Izmirlian, personally, found the Late Imperials far too melodramatic, but he supposed the subject matter was relevant.) As Izmirlian lingered by the door, another pair of azatans came in, one saying, "—utter bore, can't stay too long, got to be at Kirill's in half a bell."

At first glance, it didn't seem that the inquisitor commander was here at all, but then one azata near the fireplace called out, "I say, could we get some rakia in here if we're to be waiting all this time?"

And a gentleman who looked much the same as everyone else, even if his longvest was quite a sober black-and-silver stripe, turned and gave her a little nod. "Apologies, Azata Markani, but the staff are at present assisting our investigations. I assure you, we will be done as quickly as possible." There was a grey-uniformed clerk trailing in his wake, taking notes as the commander moved politely and pleasantly through the azatani crowd.

Izmirlian recognised his face—the commander, of course, not the clerk—but couldn't quite put a finger on where from. Could be social or in passing or even just that the commander had reported to Izmirlian's older brother on some matter. Avarair would insist on bringing his work home, as though they might not properly appreciate his importance if it weren't paraded in front of them.

Izmirlian settled himself into an armchair, and an attitude of idle and bored. In truth, he had rarely felt less of either. His skin prickled, his blood singing; it was like sailing into a foreign harbour where their welcome was unknown. Though instead of a crossbow, all Izmirlian had were his wits and his words and his name to return fire.

He'd thought this just one more evening like so many others, and now suddenly it was full of potential. He tucked the satchel down beside his feet and trailed his fingers over its battered leather. He wondered idly what *stinging his fingers* would feel like, but settled back into the chair without trying the buckles.

When the possibility of greater curiosities was dangled in front of him, Izmirlian could resist the petty ones.

Especially when he'd nearly given up on ever gaining satisfaction. It had been nearly a year since Izmirlian had last encountered a practitioner who had the skills to suggest he might be up to the task—and who hadn't already rejected or failed at it. Izmirlian had resigned himself to living with an unanswered question constantly gnawing at the corner of his mind.

And then, suddenly, Siyon Velo.

Not at all the sort of person he'd usually give a second glance. Not that Velo didn't carry off his unshaven scruffiness with a certain panache, but there were dozens of similar ruffians lurking in the city's corners. At their first encounter, he'd caught the eye chiefly because no one else in the Summer Club looked like they'd been dragged up from the lower city at the end of a three-day bender.

An unexpected package for unexpected talents, possibly. Or possibly not. But *possibly* was far more hope than Izmirlian had entertained in a good long while.

He found his fingers drumming against the arm of the chair, and he forced himself to stillness. Impatience would get him nowhere. Even if he raced out of here this moment, he could hardly prise Velo from the grasp of custody until they were ready to relinquish him, and they would likely delay as long as they could.

Izmirlian had waited eight years now, since his first inkling of curiosity on the subject. He could wait a little longer.

Finally, the commander worked his way over to Izmirlian's armchair. He took the neighbouring one with every indication of enjoying the respite from weary work. The clerk, of course, remained standing, balancing his notes carefully against their board.

"I do apologise for the wait," the commander began, with the smooth certainty of formula, then looked properly at Izmirlian and blinked. "Izmirlian Hisarani. I didn't expect to see you here."

Izmirlian still couldn't place him, but he smiled nonetheless. "I'm not a member."

The commander laughed. "I should think not. Unless you'd really started to pay more attention to chemistry."

Ah, of course. "I seem to recall you falling asleep in the back of that class along with me, Hevitani." Izmirlian had found most of school dull, to be honest; even the classes on history and geography were pale reflections compared to discovering the world for himself. "But you seem to be well on your way." Izmirlian reached out to tap a lazy finger against the silver candle badge on Hevitani's chest, with its added insignia for his rank. His branch of the Hevitani were second tier; there'd be grander things in mind for him than this position, but it wasn't bad, at his age.

"I'm getting on," Hevitani allowed, satisfaction showing in his tight smile. "What have you been up to?"

"Since school?" Izmirlian laughed along with Hevitani at the notion of summarising a decade of his life. In truth, he could very easily—*finding nothing as interesting as I may have done tonight*—but that would hardly do. "Oh, I'm settling into idle-lesser-son, much as expected. I dabbled at the family trade, but my younger brother seems far more suited."

"Dabbled." Hevitani snorted. "I heard you chartered an exploratory voyage all the way to the far end of the Storm Coast. Is it true the beaches are red as blood and they tame giant lizards to pull their wagons?"

Izmirlian just smiled. "Go for yourself, and see. The discovery is half the fun."

Hevitani laughed. "Same old Hisarani!" Behind him, the clerk cleared his throat. "Yes, well. I must move on, try and get this over with so we can all go on with our evening's business."

He hadn't so much as glanced at the satchel at Izmirlian's feet. The clerk did, as he followed in his commander's wake, but if he ever mentioned it, nothing came of it. A quarter bell later, without Izmirlian being bothered again, the commander was thanking them for their cooperation.

The entrance hall was now quiet and echoing, the non-azatani practitioners already bundled away to the Palace of Justice. The club stewards bowed them out with the usual polished murmurs of thanks and wishes for fortune in their endeavours.

Izmirlian still wanted to go straight to find Siyon Velo. It would still be a waste of time. He might as well carry on with his evening plans, whatever they had been. He paused in the street, running his hand down the satchel strap over his shoulder, and something pricked at his palm. A badge pinned to the leather, it turned out; a tree, spreading both roots and branches. One of the bravi tribes, Izmirlian thought, though he'd no idea which. Hevitani might have, but when all his schoolmates were dissecting the skills and honours of the various tribes, Izmirlian had been reading about...well, about the jungle kingdoms at the far end of the Storm Coast.

So Velo was a bravi as well as an unusual alchemist. He was full of surprises. Izmirlian rubbed his thumb over the badge, and hoped he had yet one further surprise in him.

The chance that he did was too good to let it slip away.

CHAPTER 6

By midnight, the inquisitors' wing of the Palace of Justice was seething like a kicked anthill, ascurry with humourless law enforcement still processing the assortment of Summer Club patrons caught too brazenly in the act of alchemy—or the act of not being azatani.

The holding cell was familiar in its grey stone walls, wooden benches, heavy door with thick bars across the small window. Siyon had spent long nights cooling his heels with other bravi, brought in for disrupting the peace and conspiracy to affray and public intoxication and all the other charges they slung about when the tribes had irritated the wrong people. Usually, Daruj would be on the bench opposite, tapping one toe against the bars to keep rhythm on his old rowing songs while they waited to be let go. (They were always let go. Even if the ranks of the azatani administration weren't well-spiced with former bravi of all tribes, no magistrate wanted to be the one declaring the city's favourite street entertainment illegal.)

Tonight, Siyon's cellmates were an ever-changing parade of well-dressed practitioners bleating about their family standing and how this couldn't be done to them. One by one they were free to go.

Not Siyon, of course. They *could* do this to him.

Even the mercantile and industrial alchemists were calling for their patrons to vouch for them—those who hadn't reacted with healthy paranoia and been out the back door of the club at the first tremors. Smarter than Siyon, who had run *toward* the catastrophe.

He didn't spend much time berating himself for past mistakes. He'd made too many; no one had that much time. There were more interesting parts of the evening to think about. Izmirlian Hisarani. Enkin Danelani. Those tremors, if that's what they'd been. Hisarani hadn't seemed to feel them. Astounding sea legs, or something else?

When they'd shoved the first azatan practitioner in with him, one of the fellows the Margravine Othissa had introduced (and not the one who owed him money), Siyon had asked the man, "Did you feel that lurch?"

"Of course!" he'd harrumphed, and then he'd clutched a handkerchief to his mouth and cried, "Was it *you*? Did you *do something*?" He'd hammered at the door, crying out for the inqs, who'd paid scant attention.

The next one who came along—an older gent with greying hair contributing to a ponderous air—also said, "Of course," but then added, "Such a breach of the planar balance, I do hope it hasn't caused irreparable damage, another Sundering would be irksome."

Siyon hadn't been worried about the planar balance yesterday—like Geryss had asked. But he also hadn't realised it could be *felt* like that. That wasn't the planes needing a firm grip to get a working to stick. That was...

That was the sort of thing that put *another Sundering* in a whole new, unpleasantly possible light. *Irksome*. And then some.

The older azatan harrumphed. "I don't see why we've *all* been importuned just because *someone* had a working go awry."

Siyon eyed him sidelong. "You know it was Enkin Danelani, right?"

"Nonsense." The azatan wagged a finger. "The lad is an avid supporter of the Art, but he does not practise himself. Spreading such gossip will not aid you here, sir."

He'd done *something*. In memory, Siyon stepped again into that room. Felt the air, saw the triangle, smelled the brackish residue. The triangle, like the gate Siyon drew to the Abyss. Not a delving. Not with what it had left behind. But what?

Something that took him away. Something that gave the inquisitors the nerve to lay hands on the city's rich and powerful. Something that had looked an awful lot like it was powered by the phoenix feather Siyon had sold him.

It was entirely possible Siyon was never getting out of this cell. He didn't want to think about that. Panicking wasn't going to help.

He was annoyed at the idea that his satchel might be stuck forever with Azatan Hisarani. The very pretty and fashionable and expensive Azatan Hisarani, with his commission that had been failed or declared impossible by some stupid number of other alchemists. Siyon wondered what it was. What could a young man with everything want that was so difficult? To fly? Transform into a whale? Cross the fabled moonbridge to the goblin market?

He didn't think Hisarani was that whimsical. He didn't know why he had any thoughts about Hisarani at all.

Of course, if he went down for selling the prefect's son alchemical material with which the overprivileged brat had vanished himself, he'd never have to deal with the ignominy of failing Hisarani's task and losing his chance at the Summer Club.

Always a silver lining, if you looked the right way.

Approximately a hundred and twenty years later, the door creaked open and a woman stepped in—alone, not bringing another prisoner. She had the grey trousers and tunic of an inquisitor, though no badge that Siyon could see. Her dirty blonde hair might have been wild curls if it hadn't been bound back hard enough to pull her skin taut. That skin looked cold as ice, and her face hard as a hatchet, her nose sharp and her frown intimidating.

She was instantly and almost vertiginously familiar. Siyon blinked at her, wrestling with dizziness like he'd stood up too quickly. "Have you arrested me before?"

"Come," she barked, holding the door open.

The interrogation room was just as boring as the cell had been, though to break the monotony, it had table and chairs and company.

The inquisitor looked a little familiar as well, like Siyon had seen him before. He probably had. There weren't *that* many inquisitors, and they did like to buzz around alchemy like flies on a midden. This one had the candle-badge of a captain, but he wasn't the usual lesser-tier azatani, slim and dark and sulky about having to work for a living.

This man was angry. It leaked out of him with every breath, limned every sharp movement of his fingers on the paperwork in front of him, sharpened the line of his jaw and the flash of his eyes. That jaw was a little too square, that frowning mouth too thin, those dark eyes not tilted right to be azatani.

He might have grown up in the same Dockside slums that Siyon had, blood from off the sea mixing with old-Lyraec Bezim higgledy-piggledy.

"Thank you, Olenka," he declared without looking up from the file he was perusing, twitching loose pages between his stubby fingers. "You may go."

His brisk orders seemed familiar as well. Maybe Siyon *had* been arrested by this pair before.

"My name is Vartan Xhanari," the inq said. "And you are Siyon Velo, general errand boy to the practitioners of the city and jobbing alchemist for the—" He turned back a page in the file. "Little Bracken bravi tribe."

"Bracken has no commissioned alchemists," Siyon said, glib with practice. "That would be illegal. And we aren't Haruspex."

Xhanari hummed, flicking through another couple of pages. Did the inquisitors really have that much information on Siyon? There was plenty of writing on the papers, though Siyon couldn't make out any of the details at this angle. "And the bravi of course never break the rules." Xhanari glanced up with a sharp and pointed smile.

Siyon parried it with one empty and congenial. "Bending only. We're very bendy."

None of the inqs liked the bravi much. Siyon got the idea that it rankled their sense of order, all these flashy gits causing mild mayhem in the name of entertainment and honour and other ephemeral concepts. They didn't like that bravi business gave a Dockside brat (like Siyon) a perfectly valid reason to run around in respectable parts of the city. And they certainly didn't like that the lower city loved and welcomed the bravi, where they certainly didn't the inquisitors themselves.

But Siyon didn't think that was the bee in this particular inq's grey bonnet.

"So if you aren't really an alchemist," Xhanari said thoughtfully, "what were you doing at the Summer Club today?"

"I'm having a torrid affair with a member," Siyon declared, quick and easy. "Someone very important. Someone I am far too discreet to name."

"How good of you," Xhanari said blandly, and lifted his eyebrows. "Would this be Geryss Hanlun, who signed you into the club?"

Siyon lifted his eyebrows right back. "It would be indecorous of me to say any more."

Xhanari's face said he didn't believe a word of it. Siyon hoped his face said he didn't care.

Then Xhanari sighed, and closed the file entirely. "Why are you lying for them, Velo? Do you think if you perform well enough they will *ever* invite you into their little society? You? Really?"

The memory of his interrupted membership panel only made the sting sharper. Not that Siyon was going to let Xhanari see that. Instead, he slouched a little more in his seat—uncomfortable as it was—and smirked. "Oh, I get it. Were you assigned to me so you could appeal to our common ground? Us common chaps versus the bastards, is that the idea? Is that why you haven't threatened to break my fingers yet?"

Xhanari iced over. "We are nothing alike."

"No," Siyon agreed. "We aren't."

"I can make threats, if you need them," Xhanari said, still cold. "But I doubt you need the reminder. You know how this all works, don't you? The charges we'll read in the courtroom, the evidence, the punishments. Of course, magistrates have tended more toward exile than poison in recent years for the crime of sorcery."

"I haven't committed sorcery," Siyon interjected. Ironic; if he *had* performed such an act, his membership in the club wouldn't have been in question. But at best, what Xhanari had on him tonight was trading in contraband. If Danelani's traumatised offsiders had talked, that was, and why wouldn't they? Siyon could still wriggle; he didn't have the payment on him, did he? Thin, but all he had.

But Xhanari paid scant attention to his interruption. "Still effective, of course. You can hardly practise alchemy if you've been banished from the only place in the world where the planes can be breached. But those who've been exiled are of a rather different class than you." He skewered Siyon with his black gaze; Siyon met it belligerently, though his throat felt as tight as though the poison had already closed it. "You're nothing like me, and you're nothing like them either," Xhanari continued, implacable. "Do you think anyone's coming for you? To protect you, or stand your surety? Your people are all the way down in Dockside, aren't they?"

Siyon kept up his careless smile. He didn't know if he was fooling anyone, but it felt like all he had left. "Not my people anymore."

"But you've kept the name."

"It's my name too," Siyon snapped.

Xhanari's turn to smile. "It is. And how did everyone at the Summer Club like it?" Smug as though he'd been there, seen the azatani titter over the very idea of fisherfolk. "You aren't one of them. They have protections and privileges you never will, no matter what feats you may achieve."

In the moment he said *feats*, spitting it like something twisted and dirty, Siyon realised where he'd seen Vartan Xhanari before: giving orders in the street, while Siyon and Daruj loitered in a shop, trying to flee from Tower Square.

Siyon *had* performed sorcery, though not at the Summer Club. He tried to sound nonchalant despite the sudden dryness of his mouth. "Feats? What do you mean?"

Xhanari looked at him, blank as a rock face, and Siyon wondered if everything he'd seen on the man's face before now had been merely what he was *supposed* to see. "Little Bracken bravi, wasn't it?" he said, as though thoughtfully. "Funny, that's the same tribe as had a member fall off the clock tower. Fall and apparently *not* die. Know anything about that?"

Siyon made sure to meet his eyes as he shrugged. "People love to talk shit about bravi."

"This is some story, though," Xhanari pointed out, leaning forward in his chair. "Unprecedented alchemical working, right in broad daylight and apparently spontaneous."

"Is that even possible?" Siyon asked. His voice cracked. All he could think of were the eyes turning to him in the Summer Club. All those people who knew that he'd done it. Who knew his name.

Xhanari smiled like he could hear Siyon's thoughts. "What were you doing at the Summer Club today, Siyon Velo?"

It was an invitation—break, and this will all be over. But fuck this guy; Siyon had never been inclined to take the easy way out. "Told you: torrid affair." The thunder furrowed back into Xhanari's brow, but Siyon talked on over the drum of his own fear and rage. "You can't prove anything. You found nothing on me. You've only got wild tales. You're right, I do know how this works, and I know that isn't enough."

Xhanari didn't look half as chagrined as Siyon had hoped, and that sent a trickle of unease down his spine in the moment before the inq spoke. "We have sworn testimony, actually, from a very helpful apprentice who knows her duty to Bezim."

Apprentice. Her.

Jaleh.

Cold horror and scalding anger rushed through Siyon. He wished he could just hate her, but he also understood. She wasn't azatani either, and nor was her mistress, for all Othissa's wealth. She had her own safety to consider.

"The law is quite clear," Xhanari said, with smug aplomb. "On credible suspicion of sorcery, you can be detained indefinitely while evidence is obtained, unless full surety is stood for your release." He leaned forward, his expression such an exaggeration of mild curiosity that Siyon itched to punch him in it, even before he asked again: "Do you think anyone is coming for you?"

Siyon's smile was long gone, and all his glib words with it. It was really happening; he was never getting out of here.

The door opened behind Xhanari, and Olenka stalked in. She flicked her gaze over Siyon, harsh as sand on the wind, and said to Xhanari, "The front desk sent me. His surety has been stood."

Siyon gaped at her. If Daruj had drawn inq attention by showing up here, Siyon would punch him.

Xhanari snapped, "Who by?"

Olenka said, "Izmirlian Hisarani."

Siyon felt winded, like *he'd* fallen from the clock tower, and been impossibly caught. He didn't even try to rein in the wildness of his grin. "Told you," Siyon declared. "Torrid affair. Very important person. Can I have my things back before I go?"

Xhanari watched him steadily for a moment before he said over his shoulder, "Fetch them." As Olenka went off again, Xhanari leaned forward. "This doesn't matter, Velo. Do you know what happened tonight?"

Siyon said nothing; he wouldn't mind hearing the official version.

"The prefect's son went missing from the Summer Club in suspicious, and rather alchemical, circumstances. But more than that, what happened tonight is that the inquisitors received a gilded invitation to turn the city upside down in getting him back." Xhanari smiled, a grey and unpleasant smile. "Scurry off with your important rescuer. It doesn't matter. We're coming for you, Master Velo. You and all the rest of the *practitioners*. There is nowhere you can hide from us. You'll see."

Izmirlian Hisarani slouched on the waiting room bench with his head tilted back against the wall and his long legs crossed at the ankles. Leaning against his shin was a battered leather satchel. When he rose gracefully to his feet, he hooked the strap over one shoulder. The Little Bracken badge was right there, on display.

The trainee manning the front desk seemed too busy admiring the view to even realise he was carrying anything, but that didn't stop

Siyon glaring. He did wait until they got outside to say something. "You brought it *here*?"

"You're welcome," Hisarani said, dry as Empyre, holding the satchel out.

Siyon snatched it from him, riven by rage and relief in equal measure. The leather had picked up an irritating whiff of orange blossom and fragrant wood that was not improving Siyon's mood at all. If Xhanari got hold of this, he wouldn't need the sworn testimony of Jaleh Kurit (may her next working explode on her). But he hadn't, and Siyon had it back, and he was free of custody, thanks to Hisarani.

A lucky escape, and one he intended to make the most of.

Siyon slung the satchel across his body unopened. "Thanks," he said shortly. "For holding on to it and the surety both."

He turned on his heel and strode away into the park. Mist lay heavily on the manicured lawns, glittering in the light from strings of little lanterns looped between the trees. Apparently the illegality of alchemy didn't matter so much when it was making pretty, coloured baubles. Hardly a surprise.

A scuff of footsteps, and then Hisarani was at his shoulder. "Where are we off to?"

"*We* aren't off to anywhere." Siyon shot him a sidelong glance. "I said thank you."

"You don't need to," Hisarani replied easily. "My motives were entirely selfish. You can hardly help me if you're languishing in the cells."

Siyon stopped; Hisarani took another two steps before turning to face him, an eyebrow lifted in inquiry. "Za, don't take this personally, but I am *done* with the azatani and their problems." Probably not the tone he should be taking with the man who'd just paid for his freedom. Siyon didn't care. He could still feel the scrape of panic in the back of his throat, see the sharp satisfaction on Xhanari's face.

Siyon had slipped that net, and he hadn't survived this long by not swimming fast and far when he got the chance.

Hisarani didn't seem to get it; he was pulling a complicated face of annoyed regret. "Yes, Enkin does rather seem to have made a tremendous mess this time, even for him."

Of course this azatan was on a first-name basis with the prefect's son. "Yeah, well. The inquisitors just took great pains to tell me they're coming down on alchemy like a ton of bricks, so stow whatever grand plans you have. All I'm doing next is getting down the Scarp and not coming out until this *tremendous mess* has been cleaned up."

He brushed past Hisarani, who grabbed at his arm saying, "Wait!" Like they'd let Siyon call himself bravi if he couldn't dodge that. Hisarani spat invective—with a creativity and vehemence that tugged at the corner of Siyon's mouth despite himself—and then ran after.

Ran. Siyon wouldn't have thought he knew how.

"Don't be hasty," Hisarani insisted. "After all, if things get dire, the inquisitors might venture in force into the lower city. You could stay somewhere safe *and* comfortable." When Siyon just snorted, Hisarani added, "I mean with me."

"With the person who just put his name against my release. Yeah, they'll never think to look there."

Hisarani blinked. "You think they'll come importuning the azatani?"

Siyon wanted to laugh at his reaction, but he was too busy remembering the steel in Xhanari's gaze. *A gilded invitation*, he'd said, *to turn the city upside down.* Xhanari wasn't going to care about bothering the azatani. Xhanari might actually enjoy it.

"They want me on sorcery," he replied shortly. "Do you know what they do to you for that?"

A moment of stillness, nothing but their footsteps and the gentle midnight—maybe closer to dawn—breeze in the branches of the park's trees. The lanterns lining the Boulevard were haloed by a faint mist. Hisarani said, "Well, there was that fellow Rotua who was banished—"

Siyon laughed harshly. *Still effective*, Xhanari had said, mockingly. He knew, like Siyon did, that only the bloody azatani would think being cast out from Bezim was a punishment comparable to death. "Maybe that's what they'd do to *you*. For me, it'll be poison. The old

Lyraec classic. Why change a good system, right? They'll strap me down and force it down my throat, and I'll die choking, but at least my blood won't be spilled to curse the ground."

Siyon kicked at a loose rock clattering across the Boulevard, and realised he was walking alone. He looked back to where Hisarani had stopped, shock already smoothing away beneath azatani composure. "I quite understand your reluctance."

"Oh, good." Siyon strode across the Boulevard, and gritted his teeth at the clip of those well-polished boots catching up *yet again*. "Oh, for the love of angels, can't you just—"

"I'm accompanying you to the Scarp," Hisarani interrupted. His tone was tighter now. He'd stopped making such an effort to be whatever passed for ingratiating with azatani. "The prefect's son is missing, remember? There are inqs all over the city. What if you run into them?"

"I'm insulted you think I can't dodge inqs," Siyon grumbled. "What do you think I've been doing my entire life?"

But Izmirlian had thought of it, which wasn't the sort of consideration Siyon was used to in the azatani. And Hisarani kept up with him, even though Siyon was hardly lingering.

Siyon shot him a sidelong look, as they passed beneath a street lantern that gilded Hisarani's curls and cast shadows over his sharp cheekbones. "What is it you're so desperate about anyway? What's this impossible commission?"

Hisarani tilted his chin to a carefully nonchalant angle. "I'm not *desperate* about anything, it's just a matter of curiosity."

"That has you showing up at the Palace and personally posting my surety." The more Siyon said, the more convinced he was. "Just curiosity has you running errands for me, when I was pretty sure I was going to have to track you down to get my satchel back, only to find out you'd forgotten it somewhere. So what's this *curiosity* that's so pressing?"

"I want—" Hisarani started readily enough, and then hesitated for half a dozen steps before he committed only to: "I want to leave."

Siyon didn't get it. "You want an ostler, not an alchemist."

"No." Hisarani shook his head as they turned onto the Kellian Way, heading down the hill, always down. "Not the city. Nor life, or any petty poisoner would do. No, I mean—" He waved an arm, at the Eldren Hall they were passing, but Siyon suspected more at the night and the city in general. "I mean *beyond this*."

"Another plane?" That couldn't be it.

"Beyond," Hisarani confirmed.

That—that was unexpected. Not something Siyon had ever thought of. That *anyone* had ever thought of, as far as he knew. "Four planes aren't enough? You azatani always have to sail over the horizon to see what's there, huh?"

He looked sidelong at Hisarani, tousled and tired but still polished by his wealth and status. Hisarani tilted his chin up toward the stars. "Maybe this is how our ancestors felt, sailing out to find the Archipelago. Wanting to *know* what was there."

"Your ancestors," Siyon pointed out. *His* ancestors—city-born or foreigner alike—weren't likely to have been thinking beyond something to eat and somewhere to sleep.

"Our city's ancestors," Hisarani offered, like a compromise.

Siyon snorted at that—as though this were *their* city, equally shared, whatever it was called.

There was movement ahead; all shadows were grey when drained of moonlight, but the streets had been far too quiet for Siyon to trust anyone out and about. He grabbed Hisarani's arm and tugged him down a side street that ended in a wide stone staircase. "It's an interesting idea," he allowed. "Where there's a boundary, there must be another side. I'm surprised no one else has ever considered it."

Hisarani blinked. His mouth twitched toward a little smile, slight but honest, and all the sweeter for it. "This is usually the point where people tell me I'm weird."

"You're weird, I'm weird, we're all weird." Siyon shrugged and turned down the stairs. "Doesn't change the fact I can't help you."

Hisarani hurried after him, down into the fruit market. The stalls were all covered in heavy canvas, empty bins awaiting dawn deliveries; Siyon could stride through at twice the speed he'd have managed in the daytime crowds. The lack of other traffic was making his skin crawl. Where were the late-night carousers? Where were the Flowerhouse palanquins, carrying patrons and drumming up business? Where were the *bravi*? (Safe, he hoped. He'd get a message to Daruj tomorrow. Once he knew where he was hiding.)

Hisarani caught up, elbows nudging. "I thought perhaps—since you'd already done the impossible..." He trailed off; he looked a little embarrassed about his own hope.

"What, in Tower Square?" Siyon laughed, weak and helpless. "Za, here's the truth: I have no idea what happened there." It felt good to admit it. Let go and leave behind the idea that he could somehow, impossibly, be a Summer Club alchemist.

He'd rather be alive.

"It was still you," Hisarani pointed out. "You doing something that no one else could."

Maybe. "Doesn't matter if I can't do it again," Siyon countered. He kept his voice down; in the tight streets between the fruit market and the Flower district, it was hard to know what—or who—might be around the next corner. "Just how many other alchemists have you approached about this?"

Hisarani shrugged. "A number, over the past few years. Not all of them Summer Club members in good standing, some of them demonstrable charlatans. Some told me it was impossible, that there *was* nothing beyond the planes. Some drew complicated diagrams and calculations, and then told me it was impossible. Some took the commission only to fail, or to vanish with my down payment."

They turned down alongside the Flower district's fragrant pine hedge. Laughter drifted over the trees, along with the clack of die and tiles, a lilting phrase of music, the sweet scent of herbs and incense burnt to carry away your cares. It would take more than the evening's happenings to shut down the Flowers—and the barons who profited from their trade.

Nearly there, now. Siyon picked up the pace; Hisarani kept up.

"I could take your money, if it'd make you feel better," Siyon offered. "But honestly, za, I wouldn't even know where to start. I can hop between the planes, that's just—opening a door. I don't even know where the walls *are* that you want to breach. I don't even know if they truly exist. Negedi might—"

Hisarani interrupted, dry and low. "I am starting to get very bored of hearing what Kolah Negedi would have to say."

So Siyon was laughing—unbelievably, given the rest of his night— as he turned the final corner, into the last street stretching downhill to the lip of the Scarp itself.

And stopped. At the end of the street, where it should have opened up onto the park that ran along the escarpment, feeding into the switchback staircase that carved down the cliff, there was instead lantern light and a seething crowd of people. Siyon couldn't make sense of it for a moment, in the shift of bodies and shadow, and then he realised. *That* was a grey cloak, and *this* was a disgruntled trio of bravi, and the whole thing—

Was a blockade of the Scarp. The inquisitors had a whole crowd of people at bay, everyone returning home from evening entertainments in the upper city. Grey uniforms were checking people over one at a painstaking time, asking questions, peering in bags, patting one furious woman down as though she might have Enkin Danelani hidden under her skirts. There was an inquisitor captain overseeing the operation, with the lantern light glinting off his candle badge and the metal bar in his hand.

Dowsing rod.

"Fuck," Siyon stated. He slammed a hand into Hisarani's chest and dragged them both back around the corner.

They huddled there for a silent moment, in the lee of the building. It was only when Hisarani drew breath to speak that Siyon realised he still had a hand planted against the azatan's ribs, pressing him back against the brick wall. "So if you're going to be staying a little longer in the upper city—"

Siyon cut him off sharply. "Don't you start." But what *could* he do? Perhaps he could go over the Swanneck to the industrial stews, circle down to Dockside, find a way back across the river. The Awl Quarter bravi were known to row it, now and then. But if the inqs were here, they'd probably be on the bridge as well. There were stories that some of the mansions further up the Scarp had their own private escapes tunnelling down the cliff, but Siyon didn't know which, or even who to start asking about it.

He looked back up the hill, to the tall, fragrant hedge of the Flower district. The barons had no love of the inqs. Maybe he could...

Terrible idea. The only thing worse than being in it with the inqs would be being in hock to the barons. They didn't have rules, just avarice and violence, and there was nowhere in the city, upper or lower, that was safe from their reach.

There had to be a way out. There was always a way out. Siyon just couldn't see it yet for the panicked scramble of his thoughts.

"I *can't* stay with you," he told Hisarani. "They will come looking. And they probably think we're having a torrid affair."

Hisarani blinked. "Why?"

And he couldn't fall on Little Bracken, not when Xhanari knew Siyon was a member. He'd come looking there too, and Siyon couldn't drag the entire tribe down with him.

Fuck, but he hated this. Hated that the inquisitors had him slinking and scuttling, like a rat in his own city. None of those azatani club members who'd passed through his cell were worrying about this. But that was more the *azatani* than the *club members*. The part Siyon could never achieve.

"Well," Hisarani said, sounding aggravatingly reasonable. "Where were you staying last night?"

Siyon blinked at him. "With Azatan Joddani. But that was just a one-off. I can't ask for—"

"Velo." Hisarani smiled, and it was a little condescending, but also a little bleak. "Here is the secret of the azatani: Ask for *everything*, and be appalled if you don't get it. Besides, do you have a better idea?"

Siyon didn't. Not a single one.

CHAPTER 7

Zagiri was lolling atop a monster in the garden outside the Flower district when the Tower bells chimed for Deep, halfway between midnight and dawn. The monster was stone—one of the statues in the garden, a winged lion with a scorpion's tail—and Zagiri was bored, and the Awl Quarter bravi were *late*.

"Where the fuck are they?" another of the Little Bracken bravi muttered from the lower branches of a nearby ornamental tree.

The rest of the assembled Little Bracken—eighteen of them, the first three sixes, a proper showing for a melee—muttered and shifted. Any crowd was long gone, those who'd paused to watch in interest when Bracken arrived drifting away about more entertaining business. If there wasn't going to be a fight, what was the point in staying?

Zagiri felt much the same.

A short whistle cut through the night; Voski, calling to the Bracken scouts posted on nearby rooftops. One by one the scouts whistled back: *Nothing to report.* No sign of other bravi approaching. And then one added another whistle: *Runner incoming.*

Zagiri slipped down from her lion-monster as the junior Bracken came sprinting into the garden. The runner was panting, face pale, freckles standing out on his skin like mud spatter. No one she knew; just a kid, really, still growing into his blade. "The inqs have closed the Scarp ascents," he gasped between heaving breaths. "I heard the Swanneck too. Haven't seen it."

If Awl Quarter were stuck in the lower city, that would explain why they hadn't shown up. Embarrassing, when they'd called this challenge in the first place.

"You hear why?" Voski asked the runner.

He winced. "Something about a ruckus at the Summer Club. Inqs arresting everybody."

"Inqs at the Summer Club?" Zagiri elbowed forward. The kid must have misunderstood. Maybe Haruspex had lost what passed for their minds and tried to raid the Club, and the inqs were arresting *them*. That would make more sense.

Voski shook her head. Trouble on the streets—trouble not of *their* making—could be bad for the bravi. "Form up sixes," she called. "Back to the Chapel. No showboating, but keep an ear out as you run. Savani, Josepani, not you."

As the rest of the bravi drained away like water, jogging out of the garden in small groups, Zagiri stayed behind, along with Beren Josepani. The only other azatani here, Zagiri realised, though Beren was barely second tier.

That made Voski's intention pretty clear. "Want us to go and check the Summer Club?" Zagiri asked.

The sergeant nodded. "Take the kid." She pointed at the runner, who was recovering with the alacrity of youth, but still looked a little pained when she added, "He can bring us word. Don't take risks. Brave the knife."

"Brave the knife," Zagiri and Beren returned—the runner muttered it half a beat late—and they all ran into the night.

Zagiri led Beren and the kid up the slope, then up off the street at the first opportunity—up a garden wall, up a drainpipe, along a roof ridge. She paused a moment, but the kid seemed to be keeping up fine, so they ran.

The moon hung low in the sky, light enough and more than to pick a path across the city—sliding down eaves, leaping between balconies, racing over the semi-permanent bridges across streets too wide to leap. Zagiri took them up the western side of the fruit market, atop the crenellations of the old fort wall, simply because she liked it.

At least she was getting a proper run tonight. Not all a waste.

From the old wall, they jumped down to street level, and it was shadow-work from there, the buildings around the Summer Club too tall and respectable to be worth the trouble of scaling. But remembering her visit with Siyon, Zagiri led the other two down the back laneway, dark and eerily quiet.

"Nothing to see," Beren muttered, just a darker patch of shadow. "No sign of the greycloaks. Kid, you sure about this?"

The runner shot back, "I just carry the word I heard."

Zagiri ran her eyes along the dark line of buildings. "No lights on either, though." She had to count buildings to be sure she was looking at the Summer Club.

"They're all getting an early night?" Beren suggested.

Zagiri snorted. Nihath stayed all night at the club more often than he came home, and that was just as far as Zagiri knew. Her sister wasn't precisely forthcoming about the mess of her marriage.

Personally, if Zagiri had been taken home from the wedding procession to a house already occupied by her new husband's lover, she'd have burned the damn place down, but she was not, as their mother often lamented, much like her sister at all.

Not the point right now. "No, the club's been shut early. And if it's the inqs taking a stand, we might all be in trouble." It wasn't just alchemy that existed in precarious balance with the law. Zagiri prodded the kid's shoulder; he startled, but at least didn't squawk or fall over. "Head back to the Chapel; tell Voski what we've seen."

"Hey," Beren grumbled, as the runner slipped away down the laneway. "Who said you could give orders?"

Zagiri shrugged. "Do what you like. I'm going home."

Or at least to her sister's. The door of the Joddani townhouse had been charmed to let her in after the third time she'd interrupted Nihath's work by arriving late, or drunk, or both. Zagiri tiptoed inside—

But the entire house seemed awake already. The lanterns were lit, an argument bled down the stairs from Nihath's study, and Anahid was in the hall, already dressed and deep in discussion with her house-keeper. Nura frowned at Zagiri before excusing herself, but as far as Zagiri could tell Nura frowned at everything.

"He didn't get pinched, then." Zagiri jerked her chin toward the stairs.

On cue, Nihath bellowed, "And for that, the planes must be balanced!"

Zagiri added, "Unfortunately."

Partly just for the scandalised frustration that danced across her sister's face. If she wasn't going to *talk* about this stuff, Zagiri would have to get her fun where she could.

Soon Anahid was back to tight-lipped disapproval. "What are you doing here, since it's clearly not concern for my husband? Shouldn't you be abed already? You have a garden party today."

Because of course she still knew Zagiri's social schedule better than Zagiri did. With a roll of her eyes, Zagiri stalked into the dining room and poured herself a glass of tea. However grumpy Nura might be, she made wonderful tea, minty and refreshing. "It's not like I have to be alert for that, or even awake. Children are best seen and not heard."

Anahid made that disapproving noise of hers and reached past to tuck a chased silver saucer beneath Zagiri's teaglass. "You'd not be treated as a child if you didn't act like one."

"Let's definitely have this argument again, it's entertaining even on the seventeenth iteration." Zagiri took a pointed slurp of her tea and added: "I *came* to make sure *you* were all right. And Siyon too."

It was an afterthought. He wasn't a member of the Summer Club, after all. He'd sounded quite bitter about it. Zagiri rather assumed he'd have hied himself off into the lower city before the inquisitor net came down.

But worry flitted across her sister's face, almost invisible for those without eighteen years of practice in spotting the twitch of her brows and the tweak at the corner of her mouth. "Mistress Hanlun took him to the club," Anahid admitted. "And I don't know what's happened to him."

Zagiri slammed her teaglass down hard enough that it sloshed over the gilded rim into the saucer Anahid had laid down. "And you're too well behaved to go ask him upstairs, aren't you?" She was already out the door, not slowing for her sister's exhortation to wait. "Well, I'm not!"

She took the stairs two at a time, easy in her bravi boots and leathers, as Anahid shouted, "Giri, get back here!"

Not on her life.

Zagiri swept into Nihath's study, saying, "Now, look here—" before she stopped dead in the face of far more attention than she'd been expecting. Not just Nihath Joddani and his aggravating wafty boyfriend, but another four azatans, still in their satin-sheened evening longvests, as well as two tradesmen in sensible black and another gentleman in shirt and coat with spectacles balanced on his pinked nose.

All of them looking at Zagiri with varying levels of surprise, alarm, and anger.

"Er." She scrambled for what she'd come to say. "What's happened to Siyon Velo?" It came out more querulous than demanding.

"How should I know? I wasn't even there." Nihath stomped out from behind his desk. To the assembled group, he added, "My wife's sister, don't worry."

Zagiri felt almost affronted at the way they all relaxed. She could be dangerous! "Velo saved me," she reminded Nihath, and jerked her arm away from his grip; she was sure he'd love to shoo her back out of the room. Her name was being called from downstairs as well, and she ignored all of them to set her heels and her glare and shout: "He *saved* me, and the least we could do is give a copper knuckle what happens to him."

"Thanks!" shouted a voice from downstairs, and Zagiri realised what she had been hearing—her name, being called in that Dockside drawl.

She raced back to the landing, and there was Siyon in the entry hall, wrinkled and bleary but *here*; Zagiri didn't even pause, just slid down the banister to crash into Siyon in something more tackle than hug.

Siyon laughed, tilted them back to upright, and knocked away the jab she aimed at his ribs. "Nice to know you care." If his grin was tired, it was still a grin, and it was good to see it.

"Nice to know you're *safe*," she shot back. "You'll have to stay here, of course."

"Will he?" Anahid said, standing there with her hands planted on her hips like fourteen-year-old Zagiri had got into her evening gowns again.

Except Zagiri was older now, and could stand her ground. "They've closed off the Scarp descent, Ana, and the inqs are likely to be harassing the tribes anyway, so he can hardly—"

"I don't want to cause you any trouble either," Siyon interrupted.

Turning back to him was the first time Zagiri noticed who was loitering behind him. What was *Izmirlian Hisarani* doing here? With *Siyon*?

"Don't be silly," Anahid said, just as peremptory as she was with Zagiri. "Of course you'll stay here until it's safe. But this isn't your house, Zagiri, and I'll thank you to remember it. Help yourself to breakfast, Master Velo. And my apologies for the informality, Azatan."

Hisarani returned her nod, like they could paint politeness over the wild graffiti of impropriety that was taking place here, and Anahid went off downstairs.

"Velo," Nihath called from the upstairs railing. "Were you involved in all this?"

"All what?" Zagiri asked. She looked back to Siyon—more likely to give her answers. "What's happened?"

Izmirlian Hisarani answered. "Enkin Danelani has vanished. Though probably not eloped to Lyraea with an opera singer, as the wildest gossip would have it."

Nihath sighed from above. "If only he had. Sounds like planar transference, from all accounts, but there was no practitioner working with him and I can't think where he'd get the power to effect such a thing even if he had any idea how to—"

"Er." Siyon scratched behind his ear, rumpling his hair even more. "The power was probably the phoenix feather I sold him."

"You sold him?" Nihath repeated ominously.

"Well, extorted from me might be more—"

Nihath had already turned away, back toward his study. "Utterly irresponsible... Get up here, Velo!"

Siyon pulled a face of expressive annoyance, but he still said, "I guess I'd better..."

He went upstairs. The study door closed, turning the renewed raised voices into a distant mumble. Zagiri eyed Hisarani. "What are *you* doing here?"

He fixed her with a haughty look—like she cared; her name was as good as his—but a moment later he rubbed a hand over his face. Through the windows behind him, the sky was starting to silver. It had been a long night for everyone. "I don't know," he said. "I thought there was a chance at something I'd written off as impossible, and... well, I just didn't want to let it go."

Zagiri frowned at him. Some of the other girls her age—the ones who *had* presented to the harbour master this season—had the second Hisarani son on their list of hopeful spouses. He had some sort of romantic appeal. An air of adventure in the voyages he'd apparently made during his younger merchant-venturer days. A reputation for quoting obscure books on weird subjects. That sort of thing did it for some girls. Zagiri had always thought—when she bothered to think of him at all—that he was a pretentious addition to a far too consciously fashionable set of young men, that lot who loitered in the grotto on the edge of the park during promenade.

Right now he just seemed like a person.

"Come have some breakfast," she offered. "It's usually pretty good."

"Should you be making that offer?" Hisarani's face was suspiciously bland. "I hear this isn't your house."

Zagiri narrowed her eyes and set her hand on the sabre hanging at her hip.

He raised his hands, struggling with a smile now. "I yield preemptively. You've picked the wrong Hisarani brother for an entertaining duel."

With a snort, Zagiri said, "See if I—"

Upstairs, the door to Nihath's study slammed open on a welter of shouting, then slammed closed again. Siyon came thundering down the stairs. Zagiri flinched from his expression, and the rage that boiled there.

"Good, you're still here." It was nearly a snarl; Zagiri was glad he was talking to Hisarani. "Let's do this."

Hisarani blinked. "What?"

"I'm not a *real* alchemist. I should sit still and be quiet. I can't actually *achieve* anything." Siyon grinned—or at least, he bared a lot of teeth. "So let's see just what sort of alchemy I can achieve."

"What have you two been doing?" Zagiri demanded.

Both of them ignored her, too busy staring at each other, Siyon with expectation hard as demand, and Hisarani with utter shock. "Shouldn't there be..." Hisarani waved a hand. "I don't know. Preparation? Process?"

"Didn't have any of that the last time I did the impossible." Siyon beckoned, like this was an all-blades, and he was daring the other side to attack. "Come on. You want this or not?"

Hisarani watched him a moment longer, and then his chin came up. "All right, then," he said. "Let's do it."

Miss Savani fluttered around them like a moth, which did nothing to help Izmirlian's nerves. She probably thought she sounded firm and sensible, but Izmirlian could hear the flutter of excitement and the tremor of fear both.

He knew how she felt. Izmirlian had wanted this for years, and yet found himself unprepared for it to be suddenly dropped in his lap. The horizon he'd glimpsed, and immediately wondered, *What's on the other side?* That he'd resigned himself to never seeing past. That was now rushing toward him.

Izmirlian had to assume there would be no return trip.

He'd been ready for years, and yet he wasn't ready at all. He still wanted to learn how his younger brother had fared on his venture to the North, to drink that bottle of thirty-year-old firewater, to hear Gayane Saliu perform the *Aria of the Return*. Perhaps learn what Siyon Velo was quite so angry about.

But more than all that, he wanted to see what was out there. And if this was his chance, sudden and surprising, then he would seize it.

There was always the possibility that Velo—unsettling, unbridled, and by his own admission making it up as he went along—might fail. Or succeed in a way nothing like Izmirlian had imagined.

He thought the risk was worth it. But Izmirlian was also very aware that dawn was streaking fire across the sky outside, and he'd had no sleep.

He'd chosen this course. He would sail it, and see where they ended up.

"You scold like your sister," Velo told Miss Savani, which predictably lit her up with umbrage like a lantern, even if it was accurate.

"Fine!" she shouted back. "Perform sorcery in the front parlour where everyone walking past can see, I don't care!" She just about snarled as the clock in the front hall chimed prettily; that would be the dawn bell.

"Need to get home before your parents curtail your allowance?" Izmirlian asked, not without sympathy.

Miss Savani glared at him and jabbed the orange plume on her tricorn at Velo. "Do not get my sister arrested," she snapped, jammed the hat on her head, and stalked out.

The house was well made; her vehement slam of the front door didn't make anything rattle.

Velo rubbed thoughtfully at his unshaven chin. "She might have a point about being seen. Let's go upstairs."

Izmirlian fought his sense of propriety with every step. They were planning to break the bounds of reality itself, what did it matter if he didn't have an invitation to ascend? He trailed his hand along the carved banister, letting the whorls of wood linger on his fingertips. Would there be touch, beyond the barriers he wanted to pierce? Would there be other, new and differently vibrant sensations?

Perhaps he should feel bad for not farewelling his family, but they hadn't understood any other time he'd attempted to explain this to them—his father not seeing the potential for profit, his mother thinking it far too strange, his older brother always impatient with Izmirlian's *flights of fancy*.

He'd written a letter, stowed it in his desk, the first time he'd commissioned an alchemist to attempt this. His younger brother would find it, the only one who'd care to look. It would still hold true enough.

Velo frowned at the first parlour he encountered. "This looks expensive," he muttered.

Izmirlian glanced around the room, leaning against Velo's shoulder to see. "I would never cast aspersions on Azata Joddani's decorating taste, but the furniture seems quite standard modern whimsical and that sort of geometric carpeting was fashionable perhaps ten years ago."

Velo looked unconvinced. "You can actually sit on those chairs without the legs collapsing?" He shook his head. "Never mind. The carpet. That looks perfect."

With a low table dragged aside, the carpet's pattern was actually so labyrinthine in its swirls and double-backs that it made Izmirlian a little dizzy to look at it. It took a moment for him to realise what Velo meant. "Sitting on the *floor*?"

"Sitting," Velo clarified, "in the middle of this tangled labyrinth, a perfect symbol for everything you want to escape." He threw himself down on the carpet in an easy sprawl. "Come on, who's running this ritual?"

"It's a ritual now?" Izmirlian wondered if he sounded as uncertain as he felt. The other alchemists—the ones who'd even bothered to try—had used plodding procedure, carefully calculated charts, slow and complex assemblies of glassware. This was something far more urgent, and immediate, and…well, exciting. But nerve-wracking all the same. This involved Izmirlian—personally, physically, centrally.

It might hurt. It might *work*.

Izmirlian stepped around a chaise, and sat down opposite Velo, legs folded up as he hadn't done since he was a child.

Velo grinned—smugly, encouragingly, distractingly. "Might as well be a ritual. It's not a working. You didn't come to me for structure or theory, so that's not what we're going to do. We're going to..." He sat up straighter, looking around as though for inspiration.

I wouldn't even know where to start, he'd said, walking through the dark and hushed city. "Are you inventing on the spot?" Izmirlian accused, not unamused, but also not unafraid.

Inventing on the spot, as he'd done in Tower Square, to catch the falling body. Wild improvisation, achieving the impossible.

"Ask for everything," Velo said, the very thing Izmirlian had told him. "Why don't we try it on the universe?"

"Why not?" Izmirlian echoed. A little failure could only bruise his hopes, and they were well pummelled by now.

Velo took a deep breath and settled himself into a pose much like Izmirlian's. Their knees didn't quite touch, but they enclosed a space between them. Inside, outside. That flutter was back behind Izmirlian's ribs. Fear. Excitement. Possibility.

"We're going to step out of this plane, but not into any of the others," Velo said. "The void, the space between. We'll be outside the planes. And then you can let go, and that will be that."

It seemed far too simple. It seemed terribly achievable. "Let go," Izmirlian repeated. "So I should be...holding on?"

"Good idea." Velo held out his hands, and Izmirlian took them in his own; Velo's fingers were rough, his palms edged with calluses, his grip firm. They made another circle with their arms. Inside, outside.

Izmirlian felt poised on the brink of something. Nestled inside a catapult sling, waiting for launch. He wanted to leap up, rush out of the room. He wanted to leap *forward*, to get it over with, to *see*.

"Think of what you want," Velo prompted. "What you *need*. You don't have to say it." Which was a relief, because Izmirlian had tried a dozen times or more to explain this, and had never come closer than he'd managed to Siyon Velo this night, under the stars. "You know it better than words can. You feel it. You *live* it."

Izmirlian closed his eyes, because that seemed right. Shutting out the world around him. However much he loved it, however much he'd been entertained or intrigued or engaged by the things he'd seen, he wanted—he needed—to know what *more* there was. To see something new.

"Open," Siyon whispered, barely a breath, and yet the word was also a stone dropped down a deep well, an echo and an unstoppable rush. A whirl into the tangles of the carpet labyrinth, a vertiginous slipping into the cracks between realities.

Something opened, and opened more, all around them. *Nothing* opened, and Izmirlian swayed for a moment, before Siyon's grip tightened on his fingers; Izmirlian gasped at the reminder of the physical. His eyes popped open, and then he tried to open them again, because there was nothing here, not darkness, not shadow, just *nothing*.

Nothing at all. Was *he* here? Who was he? He was a purpose. He was a body, hungry and tired and footsore. He was the twinge of his knee in this position. He was a need that he couldn't quite remember...

He was too many things. He was spinning, out of control. He was on the deck of a shifting ship, the horizon lost in storm. "Velo," he whispered, and yes, there was a Velo, there was a *someone*, holding his hand, and he held on tight, held on desperately. "I don't think this is—"

The nothing shattered. Razor shards ripped through Izmirlian, jagged across his vision, serrated across his soul. He slammed backward, sprawled on the carpet in the Joddani townhouse.

The parlour rattled around him. The chandelier tinkled; plaster dust skittered down the walls. No, it was something else entirely, the air thick with particles, fine as flour but sparkling as the stars.

As Izmirlian watched, winded and worse, the dancing motes *caught fire*. The fire was blue as midnight, and simultaneously the same delicate pink as dawn.

Something yanked at his hand—Velo, still holding on, dragging him behind the nearest sofa. As though the flimsy modern-whimsical piece offered any protection at all. The fire pelted down like rain, and ran up the walls like rats.

Beside him, Velo swayed, rocked by waves Izmirlian couldn't feel.

The door burst open, and Nihath Joddani braced himself in the doorway. "What have you *done*?"

Another man shoved past him—a wisp of a man, his pale strawberry hair billowing in strange winds as he ran into the room as though the flames weren't there. They danced in his hair and bathed him in light—blue and pink and silver—and reflected in his eyes. He grabbed hold of Izmirlian's collar and hauled him upright, surprisingly strong for someone so slight. "Go!" he shouted, and his voice crackled and popped and roared like the fire should have.

Izmirlian went, Velo's hand slipping from his as he skidded and stumbled out past Joddani and into the hall.

The door slammed shut behind him, and Izmirlian sagged against the wall, wide-eyed and panting. Already that glimpse of nothingness seemed ephemeral, gone like a dream in daylight.

It hadn't worked.

But it had certainly done *something*.

Joddani slammed the door behind Hisarani, and Tehroun wrapped cold fingers around Siyon's wrist. "Are you wearing metal?" he demanded.

"What?" Siyon patted absently at himself. He'd left his satchel in the study earlier, and no sabre hung at his hip, of course—he'd been arrested, he'd been at the Summer Club, he hadn't carried his blade *there*. What was *happening*? "No, I—"

"Here." Tehroun grabbed a heavy silver candlestick from the sideboard, shoved it into Siyon's hand; he tossed another to Joddani, who held it like a weapon as he stepped up to the edge of the rug. "Go to the other side of the room. Go! We have to contain this before it spills further."

Siyon's bones grated together, the world ill-fitting after the void. But he went as Tehroun pointed, tripping over an edge of the carpet and staggering into the far wall. He flinched back from the flames that licked and giggled against the surface, before he realised there was no heat. No sensation at all. The fire moved through his flesh like it wasn't even there.

That wasn't at all reassuring.

"Stand!" Tehroun called, and Siyon pressed his back against the wall. Held up his candlestick like Joddani was doing near the doorway, pointing toward Tehroun in the middle of the room.

The fire rushed toward him, climbing and capering, dripping from the ceiling, whirling through the air. Tehroun spread his arms, a brilliant conflagration, and inhaled. He drew the fire into him, more and more and more, until spots danced across Siyon's vision and *he* had to breathe out again, gasping as the eldritch flames whirled around Tehroun.

Until the parlour was lit only by the morning beyond the window.

Until Joddani let his candlestick fall to the floor with a clatter.

Until Tehroun's arms lowered, and his head lolled, and he fainted clean away.

Joddani lunged forward to catch him before he hit the floor. Siyon tossed his candlestick onto one of the couches. "Is he—"

Joddani looked up, and Siyon flinched back from the venom in his face. "Get out."

It was dark in the corridor, every lantern gone out and smoking faintly. Sunlight filtered through the window at the end of the hall. In the gloom, Hisarani was slumped against the far wall, arms wrapped around himself. His gaze leapt to Siyon, wide and wild, as though he'd not been sure what might emerge from the parlour. "What was that?" he asked.

Siyon rubbed a hand over his face. He felt like he should be covered in ash or grime or some other evidence of the mishap, but all he had was a faint prickling. "Aethyr flare." He huffed a laugh. "I wasn't sure they really existed. Flares happen when a working comes undone. When the power tied up in it gets loose."

Hisarani frowned. "Did we—were we using any power?"

"I didn't think so?" Siyon's body still felt ill-fitting, no room for all this energy and frustration. "Now you see the problem with someone who doesn't know what he's doing."

That only deepened Hisarani's frown. "But you got us... somewhere."

"Somewhere," Siyon repeated, and countered: "Nowhere."

"That's more than anyone else managed." Hisarani chewed briefly at his lip, knuckles whitening where he gripped his own elbows. "Was that my chance? Should I have... let go? Like you said."

Siyon rubbed at the prickling on his neck. Was it just his imagination? Was the world twitching around them like an ox bothered by flies? "I can't tell you that. You know what you want better than I do. Did that feel like it?"

"I don't think so. I don't—" Hisarani took his time to frame the thought properly, tilting his head. Siyon watched the flicker of his eyes, the twitch of his mouth; caught himself at it, and looked away. "I'm not so keen to leave that I'm willing to risk death lightly."

Siyon looked back at him. "Then wait until you're sure."

Hisarani nodded, with the faintest ghost of a smile. "Yes. So when shall we try again?"

"What?" Siyon blinked at him. How many times in the past day had Hisarani surprised him? "You still want to—?"

"What is going *on* up here?" Anahid hauled herself up the last of the stairs, skirts bunched in one hand and her eyes wild. "My house feeling like a storm, alchemists racing out through my servants' hall like someone set fire to their trousers, the oven has gone out—what has *happened*?"

Siyon winced. He'd rather hoped that this would be like the other night at the Summer Club—something only those connected to the planes seemed to feel. Apparently not. "Um," he started.

But Anahid swiped his excuses away before he could even voice them. "Never mind. I don't care what, or why, or how. I care about what's going to happen next."

"Next?" Hisarani repeated blankly.

Anahid's look suggested they were being unbelievably thick. "The inquisitors are already looking under every rock, and you lot do— whatever that was. Do you really think they—"

Right on cue, a thunderous hammering came at the front door. "Inquisitors!" a voice bellowed. "Open up!"

Cold flashed down Siyon's spine. "I'm sorry," he gasped. "I didn't expect it to do this." But what did that matter? He'd still acted blithely, recklessly, heedlessly, and now he'd brought the inquisitors down on all of them. Not just him and Joddani, but Anahid too.

Anahid looked almost startled. "You—well, thank you. Where is Nihath?"

"Still in there." Siyon nodded at the parlour door. "With Tehroun." Her face tightened with a tangle of too many things for him to decipher. He edged toward the stairs. "I should go. I should—" He had no idea what. He couldn't possibly outrun the inquisitors, not in the Avenues, where he had nowhere to go, where he stood out like dirt on a silver plate. But he couldn't just stay and let them all—

"Nonsense." Anahid grabbed his arm, her fingers pressing tight below his elbow. Her face was all icy resolve now. "You'll be caught, and they'll trace back where you came from, and the whole mess will collapse upon us anyway. No. You can hide with the other one. And you—" She lifted an eyebrow at Hisarani. "I suggest you hie yourself home, Azatan Hisarani. Your mother will be displeased should you be found here and excite comment."

Hisarani pulled himself together, managing a passable bow of courtesy. "Your wisdom graces your house." He shot Siyon a glance, even as he hurried toward the stairs. "I'll be in touch."

Another hammering at the door below, but Anahid just sighed. "Always dealing with the unpleasant necessities." She fixed Siyon with a look. "Wait here. They'll be done soon."

She descended the stairs with bewildering calm. Siyon's blood was rushing through his body, shouting with the urge to run, to fight, to hide. He sank back against the wall, deep in the shadows, and peeked around the corner to watch Anahid straighten her headscarf in the hall mirror before she opened the door.

"Inquisitors," she said, cool and precise. "Thank all the Powers that you're here. Please come inside, and quickly."

One of the inquisitors was hefty across the shoulders, sternly upright with duty, and the other had a wild halo of tight dirty-blonde curls. Of course. Vartan Xhanari was reciting official platitudes with a menacing undertone, but Siyon missed all the details when Olenka looked up, her grey eyes skewering right through the cloaking shadows and into Siyon.

He clamped down on the urge to flinch back. It was dark up here. The lanterns had been extinguished by the Aethyr flare, and all the doors were closed. She couldn't possibly see him, but she *would* see the movement.

"We've had reports—" Xhanari began.

"Yes, I should think so," Anahid smoothly interrupted. Her composure was immaculate, with just a tinge of upright privileged outrage. "I must know what's going on—in my own house! Please search thoroughly, I want to know if there's anything untoward, anything at all. Come this way."

Her hand on Inquisitor Xhanari's elbow, she drew him into the dining room as undeniably as though she'd twisted the arm up behind his back. Olenka finally looked away from Siyon, and followed in their wake.

Released from her gaze, Siyon skittered back down the corridor. He hesitated at the parlour door, knuckles raised to knock; they needed to be making the most of Anahid's delay, but Joddani had been very firm that he wanted Siyon out.

The door swung open before Siyon could decide. Joddani, carrying Tehroun tucked against his chest, glared over the spill of moonlight hair.

Siyon took a quick step back, pointing toward the stairs. "The inquisitors. Your w—Anahid is stalling them."

Joddani grunted. "The room is clean. No thanks to *you*."

Siyon gritted his teeth. "Look—"

Tehroun interrupted with a grumble and slipped down to stand on his own feet. He was so pale that he seemed almost to glow in the shadowed corridor. "Best they don't find me like this," he said, with a delicate wince. His voice was a breathy whisper again, not that crackling roar.

Joddani's hand lingered between his shoulder blades. "Are you well enough to climb the stairs?"

"Don't fuss." Tehroun patted his cheek and wafted away down the corridor.

"Wait," Siyon hissed after him. "What did you do?" No response; Siyon turned to Joddani. "What did he *do*? In there? With the—" Siyon lifted a hand, like Tehroun had done, like he was *calling* the impossible flames to him.

Joddani just glared at him. "Exercised an affinity with which he has practised to ensure mastery. Unlike *you*, who—"

Whatever came next was forestalled by a door opening downstairs, voices coming clearer for a moment—Anahid's and Xhanari's, as he tried to hurry things along and she calmly insisted on thoroughness. Joddani murmured, "In here."

Here was his library, and Siyon hurried to gather up his satchel from the side table where he'd left it earlier, storming out in a fit of pique to—well, to fuck up.

The room was empty of the other alchemists now. Fled through the back, according to Anahid, and Siyon could hardly blame them. He'd likely have legged it too, feeling that Aethyr flare so soon after what had happened at the Summer Club. He stamped on a pang of guilt. *They* could have been a little bit more inclusive, and it might not have happened this way.

Joddani lit a lantern anew with a snap of his fingers, closing the door before he rounded on Siyon, more vehement for the delay. "You utter idiot. You felt for yourself the imbalance of irresponsible power, and you go off—immediately!—and do..." He waved a hand. "What? What did you *do* to cause a flare of this magnitude?"

"I didn't *do* anything!" Siyon cried. "We weren't—there was no *power*, I used no material at all. I didn't think—"

"That much is obvious!" Joddani shouted, so loud that both of them stopped, listening to the silence beyond the room. When no hurrying feet were heard, Joddani continued, more quietly, "I don't know what has been unearthed that makes it possible for you to—" He waved an irritable hand. "To ignore all the rules. But they exist for a reason, and your willful ignorance will not save you from destruction—nor me, nor the rest of this house, nor indeed the entire plane!"

Siyon opened his mouth to tell him he was being overly dramatic, but then he remembered those midnight-and-dawn flames, the impossibility of them, their beauty and terror.

He closed his mouth again.

Which seemed to mollify Joddani a little. He sniffed, and tugged his longvest straight. "And now we must deal with the inquisitors. I don't know how they arrived so quickly, but I do not fault them for responding to this. It is just what all of Bezim must be wary of. The untrained, unready practitioner meddling with matters beyond his understanding." He actually *shook a finger* at Siyon, and Siyon couldn't even laugh in his face because there was more than one sandy grain of truth in the fish pie of his pompous grandstanding. "Were you a properly approved member of the Summer Club, you would understand—"

That was a wave too far. "Oh, fuck off," Siyon snapped back. "Do *you* understand a thing I've done? What happened *right there*?" Siyon pointed at the door—at the parlour across the hall.

"Do *you* understand the very real danger?" Joddani leaned forward, urgency in every line of him. "The planes are lurching from one extreme to another—you *felt* them, when Danelani disappeared. And for all we point at the Scarp and speak of the dangers of unregulated alchemy, we have no real idea how the Sundering happened. We could be on the verge of another, and I can't let you run around like a child with his mother's sabre!"

Siyon felt cold, as though his bones had been pulled from the depths of the ocean. "Are you turning me in?" he asked, lips numb. He'd been a fool, so grateful to Anahid for her intervention that he'd forgotten this pair were less of a partnership. Now it was too late to run.

"What?" Joddani looked horrified. "No! Of course not. I will not cast a fellow practitioner to the inquisitors. But I must insist that you make best use of your stay in this house by *educating yourself*." He waved a hand toward the shelves lining the room. "You've bargained for access anyway."

A flood of relief met a rising tide of anger in Siyon, all churned up with his helplessness. He wanted to tell Joddani he could *stick it*, this generosity that felt like punishment. But there was an entire *wall* of books. Siyon *had* bargained for this, and had congratulated himself on it. It would be stupid to throw this chance away. At least when he went back to Bracken and his life, he'd know more.

So annoying as it was, Siyon said, "Thanks."

Joddani sighed, like some long-suffering parent. "Don't make me regret it. For now, though, you'd best hide yourself as Tehroun has done. There is a painting of the investiture of the first Prefect Telmut Hisarani at the end of the hall. Knock, and Tehroun will let you up."

Siyon knew when he was dismissed. He crept down the corridor, fleeing the distant echoes of Xhanari's voice from below, until he found a picture of a fancy chap in three-century-old regalia. The painting was massive—the size of a door, and when Siyon rapped knuckles against the frame, it swung outward just like one. Tehroun wrapped a hand around his wrist and hauled Siyon through into darkness beyond.

Siyon's last thought, as he whisked past the painting, was that the fancy painted chap *did* look a little like Izmirlian Hisarani. Same canny eyes. No doubt some great-grand-relation of his.

Inside, a narrow staircase led upward. As Siyon's eyes slowly adjusted to the dark, he could just make out the angular shape of Tehroun, who'd returned to sitting as patiently as though he were waiting for an appointment. Behind him, the steps climbed up into gloom. "Where does this go?"

"Attics." Tehroun blinked. *Were* his eyes glowing faintly? Maybe Siyon was just having after-effects of being the epicentre of an Aethyr flare. "Old servants' quarters, from when this house was fully serviced."

Siyon slumped against the wall. He felt…well, like the only rest he'd had in many hours had been on a hard bench in a cold cell. "Hide in here often?"

"Only when something untoward has happened," Tehroun whispered, without inflection.

"Sorry about that." And Siyon was. Tehroun might be an eerie little wisp of lace, but he'd leapt straight in to fix Siyon's fuck-up.

Tehroun hummed vaguely. "You'll do better next time."

The words lodged in Siyon like a splinter. At least *someone* thought he could do this. Even if it was the inexplicable live-in lover with strange affectations and some sort of *affinity*. What did that even mean? He still seemed weirdly familiar to Siyon, but that seemed the least of his oddities now. "Down there, before, how did you—"

"You should be quiet," Tehroun suggested, barely a breath. "They're getting closer."

A few moments later, Siyon heard them too, the faint tramp of boots on the stairs, and Anahid carrying on like an airy azata.

Sitting silently, waiting as the inquisitors passed them by, gave it all time to sink in. Doing the impossible, and the risk of another Sundering, and all of those books behind Nihath Joddani. If Siyon was going to be stuck in the upper city, hiding here while the inqs stalked the streets, he could do that reading. See how to wrap proper alchemy around the impossibility of Izmirlian Hisarani. Why not? Doing it might still win him Summer Club membership, but mostly, Siyon just wanted to know.

What if he *could*?

CHAPTER 8

"This is stupid." Zagiri waved one net-gloved hand. "The creeping around, the disguises—"

"Yours isn't a disguise," Siyon pointed out, and she glared at him, just like a young lady might at the manservant giving her lip while carrying her shopping in the leather sacks slung across his shoulders.

Empty sacks, right now.

"We could be wearing our leathers," Zagiri grumbled. "You could just come inside yourself. You're acting like the inqs are hunting you personally."

Maybe not all the inqs, but Siyon felt pretty sure that Vartan Xhanari was. Didn't matter either way. He wasn't taking the risk of bringing trouble down on Little Bracken.

Siyon didn't argue, just unlooped the sacks from around his neck and passed them to her, keeping a careful eye on the square around them—empty, for now. "You know what you're looking for, right?"

She huffed again, but dutifully recited, "West dormitory, third bunk along the outer wall. Everything under the loose plank or in your locker goes in the sacks."

"I'll be waiting right over there." Siyon nodded to the side street. "Hey, thanks for this."

"Yeah yeah." Zagiri slung the sacks over one shoulder. They looked ridiculous with her delicate yellow gown. "Go hide, Za Paranoid. I'll see you soon."

She strode across the square and into the Chapel. Siyon lingered for a moment. He wished he could go inside. Clasp hands with Daruj, get a nod from Voski, sleep in his own damn bunk. The place he came when he had nowhere better to go—so most of the time—might be far less comfortable than the guest bed at the Joddani townhouse, but it smelt right. *He* smelt right after sleeping in it.

The square was warm in the late-morning sun, but all the residents of the nearby dwellings were about their respectable business. The quiet of the neighbourhood was part of its appeal in keeping the Chapel as the main Bracken safe house.

Siyon felt a little out of place, skulking on the corner. He tugged his broad-brimmed laborer's hat lower over his face and pulled out a pipe he'd borrowed from one of Anahid's footmen. Fiddling with it gave him a reason to keep his head down, and to loiter for as long as he needed to wait.

But hardly had he knocked the pipe out than the tramp of boots sounded. Siyon faded back, sliding along the wall a little further down his side street, as the inquisitors marched into the square.

Only four of them, but that was plenty. The one in charge—slimmer than Xhanari, at least—sent one pair down the side laneway. Covering the exits.

Siyon didn't feel vindicated; he felt a sick twist of panic. He couldn't tell Zagiri that he'd been right if she got pinched with all his incriminating alchemical bits and pieces in her possession.

He sidled away down the street, tucking the pipe back in his pocket even as he found the narrow alley running down the back of the houses. He scurried along to the houses nearest the Chapel, and then went up, hauling himself up by drainpipes and windowsills and the edges of hastily lain bricks. The alley was narrow enough that he could brace one boot against the far wall; good as a ladder, for a bravi.

Pulling himself over the gutter and onto the roof, he stayed belly-down to the tiles, looking over to the Chapel roof. It was a little higher than the house, a long and welcoming pitch, save that odd pointy spire at the front end with its little cupola.

The laneway was jumpable, but how far back from the street should he be to make sure no one saw him cross? He'd want to land lightly, or they'd hear him below. And what if there wasn't anyone within hissing distance, once he'd stuck his head down the cupola ladder?

Even as he was sizing it all up, a figure appeared in that cupola in a flash of delicate yellow. Siyon felt almost proud that she'd realised the only way out as well.

Zagiri had the leather sacks over one shoulder, holding on with a hand as she hauled up her skirt with the other to clamber out of the cupola onto the peak of the Chapel roof. She was watching her footing—those street slippers seemed ill-suited to tiles—so Siyon whistled the low, long tone meaning *friendly blade sighted*. She looked up, spotted him, and lifted a hand made pale by the net glove.

The intervening space would have been nothing in bravi leathers and sensible boots, taken at a flat run. As it was, she slid very gingerly down the Chapel roof, going slow as her gown snagged on the rough edge of every roof tile, and had to leap from a dead start and in satin slippers.

As Zagiri skidded in the gutter, Siyon darted forward, grabbed a handful of her gown and then her shoulder, and pulled her properly onto the roof. She winced and said, "I *told* you we should have worn our leathers."

Siyon snorted but led the way up the roof and away, putting another two rooftops between them and the chance the inquisitors might stumble upon them. They crouched down in the lee of a chimney, as an added precaution, before Zagiri handed over the leather sacks. They were reassuringly bulky, but Siyon resisted the urge to look inside. Now wasn't the time. "All there?"

Zagiri nodded absently. "Voski had moved most of your stuff down into the crypt. Did you know there's a whole creepy basement under the Chapel? There's a stair behind that cupboard where they keep the extra kit. I don't see why *you* couldn't have been hidden down there."

It sounded thoroughly unpleasant, really. "Still a risk." Siyon draped the leather sacks around his neck, where they pulled each other into balance, and said, "Come on, we need to get back down to the street before someone spots us up here and causes a ruckus." Even bravi didn't run the tiles in full daylight.

But Zagiri grabbed at his wrist. "I can't walk home like this. Everyone'll think I've been mugged, or worse." She pointed down at her dress, and Siyon looked at it properly for the first time. It had had some sort of lacy overlay, now snagged and torn, and streaked all over with roof grime.

The first inquisitor they passed was going to insist on coming to her rescue, and that would be that.

"We could travel solo?" Siyon suggested. "Think you could spin a story for the inqs?"

Zagiri chewed on her lip. "They might still connect me back to Bracken. And what about you? Is there another way?"

Siyon looked around the nearby rooftops. Getting Zagiri another dress might work, but this neighbourhood had communal laundry yards that would be risky to filch something from. A little way to the north, the buildings stretched into apartments and tenements, where someone might—

"Actually," he realised aloud. "I know someone who lives just over there."

Zagiri frowned. "Someone who you can trust?"

That might be pushing it. "Someone who has no interest in drawing inq attention," Siyon promised.

An easy run under the stars took nearly half a bell creeping along as the sweltering sun neared midday. Zagiri's dress looked worse with every rooftop, and she scraped her elbow when her impractical shoes slipped on the tiles. Siyon suggested ditching them altogether, but Zagiri said, "The roof's hot enough with them on."

The last bit was the worst—a jump from a chimney to a balcony, and then along the wall with only the twining ivy to offer grip. Siyon tapped on a window he desperately hoped was the right one.

The pale face that appeared was surprised, and then aghast. The balcony door was hauled open, setting the curtain of beads to rustling, and a voice from inside hissed, "What in all the Khanate hells are you doing?"

"Hello, Corbinus," Siyon said, cheerfully but quietly. He didn't want nosy neighbours getting in on this either. "Just visiting. Get the tea on, will you?"

After so long in the dazzle of the midday rooftops, it took Siyon a few moments to make out anything in the murk inside. The door closed behind them, with many mutterings in the sharp and incomprehensible dialect of Corbinus's Northern home—he never would be pinned down on which city precisely. "Now is *not* the time," he finished up.

Corbinus was even taller than Siyon and gangly as a young tree. He was all-over pale—almost white hair braided down his back, eyes like a summer sky, skin you could see the veins in. He'd probably been banished from the home he wouldn't admit to, but nevertheless he was an excellent source for all manner of little bits and pieces—alchemical and otherwise—that were found only amid the cold Northern forests. He also specialised in Aethyreal material, which meant Siyon—unable to delve the Aethyr—had called on him often. They'd kept up a mutually beneficial trade arrangement for years.

But right now, Corbinus looked nothing like pleased to see him, and Siyon could hardly blame him. "Sorry, the inqs been causing you grief too?"

Corbinus's pale eyes flicked from him to Zagiri and back again. "Not yet. But it's only a matter of time. Too many people know where to find me."

As Siyon's very presence seemed to prove. Siyon had found an unexpected place to hide, but not everyone could be so lucky. "Might be time to head back north for a bit."

The bark of Corbinus's laughter was hollow. "Haven't you heard? They're checking everyone who leaves the city, either by landward gate or on a ship."

Of course they were. Ostensibly hunting for Enkin Danelani, Siyon was sure. But it also meant finding all the practitioners who might have been seeking a safer place to weather this storm.

"Don't they just banish alchemists?" Zagiri asked. They both looked at her, and she shrugged, picking a last bit of snagged ivy out of the wreckage of her dress. "Wouldn't that work out all right?"

"Who is this?" Corbinus demanded.

"A friend," Siyon told him. "Do you have anything she could wear? Just to avoid attention on the streets. And then we'll get out of your hair."

Corbinus shot her another cold look, and stalked out of the room.

Zagiri looked at Siyon, her eyebrows drawing together. "I don't under—"

"Maybe they banish azatani alchemists," Siyon told her quietly. "And maybe they still would. But when they had me up in the Palace the other night, it was made pretty clear that clemency is off the table for the likes of me."

"That's hardly fair." Siyon could have laughed right in her face; he kept it to a snort. Zagiri blushed a little, mouth pinching in chagrin. But she lifted her chin. "There has to be something we can do. To help, I mean."

"Find Enkin Danelani?" Siyon suggested, which was unhelpful, and he knew it. At least she wanted to help. He sighed, and tried again. "You know a way to smuggle people like Corbinus out?"

"No," Zagiri admitted, but there was a slow drag to the word that suggested she was thinking very hard. "But what if there were a way to..."

She trailed off, and Corbinus said from the doorway, "A way to what?" He was holding a bundle of clothes; he shoved it at her like a challenge.

Zagiri took it. "A way to hide you. A safe place. Until we *could* find a way out of the city."

It took Siyon a moment to catch up. "No, Zagiri, *think*. You were just worrying about the safety of the tribe, and now you want to put fugitives in the Chapel's basement?"

"What good is our safety if we're the only ones who can enjoy it?" Zagiri demanded. She turned back to Corbinus. "You couldn't bring anything incriminating with you. And the sergeant of our tribe would have to agree, but I think she would if the risk was minimised. And then I'm sure we can find a way to get you out, if that's what you want."

Corbinus watched her for a moment, then turned his pale, steady gaze on Siyon. "Your tribe. Little Bracken bravi, right? I thought the bravi were just about crashing parties and having flashy duels."

"They're a lot of things," Siyon replied. "And they have no love for the inqs. I don't know that Voski will go for this," he said to Zagiri.

But if he thought he could temper the will of a young azatani, he'd clearly need to try harder. Zagiri simply said, "We can ask, at least."

Ask for everything, Siyon heard in his mind. *And be appalled if you don't get it.*

It was a little impressive, even if it was also a whole lot frustrating.

"Get changed," he told Zagiri, who slipped into the next room to do so, and Siyon added to Corbinus, "Your decision."

"I have few other options," Corbinus noted. He lifted the end of his pale braid and added, "I stand out too much to hide without help."

Like the help Siyon had already received from Zagiri and her sister, facing down the inqs. "When you meet Voski Tolan," he said, "tell her Siyon Velo asked her to help you, if she could."

The little help he could give, to bail a boat that was sinking under all of them.

Anahid and Nihath strolled across the park toward the Palace of Justice as the Merry bell rang. They were far from the only azatani couple making the journey this evening. Anahid was sure they were also far from the only couple arguing as they did so.

"To be dragged away from my work now, of all times," Nihath protested, "when the planes are particularly precarious in their imbalance—"

"Now," Anahid interjected quietly, "when the prefect is particularly precarious in *her* position, is not the time to be refusing an invitation from her!"

Nihath said plaintively, "Couldn't you represent us both?"

Anahid gritted her teeth against the simmering resentment that threatened to boil over. It would be messy, and unwise, and achieve nothing. Her palm still itched to slap him. She should slap her past self. She'd thought this marriage would be a partnership—that was what he had suggested! She just hadn't realised that for him, a partnership meant her handling society, leaving him to do precisely as he pleased.

She'd been so dizzy at the notion that someone finally valued *her*. She'd been a fool.

But here they were, and she had to make the best of it. "If you are not there," she managed to say, "it will imply that you are siding with alchemy, instead of with the prefect."

"Well, I don't think she's being entirely fair in painting all—"

"And there will be opportunities to learn more about what developments have arisen from the raid upon the Summer Club," Anahid interrupted, before he could fray her temper clean through.

"Hmm," he said, and thankfully shut up, remaining silent as they entered the grand hall of the Palace of Justice, with its intricate mosaic floor and beaten copper dome glowing gently in the light of alchemical lanterns.

They joined the other azatani climbing the sweeping staircase to the upper floor apartments where the prefect and family lived for the elected term. The Danelani townhouse had been closed up for the past three years, and would be closed for two more, though Anahid supposed it may, at present, have been reopened for Syrah's brother and his wife.

Might Tahera be here tonight? That would be pleasant.

The apartments were charmingly provisioned as ever, but Enkin's absence from the receiving line cast a somber pall over the evening. Syrah was smiling hardly at all, and her sash and headscarf were the gleaming white of her office, as though she would rather be prefect than mother to a missing son. Her husband, Eref, was beside her, a devoted pillar of support from the moment he'd taken her surname upon their marriage. (Though, gossip pointed out, his own second-tier name had little to recommend itself against the prestige of hers.)

Anahid clasped hands with Syrah, and with Eref, and murmured neutral evening greetings.

Syrah's gaze slid from Nihath to Anahid; she nodded. "We appreciate you joining us."

Not everyone had. The mirrored salon was not as crowded as usual. No doubt if Anahid knew more of the intricate movements of clerkships and committee appointments, of whose political careers were moving in which direction, she would be able to draw significance from who was present, and who absent. As it was, she was merely pleased to see that her parents were here, and equally pleased that they were engaged on the far side of the room and could only lift a glass in her direction.

Nihath, of course, wandered off almost immediately, setting direct course for Azata Kurlani. Another alchemist. Of course.

The azata's nearby spouse saw Anahid looking, and gave a welcoming wave. Azatan Kurlani was a councillor and sat upon two different committees whose names Anahid could never keep straight. Though neither had anything directly to do with alchemy or the law, he might still know what was being whispered in the Palace halls regarding the Summer Club raid.

Or, just as important to Anahid, what was known or suspected about the public spectacle Zagiri and Siyon had made in Tower Square.

Unfortunately, he was in conversation with three other spouses of azatani alchemists. Anahid knew them all, had met them previously when she'd been trying to keep closer to her husband's interests.

Before it became quite so abundantly clear that Tehroun was fulfilling the role of *partner* in that aspect of Nihath's life.

All of the people in this group knew it as well as she did. Their smiles were polite, but not friendly. The conversation stayed entirely shallow—the prospects likely in the season's trading ventures, and other azatani small talk. But finally an opening came, as one azata tittered inanely about *nervous times.*

"Here in the city as well," Azatan Kurlani sighed. "Especially for our particular interests."

"No charges brought from the raid, I assume?" Anahid asked, turning the conversation the way she wanted it.

Inexpertly, from the shrugs, the dismissive wave, even a confused look from one azatan. "Not on any of *ours*," he said, as though that were obvious.

Another chipped in, "Some foreigners. Some lower-class sorts who must have been caught up in underhanded goings-on."

Of course they must have been.

"It's so unfortunate," one azata chirped. "My Balian had something *very* delicate underway at the club, and the interruption has quite ruined it. He's had to throw it all away, which will mean acquiring the ingredients all over again, and he says the suppliers are being quite unreasonable on prices."

Sympathetic nods all around the group.

Anahid couldn't help saying, "Well, the increased inquisitorial attention makes things rather dangerous for them."

That earned her blank looks. After a moment, Azatan Kurlani said, "I suppose it might, but it's not like they're actually *practicing*, is it?"

Always that condescending tone. Like they were sure she was trying her best, but they all knew that she wasn't *really* involved in her husband's work.

She was doing this all wrong. She didn't know these people well enough. She hadn't wanted to befriend them and bear the constant reminder that the marriage she'd entered into wasn't what she'd hoped.

She tried once more anyway. "And that business in the square the other day. Was that practicing, do you think?"

"You mean that bravi stunt?" An azatan across the circle wrinkled his nose. "I shouldn't think it was anything much."

Nothing much. Just saving her sister's life.

"I'm sure you're quite right," Anahid declared, pulling up her society smile. "Please do excuse me, enjoy your evening."

She traded an empty glass for a full one, and surveyed the room as she strolled around the fringes. Perhaps she could try another angle.

Find someone she'd met at Parsola's luncheon, suggest that she was nervous about her husband's exposure if alchemy became subject to stricter regulation...

It wasn't a pretense. Anahid didn't think Nihath would spare a thought for the idea that azatani practitioners might be in any danger. Clearly, none of his cronies would. Someone should.

But before Anahid could spy a suitable azata to approach, she passed an open doorway leading to a side parlour, and heard someone inside exclaim, "A greater triad, you brazen imp! I *wanted* that run in Aethyr."

It was Tahera Danelani, at a card-scattered table with three other people. An azatan laughed, and swept coins into a pile in front of him. "Then you shouldn't have bought that deal."

Another azatan started shuffling the cards, fingers flashing fast.

Tahera glanced over at the door and brightened from her sulk. "Azata Joddani! Won't you join us? I could use some sympathetic parties at the table."

"Buy-in's five rivna," stated the shuffler, not even looking up.

Fascination pulled Anahid into the room. This did not look at all like the card games she was used to, played in careful partnership with simple rules. The shuffler tidied the deck and started dealing, flicking cards face down around the circle. He set an extra one on the table beside him, and only then looked up at her. "Are you in?"

Anahid remembered her conversation with Tahera at the luncheon. "Is this carrick?"

The azatan who'd apparently won the last hand snorted. "What else?"

"Oh!" Tahera blinked at her. "I'd forgotten, you don't play. Well, sit here and watch, if you like." She smiled sunnily and turned back to the table.

Anahid did like. She took the indicated chair, close to Tahera's side, and watched the dealer spin out more cards, until everyone had three.

That was the last thing she really understood. What followed was a complex and dizzyingly quick round of brusque utterances, coins tossed into a copper bowl in the middle of the table, cards dealt out, either face down or face up in the middle. It looked to be a standard deck—the four suits corresponding to the four planes, numbered cards and the face cards, with the Power in each suit—but Anahid couldn't make any sense of the rest of it.

The intricacy was fascinating. She watched Tahera make decisions about cards to keep, and cards to throw away, and whether she wanted to buy more cards to her hand, or to the face-up middle cards. Those were ones everyone could use, Anahid realised. And they were trying to put together a collection that was worth more points than anyone else's.

There was more to it even than that. Anahid edged forward on her chair, watching more closely.

They talked a little as they played, but almost—Anahid thought—to distract the other players rather than because the game didn't hold attention. At one point, having bought more cards, one of the azatans noted, "Say, have you heard the rumbles about the inquisitors holding up azatani trade with these new alchemy restrictions?"

The other azatan shuffled the cards in his hand, and said absently, "Syrah will have mutiny on her hands if it goes on too long, and you can tell her I said it, Tay."

Tahera just sniffed. "Are you calling or what?"

The first azatan smirked a little. "You know they say a prefect who can't control her own family doesn't inspire much confidence."

He smirked wider still when Tahera dropped her own coin into the bowl, and then widest of all as he laid down his hand, and gathered all that money to himself.

And Anahid watched it all. The ebb and flow of the cards, the faces of the players, the results as they spun out. There were patterns here, like in a conversation, or a dance, or trade. There could simply be a winner or a loser, but there could also be greater complication. You could cajole, or intimidate, or misrepresent.

You could *tell lies*.

Tahera laughed quietly beside her. "Oh, you've been bitten, haven't you? Shall we deal you in?"

Anahid wanted to. Her fingers almost itched with it. But with her concentration broken, she remembered that she had other reasons for being here. She was supposed to be out there, talking with people. Making sure the Joddani and Savani names were seen and noted and counted on the right side. Perhaps even finding out useful things.

But this... this looked like so much more *fun*.

"*There* you are."

The voice bounced Anahid to her feet by reflex; she turned to greet her mother. Kemella Savani cast a look around the table, and said nothing more than, "Please do excuse us, I must speak with my daughter."

The rest waited until Kemella and Anahid were tucked into a corner of the salon where no one could overhear Mama Savani muttering, "What in all the planes were you doing hiding in there? Your husband is nowhere to be found either, and this is no time to be misunderstood, I thought you would realise that."

Anahid wondered if Nihath had left altogether. Probably gone straight to the Summer Club too. She sighed, and salvaged what she could. "That was Tahera Danelani, you realise."

"Back from the Republic, are they? A good connection to have." Kemella nodded briskly. "I'll let you get back, but I wanted to ask about your sister. Has she mentioned anything to you about the Ball? We've not long before the sponsor register closes, and if she leaves it another year, people will start to talk."

That just prickled more at Anahid's irritation. "When does Giri ever tell *me* things?"

"Kemella, darling, don't pester her." Anahid's father, Usal, joined them with his usual placid smile. "Didn't I tell you not to pester her? Anahid, you look lovely. How are you feeling?"

But even her father's calm couldn't soothe Anahid, not when she knew that what he was really hoping to hear was that he might become a grandfather soon.

They wanted her to be happy. Anahid knew that. She loved them for it. She just wished she had the slightest idea what happy might look like.

"Not very well, actually," she said. Not even really a lie, with so much churning inside her. "I think perhaps I should take my leave. *Yes*, Mother, I will make appropriate farewells."

They had to be done in correct order for etiquette, of course. Anahid spoke with Syrah—still stiff and precise—and Eref, and with important people she hadn't managed to speak to earlier.

By the time she was done, and could peer into the little side parlour to say her farewells to Tahera, the room was empty, the table clear of cards and coins.

Anahid clenched her hands into fists, pressed her knuckles against the sash of her dress, close to her body. Only once her face was smoothed to pleasant placidity again did she turn and make her way through the party, and away into the night.

CHAPTER 9

S iyon had daydreamed many grandiose plans of impossible futures, in the long hours he and Daruj had spent lying on rooftops, waiting for the whistle to clamber down and wreak bravi-havoc. If he had the money to do as he pleased, if he lived in the Avenues, if he were an azatan...

Different from his carefully strategised plans, the things he thought might *actually* happen. If he scraped together six regular clients, who he was delving for and delivering to once a week, he would have enough money for weekly lessons with Auntie Geryss, and then he could use extra occasional clients to add slowly to his own equipment store. Little plans. Modest plans. Achievable plans.

And yet here he was, catapulted past his little plans and into those impossibilities. In the Avenues, with an immense library at his disposal and access to the workroom (and stores) of arguably the best alchemist currently working in the city. He'd refused all the sucking up and scraping that came with an apprenticeship, and now here he was anyway, tucked under an azatani wing. That was, after all, where the chances were. Ridiculous to suppose he could clamber up without their ladder.

He should make the most of this, Siyon told himself. He should *enjoy it*, while it lasted. Daruj would chortle with second-hand delight just hearing about it.

He stood in the middle of the workroom—spacious and tidy, everything sorted away on its shelves and in its drawers—and wasn't even sure how he did feel. He teetered helplessly between possibility he couldn't fully grasp and bitterness he couldn't squash.

"You just…have this here?" Siyon demanded.

Nura stood in the open doorway between this workroom and the house still room next door. The twitch of one corner of her mouth was the most expression he'd yet seen on her severe face. "The inquisitors would not be so impolite as to delve into a gentleman's service quarters."

Of course they wouldn't. Siyon looked again at jars glimmering with the Aethyr and oozing with the Abyss, at bundles of ghostweed hanging from hooks over the long benches, at stacks of specialist glassware and bronze vessels.

He felt stupid for risking Zagiri and the bravi to rescue his few paltry bits and pieces from his Chapel hidey-hole.

"That may be changing, in the current circumstances," Nura continued, impassive again. "I have recommended to the master that he consider some further discretion, but for now, simply close this door when you are at work, or when you leave." She stepped back and set a hand on the door in question. "Shall I—?"

"What?" Siyon dragged his gaze away from all of this sudden, infuriating bounty. "Oh. No, I need to—do some reading first."

The Aethyr flare had been a mad, merry demonstration of how far anger and temerity alone could carry him. Though that didn't mean he had any idea of what he should be reading either.

Siyon stood in front of Joddani's shelves, more books than he'd seen outside the Summer Club, and ran a finger down the leatherbound spines like touch could tell him more than the gilded letters. *On the Transmutation of Immutable Matter. Sublimation of Intention. Three Discourses upon Extraplanar Connectivity.*

Nihath Joddani sighed from his desk. "You *can* read, can't you?"

Rude. "Yes." Not that the master of the crowded Dockside school had imagined Siyon—or any of the fisherclan brats—would be using the skill for much beyond identifying the right ship to report to for duty, or perhaps, if they were particularly quick, checking a bill of lading.

Siyon looked at the ranks of leather-bound knowledge climbing up to the ceiling, and asked helplessly: "Can I just...read Negedi?"

Joddani barked a laugh. "Let me whip that out." At Siyon's blank look, he clarified, "The journals of Kolah Negedi are banned and locked away, if indeed they weren't simply burnt by the inquisitors entirely in the aftermath of the Sundering. So we make do with the ruminations and interpretations and counterproposals of those who did read Negedi's work. And of course those letters of the man himself that were sent to acquaintances in other parts of the world."

"Other parts of the world?" Siyon blinked. "Why would they care about alchemy? Doesn't it only work here in Bezim?"

"Vanilla grows only in the Archipelago, but we can enjoy its fruits here, and be curious about its cultivation." Joddani shrugged. "In any case, I haven't any of those letters. They are...of dubious legality."

"Oh, *that's* of dubious legality?" Siyon couldn't believe Nihath Joddani sometimes. "You know how arrested I would be if even *one* of these books was found in my possession?"

Joddani frowned over his glasses. "Why are you shouting at me? *I'd* hardly be the one arresting you."

Siyon stared up at the bookshelves. He wondered if Corbinus had been taken in by the Little Bracken, hidden in their crypt. He wondered if he'd been allowed to bring *anything* with him. Corbinus had always valued practical knowledge over that in books, but even he would have had to admit the sheer potential of all this information. Siyon wanted to open them all and run his fingers down the pages, like he could suck in the wisdom like the innards of eggs.

"What are *you* reading?" he demanded.

"A load of nonsense, actually." Joddani lifted the book he'd been taking notes from; the spine read *Sovereign Powers*. "The author is merely using an alchemical allegory to justify the so-called divine right of the monarchies that Lyraea overthrew in what we now call the New Republic. I am despairing that he has anything useful to say about the matter of Powers."

"Powers?" Siyon repeated. "Like on the playing cards? Demon Queen, Arch Dominion, Djinn Sultan, and the Alchemist?"

"The Alchemist," Joddani repeated. "Yes. The Power of the Mundane. I have long wondered about the concept in terms of planar balance; it seems particularly pressing right now. But it is difficult to find material that is not highly fanciful." He set the book down, and waved a dismissive hand. "What are you looking for? I am familiar with Azatan Hisarani's ridiculous idea. How do you propose to achieve it?"

"Not that ridiculous, surely." Siyon found himself strangely defensive. It wasn't *his* idea, ridiculous or otherwise. But maybe it had hooked curiosity into him as well. Or maybe it was just the wonder and possibility in Hisarani's eyes that had arrested his attention. He cleared his throat, and hurried to add, "If the planes border each other, then why not other borders, and something else beyond those?"

"That presupposes the accuracy of Padenz's quadrant configuration," Joddani said, as though Siyon had the faintest idea what that meant—and then he realised he did; Joddani must be referring to that common diagram of the planes as being quarters of a whole circle. There had been a rogue group of street alchemists a dozen years back who had taken the quartered circle as their symbol, before half of them blew themselves up and the other half renounced the whole business. "Which may demonstrate the sympathetic and opposing qualities of the planes, but is surely too simplistic to truly depict the multilayered nature of reality."

Siyon propped himself on the corner of the desk as he considered that. "But the planes do have those qualities. The sympathetic and opposing. That's part of what we use to harness their power into alchemy, right?"

Joddani sighed, entirely long-suffering, but Siyon was too involved in the discussion to be bothered by it. "If you had had a shred of formal education, you'd be beyond such basic questions. Yes, there are correlations between certain aspects of the Mundane and the other planes—air to the Aethyr, cleansing fire to Empyre, brackish water to the Abyss—but it is hardly the clean and easy separation Padenz supposed. After all, is not lightning more redolent of the Aethyr, though it is also fire? And in certain circumstances, tears can be of Empyre or the Abyss. So supposing that those correlations denote a deeper system of mysterious connections smacks of...of..."

"Magic?" Siyon suggested. The term Auntie Geryss had used. An interesting idea, that the body might not be entirely Mundane, that they were, like the universe, composed of parts.

Joddani interrupted his thoughts. "Negedi categorised all of this, you know. Not on any fanciful affinity theories, but in practical terms, noting the effects of all the common ingredients and bodily humours we use today."

Siyon considered the shelves. "Do you have anything on that I can read?"

That felt like a mistake by the time Joddani stacked a seventh book into Siyon's weighed-down arms, complete with an admonition that *the author's notions of planar adjacency are fanciful at best, but his methodology structures are truest to the Negedic principles.* Siyon repeated to himself that he needed the help. Needed to make the most of this opportunity, needed to make the most of Hisarani's commission, needed to wring the most out of this wild chance to not just crawl but fly.

So he took the stack of books back to his guest room—where no one would be judging how slowly he turned the pages, or how many times he turned *back* to check something he couldn't remember—and tried to get his head around it. One of the books turned out to be in Old Lyraec (and he only figured that out because the title contained the word for *sea*, which was also carved into the ancient arch that stood near the harbour master's office down in Dockside), so Siyon didn't have to bother with that one.

He still barely knew where to start with the others. He looked a little bit at this one, and then at that, and then he found a line in the third one that seemed to contradict something in the first one, which led him to looking at something he'd seen on the contents listing of the second one...

There was something thrilling about chasing an idea through paper, in a different way from chasing over rooftops or across the planes.

Some time later, he sat back in his chair, blinking in the light of the lantern he vaguely remembered lighting with a snap of his fingers when it had grown dark. Ideas spun like a whirlpool as Siyon stared at the flame. Fire called from himself by invocation of his own connection to the Empyreal. The fire of life, the spark of righteous purpose.

Maybe, just maybe, he had the edges of an idea.

His stomach growled; Siyon was so used to eating irregularly that it had barely registered before now. Even after days here, Siyon was still unsure how food worked. They *had* plenty, to be sure—often made with ingredients Siyon had only ever seen being unloaded from ships in tight-sealed caskets—but helping himself seemed impolite.

There was a glimmer beneath the closed door of the dining room, and Siyon rapped his knuckles against the door before he opened it.

At the head of the table, Anahid set another card in the spread in front of her and looked up at him. She was wrapped in a heavy lace robe, unscarved and with her hair—dark as her sister's, the glossy near-black of the azatani—in a simple braid down over one shoulder. "Yes?" she asked, as imperturbable now as ever. She'd never blinked offering him hospitality, or facing down the inquisitors with barefaced lies. Why would this bother her?

Siyon hesitated in the doorway. "Sorry," he said. "I don't want to disturb you." Any more than he had already disturbed her entire life.

She gave a rather unladylike snort. "We may as well be disturbed together, at this sort of hour. Come in. Sit down." She gestured toward the sideboard, where a trio of silver dish-covers skulked. "Help yourself."

Despite the invitation, Siyon approached the sideboard like a skittish animal. Anahid smothered a little smile as she swept her cards together and shuffled the deck. She wondered what the spouses of the azatani alchemists would make of her hosting Siyon Velo. Lowly supplier, not really at risk from inqs; lower class, up to no good.

"I heard tonight that there have been charges brought from the Summer Club raid," Anahid said, and Siyon startled at the sideboard, fumbling a fork with a clatter. "I'm told it was only foreigners and the lower class. Likely to be anyone you know?"

"Probably." He recovered the fork, shovelling more cold spiced rice onto his plate. He brought it over to the table. "Not sticking my head out to ask around about who, though. What's with the cards?"

Anahid recognised a change of subject when it was shoved in front of her, but she could hardly blame him for not wanting to talk about it. She gave the cards another desultory shuffle. "I don't suppose you know how to play carrick?"

He shrugged a shoulder. "Just bravi rules. Not as complicated as Flowerhouse."

"They play it in Flowerhouses?" Anahid wasn't sure why she was surprised. Flowerhouses, after all, offered every kind of diversion and entertainment. It just seemed odd; if Tahera Danelani had returned to Bezim so keen for a game, she could have found one easily down there.

That was beside the point. Anahid said, "Teach me."

Nihath would call the request frivolous. Her mother would think it improper. Zagiri would likely mock her for wanting to know, or not knowing already. Siyon just shrugged, wiped a smear of oil from his fingers—on his shirt, of course, because he'd not taken a napkin from the sideboard—and reached for the cards.

He started with the relative weight of the various collection of cards—a hand, he called it. Anahid chafed at this—she *knew* which cards were more important—but it soon turned out there was more nuance to it than she'd realised.

"So if my hand is all Empyreal," she repeated, picking out cards with the little red flame on them. "But my opponents are long in Mundane and Aethyr, then I am strengthened by adjacency, but they are weakened by being opposed to each other."

Siyon nodded. "A balanced hand is considered the sensible play, but sufficient strength can be worth the risk." He shifted the cards as he spoke, long fingers with their myriad burns and scars moving the eight of Abyss to half cover the four of Aethyr, then adding the two of Empyre over both at an oblique angle. He was reaching for the squire of the Mundane when he caught Anahid's perplexed expression. "Sorry," he said immediately, straightening the cards. "I got distracted—I've just been trying to get my head around Negedic alchemical balancing equations. It puts a whole new light on all this." He waved at the spread of cards.

Anahid wrinkled her nose, but she refused to be put off this fascinating game just because it had some sort of alchemical connotations. She swept the cards back together, and shuffled them anew. She had practice at *that*, at least. "Just don't spit on my cards," she commented, and wasn't sure what to make of Siyon's reaction. "Isn't that how they invoke the planes in opera? A demon bargain is always sealed with spit. They use tears for vengeance or justice." He still looked a bit horrified—or perhaps stunned. "Sorry, I once tried to learn about alchemy but it seemed—well, I stopped."

"No, you're... *I* know nothing about opera, even though Daruj is always..." Siyon trailed off, a distant look in his eyes. "Bodily humours and planar invocation," he muttered, and then blinked. "Sorry. Carrick. Let's play through a hand or three, yeah?"

Anahid had just been resigning herself to being abandoned, once again, as someone rushed away to give his attention to alchemy. The surprise was a pleasant flutter in her chest. "I—all right. We need something to wager; fetch the toothpicks from the sideboard, in that little chased silver canister. And I'm dealing three cards each, yes?"

They staggered through a few hands, arguing over the differences between what Siyon had played and what Anahid had observed. His version of the game had only one face-up card in the centre for common use; it also had far more rounds of buying, bidding, and even trading.

"I see why the bravi like this," Anahid laughed, as Siyon gathered up his handful of toothpick winnings. "Copious opportunities for bragging and bickering without having to actually commit to something."

Siyon snickered. "Harsh but fair. You know bravi so well."

"I know my sister," Anahid corrected, gathering and shuffling the cards again. "And she feels so at home in the bravi she is loath to give it up and make her presentation." She winced, and added, "Don't tell her I said that."

Siyon watched her deal out the cards for a new hand. "Make her presentation. This is the Harbour Master's Ball I keep hearing so much about, right?"

Anahid blinked at him in surprise; but of course, why would he know anything about it? The most important event of the year for azatani society, and completely meaningless outside it. Even the bravi wouldn't care. "When a girl enters society," Anahid explained, "she is formally and ritually presented to the harbour master and the prefect at that year's Ball. An older girl, called her sponsor, makes that presentation, and acting as a sponsor is how a girl indicates that she is ready to become an azata and start entertaining offers of marriage."

Siyon considered that. "You said Zagiri would have to give up the bravi to do that."

Anahid nodded as she dealt. "Youthful involvement in a tribe is entirely acceptable, but eventually we're expected to put away our childish pursuits and settle into proper adult lives." Proper adult mistakes, in her case. She sighed. "I suppose I can't blame her for delaying. Doing as we're supposed to is hardly unmitigated joy."

Siyon watched her, chewing thoughtfully at his last olive, but Anahid busied herself with her cards. This urge twisting inside her to speak further, to *confide* in him, couldn't possibly be indulged in. There was no good that could come of it.

After a long moment stretched into a few more, Siyon spat out the olive stone. "I was *supposed to* be a fisherman," he said, and there was a slant to his mouth that seemed familiar to Anahid in its bitterness. "I wouldn't expect an azata to know this, but the fisherclans of Dockside are serious business. More than just family, it's *belonging*. And the Velo clan...well, my first memories are of the scaling hall, and my brother teaching me how to catch the falling fish scales in a pan."

He stopped, staring down at his empty plate, and Anahid wasn't sure what she should say. Settled on, "You have a brother?"

Not the right thing, by the sharper twist to his mouth. "Had," he corrected. "Because I didn't become a fisherman. I fled across the river with nothing. Now I'm here." He gestured, though Anahid wasn't sure if he meant here at her dining table, or here in the midst of inquisitor attention and alchemical adventures. All of that, perhaps. More besides.

"You left it all behind." To Anahid, it seemed both terrifying and exhilarating. A more final leap even than setting sail on a trading venture; Siyon had not gone back. "Everything you'd known. Everything you'd been."

Siyon shrugged, though the tilt of his shoulders didn't seem quite as blithe as it might have. "Fish scales and supposed to. It was suffocating, and it stank. I wanted something different."

Her fingers were folded so tight around her cards that the edges were cutting in. Anahid smoothed them flat on the table instead. "How did you know what you wanted?" Her voice sounded strained to her own ears.

"I didn't," Siyon replied. "I just knew it wasn't that. So I went out looking." He picked up his own cards, fanned them out, considered them, and tossed a toothpick into the finger bowl they were using. Buying in. Stepping up to face the challenge. He looked back at her, and asked, "What do you want?"

He didn't ask as though it were a simple question, and for the first time in Anahid's life the possibilities seemed endless. Not merely *Which acceptable azatan would you like to take as your husband?* Not *Which tedious conversation with the same old people would you like to suffer through?* Not *Which allowable path would you like to take, between trade and politics and social frittering?*

What did she want?

"I want to learn to play this game properly," Anahid said, and met his gaze head-on. It might be a silly, inconsequential goal, but it was hers.

Siyon didn't laugh at her. His smile was warmer than that. Friendly, even. "Well then," he said, "you'd better buy in."

She laughed and tossed a toothpick of her own into the finger bowl.

She'd learn to play this game properly, and then... Well. Then she'd see what next.

"Izmir. Izmirlian!"

From her drawing room, their mother called, "Boys, don't bellow."

"My apologies for disturbing you, Mama," Avarair called back, turning a fierce and expectant look on Izmirlian, who was halfway up the stairs.

This was why Izmirlian preferred not to dine with the family, but when he shirked it too often, Mother started making airy remarks about not recognising him. Avair would never attack him at the table—tranquility of meals was one of their father's many requirements—but there was still plenty of opportunity for ambush in proximity.

"Yes?" Izmirlian said over the banister. "What?"

Avarair sneered with disdain; he'd practised the look, Izmirlian was quite certain, so he'd look just like the committee secretary for whom he was a clerk. (Izmirlian had belligerently avoided learning the man's name.) "You really want to discuss this in the corridor?"

Neither of them looked toward the drawing room, its door half ajar.

"I'm not coming down," Izmirlian declared. "You can come up."

He had a private study, as befitted his station and in the hopes that he'd take the hint and use it in betterment of the family name and fortunes in some regard. Izmirlian had filled it with his curiosities and his mementos of discovery. He'd amassed quite a cluttered library of history, geography, and the memoirs of explorers, now shelved amid specimens and knickknacks and curios Izmirlian had brought back from various places. A wide, woven hat from the Archipelago sat atop a marble bust of the last Lyraec emperor that still showed watermarks from its decades in a wreck off the southern tip of Prodonta. The collection of spiral shells ranged from the Storm Coast to the western shores of the Far Khanate, fascinating in their differences and similarities. Izmirlian had opals and crystals and semi-precious stones no one seemed able to name. A table shoved against one wall was layered over with copies of various maps; a few particularly fine examples Izmirlian had hung framed upon the walls, alongside a charcoal sketch of Bezim docks from the sea, cluttered and bustling with the city looming behind on its fractured promontory.

Avarair sighed as he looked around the room. "If you spent even half as much attention on the family trade as you did these whimsies—" he began, same as always.

So Izmirlian interrupted, same as always: "If trade were even *half* so interesting." Not quite the truth. Izmirlian had always been just as interested in learning about the people he visited—and their wants and needs. He'd just not been particularly desperate to exploit those for profit.

He'd been told often enough that he was a strange disappointment. The barb no longer stung.

"In any case," Izmirlian added, "I wouldn't want to step on Balian's more than capable toes." Their youngest brother, now on his third venture, was proving himself possessed of both Izmirlian's wanderlust and Avarair's negotiating nous.

"Have you heard from him recently?" Avarair asked, frowning at a Storm Coast wood carving of the lithe and dangerous spirit of the storm.

"You get his official reports. I merely get personal letters," Izmirlian pointed out, and lifted an eyebrow. "Are you really that interested in his thoughts on the silent beauty of snow lying thick on the Northern forests?"

"He's my brother too," Avarair snapped, but when Izmirlian's scepticism remained unmoved, he admitted, "There's something going on up there. The political situation seems to finally be coalescing in the closed cities. I thought he might have noticed something in passing. He's very observant."

He certainly was, but Izmirlian was equally certainly not going to betray his brother's confidence by passing on private correspondence. "I'll let you know if there's anything pertinent." A bonus that it caused that satisfyingly frustrated tilt to Avair's eyebrows. "Was Balian all you wanted to talk about? Because I have a very busy evening—"

Avarair snorted, as Izmirlian had intended him to. "That's what I wanted to talk about," he confirmed. "Things are very delicate right now, Izmir. Politically, I mean. That woman is revealed as having a tenuous grasp on control, with whatever had happened to her son—"

"Whatever *has* happened to her son?" Izmirlian asked, partly for the joy of interrupting, partly in genuine curiosity as to the view from the halls of government.

But it earned him another sharp look. "Don't you know? I heard you were there."

Extremely there, racing after Siyon Velo to the very room. Izmirlian could still taste the strange and sharp tang to the air, like the sea after a storm.

What he said was: "I was just popping by."

"And that's what I mean." Avarair leaned forward, back on track like a shark after blood in the water. "Now is not the time for you to be *popping by* all manner of outrages. There are likely to be rearrangements in the weeks to come—"

"Oh my," Izmirlian interjected. "Will you be made the second undersecretary of something?"

Avarair ignored him; he was practised in it. "And for once in your selfish and heedless life, could you just put the family's interests first? No loitering at the Summer Club, or seducing an opera singer—"

Now Izmirlian was annoyed. "That was *once*, I was barely seventeen, and *she*—"

"—or commissioning a bravi raid of the promenade, or whatever other nonsense you and the rest of your idle, frivolous bunch think makes for fun." Avarair glared at him. "We do not need any adverse attention right now."

"You mean you don't," Izmirlian corrected snippily.

They were saved from further bickering—it never achieved anything, and just made him tired—by a footman's knock at the study door. "Inquisitor Captain Xhanari wishes to see you, Master Izmirlian. Are you at home?"

Avarair's glare only intensified at the mention of *inquisitor*. He stalked out, and Izmirlian sighed. "I'll see him in the receiving parlour."

It was a prim room, stiff with the great dignity of the family Hisarani. Pride of place was given to an enormous painting of the First Colloquy, the crowd acclaiming Telmut Hisarani as the first prefect before they marched up to the Palace to depose the Last Duke. The artist had the Eldren Hall in the background, the towers dramatic enough to forgive the fact that it hadn't been built until a hundred years later.

Izmirlian found Captain Xhanari frowning at the painting, though he quickly smoothed his face as he gave greetings and a bow. He wasn't azatani himself—not with that name, and not with those broad shoulders and straight hair—but his manners were proper enough to appease even Izmirlian's mother.

"What can I help you with, Captain?" Izmirlian waved the man to a chair.

He sat stiffly. "I am seeking Siyon Velo." The name struck a spark in Izmirlian's mind, but he permitted himself only a look of mild curiosity as Xhanari continued, "You signed his surety for release."

"I did." And when he had, Izmirlian had certainly not expected that any inquisitor would have the temerity to come knocking about it. Was this Xhanari particularly tenacious, had Velo done something particularly reprehensible, or was all of this merely a product of *whatever had happened* with Enkin Danelani?

Perhaps some of all three.

When Izmirlian volunteered nothing else, Xhanari prodded further. "And the nature of your relationship with Velo is?"

"Personal," Izmirlian provided promptly, and only then remembered Velo's odd suggestion that the inquisitors might think they were *having a torrid affair*. Avarair would be annoyed, if that word got about; oh no, how terrible.

Xhanari scarcely blinked. "Do you know where he is?"

"Right now?" Izmirlian waved an airy hand. "Not at all."

Only the truth. Three days ago, Izmirlian had left Velo at the Joddanis', but *right now*, he could be anywhere.

Xhanari frowned at him. "I remind you, za, that obstructing the inquisitors in the execution of their duties is an offense."

An offense for which Izmirlian, with his first-tier azatani name behind him, could expect to merely incur a fine, were it even proven. But still, he conjured up an air of hurt innocence. "Captain, I wish I could tell you more. When I signed Velo's surety, he fled the Palace surrounds with great alacrity, declaring an intention of seeking refuge in the lower city. I tried my utmost to dissuade him."

Most of that also true.

"We have been inspecting closely all transit between the upper and lower cities," Xhanari declared. "And we have not encountered him. We have assiduously checked his usual haunts, and called upon known associates. We believe he must be receiving assistance."

He stared pointedly at Izmirlian. Izmirlian stared blandly back. The silence stretched; whatever tenacity or crisis had permitted this visit, it clearly did not stretch to allowing a search of the home of a first-tier azatani.

Not yet, at least.

"If you see him," Xhanari said, the words stiff with something like anger, "you must contact us immediately."

Izmirlian smiled. "Of course I will."

But that was a lie. He knew it, and from the tension in Xhanari's jaw, the inquisitor captain knew it also.

And there was not a damn thing he could do about it.

CHAPTER 10

Staying up past Deep playing carrick with Anahid Joddani had hardly helped Siyon's study of Negedic alchemy. On the other hand, when he finally dragged himself out of the clinging comfort of his bed and stared blearily at the books scattered all over his desk, he found himself thinking of the card game again.

Thinking of Anahid, sitting alone in the dark, looking startled at being asked what she wanted. Siyon had never even imagined that the azatani might also wrestle with that question. Until he met the Savani sisters. Until he met Izmirlian.

Find what you want. Figure out how to do it.

Siyon thought about that, and the balance of the suits, like the balance of the planes. About the connection between the body and planes. About the way a card could be removed entirely from play if it were countered in certain convoluted ways.

He could nearly see how it all fit together. How Hisarani would be pried forth one aspect at a time, like snipping strands of a net. Siyon wished he could get a second opinion; Joddani would just be rude, but going to find Auntie Geryss would be a risk. Even just talking an idea through to Daruj, who never understood half the concepts, always helped. Maybe he could—

A knock at the door, and Nura called, "Master Velo? Azatan Hisarani is here to see you."

Siyon froze, his mind skittering sideways like a crab—what was Hisarani doing here? Was he going to say he'd thought better of this involvement, now when Siyon thought he might know how to do it?

Siyon had better go and speak to him. On the way, he grabbed a coat that Nura had provided from Nihath's old discards. Siyon certainly didn't care about impressing Hisarani. But he wanted to do this—and he wanted to get paid for it as well—so there was no harm in looking a little more respectable. In the more natural light of the corridor, the coat turned out to be purple, but Siyon wasn't going back for a less lurid one now.

Hisarani stared pensively out the parlour window, framed into a perfect portrait of azatani elegance—the styled riot of burnished curls, the cloud-soft shirt, the soft-patterned longvest for afternoon visits. Manicured hands, lazy wrists, the indolent kick of one booted heel.

He was useless frippery in the shape of a man, pretty and elegant and meaningless. Yet Siyon knew Hisarani now, just a little. Had held his hands and stepped into nothingness with him. Had watched his face and seen its tiny variations. Had heard his most closely held wish.

There was more to Izmirlian Hisarani than this perfectly polished shell.

"So what happens now?" Siyon smirked to watch Hisarani startle—the twitch sliding across his face and gone even as he turned in his chair. "Do I order tea and then we make small talk about the weather and who's breeding which sort of silly yappy dog?"

"Rather not," Hisarani stated. "I've just come from three different variations of that." He tilted his head, a little annoyed line appearing between his eyebrows. "Are you going to come in properly? Or are you afraid I'll ruin your reputation?"

Siyon knocked the door shut with his heel, like that decisiveness could erase his moment of dithering—his moment of *caring* that he didn't know what he should be doing. "Sorry, am I being impolite?" He threw himself into a slouch in an armchair, and grinned.

"You're a disgrace," Hisarani said, playing up the clipped Avenue accent with a fleeting smile. "*I* certainly wouldn't behave like this in Anahid Joddani's house."

Siyon shrugged. "She's not that bad." Which he'd never imagined saying about an azata, but then again, he'd never imagined playing cards for toothpicks with one for the entire midnight bell.

Hisarani waved a hand. "Oh, I think she's wonderful. She slapped my brother once, you know, years ago, and in public too. No idea how he deserved it, but I'm sure he did. Speaking of just desserts—" And Hisarani changed tack with no more than the lift of an eyebrow to herald the shifting wind. "I was visited by a Captain Xhanari from the inquisitors last night. Guess who he was looking for?"

It wasn't really a surprise; the sudden, heavy weight in Siyon's stomach was more dread than shock. He'd crawled into a beautiful mollusk shell, wrapped in layers of knowledge and comfort and privilege for the last few days. He hadn't forgotten the inquisitors arriving at the Chapel, or the worry in Corbinus's eyes, or the crawl of his own skin as he'd scurried through the streets.

But it had been a problem for *out there*, not *in here*.

"He said they've been touring your usual haunts," Izmirlian continued. "Importuning your known associates. You chose well in your refuge. I'm quite surprised he had the temerity to come knocking on our door. Any other azatan might have taken umbrage."

"He doesn't care," Siyon said absently. "Or he thinks the prefect will allow them greater rein in the current circumstances."

"He's likely right. The Danelanis are pressed right now, my brother is quite avid over it."

Siyon barely heard the words, too caught up in Izmirlian's earlier, casually dropped news. *Touring Siyon's usual haunts*, the inquisitors had been. *Importuning your known associates.*

At the Chapel, looking for him. Had they been back? Had they gone knocking at Corbinus's door? Who else had drawn their attention, just for having done business with Siyon?

Damn Jaleh Kurit for feeding his name to the inqs.

But the fault was also his, wasn't it? *She* hadn't committed the very public, very obvious act of sorcery. She hadn't let the prefect's son go off with an item of significant alchemical power.

Siyon had made his own damn mistakes. Now everyone was paying for them. And what could Siyon do but cower here among the privileges none of his peers got to enjoy? Even handing himself in wouldn't bring back the Danelani boy.

"—not listening to me at all, are you?"

Siyon blinked. Hisarani was watching him with head tilted, elbow propped against the arm of his chair and chin in his hand. He didn't seem annoyed, just amused. "Sorry, I didn't get a lot of sleep last night." Siyon tried to pull himself together. "I've been researching your commission."

"Really?" Hisarani sat up straight. "I wasn't sure if you'd still be interested. What with Captain Xhanari's attention, and I've been hearing all sorts of complaints this morning. Someone's beauty provisioner gone missing, or that little shop that does such clever tea charms shuttered up, or some brewer of tonics nowhere to be found for days now. Lying low as well, I assume."

Or arrested. Or fled the city like Corbinus had tried. It was certainly a time to avoid an association with alchemy, if you possibly could.

Siyon couldn't. They wanted him already. Was Siyon still interested?

He smiled, tight and bitter. "Fuck the inquisitors. I'm up for this if you still are."

Hisarani's answering smile was beautiful, like sunrise over the sea. "Of course. And perhaps whatever we do could also help you find Enkin Danelani. There's a reward, you know. It's significant, with a strong overtone of name-your-prize."

A wild and wondrous idea, but Siyon preferred practicalities. "I'll take my payment upfront, rather than in what-ifs, thanks all the same." He lifted his eyebrows, expectant.

Hisarani lifted those perfect eyebrows right back. "I did pay your surety with the inquisitors. At ongoing personal cost."

"And my gratitude is boundless," Siyon countered. "But I cannot provision an alchemical work with gratitude."

"Oh, is there an alchemical work happening?" Hisarani sounded arch, but Siyon thought there was a faint edge of amusement to his tone. "I've seen no evidence that you're doing anything at all."

Siyon cocked his head, his thoughts already racing. "A commitment. A binding. Is that what we want?" The book that Joddani had recommended for its Negedic structure...hadn't that said something about beginning a working with a strong representation of the thing that needed to change?

He could see how that fit into the ideas he'd been chasing earlier.

"Commitment of intention," Hisarani said. "That's what the others did. A drop of blood, or a written statement—one asked me to bury money beneath an alder tree."

Siyon snorted. "You can just give the money straight to me and spare the tree." He sidled closer, held out his hand, and smiled something like sweetly.

Hisarani rolled his eyes, but he whisked a slender purse from a pocket of his longvest. "Is that the commitment?"

"Dunno." Siyon weighed the purse on his palm. Not as heavy as others he'd handled recently, and what was his life coming to, that he had enough experience to judge the difference? "Is this really *you*?"

Hisarani looked offended. "I think *not*."

"Then something else." Siyon tucked the purse away in his own pocket. "A drop of blood, you said?"

"It's what one of the others tried." Hisarani frowned at Siyon. "One of the others who *failed*. You appreciate that you are getting this opportunity because you are unorthodox, yes?"

"I'm getting this opportunity," Siyon parroted, "because I got closer than all the rest without even really trying." He stood from his chair and eyed Hisarani consideringly, and Hisarani eyed him right back, suspiciously. "We want to remove you from the universe, right? You, bodily, all of you." When he put it like that, he could see why that first attempt hadn't worked. There were too many ways Hisarani was connected to reality. But if he followed his idea, snipped one aspect at a time, starting with...Siyon circled Hisarani slowly. "What are you most proud of, physically? What are you *vain* about?"

"Don't be silly," Hisarani said, quellingly.

But one hand rose to touch the hair at the back of his neck. Those perfect, burnished-brown curls.

Siyon swooped in. Hisarani leapt out of his chair, fingers tangled in his hair as though he could protect it. "Wait," he said. "Now just wait a moment—"

"Relax. I'm not going to scale you like a fish." Siyon was nearly laughing; could hear it bubble in his voice. He reached out to tug at the wisp of hair curling below Izmirlian's ear, framing that stark aza-tani jaw. "Just one little lock. I'll take it from underneath. No one will see." He glanced around, but of course there was nothing useful in this parlour. "I didn't actually come prepared for this. I'll need something to tie your hair with, and—do azatans carry knives?"

It was a joke, but Hisarani whipped something glittery from an inner pocket of his longvest. "For trimming the pen when you must write an emergency love-letter," he declared, tone wry.

Siyon scoffed. "This isn't a knife, it's a confection." It was magnificently made, the handle inlaid with ivory and opal, fish leaping over each other. The blade folded perfectly inside it, small but sharp as a lady's scorn.

The something-to-tie-with was trickier; in the end, they carved a lace from Hisarani's shirt—*I'll get another*, he said, entirely unbothered.

They both sat on the chaise. Hisarani tilted his neck so that Siyon could lift up the mass of his curls and reveal his nape. Those curls smelled of orange water and cinnamon, soft and silken over Siyon's knuckles. Siyon felt very aware of the shift of Hisarani's ribs as he breathed, slow and deep. Everything seemed very alive, all their energy of mere minutes ago transformed into something else. Into potential. Into the chance of what they might achieve together.

Siyon pressed a thumb to the back of Hisarani's neck, warning him to stillness. The knife flashed, the tied-up lock of hair falling away with barely a sigh.

Hisarani's fingers flew up, touching the prickling ends of the shorn spot.

"It'll be covered up," Siyon said, quietly. He wasn't sure what to do with the lock of hair now. He pulled out the purse again, to tuck the hair among the rivna coins. When he looked up, Hisarani was poised and perfect again. As though he couldn't possibly want for anything. Certainly couldn't want to leave it all.

"How did you even think of this?" Siyon asked, the words out before he could think better of it.

Hisarani's eyes—clear and brown and beautiful—met his; he knew immediately what Siyon was asking. "Does it matter?" And Siyon could feel the answer on his lips—*Yes, of course, tell me*—even as Hisarani added, "To the working, I mean."

Siyon swallowed. "No, probably not. Not to the working." Just to him. Just his curiosity about this man.

Hisarani looked away, and opened his mouth—

A door slammed, out in the house. There was shouting, and then a familiar voice lifting above the rest. "Where is he? Siyon! *Siyon!*"

Siyon strode to the door, flung it open. Zagiri was standing in the hallway in her bravi leathers, shouting up the stairs. "What?" he demanded.

"Madame Geryss is holding a public ritual," she panted. "Down in Tower Square. She wanted you there—she wants everyone there. She's going to summon the prefect's son."

"Is this even possible?" Hisarani asked, as they shoved through Tower Square. The crowd kept bumping and jostling him against Siyon's back, but he still had to shout to be heard over the ruckus. "Wait, let me guess: How the fuck should you know?"

Siyon flashed a grin over his shoulder. "You're getting the hang of this."

He had no idea what Auntie Geryss intended to do, but Tower Square was hardly a discreet place to do it. Siyon had hesitated to come—in public, where the inquisitors would surely be looking—but Geryss had asked, so come he did. He wore the laborer's hat again, but the greater disguise was the teeming crowds. Against the masses of

Bezim, streaming into Tower Square, the inquisitors were just standing back, watching and waiting.

The bravi had been paid to spread the word—all of the tribes, all of the available pairs of legs running to every corner of the city. The square was awash with spectators, more piling in at every moment. There were people hanging out the windows of the buildings overlooking the square, and dangling their heels off the rooftops. Even the teahouse tables were packed close with azatani ringed in hired muscle protecting their dignity.

The only clear space was the stage that had been erected in front of the clock tower.

It was a sturdy wooden platform, up on barrels so it could be seen despite the crowd. Nothing on it but a workbench draped with a fancy black cloth embroidered with glinting gold. The sea breeze danced among waiting equipment—a mortar and pestle, the hulking weight of an oil torch, a bronze alembic that glowed like it was on fire. Very recognisable tools of the alchemist's trade, but also—Siyon knew from his recent reading—tools for things that took time and precision to get right.

What did Geryss Hanlun have planned?

In front of the stage, the crowd was too thick to get through. Siyon looked around for a better vantage; beside him, Hisarani gasped. "The prefect herself is over there."

By the time Siyon turned to look, the crowd had shifted between them and the café umbrellas. "She'd be a bit bloody obvious all in white, wouldn't she?"

Hisarani shook his head. "Not robed. Not *formally* present. But Syrah Danelani is here."

The prefect didn't endorse…whatever this was. But perhaps the mother of Enkin Danelani couldn't deny hope. Siyon would have a lot more sympathy if that mother's panic weren't ruining the lives and livelihoods of a lot of people he knew. But the inquisitors' lack of involvement made even more sense now.

He craned his neck, trying to see more. How was Geryss even going to get up onto the platform? There were people packed in on all sides, speculating and predicting and probably making bets. The air above them seethed with avid anticipation, brewing in the afternoon sun to an almost festival atmosphere.

Above all else, Bezim loved a spectacle. See it in the vigorous and vibrant trade of the Flowerhouses, in the regular processions out to the hippodrome, in the theatres scattered across the city both high and low, in the race and challenge and following of the bravi tribes.

The square sizzled around them, a stirred-up cauldron of steaming excitement. Like...

Like the working had already started.

Sweat trickled down the back of Siyon's neck, and a shiver went with it. What if Geryss could harvest from the crowd as though skimming smoke off a burning ingredient? What if the belief of this many people could hold her up—a crowd convinced it was seeing something amazing, with the tools of the alchemist's trade, and a public statement of intent?

All the books Siyon had been reading would decry the notion as outlandish and fanciful.

But hadn't Siyon himself done something inexplicable, just over there? He looked up at the tower, the sun dazzling off the clock face.

Magic, he heard Auntie Geryss say.

What if she *could*?

The hands of the clock knocked over with a whir and a clank. The bell struck, and the sound settled over them like a blanket. Each chime muted the crowd, until the fifth toll dropped into silence.

Geryss Hanlun appeared on the stage, simply there between one moment and the next. Siyon's breath caught with everyone else's, in a gasp of sudden belief.

She looked glamorous and strange, like some tropical parrot, in purple and green and red with wide, flaring sleeves. The golden edge on her vibrant blue turban caught the sun and crowned her in glory.

"One of us has been lost," she declared, and her voice rang off the buildings. "We will bring him home."

She clenched her hands and pulled them in, like she was gathering fishing nets from thin air. When she threw her hands down toward the bench, there was a flash, and then flames rose from the wide golden basin.

Siyon swayed with the crowd around him. Heat, or the press, or something else? He tried to stretch his arms to find steadiness, and couldn't; something else stretched instead, inside of him, with a grinding sense of stone moving against stone.

He shook his head, and the sensation was gone, but a lingering queasiness remained.

Geryss spoke—her voice as deep and sonorous as the bell that had rung—of the stability of the city, the ephemerality of the other planes.

Hisarani nudged in closer against Siyon's side. "Is this—it doesn't... *feel* like any other alchemy."

"Felt a lot, have you?" Siyon asked, a knee-jerk retort from numb lips. Probably Hisarani *had* seen a lot of alchemy, all those practitioners trying to fulfill his commission and send him away. The atmosphere of the square hung over them, heavy as a hangover. "She's... she's *harvesting* from us all, somehow. Skimming off belief and hope and expectation like it's an ingredient. Everything she says...she's telling us what to believe, and building power from the sheer mass of it."

It should have been impossible. He'd never seen Geryss do anything like this, and she'd been more willing than others to let him watch her work, to even teach him a little bit, here and there. But this...

"Is it—magic?" Hisarani asked.

Geryss added ingredients to her fire—tangible things: a dramatic handful of powder, a sprinkle of something sparkling, deep purple liquid from a glinting vial—and smoke rose in billows of lilac and pink and eggshell blue. She caught the edge of the golden basin— which must have been scaldingly hot, but that seemed the least of her miracles—and set the thing to spinning on the spot. The rising smoke spiralled around itself, curling tighter and tighter. The whirlwind of it grew sparks in its coils, bright and dark, dancing and glimmering.

It *looked* like magic; the crowd sighed in wonder.

Geryss gathered that to her as well, pulling toward her chest. Her fingers flashed in movements Siyon knew from his childhood, had seen watching women finger knit twine into new nets for the fishing boats.

A different sort of net that Geryss Hanlun was tangling and knotting out of pure energy. Siyon could nearly see it, as she hefted two handfuls of it. Drew it to herself, as the crowd drew breath in unison.

She cast it out—*across the planes, all of them at once, along the rising coil of smoke and scattering wide.*

Siyon blinked, and swayed, and the crowd swayed with him. Hisarani grabbed at his elbow, but the sensation seemed distant. Far closer, he could feel the long arc of the net, the slow drag of it across the universe.

The snag as it caught on something.

The net caught, his breath caught, the moment caught, and hung poised. Everything about the working narrowed to this one point, the focus of all the energy Geryss had created and gathered together.

It was going to work. Siyon's eyes stung with salt, and the brackish tang of a marsh tickled the back of his throat. His mouth watered, full of saliva thick and clogging. He felt a stretch, an insistence, a call that couldn't—surely—be denied.

And then it snapped.

The world jolted, nearly shaking Siyon off his feet. His head *ached*, pounded by the sun, and he staggered, jostling against shoulders around him. People shouting, Hisarani hauling at him, but Siyon could find no balance.

Another Sundering. It was all Siyon could think of: Nihath was right. They'd been on the verge of another Sundering, and now here it came.

But Hisarani was holding him tight. Holding him steadily. No one else seemed to feel the earth shaking beyond the jostling of a crowd overflowing with too much energy and nowhere to put it.

"We have to get out of here," Hisarani muttered, looking around them. But they were packed in too tightly, even Siyon could see that, for all that his vision juddered, colours smearing together.

They were packed in too tightly, all the emotion Auntie Geryss had pulled together now sloshing around like the last inch of rakia in the bottle. Ready to ignite.

"Liar!" someone shouted, and another voice added, "Witch!"

The square exploded into violence.

Hisarani hauled, and Siyon followed as best he could, when the ground still seemed to sway beneath his feet. His feet and no one else's; for all the square was chaos, no one else staggered and stumbled.

"Are you all right?" Hisarani shouted, dragging them into the lee of a tipped-over café umbrella.

Siyon leaned against the wooden post. It helped, though the world still leered and swooped like he was drunk. "Planar disturbance," he shouted back. It must be. Not a Sundering, at least. They weren't all going to die.

Yet.

But they might be arrested; through a gap in the crowd, Siyon saw a rank of grey cloaks forming up. He didn't wait to see if there were any familiar faces among them, just grabbed Hisarani and urged him onward.

"This way," Hisarani insisted, and Siyon was in no fit state to argue; Hisarani pulled them toward the buildings, where a trio of broad men were just turning in through the café entrance. Their tunics didn't match, but they moved like they'd trained together.

Oh, of course. A number of important azatani had been here. Their hired guards were getting them out.

Inside the café, two waiters shouted at each other over a line of hissing samovars; the tables had been shoved aside, chairs tipped over. The kitchen beyond was empty, a saucepan still seething on a stove, and then they were out into a narrow, noisome alley. It was busy with fleeing people, but still far less populated than the square. Izmirlian crowded against Siyon's shoulder and snapped, "Run."

They ran. Siyon could manage it now, the world only shivering around him, like a dog left out in the rain. It felt miserable and wrong, but he could run, and so he did.

Until Izmirlian flagged and slowed and stumbled to a halt in the shady fountain yard of a quiet neighbourhood. Down the end of one street, Siyon could see the dark green of the Flower district hedge; a breeze brought the pine scent of it to the lungfuls of air he was gulping.

"Are you—?" was all Hisarani could manage.

Siyon nodded. "The planes have steadied."

Hisarani winced, hands on knees. "What *was* that? What happened?"

Not the Sundering. Siyon shook his head. "It didn't happen. It didn't *work*."

"Felt like it should." Hisarani laid a hand over his chest. "It *felt* like—I don't know."

Like Geryss Hanlun's working had sunk a hook into his heart. Like the failure was personal. She'd attempted something wild and unusual, but oh, the price.

Siyon had wanted it to work. Because it was glorious, and daring, and impossible. He should've known better. That wasn't how alchemy worked. She might nearly have killed them all.

A shout rang from somewhere nearby; Siyon whirled about, couldn't see any grey cloaks.

But they'd be out there, the only stern answer, now that Geryss had failed. Siyon tugged his hat down lower over his face and said, "I need to get off the streets."

Hisarani just looked up at him blankly, and fine, Siyon wasn't waiting for him. Wouldn't blame him if this had changed his mind again about the whole business. They could—

"Wait," Hisarani said, and pushed himself back to standing. "I'll come with you." He smiled. "I have to protect my investment."

CHAPTER 11

Hisarani was back on the Joddani doorstep two days later, so early that they were still at the breakfast table. Nihath had already gone back to his study; Siyon was on his third cup of coffee, trying to feel less bleary before he returned to his own books.

Anahid looked up from her pile of letters and invitations with surprise as the footman announced the visitor's identity. "I thought he only saw this hour from the other side."

"Maybe he is," Siyon suggested.

But Hisarani's longvest was patterned for day calls, in pale green and delicate silver, not the bold colours of evening. He batted the usual azatani niceties around with Anahid for a moment or three, while Siyon drained the last of his coffee, before Hisarani said, "I think we should help Madame Hanlun."

"What?" Siyon said.

"How?" Anahid asked.

Hisarani, his serenity verging on the haughty, said, "The lockdown is lifting today. Too many azatani complaints about impediments to business. But she is still at liberty, or was last night when I was having rakia with an old friend who happens to be an officer in the inquisitors."

"Happens to be," Anahid repeated, dry as Empyre.

Hisarani ignored her, looking at Siyon. "You want to help her, don't you?"

Siyon did, desperately. For every question she'd answered that might have been covered by what Nihath Joddani called *a basic education.* For every time she'd laughed rather than shouted when he melted through her equipment. And to ask her a hundred new questions about just what she'd done—or nearly done—in Tower Square.

"But the inqs," he said.

The inqs who'd near closed the city down since Tower Square, out in such force that Zagiri had showed up last night, pouting beneath her feathered tricorn like a sulky rooster, unable to even get out of the Avenues to see if Bracken had anything afoot. (Siyon hoped Voski was keeping Daruj from getting into too much trouble.)

Regardless of azatani complaints, they would still be heavily patrolling the streets. And few azatani would complain if they grabbed Siyon.

"You've got that laborer's hat, right?" Hisarani pointed out, and then when Siyon still hesitated, his face twitched to something like regret. "I'm sorry, your risk is so much greater than mine. I just thought—she's the only one who's even really tried to help the situation. She took a risk to attempt something magnificent. I don't want this to be a city that crushes that sort of thing."

"I'll get the hat," Siyon said.

The streets were nothing like usually crowded, and those people who were out and about were hurrying, keeping their heads down. An oppressive hush had fallen over the city, each pair of patrolling grey uniforms a stitch in the smothering blanket.

The weight of it dragged at Siyon's steps, but he threw it off. Still kept his hat pulled low and his shoulders hunched, doing his best to hide his height. Hisarani, of course, breezed along like the inquisitors weren't there.

"I was going to send you a message today," Siyon said eventually, half to distract himself. "I think I have a plan for the working."

Hisarani glanced over his shoulder—they were walking with

Siyon a little behind him, to better fit the disguise. "Are you sure you want to discuss this in public?" He sounded amused.

Siyon shrugged. "If they're close enough to hear, I'm probably pinched already." It was almost freeing; he already couldn't afford to get caught, so what was there more to fear?

"Tell me your plan for this grand working, then," Hisarani invited, as they turned off the Boulevard.

"Four smaller workings, actually," Siyon corrected. Though he wasn't sure it was any less grand for that. The scope of it made him a bit nervous; was he hauling in a larger catch than his boat could hold? "One for each planar aspect, detaching part of you."

"Until the whole can be free." Hisarani was facing away from him, and speaking quietly, but Siyon thought he sounded wistful, or perhaps intrigued. "How do you achieve that?"

Siyon was still working through the precise details, but he was fairly certain of the basics. "You need to be tied to each working, and then counterbalanced."

"Tied to each," Hisarani repeated. "Like the overall working, with the hair? Or—no, wait. You mean a different part of me for each plane. They do that in opera, you know. Bodily humours in potions. Isn't that technically sorcery?"

He didn't sound troubled, merely curious. But still, Siyon asked, "You have a problem with that?"

Hisarani paused at the top of the stairs down to the fruit market, and smiled at him. "Absolutely not. What do you need first?"

Siyon nudged him to keep moving. "Tears first."

All the books had been clear on the Negedic order of workings—Empyreal first, the plane of virtue and order and justice and true, clear, elevating emotion. Bodily correlations were the thing Siyon had been chasing for most of two days, in the oblique references of books that overtly disdained sorcery. Blood seemed possibly Empyreal—hot, vital, pumped by righteous whatever—but too important for a first step. The sweat of honest labour might work, but he wasn't sure Hisarani was capable of it. And anyway, sweat was commonly tied to the Abyss, salty as it was. Shame they couldn't have started with

Aethyreal, which was clearly going to be breath. But here they were, and the only thing Siyon could think of was tears. A lot of the writers tied Empyre to what they called *exalted emotional states*, like fury or noble indignation.

Siyon had no idea how to prompt *those* in Hisarani either. He wasn't even sure if it mattered. He just needed the end result, right? "Don't suppose you're a maudlin drunk?"

Hisarani gave him a sidelong look. "No. Nor am I prone to weep over heartbreak or the fate of sweet little kittens."

"I suppose I could just thump you in the stomach." As Hisarani turned to frown at him, Siyon added, "Here we are."

The tea shop was tucked into a corner of the fruit market, under the looming bulk of the old wall and beside a small fountain watched over by a curvaceous statue draped in modesty-preserving snakes. The place he'd told Zagiri to come, to ask for Auntie Geryss, if something went wrong with the delve. It seemed half a year ago. It had barely been a week.

Siyon left Hisarani by the fountain basin, keeping an eye out for inquisitors, and wended his way through the empty tables. Near tripped over one of them. He'd been off-balance today. The last few days, actually.

The waiter didn't shift from his hard-eyed lean against the counter. "We aren't hiring."

Siyon tugged at the collar of his plain workman's coat. "I'm looking for her ladyship, actually."

"You and half the city. If inqs drank tea, we'd be dry." The waiter looked him over again, and tipped a nod toward the fountain. "What's with him?"

Hisarani had propped one polished boot on the fountain's rim and was tossing a copper knuckle into the air, as though pondering what he should wish for. "Benefactor," Siyon suggested. "Keen to offer assistance in distress."

The waiter snorted. "Keen to get a story to tell his fancy mates, more like."

Could be. Or maybe not. Siyon was starting to think there might be more to Izmirlian Hisarani. Wild and strange curiosities. A different sort of view. *She took a risk to attempt something magnificent*, he'd said. Not that it mattered. "I just want to make sure she's all right. Help her if I can."

The waiter looked sour. "You and me both, za. I ain't seen her the last few days, nor heard aught certain. And the inqs are digging into every nook and cranny, pulling out anyone they find, dragging 'em off." He turned his head and spat. "You find her, you get her out of the city, yeah? It's not safe here, not anymore."

Those words lodged in Siyon like the waiter had stabbed him. *Not safe.* His home—Auntie Geryss's home as well, for all she'd come from elsewhere. She'd loved it here, the place where alchemy worked, where wonders were possible. Siyon remembered her on the balcony of her workroom, looking out over Bezim. *This city*, she'd said, like a fond relation.

Call me Auntie, she'd said to him, to so many others, like they were all family.

Not safe. Get her out.

Hisarani looked at his face, as Siyon came back, and straightened in a hurry. "What's happened?"

Siyon shook his head. "There's one more place we could try, though I hope she's not stupid enough to have stayed there."

"Promising," Hisarani quipped, but he tossed his knuckle into the fountain and hurried after Siyon.

Even avoiding the streets with inqs loitering on the corner, it wasn't far to Sailmaker's Row, full of fashionable tailors and shops that wouldn't do anything so gauche as advertise their wares in the windows. The shoppers were unhurried and carefree as ever. Three young azatas shrieked with laughter, and Siyon nearly knocked Hisarani over with his flinch.

Was that the first laugh he'd heard in the streets today?

Siyon grabbed Hisarani's sleeve and hauled him down the alleyway that cut across the back of the block. Neat and tidy, this one, more used for access to the living apartments on the upper levels of the buildings than stashing rubbish. Siyon counted discreet grated entrances—one, two...

His heart sank, for all he was unsurprised to find the third grate already open, hanging loose on its hinges with the lock bar shattered. He set a hand on its tangle of vines—a really nice piece of metalwork, he'd admired it every time he came—and peered up the stairs. Nothing but gloom and silence up there.

"Someone's already been here," Hisarani said.

"Gone now." Siyon set a foot on the lowest step. "But you can stay down here, if you like."

He came too, climbing silently behind Siyon, and that was an absurd sort of comfort that Siyon refused to dwell upon. The door at the top of the stairs was cracked as well, splintered around the handle.

In the workshop beyond, glass crunched beneath Siyon's boots, and he had to shove aside an overturned bench to get all the way into the room. He stepped over a dented brass bowl, nudged aside a cracked jar whose briny contents had left a white stain on the floorboards. Hisarani swore quietly behind him; Siyon wanted to tell him that this had once been a bright and welcoming and purposeful room.

In the corner, all that remained of Auntie Geryss's ancestor-shrine was splinters of hand-carved cedar. The scent of it rose—green and woodsy—as he shifted aside a larger piece. The three faceless doll-figures were still there. One of them had lost its little turban. Siyon sifted through the cedar shards until he found the pink altar cloth, and he wrapped the little figures up in it. Maybe this was a sacrilege—he didn't know any more about the beliefs Auntie Geryss had brought to the city than he knew about any other religion—but he didn't want to just let them lie here.

Not safe. Not for her, nor for Corbinus so desperate to escape it. Not even for Siyon, who'd known no other home.

The helplessness curled Siyon's fingers into a fist around the little bundle.

Izmirlian tried to give Velo the dignity of space, stepping across the little room as he knelt by the shattered ancestor-shrine. (It looked like it had been an excellent example of the Storm Coast cultures within the Archipelago, but now was hardly the time for academic curiosity.)

Velo swayed a little, looking down at it, and Izmirlian wasn't sure if it was emotion, or another of those disturbances that Izmirlian himself couldn't feel. Was Siyon even aware he'd been doing it all day, just the occasional odd lean or little stagger?

It was unnerving, seeing someone struggling with something that didn't seem to exist. If Izmirlian let himself think too much about it, it opened up into a pit of uncertainty he could fall into. What else couldn't he feel? When would it abruptly leap out, like that Aethyr flare?

Or something worse.

Better to think of other things. Izmirlian looked around the apartment. The beaded curtain had been half torn down from the balcony doorway, the beads scattered or crushed. It had let dust and leaves blow in, crunching underfoot. There was dirt as well, though that had spilled from a cracked and overturned earthenware pot.

The sad rubber fig that had tumbled over behind the sofa was only just starting to wilt. "This was late yesterday, I think," Izmirlian called without thinking. Velo tucked a pink bundle into his coat pocket and came over. "Maybe even this morning."

Siyon looked stricken at the sight of the fallen fig and immediately went down on his knees, gently shifting the plant so he could right the pot and start shovelling dirt back in with his bare hands. It was useless—the pot was hopelessly cracked—but he went at it furiously. After a moment, Izmirlian swept a clear spot on the floorboards and knelt as well, picking up the bigger earthenware shards to try and wedge them back into place. He braced the side with a chunk of broken wood, and helped steady the plant—it really was a beautiful specimen—as Siyon settled it back into the pot.

"It's not going to—" he started.

But Siyon growled, "Shut up."

It stung, even though Izmirlian suspected Velo wasn't really angry at *him*. It wasn't like Izmirlian could deny that this—this destruction, this pursuit, this persecution—would never have happened if Geryss Hanlun had been azatani.

Izmirlian doubted any azatani practitioner would have even considered such a flagrant public ritual.

Velo sat back on his heels and dragged the back of his hand across his face. Dirt smeared between the constellations of his freckles. "She was the only one who ever actually encouraged me," Siyon said, voice rough as the edges of the broken earthenware. "She taught me—" He stopped, face twisting. "Can you just—?"

"Of course." Izmirlian closed the door as best as he could behind him, and went down the stairs again.

Stood in the laneway, feeling *useless*. All his will to help, and all the resources he had to offer, and still there was nothing he could *do*. Izmirlian stared down the laneway, to the sunny street where strolling shoppers went about their idle browsing with no idea what lay down here. Such a respectable area, and yet even the gossiping shopkeepers might not have been aware...

Izmirlian considered that more closely. *Might* not. But on the other hand, might be they were. And might be there were secrets they'd keep from the inquisitors that they might be more willing to share with money and custom and privilege.

He was so busy counting—doorways and windows and paces, making sure he knew how far along the block he needed to be—that he didn't realise the three young azatas on the corner had called a greeting until he was past, and beyond the chance for politeness. Too late; now there would be gossip. He could still save the situation if he went back, made an excuse, smoothed over the insult with lavished attention.

Izmirlian kept going, and a ferocious tangle of offended whispering broke out behind him as he rounded the corner onto Sailmaker's.

The shop below Geryss Hanlun's apartment was a milliner, the lone display in the window an artful twist of ribbons and feathers to crown an azata's headscarf. Izmirlian drew in a breath—and drew with it all the trappings of his name and his place in society.

Azatan Izmirlian Hisarani swept into the milliner's shop, heralded by a discreet chime over the door and causing a slight widening of the slender shopkeeper's eyes. In a moment, a pen was set down, a ledger closed, the man out from behind the counter. "Azatan, a very good afternoon to you. May I offer a glass of tea while we discuss your needs?"

Izmirlian took a long moment to drag his attention away from another display sample—another twist of ribbons, this time crusted with beads. The man's works were beautiful, but they would need a plainer headscarf than was currently fashionable. He needed a change in that fashion. He needed a patron who could make it happen.

"Your pieces are fascinating," Izmirlian said, with his best impersonation of Avarair's idle hauteur. "I shall certainly be mentioning this establishment to my mother. However, I am currently seeking something rather less tangible. More metaphysical. Is that something you could help me with?"

The milliner's chin tilted a little, and his gaze flicked to the door and back again, as though he wondered if anyone else would be following Izmirlian. Had that very zealous Captain Xhanari already been here, asking his blunt questions?

The milliner said, "At present, that is quite beyond me. I am so very sorry." Except his expression was almost more challenging than apologetic.

Izmirlian smiled. "Your discretion makes me all the more inclined to our further involvement. Perhaps you could send to me a proposal for something in the style of your window display, using any colour you wish except grey, and any other pertinent information that comes to mind." He plucked a calling card from his longvest pocket and presented it to the milliner. With their fingers gripping opposite ends of the little card, Izmirlian held on, and said firmly, "I am quite invested in the preservation of Art, you see." Just in case his comment about colours had been too subtle.

The milliner looked down at the card, where Izmirlian's name was printed plainly, no other embellishment required. "That is to your credit, azatan. I do hope I can be of assistance to you."

Izmirlian swanned back out of the shop—

And straight into Siyon Velo, staring as though he didn't quite recognise Izmirlian. Izmirlian felt a pang of fear—Siyon shouldn't be out on the street alone like this, what if an inquisitor had come by? But all he could say, with the milliner and who knew what other shoppers watching, was a peremptory, "Come."

Velo caught up with him. "Thought you'd cram in a spot of shopping?" he hissed.

This time, Izmirlian saw the young ladies coming, and gave them a tight smile and a nod on the way past. He waited until they were clear before he answered. "Thought I'd see if Madame Hanlun's downstairs neighbour knew anything about her whereabouts. Which I don't think he does, but should he get an opportunity, I believe he will let her know that I am her ally and might be of help."

"You—" Velo looked back over his shoulder, as though the milliner might have run out a flag. "Really?"

He sounded genuinely surprised, and Izmirlian wasn't sure which part had earned the sentiment. "I meant what I said about helping. And you don't have to be important to know things. We all press against our nearby fellows, and are pressed against in turn."

They walked on in silence for half a block, until Velo said, "Thank you for trying."

"You're welcome." Izmirlian smiled a little, even if Velo, half a pace behind his shoulder, couldn't see it. "And not just because you're helping me in turn."

Even if that help apparently involved making Izmirlian weep.

They reached the corner of Sailmaker's and the Kellian Way, the wide road sweeping away down the hill toward where the bulk of the opera house loomed, flying the vibrant magenta banners of the city's fervently held favourite singer.

Ah. Of course.

"Gayane Saliu's performance of the finale lament in *The Nurse of Winter*, at the close of last opera season," Izmirlian said.

Siyon, understandably, replied, "What?"

Izmirlian pulled him aside, under one of the spreading trees, as though giving his man instructions. "That was the last time I cried. It happens quite regularly, in fact. My family are embarrassed about it. They refuse to go with me anymore."

"The opera." Siyon's laugh was a little weak, but it made Izmirlian feel somewhat victorious nevertheless. "I'm not even surprised. I'm cursed with opera lovers. We can hardly go, not now, not in public. Well, I can't." He glanced toward the opera house. "Will the inqs even be letting it happen right now?"

Izmirlian was horrified at the very suggestion. "Opera is *essential*," he scolded, and Siyon looked at him like he was very odd, or maybe like he was missing the point. Izmirlian smiled back at him. "I have an idea."

Four days after Geryss Hanlun caused a riot in Tower Square, things were still nothing like normal on the streets of Bezim. Sure, there were shoppers and message-runners, and in the evenings the Flower district had scarcely dimmed at all. But the circling sharks left ripples in the water obvious for all to see.

Like the inquisitors checking every cart and pedestrian who wanted to cross the Swanneck. Zagiri and Daruj watched the impossible white span of the bridge from further down the cliff edge. The river thundered through the gorge below, distant enough that only the barest occasional breath of spray reached them.

"They're getting laxer," Daruj said, from where he was leaning against the clifftop railing with his Bracken tricorn pulled down to shade his eyes from the afternoon sun. "Not checking wagons at all, and pedestrians are showing some sort of permit to get past."

Zagiri frowned up at the bridge. Wagons and permits...of course. Hadn't Anahid mentioned something she'd heard at a party? "Trade traffic," she said, the words bitter in her mouth. "*Azatani* trade is the lifeblood of *our* city."

Daruj laughed at her, not bothering to hide it. "Feeling dissatisfied with the status quo, azata?"

Frustration warmed her face. "It's just—"

"Rubbish, yes, you said."

"*Unfair*," she countered. "They've had the first trials, did you know that? Some of the practitioners they picked up at the Summer Club.

I was at a stupid party last night and some junior magistrate's clerk thought sorcery charges made for exciting flirtation. They didn't hold any azatani practitioners, of course, but there were some foreigners, and a couple of trade alchemists who didn't have any *reputable* patrons to speak for them, and..." Zagiri trailed off. Her eyes were hot, and her fists were clenched, and she didn't want to say it out loud.

So Daruj did. "And they're going to poison them." He wasn't laughing anymore, but he seemed offensively calm, back to watching the bridge.

"Don't you care?" she demanded.

Daruj shot her a look so quick and fierce she felt sliced open. "This might be news to you, Savani, but it's always us who get it, first and hardest. The poor, the unsheltered, the foreign." He gave the Swanneck one last sour look. "Come on, we're done here. Haruspex are too smart to risk that lot."

As long as Haruspex stayed in their safe house in the industrial quarter, and the Awl Quarter stayed in the lower city, the rooftop balance of the bravi tribes was awry. But in the grand scheme of the city's problems right now, that seemed a fish too flimsy to fry.

As Zagiri fell in beside Daruj, she thought of Siyon—both poor and in hiding—and thought of his friend—Corbinus, had that been his name? The one who'd fled the city. Prescient, it turned out. But Northerners did like their prophecies.

"We should do something," she stated, as they turned away from the river gorge, winding uphill into the backstreets below the square.

"About Haruspex?" Daruj asked absently.

"About all of it." Zagiri shrugged at his sudden attention. It had always been unfair. She knew that. But recently she couldn't turn around without falling over it.

It was unfair, and she wanted to *do something about it*.

"I hate that they're getting away with it. Can't we foil them somehow? And help people along with it?"

Daruj looked amused. "I like how you think, but *somehow* ain't enough, little gull. *How?*"

How, that wouldn't rebound back on the bravi twice as hard? How, that would actually be *effective*, and not just vent frustration?

But before Zagiri could think too much about it, a trio of attackers leaped out of a shadowed gateway ahead of them, shouting and brandishing—

Wooden sabres. They were children, around ten years of age, and relatively clean and well-fed.

"Old wine!" one shouted joyfully. "And new racket!"

"It's *regret*," his friend told him. "And these two aren't Bower's Scythe, you're getting it all *wrong*."

The third one—a girl—just lunged with her wooden weapon.

Zagiri danced back, but Daruj already had his sabre out—the Diviner Prince's blade, etched with a star map. That blade was famous, and so was the wielder. He cried, "Challenge, challenge!" as though this were serious, and turned his sabre to slide along the girl's, rather than bite into the wood. Came back with a slow cut that the girl parried, her brow furrowed as she slashed anew.

Good balance, Zagiri noticed, and she didn't let herself get drawn into anything stupid.

When Daruj finally knocked the wooden sabre from her hand—tossing it up into the air and leaving it for Zagiri to catch—the girl looked furious enough to just kick him in the shins. But when Daruj said, "You've done well, little blade," she grinned like the sudden flash of a lighthouse.

Zagiri handed the wooden blade back to her, hilt-first. "When you turn thirteen, come see us. We can always use runners."

The girl scowled again. "I can *fight*."

"Bravi serve the tribe," Daruj said, warm but serious. "It's not all bladework. You want to answer to no master, then stay a free blade and seek your own renown."

She drew up. "No, I want to be a part of something bigger."

It stuck in Zagiri's mind as they continued up into the craft district. A part of something bigger. Blades served the tribe, and the tribe served...not the city, not directly. But an idea. Of wild freedom and a great levelling. An idea so precious, the bravi had endured here since before the city was even called Bezim.

"Excuse me," a voice said, and Zagiri blinked, whirled around.

The sun was setting, blue dusk creeping over the shops and stalls as the street lanterns started to spark. It was one of the stallholders who approached her, his wares folded away inside a display case turned carry case, inscribed: *Soufalla's Certainties.*

Soufalla, presumably, was Lyraec as his name, with dark hair cut short and an even neater little beard. A faint accent pinched his words. "I think you are the bravi lady I have heard about. Who runs over roof tiles in an evening dress and helps a certain friend of mine?"

Zagiri was so astonished that all she said was: "It was just a day gown."

Daruj was quicker. "Your friend was Corbinus the supplier?" Soufalla nodded; Daruj returned it. "Yes, we got him down to the docks when everyone was busy in the square. You needn't worry about him."

With a reassuring smile, Daruj stepped away, but Soufalla caught Zagiri's wrist before she could follow. He whispered, "I need safe also."

Zagiri's eyes snagged on his case again. Of course he did. *Certainties* meant prophylactics and protections, particularly for the Flowers about their trade. As with almost everything in the city, there *were* entirely alchemy-free options. But they were better with a little assistance.

The inquisitors knew it too.

The poor, the unsheltered, the foreign. Like Daruj had said, they were the first to get it.

"They're still checking everything twice and twice again," Daruj said, apologetic. "Consider refuge with one of the barons. I'm sure they'd appreciate your skills."

Soufalla shook his head, mouth pinched. "I do not like their terms."

"Let me see what I can arrange," Zagiri said, and both of them looked surprised. "I can't promise anything, but…I want to try, at least. Yes? Will you be here tomorrow?"

Soufalla looked nervous, but allowed that he would be, and then he went hurrying off into the gathering dusk.

Daruj sighed. "You get to explain this to Voski."

Zagiri was ready for it to be an argument. Sheltering one supplier had been a small risk to the tribe—trafficking more would be a greater and ongoing problem. But Soufalla would hardly be the only person who needed to escape. The poor, the unsheltered, the foreign.

And the bravi, serving an idea bigger even than the city. An idea of freedom.

By the time they made it back up to Tower Square, and Zagiri slid into the supplicant's chair at Voski's café table, she thought she had a plan.

They weren't checking wagons on the Swanneck, after all. Azatani trade shipments, but they were hauled by regular wagoners who might be persuaded to look the other way while additional cargo was added on one side of the river, and removed on the other.

Voski listened, her face impassive as ever, and just asked, "Who does the removing?"

Zagiri hesitated. There was only one chance that she could see. "What if we got Haruspex and Awl Quarter involved?" In the industrial quarter, or even down in the docks themselves.

Voski considered that, and tilted her head across the square. "You convince them, and we'll do it."

Zagiri just gaped at her for a moment. Taking this wild idea to her *own* sergeant had seemed outrageous, but at least she knew Voski. Knew Voski knew her own mettle. But talking to the other sergeants...

Voski lifted an eyebrow. "Just how much do you believe in this, Savani?"

Her discomfort against the lives of practitioners. No comparison at all.

Zagiri stood, and set her sabre straight on her hip, and gave her sergeant a nod. "I'll be right back," she said.

She was a part of something bigger. She believed in something bigger. And she was going to make this happen.

CHAPTER 12

Izmirlian Hisarani hired a palanquin to foil inquisitor scrutiny, and it was the most ridiculous way Siyon had ever travelled in his entire life.

"Are you telling me," he snarled, trying to find a position on the ridiculous cushions that didn't leave him lolling about like a lobster in a pot, "that all I needed to do to escape to the lower city was get one of these things to take me?"

Hisarani, of course, looked entirely comfortable reclining amid the red and blue and yellow cushions. "Could it maneuver down the Scarp ascent?" he wondered, and he probably had a point. This was a big one, for two people, and there were six burly men carrying it, propped up on crosspoles and all done up with gilding and drapery. "Probably if you tried, the inquisitors would check the occupants, propriety be damned." He frowned at Siyon. "Are you quite all right? I thought you were a fisherman's son; you don't get seasick, do you?"

Siyon was *not* all right. "I'm a fisher*woman*'s son." He closed his eyes—no, that was worse. "And this is nothing like being on a boat."

"Not really, no," Hisarani admitted. "But it's getting us there without the inquisitors seeing."

"I could have worn my disguise," Siyon grumbled.

"You could not," Hisarani said firmly. "Not to the opera."

So instead, Siyon was wearing Nihath's old purple coat again, Hisarani having deemed it an acceptable compromise if Siyon was going to resist being put in a longvest—and he most certainly was. "I thought you said no one would be able to see us."

"It's the principle of the thing," Hisarani sniffed.

He clearly took opera even more seriously than Daruj—who'd mostly, though not entirely, been enthusiastic about the magnificent legs of the opera dancers, and the magnificent everything of Gayane Saliu, the city's favourite soprano. He'd dragged Siyon in a time or two, to the cheap matinees when they touted the leftover stall seats at a fraction of the usual price. The atmosphere tended toward raucous on those afternoons, and Siyon had never paid too much attention to the actual show.

He didn't think Izmirlian Hisarani would allow that tonight.

Ridiculous to even be going to the opera, with the city still half shut down, the bravi doing who-knew-what (Siyon certainly didn't), and Auntie Geryss still nowhere to be found—but at least not caught.

"No word from that hat guy?" he asked, with scant hope.

"Milliner," Hisarani corrected, almost apologetically. "And no. It was a long shot."

The palanquin finally wobbled to a halt, and Hisarani swept aside the diaphanous curtains. Siyon clambered out after him, and had to let the world steady itself around him.

They were in an alleyway—cleaner than many Siyon had frequented. The massive building that ran along one side was all of golden stone, and when Siyon tilted back he could see the little opera house turrets silhouetted against the purpling evening sky.

Hisarani rapped his knuckles against a door, and it swept open with a wash of orchestral music. "Oh no," Hisarani almost yelped. "Have we missed the beginning?"

"The overture has just commenced," the steward replied. "And the widow box is ready for you, za."

The room they were shown to was small and dim, with only a single lantern barely illuminating the pair of velvet-covered chairs. The music was louder, streaming through the fine and intricately patterned grate in the front wall. Siyon peered out through it, looking over the stall seating to the stage. They were inside the wall that bound the floor seating, beneath the first level of elevated boxes. Even if anyone looked their way, the grate and the low lighting would keep them invisible.

"Oh, the sound is really quite good." Hisarani settled happily into one of the velvet chairs. "I'd heard it was, but I worried. There, does this salve your paranoia?"

The boxes lining the upper levels were all brightly lit, as though the occupants were as much on show as the dancers whirling around the stage in the final tumult of the musical overture. Over there an azata laughed with a constellation's worth of diamonds spangling her headscarf; over here an azatan whose longvest glittered with thread-of-gold poured more djinn-wine for his guests; in a box next to the stage, three princesses from some part of the Khanate sat wrapped in shimmering silks and positively glittering with jewels.

Somewhere up there was the Hisarani family box, where they could not possibly have watched the opera without everyone else watching *them*.

"This is fine," Siyon said, and took the other seat. "What is this even for? Widows?"

Hisarani waved a dismissive hand. "The Republic have rules about women whose husbands die not going out in society. This is a way around it. Though I understand these boxes are also available for surreptitious meetings or timid foreigners. Now hush."

The black curtain behind the dancers swished aside, revealing a brightly lit backdrop of a charming country village, and a woman began to sing.

Izmirlian Hisarani shifted in his chair, a tension coming into every line of him. His eyes fixed on the stage, and his attention narrowed like a lens refracting sunlight to a fire-starting pinprick.

A dozen women in fancifully rustic dresses danced around the painted village green. A dozen men, far too clean to be coming from their day of work, joined them. Siyon tried to pay attention, but the song was in Old Lyraec, and the words stretched to breaking. They were all looking forward to something—a wedding? Perhaps between a strapping young tenor with a red neckerchief and a bright-eyed woman who Siyon assumed was the famous Gayane Saliu. When she stepped forward, the first few notes of her song were drowned out by a roar of adoration from the audience; two of the dancing girls darted forward to gather the thrown bouquets.

It was all bright, and beautiful, and charming, and Siyon didn't really see the point. Daruj should have been here instead; he'd have loved it all. As his eyes grew used to the darkness in here, Siyon found a low table with platters of little nibbly bits of food, and an ice bucket holding a bottle of something, though when he shifted that, the ice clinked and Hisarani hushed him absently, so Siyon left it alone for now.

He *did* enjoy the part of the opera where a woman in skintight black snakeskin leapt out of the well and strutted about, singing lasciviously and brandishing an impractically small trident.

All in all, Izmirlian was far more interesting to watch than the theatrical goings-on. His eyes shone, fixed on the stage; the hand laid on the arm of his chair was rarely still, fingers tightening their grip, flexing, tapping, smoothing over the upholstery. He drew breath as the young tenor sang earnestly; he bit his lip as the demon danced into a frenzy; he swayed with the wistful soaring soprano.

Beneath it all ran the susurrus of the audience—in the boxes, gossip continued unchecked; in the stalls, ladies flitted from seat to seat and men passed flagons of rakia. But here, in the private world of the widow box, nothing existed but the opera, as the second act built itself to a feverish and desperate close.

In the captured intensity of Izmirlian's attention, Siyon could see the edges of what he wanted so desperately. To be lifted up and carried away—like this, but further, and deeper, and more permanently. Carried away, and never brought back to earth.

Siyon should give Izmirlian privacy; there was more on show here than he—a relative stranger—should be witnessing. Izmirlian was laid bare, entirely free of the mask of azatani disinterest. He looked sharp and keen and eager as the fine prow of a ship, cutting through the sea.

And Siyon couldn't look away.

The soprano and the tenor twined together, vibrant with need and with sadness. Siyon wasn't even watching, and still he felt it tug at his heart; he saw the glint in Izmirlian's eyes, and was already reaching for the square of linen he had tucked in his coat pocket when Izmirlian gasped.

Siyon reached across gently, and caught the tear spangling Izmirlian's lashes with the handkerchief. The song spiralled into its conclusion, the chorus singing together in glorious harmonies. Izmirlian caught Siyon's wrist, held his hand carefully steady as he blinked the droplet free. He sighed, and his breath warmed Siyon's wrist, sent the ghost of sensation skittering along Siyon's skin.

"Perfect," Siyon whispered.

Izmirlian looked at *him*, all that emotion still churning within him. It made his eyes shine with more than incipient tears. It made his face fierce and yearning. It made his mouth soft.

Siyon wanted to touch him again. Not for alchemical purposes, but to know what this felt like, even if just second-hand. He hesitated, the moment poised around them, wrapped up in song.

Then the orchestra crashed into the final chord, and the audience erupted into cheers.

Siyon leaned back, and Izmirlian's grip fell away from his wrist. Izmirlian added to the applause, while Siyon folded the linen up again, tear trapped inside, and tucked it back into his pocket. When he looked up, the curtain was down, the audience all in a hubbub, and Izmirlian was smiling sidelong at him. "You didn't understand that at all, did you?"

Siyon shrugged. "Blondie was upset because she couldn't marry the guy with the moustache, right?"

"That's her *brother*, Siyon. He's a fallen angel only just realising his true nature—"

"He what?" Siyon interrupted, unable to help a laugh. "Is that a thing that happens, then?"

"You tell me, you're the sorcerer." Izmirlian laughed as well. "It's all an allegory, anyway."

"I gathered that when the Demon Queen jumped out and threatened to invade with her hordes of hungry demons." Siyon nodded to the ice bucket and its mysterious bottle. "What's in that, then?"

Izmirlian wrapped a hand around the neck of the bottle, but paused. "We don't have to stay. You got what you need, right?" He said it carelessly, as though it didn't matter a jot to him.

"And miss out on free booze?" Siyon replied, just as lightly. "Don't be silly."

Izmirlian ducked his head to open the bottle, but it didn't quite hide his smile. "You'll like the second half," he said, passing Siyon the glasses to hold steady while Izmirlian poured. "There's a dragon."

There was a dragon, for no reason that Siyon could see, but it was very impressive nonetheless, descending on creaking ropes and levering open a fearsome black jaw to roar like a blacksmith's bellows. There were also two stabbings and a death by poisoning that lasted long enough to sing a whole song. Three of the ladies—including the Demon Queen—kept changing into each other's costumes, sometimes actually on-stage, and in the grand finale number, a hefty bass who Siyon had thought dead in the first act put on a jaunty purple hat and declared himself the Alchemist (one word that Siyon could recognise in Old Lyraec, and with the hat and a big wooden staff he looked just like a playing card Power of the Mundane). He threw the Demon Queen back down the well before climbing atop the dragon and being carried off the stage.

It was ridiculous. Siyon couldn't help wondering, as sulphur smoke belched up from the well, how much money and ingenuity was being wasted on this idle entertainment for people who weren't even watching it.

But Izmirlian was watching like his soul depended on it, and reflected in his eyes, it looked almost necessary.

There was dancing going on in the grey parlour, so Anahid avoided it—honestly, not having to dance anymore was one of the chief virtues of being married. Instead, she went around the long way, through the paltry library and the not-at-all-hidden door into the green sitting room.

Unfortunately, the sitting room was occupied. Polinna Andani and half a dozen of her cronies were nursing half-empty glasses of applebright and passing around gossip like the dish of sugared rose-water delight they'd brought in with them.

"Ana, darling," Polinna greeted her expansively, and Anahid instinctively tensed. "Is it true someone in a *palanquin* called upon you earlier this evening?"

Anahid might have been angrier at Izmirlian Hisarani if he hadn't been so very focused on protecting Siyon, and therefore not thinking at all about anyone else's reputation. If he ever did. It had never been her experience that any of the Hisarani boys were all that considerate.

She couldn't even blame this on her neighbour; the Andanis *were* her neighbours.

"Some prank, I think," she said instead, with an airy shrug of one shoulder. "One of Nihath's associates making some point or another." If he wasn't going to come, he could at least be useful for something.

"Can't they only be hired from a Flowerhouse?" Polinna asked the question artfully, as though inspired by innocence and not at all maliciousness.

Anahid widened her eyes as well. "I'll take your word for it. I'm sure I wouldn't know."

That sent a sizzle of gasps and whispers through the group that gave Anahid a stab of satisfaction as she swept toward the door.

She didn't make it before Polinna's voice sliced across the other noise, saying, "I'd have thought you'd be more careful, in the present circumstances."

Not close enough to escape to pretend she hadn't heard, and Anahid couldn't afford—in the present circumstances—to ignore Polinna Andani. She stopped. Turned. Said, "And what circumstances are those?"

Polinna's eyes were wide. "Haven't you heard? They *dealt with* the first of the arrested alchemists this afternoon. No question of her guilt, even though she was a member of the Summer Club. Isn't Nihath a member there also?"

She knew he was, of course she did. Polinna's smile was sweet as the poison they'd fed to whatever poor woman they'd executed today. Anahid's stomach twisted. Foreigners or the lower class, the azatani alchemists' spouses had told her. "Was it anyone we know?" A weak sally, trying to remind them that *everyone* in azatani society knew alchemists.

Polinna shrugged, unconcerned. "Some noble from the Republic. A Marquesa? A Margravine?"

Anahid's mouth went dry. "The Margravine Othissa." She barely heard Polinna's triumphant agreement, her almost purring assertion that she'd been sure that Anahid would know just who she meant.

Anahid did know the woman. Had met her, shortly after she'd married Nihath, soon enough that she was a little jealous of this overtly feminine, wildly generous specimen of Republic womanhood. Othissa had kissed both her cheeks, left her scent on Anahid's headscarf, set Anahid's teeth on edge with her gay laughter ringing from Nihath's study.

Poisoned. She was dead now. She'd never laugh again.

Anahid found herself at the foot of the stairs with no real memory of how she'd left the room. The front door was just there. She could leave. She could flee. She wasn't sure how she could stay here, make all the usual azatani small talk, when a woman had been killed this afternoon for doing nothing that dozens of azatani practitioners didn't do every day.

Not any of ours. But how long would that last?

"Ana *darling!*" someone called, and Anahid whirled around, fists clenched, almost ready to *scream* at Polinna Andani.

But it was Tahera Danelani coming out of the front parlour, one hand extended eagerly. Anahid took it, held it tight as a lifeline. "Tahera!" she gasped.

"Call me Tay, we're friends now," Tahera declared, and squeezed Anahid's fingers with a cheery smile.

An azatan brushed past, on his way up the stairs. "We'll be in the yellow parlour," he told Tahera.

Anahid recognised him; he'd been at the carrick table at the prefect's party. "What is happening in the yellow parlour?"

Tahera dismissed the matter with a flip of her hand. "We're playing a few hands. But let's talk first, I missed you almost entirely at Syrah's little thing."

"Actually." Anahid felt a flutter of quite ridiculous nerves to be saying, "I've learned how to play. A little."

Tahera's eyes lit up. "Would you like to…?" Her smile widened; she had an impish dimple in one pretty cheek. At Anahid's nod, she laughed out loud. "How marvellous! What a wonder you are. Come. Let's."

She tucked a hand into Anahid's elbow, and they almost ran up the stairs. This was just the distraction Anahid needed, the thrill of anticipation muffling her shock and fear. She could deal with all of that later.

In a parlour papered in pale lemon, the familiar azatan was waiting, along with a gentleman who seemed to have styled himself after the most lurid romantic poetry of the street press. His straight dark hair was pulled into a tail at the back of his neck, and he wore no longvest, but a heavy coat with wide turned-up cuffs extravagantly embroidered in silver and midnight blue. He was far too polished to really be a pirate, but he seemed interested in being mistaken for one.

"Your little friend from last time joining us too?" the azatan asked, as he cut a deck of cards into two, and shuffled the halves back together.

"Yes, actually." Tahera nudged Anahid toward a seat. "Anahid, this brat is my cousin, Hasan Melani, and this is the Captain."

For all his churlish manners, Melani tipped her a nod entirely appropriate for a junior family branch greeting a first-tier azata.

Whereas the Captain merely snapped a pocket watch closed, tucked it into a little pocket of his coat, and said, "Let's get on, I've other business at the midnight bell. Buy-in is five rivna, azata."

Anahid fumbled at her waist sash, retrieving her purse, and fished out a handful of coins. They had a beautiful glass bowl in the centre of the table, and Anahid added one of her coins to the others already there.

And then the cards were being dealt, and she needed to concentrate. This wasn't casual carrick with Siyon at her dining table, laughing and arguing and playing for toothpicks. Nor was it precisely the rules she'd learned, as she realised when Tahera said, "You need to discard one, darling," as Anahid reached for a new card.

So Anahid kept her bets very conservative for the first few hands, as she watched closely the shifts of the cards, the coins, and the players. It was a relief to have to concentrate so hard; she had no space left to think of anything else.

Melani, she noticed, chivvied the play along regardless of what sort of cards he was holding, but he used their names more when he had something of value. She felt quite smug about observing that, when she bowed out of a round of betting spiralling higher, and watched him slam a greater triad—the Squires of Aethyr, Mundane, and Empyre—down on Tahera's lesser run in Empyre.

"Oh, damn you!" Tahera laughed, and sagged back in her chair. "And that's all the money I brought with me. I wasn't expecting such lively company! I should go down and do my society duty in any case."

Indeed, she only had a few silver bits remaining in front of her. Anahid's heart twisted—she didn't want to give up playing just yet, and she could hardly stay up here with the men alone. "I can spot you a little," she said, the words out before she'd really thought them through. But yes, why not? They were friends, after all. She smiled at Tahera's hopeful expression. "Though if you'd rather go back downstairs, we could—"

"Please," Tahera interrupted, vehement, and they all laughed.

In the end, when the midnight bell finally rang in the distance and the Captain called an end to the game, Anahid thought she'd probably loaned Tahera eight rivna, or maybe six, after factoring in Tahera's end winnings, which she'd shoved into Anahid's pile without counting. It was hardly any sort of significant amount, really. She was far more pleased with her own result—she'd bought in with five, and come away with seven, won by her own hand.

"Good game," the Captain declared. "I'm headed down to the district, if you want to join me. Melani? Ladies?"

"The district?" Anahid asked.

Melani smirked. "The Flower district."

Anahid felt the flush bloom on her cheeks, and was glad none of Polinna Andani's circle were here.

But the Captain just said, brusque and without any hint of innuendo: "Best play in the city. Or anywhere else, for that matter. You want to play seriously, that's the place for it." He was looking at Anahid as he said it, and Anahid had the impression that someone, at least, had noticed her noticing Melani's little habit.

For just a moment, she let herself wonder. This had been *thrilling*; what might the best play in the city be like?

Then Tahera said, "*Seriously* is the word, my goodness, they're absolutely *no* fun about it at all. I'm parched. Anahid, shall we go and find something to drink?"

Anahid gave the Captain a parting smile. "Good evening, sir."

He nodded. "Until next time."

Yes, Anahid thought, as she accompanied Tahera back downstairs. Yes, there would be a next time.

This had been the most fun she'd had in months.

To Siyon's relief, they walked home from the opera, slipping through the late-night shadows like any other pair of azatans returning home. There was just enough traffic to blend in a little, everyone moving quickly and minding their own business. Siyon kept a sharp eye out for patrolling inquisitors, but Izmirlian's careless saunter was the most effective camouflage.

How was Auntie Geryss managing, still at large on these streets? She was as canny as Siyon, if not more, but did she have help, azatani or otherwise? Siyon couldn't help worrying, though there was nothing he could do.

As they crossed the Boulevard, Izmirlian was still humming the Alchemist's triumphant finale number, all about putting everything in its right place. Siyon thought of the book Joddani had been reading. About the Powers and planar balance.

There were lots of old Lyraec stories about the Powers. Allegories, as Izmirlian had said, rife with morals. Don't be overcome by vice. Mundane justice must always be fallible. Too much fascination with mystery can lead you astray.

Joddani had no doubt considered all that already. He—as he was so fond of pointing out—knew a lot more about this sort of thing than Siyon.

It wasn't late yet—not by city standards. Barely midnight. But the teahouses were closing already, and the rooftop gardens were dark and silent. There were no sounds of merriment drifting down from the university hill, and no tipsy groups dallying between parties on the corners. A mist was rising, wreathing the alchemical street lanterns in softened focus, making the empty streets even more eerie.

"Where are the bravi?" Izmirlian looked down a side street as they passed.

"You're looking in the wrong place." But Siyon hadn't heard any clatter on the roofs either, and he'd been listening. "I hope they're all lying low. Inqs have never liked us much either."

"Don't they dislike the barons as well? I hardly think the Flower district will be quiet." Izmirlian considered Siyon. "I'd forgotten you were bravi. I saw the badge on your satchel, but I must admit I can't tell them apart. I've seen the staged melees at parties, and I even got dragged along once to an all-blades—that's what they're called, yes? When it's all a chaotic jumble? Who do you run with?"

"Little Bracken." *Chaotic jumble* was a bit rude, but not actually imprecise. "I'm fairly rubbish with a blade, to be honest. Not so much my thing. But my mate Daruj was keen, so—" Siyon shrugged. "You've probably heard of him. The Diviner Prince."

"I have." Izmirlian looked surprised at the admission. But there was no escaping word of the dashing exploits of named blades, and Daruj was as famous in his own way as Gayane Saliu was in hers. "I've never been clear—do the bravi pay their members?" A delicate and awkward cant to that word—*pay*. Like he didn't use it that often.

Siyon was less annoyed than usual about that, in the mist-softened streets, after what he'd seen in Izmirlian's face earlier. "If you're good, you can win enough prize money to make a living. But a tribe might also pay for a few bits and pieces of alchemical help. Charms on the blades, quick-heal salves, other cheap parlour tricks. And they give me a bit of space to pursue my own stuff. Or gave, rather."

"They haven't disavowed you!" Izmirlian sounded genuinely outraged.

That made Siyon laugh, at least. "I don't know, do I? I've not seen any of them save Zagiri for more than a week. I've been—" He waved a hand at the quiet avenues now enfolding them. These tall town-houses had lights on in their windows, figures moving inside. Life carried on, up here. Siyon sighed.

"Is this not what you wanted as well?" It could have been an imper-tinent question, but Izmirlian sounded genuinely curious. "When we first met, at the Summer Club, you said—well. I rather got the impression that this chance to become a member was something you might want."

This was everything Siyon had wanted. It was nothing like he'd wanted. He'd thought he could work hard, and one day earn this for himself.

Instead, he'd been catapulted into the middle of things he didn't understand, among people he...didn't entirely hate.

"Turns out getting what you want isn't without complications," was all he said.

They paced on in silence, four of Izmirlian's steps to three of Siy-on's, until Siyon paused at the laneway that cut down behind the Jod-dani townhouse. "Good night, then. I'll be in touch when it's time for the next step."

Izmirlian frowned—at the laneway, rather than him. "You're not still coming and going by the servants' hall, are you?"

Siyon's mouth twisted, like he'd reached the bitter lemon dregs of a long glass of tea. "Don't get confused, za. I'm still the hired help."

He stalked away. At the Joddani gate, he looked back, but Izmir-lian was gone.

Why had he even looked? And when had he started thinking of him as *Izmirlian* rather than Hisarani?

The last of the late staff were in the servants' hall, gossiping over fortune-telling cards, as Siyon went past. He looked through the still room, to the closed door of the workroom, and paused, one hand laid over the pocket of his coat where he had tucked away the handkerchief with Hisarani's tears. (From his eyes lit with emotion, his mouth soft, his lips parted—*focus*, Siyon.) His mind was already turning over the first planned working, the ways in which the Empyreal essence of those tears could be gently counterbalanced out of Mundane alignment.

He could get started right now. He could. Why not?

Siyon lit the workroom lanterns with fingers that trembled a little from the excitement. He was going to do a proper working. A Negedic working.

Starting was daunting. He thought he'd planned it all, but now endless details crept out of the cracks. Should he use the whole handkerchief, or would that be too much? Ending up with another Aethyric flare—or maybe it would be Empyreal, in the circumstances? Anyway, it would be embarrassing. He wished again—always—that he could ask Geryss for her advice.

Siyon rummaged in drawers until he found a delicate little pair of embroidery scissors and sliced the linen into strips. A more manageable amount. Plus, now he had backups in case he made a little mistake.

That reassurance soon became a bitter comfort. The first attempt instantly turned to brackish sludge when he added Abyssal ichor, and only got worse when he spilled a handful of stardust on top. (Too strong a counterpoint? Siyon flipped through his notes, swearing under his breath.) The second attempt he only added seawater, and a pinch of fine red farm dirt (air for Aethyr, dirt for Mundane) and made mud. Too subtle now? He tried again, with stardust, and just made *sparkly* mud.

Siyon shoved the ruined dishes aside and pored over his notes again. The words swam, tangled up, stopped making sense. He tried *sidelong* planar affinities, and *then* the crosswise counter, but the farm dirt and stardust wouldn't stick to dry linen. Sprinkling over a mix of seawater and Abyssal ichor just increased his supply of sparkly mud.

He dragged his hands through his hair. Get back to basics. Try just one planar evocation at a time.

Siyon started with Aethyr, often his strongest plane, but tonight a fifth attempt showed no interest in being evoked by the fanning of his page of notes, or a dusting of Nihath's steadily depleting stash of stardust, or by the night air, when Siyon tramped down the corridor and waved it around in the back courtyard. He had to take his lantern with him, when he was doing that, because the servants had retired and all was pitch-black.

He switched both linen strip and lantern to the one hand, as he tried to close the door silently again, and there was a sudden *flare* from the lantern that made him fumble the lot, drop the linen strip, singe his thumb on the suddenly hot lantern glass.

Oh. *Oh.* Aethyreal *with* Empyreal. Air with fire. The counterbalancing *with* the matter to be balanced.

Finally, he was making progress.

The sixth attempt caught fire in the lantern flame, going up in a flash as the planes tilted—just a little, just too much—around Siyon. He swore, shaking out his burned hand, and set the lantern aside altogether. He found a fine white beeswax candle in Nihath's stores, and tried again slowly, carefully, bracing against further planar skittishness. This time the linen gave off a strange and subtle scent, as he dangled it over the flame—old brass and wood polish and something a little like rakia—before it also caught alight, flying up toward the rafters and crisping the edges of a bundle of dreamweed.

Siyon only had two strips of linen left now. Nine had seemed like far more than he could possibly need, back at the start of this. Siyon felt like that had been days ago. Maybe he should stop. Rest.

No. Fuck it. He'd started this, he was finishing it.

He wanted heat, but not actual flame. Maybe he was trying to be too subtle here. After all, he knew Nihath had a whole heap of…ah-hah, there it was, tucked into little velvet-lined cases in a drawer.

Vials of firesand. Provided by one dashing planar delver, if he did say so himself.

Siyon found a wide and shallow stone dish, and shook out a thin layer of the firesand. It ended up taking the whole vial, whoops. How much of Nihath's stores had he used up tonight?

Ignore that. He could fix it tomorrow. Go delving. Just get this done now.

The firesand shimmered and gleamed like it *should* be hot, but didn't actually sear the fingers, not in this plane. But when Siyon laid the eighth strip of handkerchief carefully across it, the edges of the cloth fluttered and curled as though it *were* hot. Smoke curled around it—though there was no sign of flame—and faint brownish marks appeared on the linen, unfurling and writhing, somewhere between words and a dance.

This. This was it.

When the marks faded, Siyon lifted the linen carefully by the very end of the strip, heart racing. Mundane now, yes? But with an Empyreal flavour as well, the basis of the working. Siyon didn't know if that was very Negedic—wasn't sure he cared. It *felt* right.

He found a ceramic bowl—fired earth, the perfect blend—and dropped the little strip of linen into it. It curled up in the bottom like a contented cat. After a long moment of thought, Siyon trekked back out into the servants' hall, toting his lantern, hunting a bottle of rakia. The good stuff was locked away, but one of the footmen had a half-empty bottle tucked behind a cupboard. Intoxication and a fiery burn—the Abyss, and Empyre.

Siyon poured in just enough to cover the linen, and watched for a moment as shadows shivered beneath the surface. The liquid hissed, as though quenching, and the barest breath of that scent rose to him again—warm wood and something sharp.

He let out a satisfied breath, and set down the bottle. He'd done it. He thought.

"Next time you could just ask me."

Siyon yelped, smacked his wrist against the workbench, knocked over the rakia, and caught the ceramic bowl just in time. The inch of liquid inside sloshed sluggishly from side to side, and he set the bowl down carefully before he whirled around.

Leaning in the open doorway that Siyon was sure he'd closed, Tehroun lifted a moon-pale eyebrow. "Sorry," he breathed, not sounding a bit of it. "I thought you knew I was here."

Siyon's heart was still racing. "What are you doing here?"

"Came to see," Tehroun whispered. "Impossible to sleep with you hammering away. You got there eventually, I suppose."

"Fuck you," Siyon declared, pointing a finger. "You weird pale freak. I *got there*." Never mind that it had taken him eight attempts, that he'd very nearly run out of handkerchief. "It's the first time I've ever—hang on, what do you mean, ask you?" He stared at Tehroun, who'd smothered an Aethyreal flare, who'd felt so strange and familiar, who *was* so strange.

Who'd *heard* Siyon down here, far from the bedrooms, and making very little noise.

Tehroun's mouth curved in a fey little smile. Almost like he was *encouraging* Siyon.

So Siyon asked, "Who are you?" Not quite the right question; Tehroun's smile curved a little deeper, and Siyon corrected: "*What* are you?"

Tehroun looked the closest to pleased Siyon had ever seen. "Exactly what you think," he whispered, each word fluttering through the night. "A being of the Aethyr, now come to the Mundane."

Is that a thing that happens, then? "A fallen djinn." Something from an opera. Something from an allegory.

Tehroun yawned, jaw stretching wide as a cat's. "Just so," he murmured. "Since you're done, I think I'll get some sleep. Good night."

He left Siyon there, in the lantern-cut dark, as though he hadn't just claimed the impossible.

CHAPTER 13

Siyon woke up to late morning sun slanting through twitched-aside curtains, and the crunch of someone biting into celery. He squinted; Zagiri was sitting at the table in his room, with the beaded slippers that matched her blue-and-red dress up on the other chair.

"Are you eating my lunch?" he demanded.

"I think it was breakfast." Zagiri pointed the stick of celery at him. "Are you carrying on with Nura? She never brings *me* breakfast in my room when I stay over."

Siyon scrubbed a hand over his face. It had been dawn, at the earliest, when he finally fell asleep, caught in an endless cycle of wild ideas. His dreams had been full of the planes tilting and slipping around him while he clung to things that changed shape under his hands.

Was Tehroun serious? Could he be? Were fallen beings not just an operatic device? (Was everything else also true? The Alchemist, the dragon, the demonic invading hordes?) Was "falling" what had happened to Enkin Danelani? Was it what *could* happen to Izmirlian Hisarani? And most importantly: Had Siyon's first proper alchemical process really worked, or had that just been a late-night hallucination?

Siyon wrestled his way out of bed, hauled on a shirt, and grabbed the plate away from Zagiri on his way to the door.

"Hey!" She hurried after on whisper-quiet slippers. "Where are we going?"

Siyon glanced sidelong at her, then back to the one-handed sandwich he was making out of the various goods Nura had apparently left him. "Why are you wearing a dress?"

Zagiri pulled a face. "Because I'm supposed to be at a luncheon right now. Nothing interesting'll happen until after the cucumber tea is served anyway, so I decided to come and check on you." She prodded him in the shoulder with one sharp finger, as they turned and turned again down the cramped servants' stairs. "You were out with Izmirlian Hisarani when I came by the other day. Are you carrying on with *him?*"

Siyon thought of Izmirlian's fingers around Siyon's wrist, so close in the quiet dark of the opera box, and ignored that question. "You're checking on *me?* I'm not the one who fell off the clock tower."

"No," Zagiri countered, "you're the one the inquisitors want for catching me. So are you?"

Siyon skirted the busy servants' hall and ducked through the still room to get to the workroom. "Am I what?"

Zagiri followed. "Carrying on with Izmirlian Hisarani. From what I hear, you are extremely his type."

"Of course not." Siyon stopped beside the bench. "What's his type?"

She grinned. "Wildly inappropriate."

Siyon turned away to hide his smirk, and reached for the bowl he'd tucked away carefully into a corner of the workbench. Speaking of Izmirlian Hisarani . . .

As he pulled it into the light, excitement sparked again in Siyon's veins. The rakia had turned thick as jelly, with strange golden highlights crawling through it. They caught the light as Siyon tilted the ceramic dish, curling and coiling around the linen strip. They looked like . . .

Well, they looked like magic. *He'd* done this.

"So," Zagiri said, with far too much careless drawl. "If Hisarani isn't *your* type, what is?"

"I didn't say—" And then her tone—the words—caught up with him and Siyon set the bowl back down, giving her a wary look. "Zagiri, please don't take this the wrong way, but you're a little young for—"

"What?" she yelped. "No. *No.* You're—old, and I don't— No. I meant my sister." The words were tripping over themselves to get out of her, a desperate flood of explanation. "You've seen the gullshit going on in this house, the girl needs some fun of her own, and she likes you, she was *barely* sarcastic when I came asking after you—"

"Zagiri," Siyon tried to interrupt.

But she just kept going. "But of course *she's* not going to unbend, so I just wanted to, you know, encourage you to—"

"Zagiri," Siyon stated, "*please* shut up."

She glared at him mulishly. It was far less effective in the dress than it might have been in bravi leathers. "Ugh, you *are* all bothered by Hisarani, aren't you?"

Siyon thought again of Izmirlian's breath against his wrist. He cleared his throat. "I am *not—*"

"What *are* you pair shouting about?" Anahid asked from the doorway.

Zagiri yelped and clapped a hand over her own mouth; Siyon started laughing.

Anahid sighed. "Zagiri, you were supposed to be at the Prishtanis' half a bell ago."

"Wait." Siyon looked quickly over the rest of the mess he'd left on the bench. He'd need to tidy up, but more importantly, he needed to restock. "Can you come back later? I need to delve."

Anahid frowned. "You aren't taking my sister to another plane. What have you been getting up to?" she demanded of Zagiri.

Who pulled a face. "I just hold the tether. And I can stay, it's not really important that I—"

"No." Anahid spoke quietly, but firmly. "You have made a promise to attend. *Try* to remember your manners, Giri. I am sure I can manage whatever Master Velo requires."

Siyon opened his mouth to protest—and then closed it again. He couldn't ask an azata to hold his delving tether...except he already had, when Zagiri had done it, and it wasn't like Anahid was delicate or distractible. She'd probably keep her head better than Siyon had done the first time he'd tried delving. Which wasn't saying much.

"Fine," Zagiri said, and sulked her way out with her sister in implacable escort.

Siyon took the chance to tidy a little. He replenished the Mundane ingredients—the farm dirt, the pure seawater—direct from his satchel. He didn't want to think about the Aethyreal things—didn't want to think about Nihath's apparently tame djinn—but the firesand was a problem. Siyon didn't want to owe Joddani any more than he had to.

In the bottom of his satchel, Siyon's fingers brushed up against something cold and heavy that made him pause. Oh, of course: Enkin Danelani's signet ring. Siyon turned it over, letting the light catch the trident symbol on the heavy square face. It had seemed such a cunning trade at the time, buying himself the protection of the prefect's son. It'd be just another brick in a wall of inquisitor suspicion, now.

Anahid came back, and Siyon dropped the ring back into the depths of his satchel.

"Delving," she said, as though discussing nothing so unusual as going out shopping. "Not down here, I think. I don't want to disturb the servants at their work. And I think you've made enough of a mess of my parlours already. Your sitting room, I think."

Siyon blinked. "I have a sitting room?"

Of course he had a fucking sitting room. There was even a connecting door in his bedroom that he hadn't noticed because it was so perfectly set into the wall. The sitting room wasn't large, but it had the same quiet—*expensive*—taste as the rest of the house.

"Great," Siyon said brightly. "Let's trash it."

Anahid gave him a glare, and he gave her a grin, and they settled down to work.

Actually a lot easier than the last time he'd tried this. He wasn't hungover, and the floorboards in this parlour—once they'd rolled aside the grey-patterned rug—were straight as honesty and regularly sized, so it was simplicity itself to measure out the square and draw the lines with ash from the little pail Nura provided from the kitchen.

"Siyon," Anahid said, far too carefully, as he finished the last side of the square. She was twisting her fingers up in the ball of kitchen twine Nura had also brought up, and between that and the tone of her voice, Siyon set the ash aside and sat back on his heels to pay attention. "Did— Do you know the Margravine Othissa?"

Who didn't? "The Margravine Lyralina-Othissa de Ivory Something-or-other the Third, you mean?" And Jaleh Kurit's alchemy-master. He didn't want to think about *that* right now.

Anahid swallowed. "They poisoned her yesterday."

Siyon blinked. He must have misheard, but her eyes were so serious, watching him. Her face full of sadness. "What?" he said anyway. "But she's . . . she's *nobility*."

"What do we care for foreign nonsense like that?" Anahid said, her voice hollow. "And she'd been here for long enough that the title was renounced. Just a foreigner. Not really one of us."

Siyon's thoughts skittered like they didn't know where to settle. From Othissa tucked against his side at the Summer Club, simpering about what a thrill it all was, to Xhanari snarling across the table at him about Jaleh selling him out. This was what she'd earned: her master executed and her apprenticeship over. He rubbed a hand over his face; everything smelled of ash.

"I'm sorry," Anahid said.

Siyon shook his head and tried to drag himself back to the here and now. "Doesn't matter." It did matter, a person was *dead*, but there was also nothing he could do about it. Add it to the long list. "Let's get this done. You have the tether?"

Anahid frowned at the twine, unravelling it from her fingers. "*This?* I thought Zagiri said you used a rope. Actually, she used the word *hawser*, which I don't believe she knows the technical definition of."

"Physical strength isn't what's important, for a tether. It's a symbol. And that"—he nodded at the twine—"is made by machine from plants grown in the earth. It's as Mundane as it comes. That's what will matter. It has allegorical strength."

"Allegorical strength," Anahid repeated, like she suspected he was taking the piss—for once, unjustified. Auntie Geryss had taught him this, and it was as solid as all her advice. "Well, you're the one at the business end of it. What now?"

The twine was far easier to tie knots in, though it pinched at Siyon's skin. Anahid held the ball of it in her hand, wrapped twine around her fist once, twice, thrice. She was all business, and Siyon found himself glad she'd insisted on this. He wouldn't have blamed Zagiri if she panicked at the first sign of Empyreal heat haze, after how last time turned out.

"All right?" he asked.

Anahid nodded. "All right."

Siyon set his feet, looked down at the square of ash, and focused. Sun and fire and a keen blade of duty.

Siyon stepped into the ashen square—

—and his foot hit the floorboards, hard and jarring where he'd expected the give of sand. His heel skidded, he went down on one knee, steadied himself with a hand that smeared through his careful line of ash.

What?

"Um." Anahid frowned. "Have you been and come back? Is that how it works?"

No. No, it wasn't at all. This was like—

Siyon pushed that thought away, and repaired the ash line with quick swipes of his already-dirty fingers. "It's fine. I just need to focus."

He dusted his hands on the sides of his trousers. Focus. He took his time—as he hadn't bothered to do for years now, delving the Empyreal as easy as breathing. Think of the sun on your face, turning your closed eyelids red and burning. Think of the need that drives you; a debt to pay was something Empyre could bend itself in approval of. Hold all of that, on the verge of reaching. And then—

His foot hit the floorboards again, a dull and flat feeling inside him like walking into an expected door.

He knew that feeling. It was the nothing that happened every time he tried to delve the Aethyreal plane. He didn't even feel the plane skewing the way it sometimes did, needing to be held steady and strong. He didn't feel it at all.

Siyon rubbed at his face with trembling and ashy fingers. He smelt the ghost of the fire, and vertigo yanked at his senses, a scream echoing in his ears. Like standing in the square, watching Zagiri fall, like hurtling back across the planes with a flaming broadsword slamming after him.

Fuck, had something happened, when that sword came slicing down? Had it somehow severed his connection to the Empyreal plane, like his Aethyreal connection was already severed? Was Siyon now *broken*? Maybe he'd always been broken, and now it was eating up everything.

"*Siyon.*" Hands on his shoulders, giving him a shake. He looked up, into Anahid's worried frown. "Is it not working? Is this because of that planar balance Nihath keeps going on about?"

"I don't—" Siyon hadn't felt that at all, but hadn't both Nihath and Geryss said it was getting worse? Was this what happened when the planes got too far out of alignment? They weren't reachable at *all*?

"Fuck," he muttered. If they couldn't get to the other planes, couldn't get the material, would alchemy even be possible at all?

Would Bezim lose alchemy entirely, like the rest of the world already had?

"I have to talk with him," Siyon gasped, lurching to his feet, fumbling at the twine still knotted around his waist.

Anahid handed him a penknife—bless her—and then also the ash-pail with a little brush inside. "First," she said sternly, "you clean this up."

Joddani's desk had become a fortress, flanked and buttressed with books that he flitted between like a malcontent butterfly. A bedsheet had been pinned across the closed curtains, and three columns drawn in charcoal—Empyre, Aethyr, Abyss. Across the bottom, in vehement capitals, was written: INTENT→ POWER→ CONTROL.

Siyon was surprised to understand some of the other notes. Balancing calculations like his figuring for Izmirlian's task, though on a much more complex scale. And everything seemed to feed back into itself, slipping from column to column in a dizzying sort of spiral.

"What are you *doing*?" he asked from the doorway.

Nihath glanced up, hands marking places on two different books. "There you are. I sent Tehroun to find you."

Why? Siyon very nearly asked, but the other matter distracted him first. "Yeah, about him. Is he—ah—"

Nihath looked over his spectacles, at Siyon's inability to phrase the question. "Shared his little fancy with you, has he?"

"So he's not a fallen djinn?" It seemed bizarre, spoken out loud.

Nihath's fond and amused smile was reassuring, like they were discussing the foibles of a favourite but eccentric friend. "Something out of an old Lyraec fable, isn't it? But it pleases him, and it's harmless. He certainly has an affinity. What is it to me how he wants to name it?"

"Affinity," Siyon repeated. "Is that how he controlled the Aethyreal flare?"

"Of course," Nihath replied absently, peering at one of his books again. "Negedi outright refutes the notion of fallen beings—we know that from the calculations in the Brescian treatise."

"Of course we do," Siyon muttered.

Nihath ignored him, lost in academic ruminations now. "But affinities are mentioned in one of his letters. I considered making a formal study, after I met Tehroun. There was an enforcer for one of the crime barons, years ago now, who claimed an Abyssal affinity. I wondered if perhaps affinities might exert influence—the Abyssal toward crime and the Flowerhouses, for instance, and the Empyreal to the inquisitors. But other matters caught my attention, and I never looked into it further." He pushed his glasses up his nose, and added, "So if you wish to dissertate in the area, the field is quite clear."

Bloody hell. "Thanks, I'll bear that in mind," Siyon drawled, letting the dock mud rise through his accent. But it wasn't why he was here. "Listen, about the planar imbalance business—"

"Ah yes!" Nihath left off the books to grab a card and thrust it in Siyon's direction, flapping it insistently until Siyon took it.

The card fit nicely into the palm of Siyon's hand, on smooth and expensive stock, elegantly printed. *Your presence is solicited as Za. Nihath Joddani attempts to balance the Powers of the Planes.* When Siyon turned it over, there was the address of the Summer Club, and a date three days hence—no, wait, that was tomorrow. He was losing track of time, cooped up here. "You're going to balance the planes?" It was both a relief—the problem was well in hand—and a strange disappointment. If it was so *easy*, how had it been allowed to get this bad?

"I *hope* this will balance the planes," Nihath corrected. "I expect it will. I have checked through all my calculations. But I believe Madam Hanlun may have stumbled upon a useful notion with her use of an audience, so I seek the witness of as many cognizant practitioners as can be mustered. I suppose that includes you."

Which left Siyon annoyed—on his own and Auntie Geryss's behalf—and yet pricked by pride, that he counted as a *cognizant practitioner* now.

"Hang on. Your claiming of Power?" He looked back at the card, and at the careful capitalisations. "You're going to become the Power of the Mundane? The Alchemist, like the playing card? The guy in the purple hat who rode off on a dragon?"

Joddani nodded. "Yes, just like the cards. Each suit with its own supreme card, each plane with a Power. The necessity of the Alchemist as a balancing force has long been recognised in folklore and mythology, and while such things are not, as Negedi teaches us, to be trusted, in this case life may need to follow art." He looked over the strata of open books layering his desk, and sighed. "I wish Negedi had continued his work in this area. Perhaps we could have avoided the Sundering altogether. But we must, at the very least, try to avoid another."

Siyon frowned. "Is that what caused the Sundering? Planar imbalance? I just—didn't you say the imbalance was a more recent thing? And I always thought the Sundering was some massive flare of one plane or another."

"A common view," Joddani said, with the blunt disapproval he might give to those who insisted on picking their nose. "And the inquisitors encourage it, for it suggests any untoward working might have similar effects. But I have never seen any flare, be it ever so vigorous—such as your misadventure last week in the parlour—interact directly and violently with the Mundane. I believe the Sundering was the Mundane manifestation of a planar cataclysm, the jolt that knocked the whole system out of alignment into the spiral of slow decay we have witnessed since. Had there been a Power of the Mundane then, he might well have operated as a lightning rod, absorbing the damage."

And then...no Sundering. Siyon could barely consider the city without the Scarp carving across it. Couldn't conceive of the shape of his own life without that divide. He'd seen old paintings, of Bezim from the sea, and it had looked like some other place entirely.

Joddani sighed. "But the past is useful only inasmuch as it teaches us. What we do next is the important thing. I must get back to work. It is vital that every little detail is perfect. Was there something you came in here for?"

Siyon looked over at the sheet of Nihath's notes, the twisting and interrelated tangles of his massive calculations. In the middle of one column, the word *firesand* leapt out at Siyon.

Vital that every little detail was perfect. Essential that Nihath have everything he need for this. Embarrassing, and more than, if the universe fell to pieces, or the whole city slipped into the sea, because of Siyon.

"Never mind," he said. "I'll sort it out myself." And taking the invitation card with him, he closed the study door quietly behind him.

Siyon needed to get more firesand. And if he couldn't delve for it, he'd have to go out into the city and find it.

⬦

The streets were the sort of empty Siyon associated with summer heatwaves; where anyone lingered, it was in wary twos and threes, conversations hushed and hurried. Siyon—with his laborer's hat pulled low and his satchel slung across his body—cut through the fruit market, and half the stalls were still covered over with canvas.

The teahouse near the fountain was open, but the tables were still stacked. The same waiter stood in the open doorway, arms folded over his chest; his gaze skipped over Siyon, but he looked ill-pleased with the entire world.

The first shop Siyon tried—a chandler with a sideline in alchemical provisioning—was also closed up, the shutters over the window, a padlock on the door. Siyon didn't even pause, just kept walking.

The second shop, up in the narrow and quiet streets below university hill, had a woman at the counter who Siyon had never seen before, though the same bouquets of roses and garlands of marigolds and bundles of dock festooned the little space. When Siyon asked for Tommas, her smile never twitched as she said brightly, "Who?"

"Sorry," Siyon said, already backing out again. "Must have the wrong place."

He loitered on the street corner for a moment, chewing at his lip and his options both, before heading up the hill.

There was an alchemist who lived just off campus and specialised in memory philtres and wakefulness powders and other necessities of academic life. But as Siyon came up the hill, he noticed that the teahouse on the corner—usually stuffed full of argumentative scholars—was as quiet as the rest of the city. In fact, there was only a single lone customer sitting outside, the brown robes of a student pulled tight across very hefty shoulders. He had a book open, but he was scanning the street over the top of the pages, and his casually crossed feet were encased in the thick-soled boots of the inquisitors.

Siyon kept walking, straight past the building of the alchemist he was seeking.

He wondered if the alchemist had already been arrested, or if they were waiting to see who else they could catch. He wished there was some way to find out. Perhaps warn the guy.

Like Xhanari had said: They were coming for him and all of his kind. Seemed that even stretched to the street-corner hedgewizards with one or two tricks to ply. Siyon wondered what the people of Bezim were doing to soothe their headaches and prevent pregnancies and keep the edge on their kitchen knives.

Little problems, compared to some. Othissa had been poisoned; Anahid had told him that. Had there been others, not as important, not as gossip-worthy, that she hadn't heard about? Who was still waiting in lock-up, wondering if every footstep was the poisoner's approach?

Siyon kicked at a rock, sending it clattering down the street, bouncing up—

Into a dark, long-fingered, familiar hand. Siyon looked up, blinking in surprise, as Daruj said, "Brother! Fancy meeting you here."

Outrageously good to see him. Siyon nearly fell into the offered hug, Daruj's arms wide and his grin wider. Daruj ruffled his hair; Siyon jabbed him in the ribs. "What are you doing here?"

"Same as you, I think." Daruj lifted a hand to point up the way Siyon had come from. "Here to see—"

"Ah." Siyon caught his hand, dragged it down again. "Let me save you the trouble. A *lot* of trouble."

Daruj didn't fight, turning with Siyon to go back down the hill. "Inqs on site?"

"In the teahouse opposite." Siyon eyed him sidelong. "That happening a lot?"

Daruj shrugged. "Auntie G. isn't the only person of interest. But they can't stake them *all* out. Sometimes they just terrorise the neighbours, let them pass the scare on." He knocked knuckles against Siyon's shoulder and gave him a stern look. "You should be staying safe."

"I need some trade," Siyon admitted. "Urgently. But if everyone's been shut down..." He didn't know. This morning, with one part of Izmirlian's working magically complete, everything had seemed so rosy. Now, it hardly mattered what he might achieve, because he'd probably not have the chance before the planes fell apart, or the city Sundered again, or—

"Not everyone's shut down." Daruj caught his arm, pulled Siyon onward when his steps started dragging. "Some are blending in, when they can. Some are getting out; there are ways. And some are going to the barons for protection." He tipped Siyon a look, both of them knowing *that* for what it was: asking the sharks to save you from the fisherman. "But some are still business as usual, if you know where to look. Come on."

Siyon sighed, and fell back into step beside Daruj, the rhythm familiar and soothing despite everything. He'd missed this—missed the brotherhood, but missed *Daruj* in particular.

So when Daruj said, "What are you *doing* up there anyway, that you need trade?" Siyon told him everything. About the Summer Club and Enkin Danelani—and that Siyon had sold him the power for it. About Hisarani's commission. About hiding with the Joddanis.

Even keeping brief, it was a tangled mess.

"You saw Gayane Saliu?" was of course the first thing Daruj asked about. "I hear she's *angelic* in this show."

"You're talking to the wrong person about angels," Siyon pointed out. "Last one I met tried to kill me."

"I'd let Gayane Saliu try to kill me any day," Daruj suggested, with lascivious emphasis.

They laughed, and it felt like a tiny island of normality in a rolling sea of strangeness.

Daruj prodded at Siyon's shoulder again. "I worry about you up there in the Avenues, brother. What if they get frightened? What if it gets worse? I hear the inqs are still pushing, that they want a curfew next."

Siyon snorted, waving a hand at the empty streets—they were skirting the Kellian Way, but there was still none of the traffic of a normal day. "What's the point?"

Daruj shrugged. "Maybe it won't happen. There'll be warning, anyway, for the azatani and their precious trade. That's what they care about. You"—and he prodded a finger into Siyon's shoulder—"need to look after yourself. I know you don't like them, but you might be safest down with your own people."

Took Siyon a moment to realise who he was even talking about. "You mean my *family*?" He couldn't keep the scorn from his voice.

"No." And when Daruj opened his mouth, that wheedling look on his face, Siyon repeated, "No. 'Don't like' is an understatement. I'm safer anywhere but there."

Daruj shot him a look, but didn't push it. "Maybe it won't get so bad. Can't go on forever, right?"

"I don't know," Siyon admitted. "There are plans underway, by serious practitioners, but I don't know if they'll get Enkin Danelani back. I don't know if they can."

"Getting him back matter so much?" Daruj asked. "My mother doesn't still demand I come home. Children leave. We adjust."

But Syrah Danelani swung a bigger stick than the matriarch of an Archipelago village. And Syrah Danelani wasn't the only one involved here. "The inqs won't let go easy of the extra chance they've been given here."

They turned down a short, shallow staircase, skirting the square, and the river chasm came into view. The Swanneck Bridge sliced across to the noisy, smog-clinging industrial stews on the other side. Siyon realised where they were going, what Daruj had in mind. The azatani *did* get upset if their trade and industry were disrupted, and the industrial alchemists were essential to their workshops and factories. "But how do we get across?" he asked out loud. "Aren't the inqs—"

"We have ways," Daruj declared, and steered them down toward the Kellian Way.

The major thoroughfare still rattled with ox-drawn carts, carrying goods raw and processed up and down. Stepping to the edge of traffic, Siyon close behind him, Daruj tipped his tricorn forward, afternoon sunlight flashing off the Bracken badge.

The driver of the oncoming cart gave a return nod, and Daruj flipped a coin up to him as they walked past. And then he jumped up onto the back of the wagon, pulling Siyon up behind him.

As they nestled among the strapped-down barrels, Siyon hissed, "You're just trusting the driver?"

"There are arrangements," Daruj murmured, and then gestured Siyon to stay silent.

Siyon hardly needed the urging, as they rumbled down the hill toward the bridge. There were inquisitors flanking the approach, beckoning over every pedestrian, turning back anyone without some piece of paper.

But Siyon, peeking between barrels, noticed they weren't stopping the carts at all. Trade must run freely. This was Bezim.

The cart didn't even slow, and they went from the bump and clatter of cobbles, to the smooth low rumble of the bridge itself.

As always, it took Siyon's breath away. The single span of stone—or something like it, veined like marble in pale green and pink—cut straight across the chasm, flat as the bottom line on a trade sheet, and wide enough for two lanes of wheeled traffic and usually a flood of pedestrians besides.

The Swanneck was a relic of a time when the Art was not only legal, but studied at university. The pinnacle of Kolah Negedi's legacy, before the Sundering. Which hadn't, Siyon wanted to point out, so much as cracked the bridge.

No inqs on the other side; anyone could come in, it seemed, unless they wanted to get out again. Daruj simply called out, "Cheers!" and received a wave from the driver, before they leapt off the back of the still-rolling wagon.

They turned uphill, into the stews, where the road became hard-packed dirt rutted with wagon tracks. The factories were all function and no care for prettiness, undressed brick and cold stone caverns. The stink and clangour clung like wet linen; Siyon squinted at the smokestacks and warehouse fronts and tried to think who might have what he needed.

He heard the high whine of the big saws first, their alchemy-sharp teeth chewing through wood, and dragged Daruj into the lumber yard. Sawdust hung in the air like mist, and Melis sat on a stack of dressed timber. She looked no happier with the world than she had at the Summer Club, and her frown didn't ease at all when she saw Siyon.

"What do *you* want?" she snapped.

Siyon spread his arms and smiled. "After all the good trade we've done, Melis, this is how you greet me?"

"The inqs have been here twice, asking if I know where you are," Melis shot back. "So yes, that's how I greet you."

Siyon winced. "I'm sorry, but I need the trade. Not even for me. Nihath Joddani's going to—" Siyon reached for his satchel, where he'd stashed the invitation card to Joddani's intended ritual.

"I don't care." Melis sliced a hand through his explanation, but glanced around, and then jerked her head toward a door in the side of the factory.

Inside, her workshop was narrow and utilitarian, with offcuts of wood and drifts of sawdust alongside the big stoppered jars of glittering powders and stacks of copper bowls. Melis opened a cabinet with a key that she tucked back into the severe knot of her greying hair. Her material was limited, but plentiful. "You're welcome to anything I've got. Moonglimmer aplenty. The firesand's getting old, but there's a chunk of hammer-rock you're welcome to as well."

"Really?" Siyon eyed the jar of moonglimmer—an unexpected bonus. "What are you asking?"

But Melis turned to Daruj as she said, "I want out, that's my price."

Siyon abruptly felt like the world was moving beneath his feet again. "Out?" he repeated. "Of the city?"

"No, of an unfair marriage." But the quip lacked any humour; Melis's mouth was a flat, thin line. "They *poisoned* Othissa, you know that, right? And Talyar's not shown at the textile mill for three days now. No one knows if he's gone or been got, and the inqs take a dim view of questions. All this shit, and the planes near too slippery for a reliable working—" She grimaced, and looked back to Daruj. "I want *out*. Whisper is you lot are good for it."

You lot. The Little Bracken bravi, she meant. *Some are getting out; there are ways,* Daruj had said.

Daruj pulled the workshop door fully closed. The noise of the factory wrapped around them, like being inside a purring cat.

"You're smuggling alchemists from the city?" Siyon demanded, and just got the flick of a glance as confirmation. Daruj had his serious face on, not the cocky smirk of the Diviner Prince. Siyon asked, "Including Auntie Geryss?"

"She hasn't come to us." Daruj looked as concerned as Siyon felt, but then he turned to Melis. "We can get you out, if you're ready to go tonight."

Melis shook her head. "Tonight is too late. Haven't you heard? The curfew comes in at sundown."

"What?" Daruj barked.

Siyon gaped. "I thought you said there'd be warning."

Melis's frown deepened. "They came around first thing this morning, making the announcement."

And of course the inqs wouldn't be making an effort to tell the bravi—children of the night, thorns in their sides—about a curfew. Of *course* the factories would be told, so they could arrange their transportation and ensure commerce—and the flow of money into azatani pockets—was not interrupted.

The sun had been lowering toward the bluff as they'd crossed the Swanneck. Sundown couldn't be that far away.

Siyon grabbed for the goods in Melis's cabinet and shoved the jars straight into his satchel. Daruj was chivvying Melis, as she snatched up this and that, hooked a satchel of her own over her shoulder. "Ready when you are," she stated, crisp and businesslike, and tipped a nod to Siyon's bulging satchel. "Hope you're going to use it to give the bastards a hard time."

She slipped out, but Daruj paused to set a hand on Siyon's shoulder. "What?" Siyon asked, with a jar in each hand.

That serious face on his friend had Siyon's stomach sinking. It was a face that had responsibilities now, and people depending on his common sense. When had the boy Siyon had run the lower city with become this man?

"Come with us," Daruj said. "We can get you out too. If you come now."

But Siyon couldn't. Nihath needed this firesand for the only chance they had to keep the planes balanced and the city whole. Maybe the world too, maybe the universe, but all Siyon really cared about—all he really knew—was this city. He couldn't just leave it.

"Thanks," he said. "But I'm staying."

Daruj frowned. "You can't get back up to the Avenues before sundown."

"Not if you don't get out of my way," Siyon snapped, and crammed the rest of Melis's stores into his satchel, until it bulged so much he could barely buckle it closed.

When he looked up, Daruj was gone; the doorway and the yard beyond were empty.

CHAPTER 14

"Curfew?" Voski Tolan repeated, like she couldn't believe what Zagiri was telling her.

Zagiri, still catching her breath from her frantic sprint back to the Chapel, had barely believed it herself, when the girl from the other day—the bravi hopeful with the wooden blade and good style—had come to tell her. But the girl had it from her father. "Merchants are being informed."

"But not us." Voski frowned.

The main door banged open, and two more runners came shoving through the press of gathered Little Bracken. One of them was clutching a written notice. "Being posted in the markets," he reported.

Voski crumpled the paper in a fist with a snarl. At the rare display of emotion, the gathered bravi quieted even further. They were all here waiting for sundown, and the business that awaited. No parties or raids, no tracking other tribes or parading to draw ambush. They hadn't been doing any of that for the past week.

Instead, they were smuggling alchemists down to the docks and onto ships waiting to receive them.

Zagiri glanced down at the stone floor, as though she could see through, into the hidden crypts holding nearly two dozen practitioners, suppliers, and their families. What had started with Corbinus had grown; Soufalla the Lyraec prophylactic specialist had been the first drop in what had turned into a steady trickle of desperate refugees.

Each one was a spark of victory, a life that the inqs couldn't smother. But each one was also a prick of failure. If Bezim was so inhospitable that people had to flee, whose fault was that but the azatani's?

Voski braced hands on her hips. "Right. Give me options."

"Chance it," Tein suggested immediately. "They can't watch every street. We send small groups and decoy distractions."

Voski shook her head. "Swanneck's the problem still. Or the Scarp. They'll be camped there like a spider in a web, bet your blade on it."

Zagiri stepped forward; this was her plan and her responsibility. "We could leave it until tomorrow. Move them down in daylight?" It had been considered too great a risk before, but things had changed.

Tein frowned. "The ships sail with the dawn tide. We've spent money and goodwill on making these arrangements—"

"They're already lost." Voski drummed her fingers against her leathers. "I know we said the overland caravans were too slow, but it's better than nothing."

Tein tilted his head, considering that. "Caravans gather at the Western Hill depot. Still got to get them out of the city."

With the inqs checking all departures at the city gate. But the depot, Zagiri remembered, was not far from the hippodrome. And she knew horse-mad azatani boys who stayed overlong at the races...

"Actually," she said, and the argument broke off; Voski and Tein both looked at her. A bit daunting, but Zagiri forced herself not to flinch. "Some lads I know must have a way to sneak back into the city."

"Lads you know," Voski repeated, and looked around.

Zagiri was also scanning the crowd, but azatani bravi were thin at the moment, many kept home by nervous families. Or maybe they'd not found the recent work of the Little Bracken as interesting as usual bravi fare.

"Malkasani?" Voski shouted, and there was no answering call. "Hildani? Josepani?"

Finally, blessedly, a voice called back, "Yeah!"

Beren Josepani came through the gathered crowd, sullen as ever; or maybe that was just his reaction to Zagiri. "You know about the Palokanis' secret bolthole in the landward wall?" she demanded.

He pulled a face. "They'll skin me if I spill."

Zagiri laid a hand on her sabre hilt. "Guess what I'll do if you don't?"

Between that, and the hard clench of Voski's jaw, Beren gave a terse report on a tunnel beneath the wall from the basement of a teahouse. A party was hastily put together—Beren as guide, a half-dozen blades as scouts and escort, and Voski herself to bring the full weight of Little Bracken to any negotiations.

Tein was in favour of sending all their gathered alchemists right now, getting them out to the depot, where the inqs had less sway. Zagiri didn't think they had time before the curfew came down, and what if this secret route didn't work? It was unchecked, and she'd never rely on the Palokani boys, if she could help it.

But as the bravi party raced out into the imminent sunset, Zagiri wondered if she'd just condemned all their sheltered alchemists to being imprisoned forever in the crypts.

"Stop second-guessing," Tein grunted from where he was writing messages.

Zagiri opened her mouth to snap at him, but the Chapel door banged open again. She had a sudden pang of panic—the inquisitors, launching early upon them?—but it was Daruj who came pelting in, grim and with a stranger in tow. She was a hard-faced lady in practical industrial dress, though her grey-streaked hair was starting to fray out of its bun and she was staggering and panting from the speed of their run.

Daruj had breath enough to shout, "Savani!"

Zagiri shoved through the crowd. "What?" She got a proper look at the woman with him, doubled over now and heaving breaths, but carrying a satchel much like Siyon's. "Get her downstairs," she snapped, and a pair of blades hurried forward to show the way.

Daruj grabbed her arm. "Siyon was with me. We were down in the stews."

"Velo?" someone behind Zagiri said. "He can't come here, they've gone over us twice already looking for—"

"Shut it!" Daruj snarled. Zagiri had never seen him this angry, not even when they'd lost that all-blades against the Bowerboys. "He wouldn't come. Seems to think he owes some stupid loyalty to your family." He was glaring at Zagiri like she'd done this personally.

"He'll hide," she suggested. He'd never make it back up the hill in time. It would be stupid to try.

"Where?" Daruj demanded. "If he had another place, you think he'd be with you at all?" That pinched, like Daruj's tightening grip on her arm as he leaned closer. "An azata could be late though, right?"

An azata could. Zagiri was sure of it. More than one of her neighbours would be caught out and about this evening, and no doubt the most that would happen would be a reminder of the new arrangements, and a suggestion that she keep safe.

"I'm not an azata," she said, the words bitter in her mouth. She hadn't made her presentation, didn't wear the headscarf. Didn't have the full weight of adulthood behind her. Couldn't save her friend. "I know someone who could do it, though." And more importantly, someone who *would*.

If she could get there in time.

"Go," Daruj urged.

Zagiri went, leaping down the front steps of the old church, pelting across the square in a flat sprint.

The sky was streaked with fire, and dusk lurked in the long shadows of the buildings. Lights were coming on in apartments and tenements; shutters coming down on shopfronts; teahouse waiters lighting lanterns on the street tables. Children stopped their fountain games to watch her streak past; one whistled in her wake, not any signal Zagiri recognised, just a wild blast of noise.

She ran, and the wind whispered over her skin, the rhythm settled into her bones, the thrill of it pulled a smile to her mouth, despite the dire circumstances. There was a reason she'd joined the bravi, and it hadn't been just to make her father *tsk* into his morning newspaper.

Zagiri ran—in a curve around the lower university wall, leaping down the staggered sections of the Bankers Stair, skidding pell-mell through the winding alleyways that spat her out onto the Kellian Way. The sky was indigo now, deepening with every breath she dragged behind her ribs, and the street lanterns were coming to life. Where was Siyon now? Would Hisarani know? Could she reach him in time? Could they—?

"You there! Stop!"

Zagiri ignored the call. She was fast, she knew it; she could keep this up, and the inquisitor was behind her already, even if he had fresh legs to chase her with.

Then another pair of grey-cloaked figures stepped out of the lee of the Eldren Hall ahead, hurrying to block the road. "Inquisitors!" one shouted. "Stop!"

So she slowed to a jog, and then to a halt, bracing hands on her hips as she pulled in big gulps of cool evening air. "I'm just on my way home," she told them, and pointed—up the hill, to where she could *see* the trees silhouetted, black on purple night.

"Name?" One of the inquisitors demanded. He had a lantern; he lifted it to look at her face, and then amended, "Miss," to that request.

Of course he did. Her face was azatani, and her head was bare, which made her no azata yet. "Zagiri Savani. I just learned about the curfew. I'd be home by now if you hadn't stopped me."

None of the inquisitors—not this pair, not the pair from behind who'd finally caught up—seemed to care. "I'll need to see you there, Miss Savani," the first inquisitor said.

Zagiri swallowed the urge to point out that she wasn't a *child*. Technically, she still was.

"Come on, then," she said, and set out at a brisk walk. He hurried after her.

It really was no distance at all, just up the Kellian Way and along the Boulevard. She'd nearly made it, but now the sun had slipped away entirely. "I don't want anyone to worry about me," Zagiri tried, but the inquisitor wouldn't go faster than a frustrating walk, as they took the first avenue down the edge of the parkland.

There was a little grotto there, commemorating some piece of history that a committee of generations past had thought important. It was the favoured promenade haunt of a certain crowd of young dandies, and Zagiri's eyes skittered desperately over their matching haircuts, their jewel-bright longvests, searching for—

Oh, thank all the angels.

"Izmirlian!" she called, and one of them turned; the inquisitor grabbed her arm. "That's my *cousin*," she declared, loud enough to carry. "Surely you could just leave me with him."

"Got yourself in trouble again, Giri?" Hisarani asked as he strolled over. "Yes, I'll take custody, but you'll owe me a double favour this time."

The inquisitor wasn't only willing, but downright eager to be of service to the young azatan, and Zagiri wanted to kick him long before he'd finished taking his overly solicitous leave.

Hisarani turned his smile on her. "What was all that ab—?"

"There's a curfew, and Siyon's still out there," Zagiri interrupted. The words tasted bitter; they were safe, Siyon was not.

The amusement fell from Hisarani's face, and he turned immediately down the avenue. Someone called from the grotto; Hisarani merely waved a hand, not even looking back. "Do you know where?"

"No idea," Zagiri admitted.

"Never mind, I have a notion or two." He shot her a quick glance. "I'll find him. I promise."

He strode back out into the Boulevard, and Zagiri stopped. She had to. She'd done all she could.

For now.

Maybe Siyon should have gone with Daruj. Got to safety. Left the city behind. He'd done it before—left Dockside, left with nothing, built a new life.

But he had already built *this* one. Had fought to have it. Wasn't going to just run away from it, or his responsibility to help Joddani fix it all.

Couldn't help by agonising about it. He needed to get moving.

The traffic on the Swanneck was even thicker now, seething crowds jostling around shouting wagoners and inexorable oxen, everyone desperate to get where they needed to go before the sun slipped all the way behind the distant hills. Just looking at the press was exhausting.

Siyon hesitated in the shadowed lee of a factory wall. He *didn't* have time to make it to the safety of the Avenues. Was Daruj right? If he turned the other way, the road led down to the cramped neighbourhoods near the docks, where Siyon could disappear into laneways and compounds and gutter shops where neither inquisitors nor curfews were welcome.

A different sort of law was kept down in Dockside. Siyon knew well. He'd fallen foul of it at fourteen.

Rather take his chances up here, frankly.

Siyon dashed out into the traffic, clambering aboard a wagon at random, wedging himself amid bales of cloth. They trundled across the bridge, slow but with the unstoppable force of commerce. Siyon thought he'd just get across the span, and then sprint like a bravi.

But the inqs would be looking for people on foot, wouldn't they? If this were a plan to trap the undesirable, then they would be out on the streets in numbers, grabbing every fleet-footed bravi or suspect baron-runner that they could lay hands on.

The muted rumble of the cart wheels changed to the familiar rattle of paving stones. The sun crouched orange and heavy on the horizon. Siyon still didn't have a plan.

The cart tilted up the hill, and Siyon wedged himself more deeply. There were worse places to stay than right here, tucked between bales, but he'd need to get off sooner rather than later. The cart couldn't leave the city before sunset, and wherever it *was* going, Siyon needed to be gone before it got there. No sense giving the wagoner the chance to turn him in to the inqs. Far better to slip away, preferably on a quieter side street, when the opportunity presented itself. If the opportunity presented itself.

Difficult to tell just where they were, in the chinks of visibility between the bales. The cart turned a corner, onto the well-laid pavers of the road that curved around the back of the Flower district (all the better to make deliveries). Then came the more irregular rhythm of the older roads past the fruit market. From here, the road would veer south toward the districts near the Scarp and then—

Wait. They turned a corner, Siyon bracing against the bales and the cart starting to rock and bump. Over cobblestones. They'd turned off the main road.

Siyon eased a little closer to the tail of the cart and peered out between the bales of cloth. It was deep dusk now, and the street lanterns cast a golden glow over the ostentatiously modest buildings around them. Doors were shut and curtains drawn closed, but Siyon thought they were somewhere near Sailmaker's Row. Near to the Summer Club, but surely the inquisitors would be watching that. Near to Auntie Geryss's apartment.

What had she been doing, with all the inqs after her, in all the days since Tower Square? They hadn't caught *her*. Then again, if Siyon were as canny as Auntie Geryss, he might not be in this position in the first place.

Still, he knew where she *wasn't*. He knew the place the inquisitors had already searched. They might be on watch, but if he could get past them…

Before he could think himself out of it, Siyon slipped out from between the bales, leaping down to the cobblestones. It was dark here, easy to slide into the narrow lane and press against the cold brick wall.

No shouts, no running feet. Just the diminishing rumble of the cart as it continued down the street, fading away toward silence. Eerie and unnatural, to hear nothing in the city at night. There should be footsteps and chatter, laughter and shouting, bravi whistles and drunken singing and an endless burble of humanity, like the sea lapping never-ending against the shore.

Siyon's breath felt too loud, like the scrape of his foot against the cobblestones, the brush of his coat against the brickwork. He slunk down the alleyway as silently as he could, looking up at the buildings.

If *that* was the back of the cobbler on Glass, then this tailor up here was the one who always had something astonishingly fuchsia in the window, so if Siyon went *this* way—

He turned a corner and spied the dark lantern over the gate to Auntie Geryss's apartment. Then the shadows shifted, and he spotted the inquisitor standing on the opposite wall, and Siyon froze.

Right. If they were *there*, then he could find another way up. For the bravi, the ground was just one option.

Siyon edged carefully backward, keeping his eyes on the lurking inq, who seemed more interested in scraping something off his boot than keeping an eye out. He slunk back around the corner and looked up, assessing the climbing potential of the wall.

And then skinned his chin startling when the other inq grabbed him by the elbow. By the time Siyon thought to yell, the arm was twisted up behind his back, and he was shoved against the wall. Only enough air left in his lungs for a huff rather than a holler.

His assailant had better luck. "Got one! Get up here with the lantern."

Boots coming up the alleyway. Siyon would have scant chance getting away from two of them, but wriggling and bucking did nothing but leave more of his skin on the brickwork. "I'm going *home*," he objected. "I only just heard about the curfew. If you'd just let me—"

The inquisitor hauled him back by the collar, and Siyon cursed and squinted in the sudden glare of a lantern. "Anyone we know?"

Siyon held his breath, hoping with everything he had that it wasn't Vartan Xhanari holding the lantern. But it was a lighter voice that answered, clipped with the Avenues, saying, "Don't think so. Bring him along, the wagon'll be by soon."

The inquisitor kicked him into stumbling motion. His partner held the lantern high, lest there be anything else on the largely clean cobblestones to trouble the state of his polished boots.

Siyon's face stung like the embarrassment of falling into the clutches of these two. Melis hadn't mentioned the punishment for breaking curfew, but it hardly mattered; once someone recognised Siyon, far worse things awaited.

He needed to get away somehow, and before this wagon showed up. He needed to calm down enough to manufacture a distraction—a snap of Empyreal spark right in the face of the guy holding him would do nicely, if the planes would stay still enough to cooperate—but where could he go? Duck up the stairs to Auntie Geryss's apartment and get to the roof from the balcony? And then what? *Fly* across the Boulevard to the Avenues?

He had to try anyway. But as Siyon gathered himself to reach, tried to hold himself and the planes still, he heard a new sound. Crisp, well-shod heels on the cobblestones, approaching the alley. A figure stepped into the entrance, just a person-shaped shadow given a faint golden limn by the street lantern. Shit, a third one.

But the tailoring was far too fine for an inquisitor's tunic. And there was a burnished sheen to those dark curls.

Siyon's heart leapt a moment before a haughty and familiar voice said, "Just *what* are you doing with my man?"

"Who're you when you're at home, then?" the inquisitor grappling Siyon demanded.

But his partner lifted his lantern, and cleared his throat when the light fell on the face of Izmirlian Hisarani. "Azatan, good even. This is not a good night to stray from your evening entertainments."

"So I am learning." Izmirlian's tone was icy as a winter blade. "You," he barked, and snapped his fingers at Siyon. "Come along."

The grip on Siyon's arm didn't lessen. The inq holding the lantern—minor azatani himself, Siyon guessed, from the boots and the accent and how quickly he'd recognised Izmirlian—winced but said apologetically, "I'm afraid there are procedures that have to be followed. If you'll wait for the wagon I am sure this can be—"

"*Wait?*" Izmirlian filled the word with such outraged disdain that Siyon had to swallow a hysterical giggle. "No, I've wasted enough time already. You, sir, what is your name?"

Lantern-bearer twitched his shoulders a little straighter. "Hildani, azatan."

An azatani name. Siyon loved being right. Izmirlian gave the inq one of those little nods that he and Anahid loved to exchange. "I'm sure you understand the need for urgency. I've—" He pulled out a purse, lifted the flap with an idle finger, and shrugged. "Five rivna for your trouble, and another five to thank your colleagues for their assistance as you see fit. I am sure I trust your judgment."

Ten rivna! Just tossed easily to an inquisitor who caught it with the flush of someone who wished he was worth more than this. Siyon was outraged at the casual money, impressed with Izmirlian's deft mix of flattery and bribery, absolutely livid that it was *working*—the azatan inquisitor made a gesture, and the one behind Siyon shoved him forward, letting him go. He staggered forward a few steps, his abruptly untwisted arm shrieking with djinn-prickles skittering up and down the nerves.

A hand steadied his shoulder. Siyon looked up into Izmirlian's clear brown eyes, that contained just for a moment a bolt of worry, and surprise, and relief.

The relief was mutual. "I could kiss you," Siyon breathed, fervent and giddy and unthinking. A twitch at Izmirlian's eyebrows, a flick of his gaze down to Siyon's mouth.

Then the azatan mask was back, Izmirlian shaking his fingers as if Siyon were sticky, wrinkling his nose. "Now, I said *come along*. Good evening to you," he added to the inquisitors, and strode away down Sailmaker's Row.

Siyon jogged after him.

Back in the Avenues, the evening promenade was underway. The azatani sauntered slowly along, seeing and being seen. Alchemical lanterns were strung between the leafy trees, and the light struck sparks off the beading on headscarves and the embroidery on longvests. It was a glorious, useless parade, and curfew was something that happened to *other* people.

Siyon was already a queasy churn of gratitude over his rescue and bitterness at how easily Izmirlian had done it; the blithe disregard of the azatani scooped resentment in atop it all. Angry words crawled up his throat, pressed against the inside of his gritted teeth.

Izmirlian's hand tucked around his elbow. "This way," he murmured, nudging Siyon off the street and down a laneway. Not one Siyon knew, nor the gate Izmirlian laid a hand on. The wood around his hand flashed briefly—an alchemically charmed lock, of course; they all seemed to have them up here—and the gate swung open. Izmirlian gave a rueful little smile as he waved a hand toward the house. "Welcome to the Hisarani home."

"You're bringing me home?" Siyon asked.

"*Not* to meet my mother," Izmirlian said, his mouth slanting. "They'll all be on promenade. And to dinner afterward. I thought perhaps we should get you off the street before too many people saw you." He cut a look toward Siyon. "Or you stabbed someone."

Siyon looked up again at the enormous house. It was wider than the Joddanis', and possibly taller. It had weight beyond its dimensions, and Izmirlian carried that with him, could bring it to bear upon inquisitors who knew what it meant. Siyon had been slammed against brickwork just for being outside after dark. All the residents of this house, save one, were currently not just outside but drawing as much attention to themselves as possible, making sure everyone knew who and what they were.

But Izmirlian had come looking for Siyon. "How did you even find me?" he asked, his voice a strangled thing.

A lantern near the yard door of the house cast orange light over Izmirlian's face. "Miss Savani found me not long after the sun went down and explained the situation."

Just after sundown. She must have sprinted the entire way from the Chapel, left the moment Daruj had arrived. Used her own azatani clout to make it, perhaps. "But how did you know I'd be there?"

"I didn't. I thought—maybe. And it was closest. I was going to try the fruit market next, and then...then, I had no idea." Izmirlian cleared his throat, and pulled up a little smile. "If you were actually *thinking*, you'd have gone to the university. The inqs won't be enforcing the curfew on campus, not with all those law candidates dying to prove themselves by overthrowing a tyrannical imposition on the natural rights of a citizen."

It was light, even teasing, but for a moment Siyon had seen a shadow of something wild and desperate in Izmirlian's clear brown eyes. He'd thought *maybe*. He'd had no idea.

He'd come out, and he'd found Siyon, and he'd thrown everything he had at getting him out. Maybe generosity was easy, when you had such abundance. But most of the other azatani were doing nothing more useful than parading like peacocks.

Siyon swallowed hard against the bitter, burning rage lodged in his chest, and said, "Thank you. I owe you ten rivna."

Izmirlian shook his head. "I'm sorry. About all of it." He set a hand on the door of the house, and hesitated. "Come in? Until all that nonsense is over and it's easier to get you back to the Joddanis'?"

Their proximity back at the alleyway prickled fresh in Siyon's memory. This felt almost like a bad idea. Maybe that was part of why it also felt so compelling.

"Sure," Siyon said. "Got anything to drink?"

Of course they did. They had a whole cellar, well-dusted racks of carefully labelled bottles marching back into the gloom where Izmirlian's lantern didn't reach. "Appalling, isn't it?" Izmirlian's smile crooked at the corner. "Worst part is that Father doesn't even drink, hasn't the head for it, and Mother hates hosting. Apricot brandywine from the New Republic?" He lifted the bottle, shining golden in the lantern light. "It's sour as a sore loser. Come on."

They went up through the house—climbing thick-carpeted stairs with polished wooden banisters, passing plush sitting rooms where silence lay heavy—and up again, until Izmirlian reached a pair of tall doors at the end of a corridor, flanked by velvet curtains and inset with darkly glittering glass. He opened one door and stepped out onto a stone balcony. Below, the promenade was still in full, ponderous swing, laughter rising delicate and fake on the evening air.

"Don't worry," Izmirlian said, handing Siyon the bottle of wine. "No one ever looks up."

And he laid hands on the trellis of a star jasmine creeper, and climbed straight up the wall.

Siyon stared after him, the heavy sweetness of disrupted flowers drifting down behind him, until Izmirlian swung a leg over the heavy stonework parapet of the roof and hauled himself up. He reached an expectant hand back down, and it took Siyon a moment to realise what he wanted; he handed up the bottle and grabbed the trellis. It was solid beneath his grip.

"I thought you said you didn't run the tiles," he called up, as he climbed.

"I hardly think this counts." Izmirlian grinned as he helped Siyon over the parapet at the top. Siyon teetered close for a moment, and the wood-and-orange-blossom scent of him overpowered the star jasmine, before Izmirlian turned away, picking his way up the pitch of the roof.

The view from up there was incredible. The house was taller than many—certainly than its neighbours—and the Avenues spread out around them like silent stone waves. Over there, the Palace of Justice with the dome lit up like a lantern. Over this way, street lanterns speckled the darkness between here and the multicoloured blooming of the Flower district. Curfew didn't apply to them either, it seemed, or the barons were just daring the inqs to make a thing of it. Out that way, nothing but darkness, past the quieter, crumbling neighbourhoods, where the Scarp fell away to the lower city. The moon was rising over the restless sea beyond.

They sat on the tiles, feet braced on the parapet. The wine was indeed sour—big and bold and just on the verge of being far too bitter, but the scrape of it against Siyon's tongue was nearly perfect. They passed the bottle back and forth, and the furore inside Siyon banked down to a simmer.

"Sitting on a rooftop, drinking something stupid, waiting to go out later," he listed. "Tell me a wild fabrication about who you slept with last night and this basically is a bravi evening." He said it with a pang; would he ever get to run the tiles with his tribe again?

Did he even still want to? There were so many other fascinations at hand.

"The Precarious Perch tribe." Izmirlian crossed one long leg over the other at the ankle. "Though I am a liability with a sabre. Always my brother's thing, so I made sure to be *aggressively* bad at it. Fencing, picking winners at the hippodrome, and politics." He took a long swallow from the bottle, winced reflexively as he lowered it. "Do you have brothers?"

Siyon stared out into the night. The stars were out now, scattered across the chasm of the night sky. "Four," he admitted.

"*Four.*" Izmirlian shifted beside him. "I shall start giving thanks for only having two. All down in—where *are* you from?"

That curved Siyon's mouth in a sardonic smile. Not sure where, but sure it was *down*. Wasn't everywhere, from here? And it wasn't like Siyon tried to hide his origins. Wallowed belligerently in them, rather. "Dockside. They'll be there. Haven't seen them in years." Since fourteen. "Families like mine...we don't leave."

Siyon waited for the words—*You did*. Waited for Izmirlian to ask. Wondered if here and now—tipsy and simmering in bitterness and with the long warm stretch of Izmirlian beside him—he might actually answer honestly.

"You know what?" Izmirlian said instead. "Why should Avair get all the fun? Come on." He started levering up to his feet. Siyon laid a steadying hand on his hip, knowing how slick roof tiles could be, and Izmirlian grabbed it, hauling Siyon up. "Come *on*. Teach me to fence."

"What?" Siyon blinked at him. "I'm rubbish too, you know."

Izmirlian grinned at him, and it was remarkably difficult not to smile back. "Not compared to me."

There was, of *course*, a whole bloody *fencing gallery*, lined with portraits featuring the haughty Hisarani nose. Siyon could feel his anger clawing back up again—there was a whole *rack* of blades, from the decorated swish of a sabre through hefty Northern longswords and the slender knitting-needles of the New Republic—but it had to fight against laughter as Izmirlian pranced about doing his best impersonation of a bravi from an opera.

Siyon stepped forward to adjust his stance and correct his grip. Their fingers slipped and entwined beneath the basketwork of the sabre hilt. Siyon wrapped his other hand around Izmirlian's wrist. "Like *this*."

Izmirlian's laughter was warm against Siyon's neck; Siyon nudged his feet back into position.

He *was* rubbish. But he got the hang of it quickly—had good posture naturally, or through strict instruction, and followed easily when Siyon demonstrated. "Just like dancing," he quipped at one point, and maybe it was. A bravi duel was only partly a fight. It was also a conversation, a flirtation, a performance—yes, a dance. With a chance of blood.

They sparred back and forth, nothing like serious, barely safe. The way Siyon and Daruj had done, back at fifteen, cheap second-hand blades in their hands and wild, improbable dreams in their heads. Izmirlian kept indulging in dramatic swings, so wild that Siyon could reach in and prod his side with a finger, which made Izmirlian yelp. Siyon found himself laughing, free and easy, bubbling up from his chest unimpeded by anger.

It felt good.

After, they slumped against the wall, finishing off the bottle of wine, beneath the disapproving gaze of a fearsome azata in the full finery of a court magistrate. ("My grandmother," Izmirlian said. "We used to call her The Full Bench. Not where she could hear.")

"Why?" Siyon demanded, before he could think better of asking. "Why do you want to leave all this?"

Izmirlian lolled next to him, a sneer stretching his mouth. "Why not? Because I have ridiculous wine, and a whole rack of swords, and gilt-framed family?" He turned those big, clear eyes on Siyon. "I want to leave because—"

"No." Siyon suddenly didn't want to hear. Didn't want to carry any more of this man inside himself. "No, it's—it's none of my business. Doesn't matter for the working." The working. "We could take the next step," he said.

"What?" Izmirlian blinked back at him, setting down the empty wine bottle with exaggerated care. "Oh. The next step. *Now?*"

"Why not?" So many reasons; they were both *drunk*, for starters. Siyon waved a hand. "Not to actually *do*. I'm not going to do tritay—" He stopped, and lined up the right sounds. "Titration like this. But like I said, with each bit having a sample of you. We could take the sample."

Izmirlian chuckled—it was almost a giggle. "Sample. Right. Almost afraid to ask, after *tears*."

"Aethyr, this time. Just breath. You just have to breathe into—" Siyon fumbled with the buckle on his satchel, stretched tight by Melis's wares, when his eyes fell on the empty wine bottle. Yes? Yes. It *felt* right. A part of this already.

Of course, he would still need something to stopper it with, and they'd used the cork for slicing practice. (It had bounced off, unsliced, somewhere into a dark corner; Siyon wasn't hunting for it now.) He squinted at the bottle. "Do you have a handkerchief?"

"I'm offended you even ask." Izmirlian produced a lace-edged square with a languid hand. It was monogrammed and everything; even better, right? *Ownership*. That sounded good.

Siyon draped the handkerchief over the neck of the bottle, pulled it taut. "Right. Breathe away."

Izmirlian's eyes glittered inscrutably beneath his lashes. He reached for the bottle, wrapping his long fingers over and between Siyon's around the neck of it. He drew breath in, eyelids fluttering fully closed, and pressed his mouth to the linen to exhale, long and slow and unhurried. It seemed to stretch even longer than Siyon had anticipated; his vision swam, and he pulled air into his own lungs. It tasted of the bitter tang of the wine, of the sweat of their exertions, of Izmirlian's orange-blossom and fragrant wood cologne.

Izmirlian released the bottle—and Siyon's hand—and slumped a little more against the wall as he drew breath again. Siyon hurried to shove the handkerchief into the neck of the bottle, fold upon fold of it. Not really airtight, but *symbolic*.

Izmirlian began to cough, shallow and rough. Siyon put down the bottle, set a hand on his shoulder. "It's fine," Izmirlian managed. The words were thin and stretched; he coughed again. "Just a catch in my throat."

Siyon realised he was hovering, hand still on Izmirlian's shoulder, thumb stroking along the collarbone bared by the lacing Izmirlian had undone during their fencing.

Izmirlian smiled, and Siyon didn't lean back.

"You need a drink," Siyon murmured.

"We drank it all already," Izmirlian whispered back. He tangled fingers in the front of Siyon's shirt, and pulled him closer still.

Pulled him closer, then hesitated, barely a breath between their mouths. As though, with the entire city his for the taking, he didn't want to just take this.

Siyon leaned the rest of the way and kissed him first. Slid his hand from Izmirlian's shoulder up to his jaw, as the kiss slanted quickly from gentle to hungry. The touch of Izmirlian's tongue, a graze of Siyon's teeth.

One kiss slipped easily into another, and another. Siyon curled his hand into Izmirlian's hair, as soft against his knuckles as it'd been to harvest. Izmirlian's fingers skirted under Siyon's collar, thumb stroking at the pulse in his throat.

This was a terrible idea, really. They had nothing in common, save the business they were about, trying to banish Izmirlian from reality. There was literally no possible future in this.

Perhaps that was why this moment felt so precious. Siyon seized it, stretched it, savoured it. Izmirlian Hisarani tasted twice as expensive as he smelled, rich and sharp and intoxicating. And yet, tonight, so very real as well. Sour wine on his tongue, roof dust in his hair, sweat in the hollow of his throat from fencing.

A door opened, far below in the house. A burst of voices. Izmirlian tensed; Siyon sat up. "Your family?"

"Home already," Izmirlian sighed, and tugged the collar of his shirt straight. "I should—"

"Yes," Siyon agreed. "Of course. Do what you need to. I'll be fine from here."

"Are you sure?" Izmirlian asked hurriedly. "I could—"

Siyon shook his head. There wasn't any danger, after all, from the inquisitors here in the Avenues. However bitter that made him feel, it also made him safe on the streets. Izmirlian could stay here in his plush townhouse while Siyon skulked through the back alleys and—

"Fine," Izmirlian huffed, and ducked in to press a fleeting kiss against Siyon's mouth before he hurried away down the corridor.

At the end, he glanced back, and Siyon—still standing there like a fool—saluted him with the bottle, empty and yet not. Then he turned and headed for the servants' stairs, because that was just the way the world was.

CHAPTER 15

As the afternoon dragged on, Anahid tried to concentrate on her correspondence. There were the usual letters—from old school friends now on trade routes for their families to Lyraea, the Archipelago, the Republic, and Northern ports—but also more pressing business closer to home. The scarcity of invitations received might be related to how rarely Nihath had socialised recently, too busy with some alchemical business. But more likely it was about that alchemical business. Nihath's predilections were too well known, the current climate too hostile to alchemy, and the inquisitors had already been seen on their doorstep.

It was up to Anahid to solve, as usual, but dashing off an airy note downplaying their concerns was difficult when her attention was snagged by every noise from the street. The patter of quick footsteps approaching their door had Anahid hurrying to the window of her upstairs sitting room; too slow, for there was only a twitch of movement below, and the sound of the door opening.

Anahid had sent another message already today, just after breakfast, to Tahera. It was the least important of all, but the one that had her on tenterhooks awaiting a response. This wasn't it; a message-runner would have knocked.

Soon enough, Zagiri came into the room. She was wearing a pretty black-and-pink day gown and a strangely thoughtful expression. "Oh good, you're here." She cast herself into one of the armchairs with her usual excess of vigour. "I thought you might have gone to that thing at the hippodrome as well."

"Not if I can avoid it." Anahid took the other armchair, sitting with exaggerated care, even though she had no reason to expect Zagiri would note the example when she hadn't in the past eighteen years. "What are you bothered about now?" For clearly, her sister was bothered.

"Nothing." But the frown on Zagiri's face deepened, and Anahid waited patiently while her sister worked past that initial knee-jerk denial. She sounded almost belligerent when she demanded, "How did *you* decide to do this with your life?"

Foolishly, Anahid didn't say. What use in voicing it? "Marriage instead of trade, or scholarship, or politics, you mean?"

"Trade was always out, of course," Zagiri considered. "You turn green just being rowed across the harbour."

Undeniable, though Anahid still wanted to deflect. In ocean-going Bezim, seasickness was quite the curse. "I did consider warehouse overseer," Anahid said instead, "but Cousin Telmut is so protective of the business that it didn't seem worth the fight. *You* don't get seasick, though."

Zagiri pulled a face. "I don't have the patience to haggle with the dressmaker, how am I supposed to wrangle in the family's best interests in foreign ports?"

Anahid couldn't help her laughter. "And I don't think the university would be a tranquil or natural home for you either." But for a child of the azatani, even or perhaps especially at the first tier, there were few other options. Anahid hesitated to pry further. Zagiri was inclined to react to questions like they were attacks with a sabre. But they seemed to be *talking* for once, and Zagiri had brought it up, so Anahid took the risk. "Have you considered politics?"

Even if Zagiri as a clerk—sitting through the interminably detailed meetings of the endless committees that comprised the azatani government—seemed just as laughable as academic diligence.

"No," Zagiri huffed. "Yes. I don't know. I want—" She jumped up again, and started to pace. Always needing to be *moving*. "I *want* to not have to choose. To stay like this forever. But this—" She waved her arms wildly, and Anahid didn't think she meant just her life. "This is only all right for *me*."

Anahid blinked. "As opposed to…?"

Zagiri stared like she wasn't getting it. Fair; Anahid clearly wasn't. "All right for *everyone*."

There came the sound of running feet in the street. Anahid leaned to the window, watching the message-runner carry on down the avenue—not for her, clearly—as she tried to rearrange her thoughts to her sister's wild pronouncement. "You don't have the patience for trade, but you think you could try and turn the balance of the entire city?" Zagiri sagged a little, her frown turning abruptly sad, and Anahid stepped closer to take her sister's hand in hers. "I think you should do it," Anahid said, and smiled at Zagiri's surprised expression. "You must do something, and I'd miss you if you ran away to the Inner Khanate to be a lady brigand."

The bark of Zagiri's laughter made Anahid feel unduly proud. They had laughed together often, before Anahid had presented Zagiri to the harbour master, and both of them had grown up. Grown apart.

Anahid took a deep breath, bracing herself. "You should set your sails on a course that excites you. For *you*. I—I thought I could build a life that mattered to me with a suitable partner, but that has proven… more difficult than I anticipated."

Zagiri snorted, and Anahid couldn't even scold her. Her sister had a point. "Why," Zagiri asked, and then stopped. She looked down at their linked hands—Anahid's long and smooth, Zagiri's shorter and scuffed with the calluses and scrapes of the bravi. "Why do you stay with him?"

The question stole Anahid's breath for a moment; Zagiri always ventured where others were too polite or timid to dare. But this Anahid had avoided even asking herself.

"It's only been a few months," she said, almost breathless.

Zagiri's look was quick as a blade in the dark. "You think he's going to change?"

Anahid swallowed. Her throat was still dry as she said, "And go where? Do what? Back to our parents, to try again?" Because she'd had *such* a wealth of offers from which to choose in the first place.

"So you just make the best of it?" Zagiri sounded more than grumpy. There was an edge to her voice.

They'd been talking about *Zagiri's* future. Maybe they were still. Didn't she want better for Zagiri than she'd managed? *Someone* should do better.

But the truth was: "All any of us can do is make the best of the cards we are dealt."

"Why? Why can't we—" Zagiri waved her free hand wildly. "Draw blade on the dealer. Seize the deck. Make the best *better*. For everyone, not just us."

Anahid opened her mouth, but she found no answer. Because it wasn't possible. And yet, why not?

Zagiri's laugh was short and bitter. "Fanciful," she snarled, and pulled away from Anahid to pace once more.

Anahid wanted to tell her it was noble and worthwhile. Her sister had wild dreams, and she didn't want them crushed. But she alone couldn't stand against the world.

Running feet in the street, and Anahid's attention darted to the window before she could help herself. Too far to see out through the lace curtains, and she didn't want to step away from Zagiri, not now.

But Zagiri had noticed, was laughing like she was grateful for the distraction. "You are so *twitchy* this afternoon! Are you getting clandestine messages? Don't tell me you've finally got a lover."

"Giri!" Anahid felt the blood rise in her face; she glared at her sister.

"What?" Zagiri waggled her eyebrows. "You could use one."

Anahid drew breath to scold, but a tap at the door interrupted her. Nura slipped in with a folded letter on a tray. Anahid snatched it up and quickly opened it, too eager to know Tahera's response to be bothered about Zagiri on tiptoe behind her, peering around her shoulder.

"*Your suggestion is not appropriate for—*" Zagiri read aloud. "Ana, what *are* you engaged in?"

Anahid had lost her voice. There seemed something small and cold lodged inside her, like she'd swallowed a pebble. She had no strength in her grip to stop Zagiri plucking the letter away to read properly.

"Who's *T*?" Zagiri demanded. "*Impertinent*, you? I'm going to break their windows!"

"Giri," Anahid chided weakly, but the wild support made her feel a little better. "She's just making clear that her refusal is not negotiable."

Zagiri blew a noisy raspberry. "What did you propose, a wild odyssey through the Flower district?" Anahid looked away, and Zagiri gasped. "You did?"

"Not an *odyssey*." Anahid snatched the letter back, though she didn't actually want to look at it again. She folded the paper and set it on her desk. "I thought Tahera and I might...just a little visit. To one House, of reliable reputation, to—to play carrick."

"Carrick?" Zagiri looked astonished, her eyes huge with it.

Anahid felt more defensive than ever. "She knows those who play it in the Houses. She introduced me, we played together at a party. She didn't seem so *set* against it when the Captain suggested—" Anahid sighed. "I was curious."

More than that. The idea had been bubbling up inside her all day, anticipation setting her to pacing. What would it be like, to sit to serious play, not half-hidden but free of society supervision? To really explore how fascinating the game could be.

She couldn't remember when she'd last *looked forward* to something.

Zagiri grabbed Anahid's hand, her chin tilted up, her mouth pressed tight with furious challenge. "Fuck her. Tahera, whoever she is. Go out and have some fun, for once. Do it by yourself, if she's going to come over all prissy. Don't know why, if she's all right with the rest of it. But I know which Flowerhouses to avoid, and you can—"

"You do? How?"

Zagiri shrugged. "You don't run with bravi without learning a thing or two. I can even go down with you, if you want. I can't stay, there's a thing on tonight."

Anahid frowned. "You shouldn't be out. Isn't there a curfew?"

"Says the lady prancing down to the Flower district." Zagiri smirked.

Anahid found that expression a little contagious; it tugged at the corner of her own mouth. "I'm not going to prance."

"But you are going to go." Zagiri squeezed her hand. "Right?"

She was. She *was*. Anahid's smile widened, and she gripped her sister tight.

Sitting down to contemplate alchemy with a hangover skulking around the back of his skull felt downright familiar to Siyon. Fortunately, the headache was mild. Unfortunately, the alchemy wasn't.

The second working, this one. Aethyreal where the last had been Empyreal. Siyon had his focus—the wine bottle full of Izmirlian's breath—and now he just had to figure out how to counteract and balance it out, like he had the tears.

Of course, that had taken eight attempts. How did he divide up a bottleful of breath?

(If he messed up, they could harvest more. Siyon could watch Izmirlian's lashes flutter on his cheeks, tangle their fingers together, get entirely distracted all over again. Would that be bad?)

Siyon pulled his thoughts back to business, pulling things out of his satchel. The firesand—he tucked that straight back into Joddani's organised ranks of ingredients—and the moonglimmer and the hammer-rock and even some cedar wood shavings because you never knew what might come in handy. He'd vaguely intended to unpack all of this the night before, but when he'd come in Nura had taken one look at him, sniffed pointedly, and stated, "I *said* there was no reason to worry about you. Now up to your room! No more mischief!"

It had just seemed easier to do as she said.

Siyon wondered now, as he lined it up on the bench, where Melis was. Had she and Daruj made it safely away? Was she out of the city already? How were Bracken even getting them out?

A shame to miss this grand adventure—tweaking the inquisitors' noses would have been a thrill. But this was his own adventure, hardly devoid of thrills.

All right then, what had he learned from the first working? It now seemed stupid not to have written more notes as he went. Siyon flipped to a new notebook page and scribbled: *Take more notes.*

He stepped back through his memory. *Sidelong planar affinities, then crosswise counter.* So for Aethyreal, that meant Empyre and Abyss first. One, then the other. And then counter with the Mundane reference.

But was Izmirlian's breath the Mundane or the Aethyreal? He *was* Mundane, if not at all mundane, but the purpose here was to evoke the Aethyr, so the sample itself should be considered the subject of the working, not a reagent.

…right?

Siyon buried his face in his hands and groaned. If he were a *proper* alchemist, if he had more experience with this, if he had *any idea what he was doing*…but none of those things applied.

"I need help," he muttered into his palm. And in the absence of Auntie Geryss, that probably meant Tehroun. He'd offered, hadn't he? And even if he was…whatever he was. Delusional but with an affinity. Or actually a fallen djinn. Impossible, Joddani said—*Negedi* said, apparently—and yet there was something about him. What did *affinity* even mean?

Whatever. He should be able to help.

Siyon strode out of the still room, mentally listing the places he could try—Joddani's library, or the dining room still loitering over lunch, or upstairs wherever he slept. The serving staff would probably know, but he hated to interrupt their work, and then he stopped so suddenly his heels skidded.

Tehroun was sitting on the stairs leading up into the house.

Lounging would be a more accurate word, sprawling propped on one elbow. Tehroun cupped a pale hand around his ear, and turned toward Siyon as though waiting to hear something.

Siyon sighed. "Could you help me with the working, then?"

Tehroun wafted to his feet with no apparent effort. "Of course." He whisked past Siyon with a blithe smile, back into the workroom.

When Siyon caught up, closing the door behind them, Tehroun was fluttering his fingers around the wine bottle, prodding at the handkerchief plugging the neck. "Ingenious," he murmured, and Siyon couldn't help a little flutter of pride. Right up until Tehroun added, smug as a whisper could be, "But now you're stuck."

Rather than do something unhelpful, like smack him upside his pale and irritating ear, Siyon folded his arms. "I already asked for help."

"Of course," Tehroun breathed, and stepped back from the bench. "You want a bowl of wood—hard, not soft—and to render that hammer-rock down to powder within." He looked at Siyon. "Are you going to just stand there?"

The first three bowls Siyon pulled down from the shelves were unsuitable—soft, soft, and the third Tehroun ran a finger over and pronounced, "Lacquer," like it had done something unspeakable to his mother. Tehroun at least knew where Joddani kept his heavy file, for grinding down the hammer-rock. It was a hideous job, with Siyon's fingers cramping after two minutes of effort, which was about ten minutes sooner than Tehroun finally stopped saying, "Not enough."

Siyon ground up seagrass with a little brackish seawater, adding it drop by drop while Tehroun tasted with the tip of his littlest finger, making increasingly revolted faces. Then it all mixed up in the wooden dish into a thick, gooey paste, which Siyon painted over the neck of the bottle—handkerchief and all—with a delicate little featherbrush. It went on obligingly thickly, and started to seethe at the neck.

"That's the paste eating away at the linen," Tehroun whispered mildly. "You'll want to get it over a flame."

"What bloody flame?" Siyon demanded.

So then there was five minutes of frantic activity, getting the little torch lantern from the distillation equipment set up and burning evenly, getting the stand steady at the right height above it, to suspend the bottle to heat but not crack.

But it worked—it *worked*. At the mouth of the bottle, the thick-painted paste bulged outward, stretched and distended. But it held, and inflated slowly into a bubble just the size of a small, ripe apricot... if an apricot were deep purplish black and smelt of sun-baked dust.

Siyon eased the bubble off the neck of the bottle with delicate fingers, and his breath caught in his throat. It came, whole and unburst, and as he held it up, there were patterns striating across its surface. Like the markings that had appeared on the linen. It felt *right*.

He set it in a little ceramic dish of its own, next to the one with the linen and rakia from the first working. A pair of them—*two* successful workings, a half of a whole complex undertaking.

Two weeks ago, Siyon would never have imagined he could be here, making a multi-planar working with Negedic principles and innate inspiration. He still felt wildly out of his depth, but for the first time he thought perhaps... perhaps he *could* do this.

Tehroun sniffed. "Adequate, I suppose."

Siyon cleared his throat. "Thanks. Guess you learned a whole lot of stuff from Nihath, right?"

A gentle laugh from beside him. "You don't believe me. That I am what I said I am."

Siyon leaned back against the bench, so he could look at Tehroun properly. In person, it seemed both more and less plausible. Tehroun was so slender and strange, his hair pale and wisping, his posture curled and languid, his eyes arresting. But he *had* body and hair and eyes. He was a person.

And yet.

"*He* doesn't believe that you are what you said you are," Siyon pointed out.

Tehroun smiled gently. "Of course he doesn't. Nihath Joddani is safe within the boundaries that Kolah Negedi drew around the Art. And within those bounds he does such marvellous things." He sighed, like an autumnal breeze carrying regrets of summer. "But the world is never so simple or tidy as we would like it to be."

Siyon frowned. Was Tehroun suggesting Negedi was... *wrong*? Surely he hadn't mentioned that to Joddani, or the whole house would've heard the resulting argument. "So if you *are* a djinn, then how?" Or more importantly: "*Why?*"

"Am I here?" Tehroun cocked his head like a bird. "I don't know. The memories of that transitional time are clouded, neither clear as my Aethyreal life nor strongly felt as the Mundane. The first thing I really remember is the docks." His smile was sharp. "A fitting arrival point, yes? Before that…there was need. And an opportunity. And then I walked out of the water and into a human life." He looked far away, walking through memory again. "I knew that the Sultan desired more of us to cross over."

More and more like something from an opera. "You can just do that? Cross over? Why don't we have djinn all over the place?"

Tehroun rolled his eyes. "Because I'm no longer djinn. You—" He waved one finger vaguely in Siyon's direction. "You go delving on a whim; did you think that was a one-way possibility? But with the planes as they are, it is difficult. This—" And he laid his hand against his own chest, narrow and pale but very human. "This is more certain. Not difficult, but irreversible, and thus not undertaken lightly."

"Falling," Siyon named it. As good a word as any other. He still didn't quite believe it. *With the planes as they are*, Tehroun had said. "Is planar imbalance a problem for the other planes as well?"

The look Tehroun gave him was unimpressed to the point of pitying; even as Siyon had asked the question, the answer seemed obvious. Of course. Balance required all four planes. They were all in this together. "There is a limit to how much support we can give you," he said, "if you remain beyond our direct control."

Siyon's wavering doubt was sluiced away by a chill wash of fear. "What does *direct control* mean?"

Tehroun shrugged, like it was of no interest to him, but as he opened his mouth, something seemed to snag his attention; he looked abruptly at the still-closed door.

A moment later it opened, and Nihath Joddani said, "There you are!" He frowned, at the pile of bowls on the floor, at the dusty mess of the hammer-rock and file, at the scattered scraps of seagrass stem. But his face cleared as Tehroun sauntered across and curled long, pale fingers around his arm. "Yes, right. Are you both ready?"

"Ready for what?" Siyon asked, even as Tehroun whispered, "Of course."

Nihath Joddani looked pained. "I gave you an *invitation*, Velo."

And Siyon had shoved it in his satchel and forgotten about it. "Right," he said. "*That*. You becoming the Power of the Mundane. Let's go."

He eyed Tehroun's back uneasily as they all climbed the stairs. What *did* that *direct control* mean? It sounded, even in Tehroun's weak and wafty way, like a threat.

But he didn't need to worry, right? Negedi wasn't wrong. He couldn't be. Tehroun was just embroidering wild fancies. Joddani would fix this.

It would all be fine.

CHAPTER 16

It was the promenade hour again, but even that self-indulgent fete of gossip and glitter paused to consider the wedge of alchemists who formed up outside the Joddani townhouse. Siyon was the least among them, back in Nihath's old purple coat and squashed in among the lower-tier practitioners. At least in the middle of this school of fish, he'd be less visible to the inquisitors as they left the Avenues to get to the Summer Club.

Siyon wanted to see this. Nihath Joddani—undeniably the most skilled alchemist currently practicing in Bezim—doing something unprecedented. Something that could fix it all. If Nihath became the Alchemist, the Power of the Mundane, then surely he could get Enkin Danelani back, call off the inqs, fix the planar imbalance. Solve the problems Siyon had been having with delving the Empyreal plane, maybe even let him see the Aethyreal. Declare a holiday with free pastries.

Yes, Siyon wanted to bear witness.

And he wasn't the only one. Curfew be damned, the Summer Club was humming like a festival, lanterns blazing behind every window. A wild hubbub of speculation and acclaim greeted Joddani. Siyon slipped into the crowded library in Joddani's wake. There weren't a lot of plain coats in the crowd, no merchant brown, not much industrial black. Had they fled, or been arrested, or just stayed home?

Only one table remained on the library floor, set up with an array of equipment. Siyon was already tired of craning over the crowd, so edged back until he could pull himself up to sit on the sill of one of the wide windows, curtains drawn back on black, reflective night.

There was someone already up there, tucked into the other corner of the windowsill, and Siyon said, "How in the Abyss did you get up here so fast?"

Tehroun gave him an amused look. "The Abyss had nothing to do with it," he said, though his smile faded as he looked back over the room. "He's going to fail, of course."

"What?" Siyon followed Tehroun's gaze to the central desk. Someone helped Nihath off with his coat; someone else clapped him on the shoulders, like a prize fighter entering the ring. "He's the best alchemist in the city."

"He is," Tehroun agreed. "But he, alone, is not enough."

Siyon opened his mouth again, but a gong rang, and the seethe and hiss of the crowd subsided. Siyon turned away from Tehroun with relief.

Nihath Joddani set his shoulders, spread his hands. There was the same sort of anticipatory energy as Auntie Geryss had had in the square. "Colleagues, thank you for joining me for this endeavour, and thank you further for your aid as I prepared. You know my purpose already, but the great Negedi stresses the value of clarity at the outset of any working, and so let me be clear."

He started to pace around the table, slow and steady. "The planes are imbalanced; we can all feel them slipping further awry with each imprudent imposition. It will only worsen until and unless there arises a counterbalancing force. Gentlemen"—and then he added, as an afterthought—"and ladies, there must be a Power of the Mundane. There must be an Alchemist. This evening, I will take on that mantle."

Genteel applause at that pronouncement, as though he'd made a good play at tiles. Joddani ceremoniously turned his shirtsleeves up toward his elbow. Not quite as theatrical as Auntie Geryss, and this crowd weren't participants so much as witnesses.

He whipped the velvet shroud off a round glass vessel, and Siyon nearly laughed out loud. There was a piece of rope in a glass fishbowl, smouldering gently with a wisp of smoke rising from it, from where an angel had tried to murder Siyon.

"Angelfire," Joddani announced, and a shiver passed through the audience. "Intrinsic matter of the Empyreal plane. Too fierce and pure for Mundane matter to resist, of course. But with a little additional balance..."

He pulled up a dish of dark clay, the rich sort cut out of the marshes for the use of potters and tilers. The liquid he poured in carried a whiff of salt and sulphur, but Siyon wasn't sure if it was proper Abyssal brine, or merely the Mundane equivalent. He didn't begrudge Joddani his secrets; this was something unprecedented, after all.

Siyon had a certain sympathy.

Joddani coated his palm with a thick layer of clay slip, then another and a third. Angelic fire would burn straight through any amount of plain old mud, of course. But when Nihath reached into the fishbowl and closed his fist, armoured in alchemical clay, around the still-burning rope, there was a faint hiss of extinguishment. He unfurled his fingers to show the ashen rope-end. No wisp of smoke.

The crowd shifted and murmured; Siyon leaned forward. This was not unlike what he had underway—smaller workings making a bigger whole. That was only the first step, but Joddani had done it so calmly and confidently, and surely, surely...

This would happen.

A second fishbowl was a quarter full of dark liquid, blacker than black, shifting nacreous into purple and green, sheening pearl and vitreous orange. Even Siyon gasped when this was unveiled. How had Joddani got hold of kraken ink? Siyon wouldn't know where to start finding the stuff—well, in a *kraken*, presumably, but how would you harvest it?

Joddani set the bowl on a stand over a brazier fed with peat and charcoal that made a thick and earthy smoke. The ink wouldn't so much as simmer, of course, until Joddani tipped into the bowl a hefty vial of sand—that Siyon had got from Melis. It thickened and clogged the ink, and the mixture soon bubbled into a seething boil. Joddani attached the distillation apparatus—and Siyon was proud to be able to follow the process through each piece to the inevitable drip-drip-drip into the final beaker.

The liquid was entirely clear.

Joddani held it aloft for consideration, and then—with a smile and a performer's flourish—poured in a measure of whiskey and took a large mouthful.

The ripple of laughter only wound the anticipation tighter. Two pillars complete, and all was proceeding with precise Negedic inevitability. Surely, *surely*...

Siyon had nearly forgotten about Tehroun next to him, until Joddani reached for the third shrouded fishbowl, and spider-long pale fingers clutched at Siyon's arm.

"Unwise," Tehroun whispered, between tight-pressed lips.

The third fishbowl seemed entirely empty, capped with a thick cork. But inside, the empty air *twisted*, pulling in the gaze and tying it up, tangling an impression of anything, of everything, of nothing at all—

Siyon pulled his gaze away as Joddani announced, "A will-o'-the-wisp."

An actual *creature* of the Aethyreal plane, not fallen but somehow, genuinely, here. A lesser creature, but it could still tear the roof off the entire building if it got free.

The audience shifted uneasily, but Joddani moved confidently to set the corked fishbowl atop a slender slab of square-cut marble. He set similar slabs as walls, mixing mortar from the angelfire ash and the mess left over from the sanded kraken ink, working with greater skill than Siyon would have expected from an azatan facing manual labour. Soon he was readying the roof tile, mortared on all edges and held balanced with one hand, as he dipped a finger in his whiskey-and-water and traced a nullification sigil on the fishbowl cork.

It began to fracture; the crowd shifted uneasily.

Joddani dropped the marble down atop his cube, just as a shriek like a furious kettle started within. He leaned his weight against the cube, but still the edges ground as the marble tried to shift. The keening from within was faintly audible; the crowd edged backward, as though that little distance would matter if the wisp got free.

No one fled.

In the space between one breath and the next, the whistle dimmed to a whisper, and then was gone entirely. Joddani lifted his hands from the marble, which did not move.

Until Joddani hefted a mallet—taking both hands to lift, and a grunt of effort to swing—and shattered the marble asunder. Siyon flinched along with everyone else, but nothing came shrieking out. The shards of marble were coated with a glittering grit.

The crowd shifted and murmured. A primal force of each plane, now subdued. *Surely...*

Joddani added a pinch of the grit to a pinch of the ash, moistened with his kraken ink distillation. He worked the concoction together in a little golden bowl, squishing it into a tight little pellet. He lifted it like a trophy of a victory no one here would dispute.

"I have mastered each of the other planes, subsuming its fury into the Mundane. With this, I assert my power. I am of this plane, and it is of me. I lay claim to the Power of the Mundane."

Joddani placed the pellet on his tongue, and swallowed.

Silence fell over the library, an utter stillness, as they all awaited... something. Anticipation ran along Siyon's nerves, echoed in every face around him. It must happen. What would it—?

The universe skewed and snagged. One blink, one moment, one breath that stretched, and teetered, and hitched—

—and then snapped.

The universe staggered, the planes shuddering around them. The crowd swayed and grabbed at each other; Siyon fell from the windowsill, slipping down the wall, and barely noticed for the headache that slammed down through him like a strike from that mallet.

The chandeliers did not so much as sway.

Joddani was standing, and then he fell like a tree in a forest.

Someone shrieked, and the crowd started shoving, some pushing forward, others lunging for the door. Siyon leaned heavily against the wall beneath his windowsill; Tehroun was gone, vanished into thin air for all Siyon knew. All was chaos.

Not so different from Auntie Geryss's ritual at all.

The headache still throbbed as Siyon staggered out of the Summer Club's library. He had to stop and clutch at the doorway as the world shifted and skewed around him; someone jostled against his shoulder, and two women in the hall clutched at each other. But the clerk behind the front desk merely watched them all with faint puzzlement.

Not the world moving, but the planes.

Very few people seemed to be leaving; they'd all crowded into the general parlour, huddling in little knots of concern and distress. The club stewards were bringing out trays of fortifying rakia.

Siyon didn't know where to go or what to do. Everything was supposed to be in hand. Nihath was supposed to fix it.

Nihath was still out cold, now being laid out on the table by his increasingly hysterical friends. Their rising shrieks and hissed imprecations sliced into Siyon's aching head; he moved toward the bottom of the stairs just to get away from it all.

He wanted—suddenly and desperately—to go home. He didn't even know where that was. The Joddani townhouse, which *wasn't* home? The Little Bracken safe house, which wasn't safe? One of the lower-city squats where he'd slept now and then, that he could hardly remember?

The narrow, neighbouring houses of the Velo clan, buried in the warren of Dockside, cramped and crowded, where he hadn't been for years?

Siyon didn't know where he belonged. He didn't know who he was.

"Hsst!"

Siyon thought it was just the clock; he glanced up and froze.

Auntie Geryss was at the top of the staircase. Just standing there like he'd conjured her from his own fervent wishes.

Standing there and beckoning impatiently. "I want a word with you," she called.

Siyon sprinted up the stairs, but she was already disappearing through the doorway leading into the upper level of the library. He wondered if maybe she *was* a fancy, but he followed into the library's sudden dimness. The lanterns up here had been doused, the better to focus on what was happening down below. There was a great view over the railing of the prone body of Nihath Joddani. Accusations were starting to be thrown around, jabbed with pointing fingers: *You* didn't really believe; Well, *you* have betrayed Negedic practice!

They all cut off in a gulp—and Siyon grabbed hold of the railing—as the planes bulged and ebbed like a wave probing the shore.

"Easier if you're sitting down," Auntie Geryss said from behind him.

In the light of a single lantern, she sat and picked over a plate of supper—grilled vegetables, cheese, olives, salt fish. She looked just the same as ever, a wry and spry woman aging into her wicked elder years, carved of teak and wire and will.

Siyon lunged forward to grab her up in a hug, nearly tipping her chair over backward. She laughed in his ear, and the sound brought tears to his eyes. She smelled of ash, and dust, and beneath it all, her own faint frangipani scent. She was wearing a different turban—swirled in red and black—but the same rumpled under-robe from her ceremony in the square. She was *real*, and really here. Safe.

"What are you doing here?" Siyon demanded, letting her go to fall into a chair of his own. The planes were still jittering around them, and he didn't even care.

"Here for the show." Geryss nodded to the railing. "Not sure why he bothered. If you could reason your way into being the Power, Negedi would have already done it, wouldn't he?"

Siyon remembered Nihath in his study, with his books and his plans, saying, *I wish Negedi had continued his work in this area.* But he hadn't. Hadn't, or couldn't?

The world is never so simple or tidy as we would like it to be. That had been Tehroun, whispering in the darkened still room, suggesting the impossible.

Geryss sighed happily as she carved a slice off the cheese. "Best I've eaten all week." She pointed her little knife at Siyon. "How have you been?"

"Me? *I'm* not the one the inquisitors are overturning half the city to try and find."

"Not just them, yeah? Heard you came looking, with a friend flashing his name and his card. The inqs look for things like my first husband did—poke, poke, poke, and then crying that it's gone forever. I won't say they aren't a bother, but compared to some places I've been in hiding…" She shrugged a shoulder, though her mouth got a sour twist. "Worth the risk, if it had worked."

Her ritual in the square. Her wild, public, audacious, entirely non-Negedic ritual. Siyon rubbed at his head. The ache wasn't going away. The planes flipped and flopped, like the half-hearted throes of a dying fish. "It nearly did. Work, I mean. You caught something, I felt it snag."

Geryss cackled. "Felt! Listen to you. I thought you'd gone Negedic, locked up with Joddani and his books of theory like prison bars, and then you come out with *feelings*."

Siyon hunched. Why was nothing steady anymore, not the planes, not the city, not the granite surety of Kolah Negedi's primacy? "I thought all alchemy was based on his work. But you—you were working with intangible ingredients. Emotions and belief."

"Numinous, is what the ancient Lyraec writers called it." Geryss dragged a piece of bread thoughtfully through the oil on her plate. "Got the idea from you, you know. Doing the impossible, right in front of everyone. Negedi even assigns emotions to the planes—the exalted emotions, the base emotions, the intangible sensations—but then he declares they don't matter."

Siyon had used that in figuring out the steps for Izmirlian's commission. He had to take a moment to think through the rest. "Are you suggesting I could catch Zagiri because everyone in the square wanted me to?" The memory was too much of a blur, a screaming moment of desperation. *Had* he felt a surge from the crowd? That scream he'd heard—or thought he heard—might have been the sound of their collective horror?

He didn't think so. He wasn't sure why.

"Maybe." Geryss shrugged. "Maybe not. Maybe we're being unfair to Negedi. Maybe there's more to his work than has survived. Not like anyone's actually set eyes on his stuff in a century and more. We need to work with what we *can* see."

She fixed her gaze on Siyon, expectant like she'd been when teaching him in her apartment. Her insistence that he *could* find the next logical step made Siyon twist his mind to do just that. What could they see? What did it suggest? "There *was* power in your Tower Square working. And it snagged, but then came loose. Or maybe broke." And in the aftermath, Siyon had *felt* the power loose in the square, not quite a flare, but something similar. Geryss beckoned, urging more. "You had power, and you caught something, but couldn't pull it back. So is there... *more* power holding Enkin Danelani wherever he is?"

Geryss nodded. "A question I ask also. He *is* out there—in the Abyss, if I had to narrow it down. The backlash—" She rubbed her fingers together, wrinkled her nose. "You know what I'm talking about, an aftertaste of salt and regret."

Siyon had felt that, remembered it washing over him. The Abyss, and power holding him. Power or *Power*? "Does the Demon Queen have him?"

Geryss didn't dismiss it. "Sounds like a bad opera, but maybe. Or maybe there's something we don't understand because we're too focused on Kolah Negedi."

An idea surfaced from the roiling possibilities in Siyon's mind. So many new things recently. "Is it possible," he asked carefully, thinking of Tehroun. *Not difficult, but not undertaken lightly.* Enkin Danelani, that last evening at the Summer Club, throwing around money and influence; like a brattish azatan, or like a man making a massive decision? "Is it possible that he's *fallen*?"

Auntie Geryss closed her mouth and thought about it—really thought, and Siyon felt proud to warrant that much consideration. "Maybe we've all paid too little attention to the ways the barriers between the planes can be crossed." She gave him an assessing look. "More your specialty than ours, isn't it?"

And he was drowning in his ignorance. "However he's there," Siyon pointed out, "we need him back." Or the inquisitors would continue to run amok, and the prefect would let them.

Geryss didn't argue with that; after all, she'd already tried to get him back. "If I'd had a better focus, a way to grip tighter, or maybe if I'd been able to hold it longer…" She shrugged. "If *I* were his mother, I'd have an altar-figure for him. That would've been perfect."

"Oh! We went to your apartment, the inqs had broken the altar, but the figures—" Siyon patted at his coat—but this was the old coat of Nihath's, purple and fancy, not the laborer's disguise he'd been wearing that day.

Geryss lay a hand on his arm; her smile was gentle and sad. "Thank you for the thought. I'm glad they'll be travelling with you, rather than lying forgotten."

"I can get them to you," Siyon argued. "They'll be in my satchel. I didn't bring it tonight because there's too many incriminating things—" He stopped dead as his thoughts snagged like her ritual had. Things in his satchel. Including the personal signet ring of Enkin Danelani.

"What?" Geryss watched him with no little amusement. "You look like you've just sneezed on Gayane Saliu."

Siyon felt a little like it too—unbelieving and awed and mildly horrified by possibility. "If you *had* a better focus, for the prefect's son, what would you do with it?"

Geryss tilted her head, like a blackbird considering stealing his lunch. "I'd have given my ritual more punch, but could be I was taking the wrong approach all along, given what we've talked about here. Maybe I should have done something more subtle, and maybe I could, with that better focus. Used it like—like—" She touched a finger to her nose. "Like getting the scent, yes? Delve *to* him. See what's keeping him there. See if he can't be got back." She smiled. "What have you got, boy?"

"His ring. Traded with his solemn promise of protection, all of a quarter bell before he fled the plane." She barked a laugh, and Siyon nodded ruefully. "I know. But would it—?"

"Oh yes," Geryss agreed. "You could hunt him down anywhere with that, sure as eggs."

Siyon blinked. "Me?"

But before Geryss could say any more, a hollow, demanding boom shattered the stillness of the house. Something downstairs, something heavy, something thudding against the front door of the building. Once, and twice, and then on the third stroke there was a crash and a splinter.

Clamour from below. Shouts and drumming feet and the shattering of glass. A powerful voice rising above all of it: "This is the inquisitors! Stand where you are!"

Across the table, Geryss Hanlun started to laugh, lolling back in her chair.

The voices from the library rose into shouts—*Get him out of here; This is an outrage; Get your hands off me*—and Siyon lurched to his feet. He had to get out of here. They'd poisoned Othissa after the last raid of the Summer Club. He wouldn't be getting off on surety this time.

A bony hand closed around his wrist; Siyon tugged against Geryss's surprisingly firm grip. "There's a back entrance," he gasped.

"You don't think they've come that way too?" she challenged. "They'll be playing for keeps, this time, and doing it right." She stood up, still holding his wrist, and dragged him down an aisle between shadowed bookshelves. The wall at the end had a window, and she hauled at the latch. "But they don't think *up*."

She shoved the window smoothly open on oiled hinges. The night air poured in, crisp and laden with ruckus—shouts and another wooden crash. There were stomping feet on the stairs, climbing heavily.

"What sort of bravi are you?" Geryss demanded, and jerked her head toward the window. "Get out."

The steep tiles of this part of the city rarely saw the race and clatter of the tribes, but they were clean and well maintained, giving good purchase to the soles of Siyon's boots as he swung a leg out over the windowsill. Almost easier climbing than the Hisarani rooftop.

Siyon hesitated, half in and half out. "What about you?"

Geryss laughed. "My tile-tripping days are done. And I've got my own ways out of this. Out of all of it."

"No," Siyon gasped. "Wait. Auntie, they're *killing* people. Othissa—"

"Was a foolish girl," Geryss said harshly, and her mouth twisted. "Poor thing, but she was. I'm cannier. *You're* cannier. And you need to be." She laid a hand on his shoulder. "You need to stay free. You need to use that ring and the promise made to you. You need to make your turn count."

"I will," Siyon promised, the weight of it settling on him like a tangible thing.

"Good." Geryss smiled, grim and satisfied. "Now fuck off."

She shoved him out, and hauled the window closed while he was still teetering. Siyon grabbed at the edge of it, just caught it enough to stop it slamming closed, enough to stop himself going over backward.

Behind the glass, Geryss was already gone, just a shadow flitting between the dark shelves. Those booted feet sounded closer still, and light slanted across the library. "Hold there!"

Siyon ducked down on the tiles beneath the window, still open a crack. He braced hands beneath the sill and prayed to the dark to keep him hidden.

Inside, Geryss Hanlun said, "Hah, come yourself to see us all brought to justice?"

"Come to make sure," another voice replied. It was cool and calm and collected, a woman with no need to rush, and yet a tight-wound tension coiled in the azatani clip of her consonants. A voice Siyon recognised, though he couldn't think where from. "There are many who would invoke my name and wriggle out."

Geryss laughed. "What, me? You've made it perfectly clear those days are behind us, Syrah."

Siyon gaped in the darkness. Syrah *Danelani*?

Inside the library, the prefect herself said, "Actually, I mean him down there." Down there? Oh, of course, on the library floor: Nihath Joddani, alchemist prince of the Avenues.

So much for the privilege of the azatani. They were all fucked together.

"I thought you'd already fled the city," Syrah Danelani said. "It would be better if you had. If you did, right now. I am grateful, Geryss, for all you've done. For all you've tried to do. But I cannot let this stand."

"'Course you can't." Geryss sounded tired. "If a mother can't even keep her son, how can she keep her city?"

Not silence then, but no more speaking. The tramp of feet, the rattle of books in their cases, the skew and leer of shifting shadows and hand-carried lanterns against the window. Below, in the yard, the to and fro of inquisitors never quietened. Siyon couldn't see them from where he crouched below the window; they couldn't see him either.

He could try to clamber up the drainpipe, onto the upper roof, over the crest…but who knew what was over there, and all it would take was one body below looking up. No, all things considered, Siyon stayed put. At least the planes had settled down, but it was cold and cramped, as the stars wheeled and the Summer Club was scoured. The people trickled away in twos and threes, practitioners escorted away to the Palace of Justice, in their azatani finery, with their azatani protests unheeded.

The night stretched toward a new dawn, creeping grey and bleak over the sea, as the front door of the Summer Club slammed shut for the last time.

CHAPTER 17

Anahid prepared carefully for her foray into the Flower district. She studied a map of the Houses that Nura had confiscated from one of the footmen and noted those Zagiri suggested she avoid. She even dressed modestly, determined to avoid being mistaken for a Flower herself.

She realised how ridiculous that fear was with her first step through the hedged archway into the District. The Flowers who wandered the street—on the arms of patrons, or on their own business—were sumptuous and decadent beyond anything even the most decorated azata would try. *Flower* was quite the right word; the elegant entertainers of the District were brightly coloured, beautifully perfumed, and gathered in dizzying bunches designed to turn heads and win interest. Anahid dragged her eyes away from a young man with crushed flicker-beetles lining his pale and pretty eyes, whose loose shirt slipped off one pale shoulder.

The streets outside had been quiet, as the curfew laid its smothering blanket over the city, but here within the fragrant hedges, the Flower district laughed merrily at the idea that the night could be vetoed. There had been inquisitors at the entrance, but they hadn't been at all interested in stopping people going *in*.

Inside the Flower district, wide streets wound between little blocks of shops and arcades—selling everything from sweets to fortunes to indulgences Anahid could hardly begin to imagine—and the larger, walled compounds of the Houses themselves. Each was different, this one fronted by balconies in the style of the southern Republic, that one tiered with verdant plants and cascades of water splashing down around a statue of a mermaid winking salaciously.

All of them with doors open wide upon their merriments—loud with music, laughter, conversation, the clack of gaming tiles.

But Anahid wasn't here to be distracted by fire-breathers, or musical fountains, or a square housing a massive nardi board, populated by giggling people instead of counters. Anahid kept her memory of the map firmly in mind, and her hands folded against her waist sash.

She bypassed Sable House, which looked rather unnervingly like a squat fortress, even with its massive jet-inlaid double doors thrown open. The House of Gossamer was more inviting, with pale curtains wafting from the arched entrances in its golden sandstone facade. Inside, layers of diaphanous fabric shrouded the ceiling, draping over the tables in the main gaming hall.

There were so many tables. So many games in play. As Anahid hesitated, she was approached by a woman who introduced herself as the gaming floor mistress. She easily ushered Anahid through signing the House's buy-in ledger to receive an account token, and then escorted her to the back of the hall, where there were three round tables for carrick.

One was empty—no dealer and no play—and another was crowded with students from the university involved in more shouting and drinking than actual playing. Anahid slipped into a vacant chair at the third, between the two existing players, and passed her account token to the dealer, to receive a stack of play tokens in return.

They didn't play for money on the table, the gaming mistress had explained, but settled accounts at the end. As Anahid turned the lacquered tokens over in her fingers, she thought this might make it very easy to lose a great deal of money without noticing.

But she didn't intend to lose at all. She would be careful.

Anahid started cautiously, as she had at the party game with Tahera and the others. She kept her additions to the central golden circle to the minimum required and used the first few hands to consider her fellow players. One was a merchant captain, or a retired one, with a battered tricorn atop his head and large stacks of tokens in front of him; he lifted his mug of drink to her in a welcoming toast. The other player, who had the neat and unremarkable air of a prosperous clerk, ignored her entirely, eyes fixed on the cards at all times.

After a few hands, the merchant captain drained his mug, swept his remaining tokens into his tricorn, and left the table without a word. Anahid shifted in frustration—she had just determined the way he turned a token between his knuckles when he was taking a risk, and two players was hardly an interesting game. But very quickly they were joined by a pair of ladies dressed bright as parrots in the wide necklines and wider skirts of the Republic. They chattered constantly to each other in some dialect that Anahid could almost but not quite understand, and they played just as fast and loud, buying extravagantly, bluffing outrageously, and glaring through darkened lashes when she edged them out on a close-fought hand.

One snapped her fingers, and when a waiter popped up at her elbow, declared, "Another glass of what we're having for our new enemy."

That was almost flattering, and the glass turned out to be Northern bluewine so pale it barely seemed to be there at all. Anahid sipped it to be polite, and then again when it turned out to be fierce and cold and quite refreshing. The Republic pair toasted her with their glasses, and they returned to play.

Anahid was halfway through the glass, and her pile of tokens had grown a little more, when a new arrival took the seat next to her. Her honey-dark hair was braided around her head and strung with glittering beads, and her pale blue gown had the gauzy shawl collar of the southern Republic. She exchanged familiar greetings with the parrot-ladies, and lifted her own glass (of something a deep ruby-red) before turning to Anahid.

"The Vidama Yilma-Torquera Selsan de Kith," she declared. "Selsan, please, or call me Sel. All my friends do, and I'm quite sure you and I are going to be friends."

Anahid had been assured so in drawing rooms before, and it had never turned out to be the case. "Anahid Joddani," she returned nevertheless, and touched her glass against the other woman's. "But I'm here for the cards, rather than friends."

Selsan's smile widened. "And that is exactly why. Yes, darling, please buy me in for the usual," she added to the dealer, who as far as Anahid could tell hadn't even asked. He did bring out a stack of tokens, however.

The Vidama, Anahid noticed, didn't have to produce an account token for them.

Within three hands, it became apparent she was also a fiendishly good player. She chattered the entire time—sometimes to her countrywomen in a variety of dialects, sometimes to Anahid, sometimes only to herself, about the weather, about the curfew, about the drinks, about her hair. But as careless as her tossing about of tokens seemed, every time she bought, she earned back, and every time Anahid thought she had a hand capable of carrying a big win, the Vidama casually edged out of the game leaving very few tokens behind.

It was infuriating, in the most invigorating way possible.

"Darling," the Vidama laughed, when Anahid finally managed to lay down a better hand than hers. "Have you been hiding in the Avenues all this time? It's so delicious to have an unexpectedly good game."

Anahid knew just what she meant. "I only learned to play recently," Anahid admitted, as the dealer gathered up the cards again and shuffled. "With a new friend. I was hoping she'd come down with me, but she seems reluctant to do so."

"You must bring her along next time!" the Vidama declared. "Now that you've seen we don't bite."

"I wouldn't have thought Tahera one to be scared," Anahid said, watching the cards come out again. It was strange, really, that Tahera—who'd been so casually dismissive of society's strictures—had been so harsh about this.

"Tahera?" Vidama Selsan repeated, and set down her glass. "Tahera *Danelani*? I imagine she would be reluctant to come down, considering I think she still owes money to half the Houses."

"She—" Anahid realised she was gaping, and closed her mouth. "She has debts?"

"Old now." The Vidama picked up her cards, frowned at them in that way that Anahid hadn't yet figured out the significance of. "This would be, oh, two years ago? She was in *such* a pickle, but then she disappeared. Did her husband get sent overseas? Anyway." Selsan shrugged a shoulder. "Are you playing this hand?"

Anahid was still reeling from the news of Tahera's debts. For the azatani of Bezim, born to cut deals and arrange trade, debt and the poor judgment that it denoted was quite the scandal. *Unpaid* debt could ruin a reputation entirely, let alone owed for such a reason. How much did Tahera owe, that she fled rather than pay?

"Za?" the dealer prompted, and Anahid fumbled a token into the golden circle. She surveyed her cards with barely half her attention. No wonder Tahera wanted so vehemently to keep her play in the Avenues. She could hardly show her face down here, and she wouldn't want anyone to know about this.

Now Anahid did. Not that she cared, personally. She knew about making mistakes. She knew about things you'd rather hide from than face. She understood.

Anahid stumbled through the hand, and then the clerk—who Anahid had half forgotten about, so unremarkable was his play—took his depleted stack of tokens and left the table with a murmured, "Ladies, azata."

The Captain took his seat, looking just as romantically piratical as he had when Anahid had met him at Tahera's game at the party. Tonight his extravagant coat was bottle-green and decorated with pearls. "There you are," he said to Vidama Selsan, huffy and aggrieved. "I thought we were meeting at the Ember." His gaze flicked to Anahid, and then came back with a blink. "The azata's decided to play seriously after all."

"You know Anahid Joddani?" The Vidama sounded delighted about it. "Maybe we can all go on to the Ember, then."

But the Captain was frowning now. "Joddani," he repeated. "Any relation to the bloke the inqs wheeled unconscious out of the Summer Club earlier?"

Anahid gaped at him. "What?"

"The Summer Club!" Selsan trilled. "This sounds positively lurid. What has happened?"

"They've raided the place. Shut it down, I heard. Not before time." The Captain answered Selsan's questions still frowning at Anahid, like he could hear the ringing that had started in her ears. "Here, you aren't going to faint, are you? Don't have the temperament for a proper game?"

"Oh shut up," Selsan told him. "She'd been steadily fleecing Torbeld until he ran away."

The Captain snorted. "*Anyone* can fleece Torbeld, he's got the imagination of—"

Anahid lurched up from the table. They all stared at her—as they should, unaccountably rude, but she couldn't find more words than, "I have to—" before her tongue stuck itself to the dry roof of her mouth.

Wheeled unconscious out of the Summer Club.

She'd known Nihath was going there tonight. He had some very significant thing to do that she hadn't paid the least attention to, because she'd been more focused on *her* plans for the evening.

Anahid shoved through the crowd, grown ever more thick and merry in the time she'd been playing, unaware of the world turning upside down. She pushed out of the House, into the cooler air of the street, and then stood there gasping.

The Captain had known her name. If she gave it to the inquisitors at the gate, to let her out into the curfew night with her azatani authority... would they arrest her too? What had Nihath pulled down upon them?

"Anahid!" the Vidama Selsan came striding out of the House of Gossamer behind her. She caught at Anahid's wrist, dropping a white velvet pouch onto her palm with a liquid clink of hard currency. "Your winnings. And I took the liberty of calling a House palanquin for you. Here it comes now. Quicker and far less bother, you'll see."

Here it came, draped in pale curtains and carried by burly young men. It would be quicker, and get her past the inquisitors. But Polinna Andani would gossip for days.

If only that turned out to be the worst consequence of tonight.

"Thank you, Vidama," Anahid said, closing her hand around the velvet pouch.

Selsan helped Anahid into the palanquin. "I told you, call me Sel. We're certainly going to be friends. Next time, you should join me and my other friends in the back room at the Banked Ember."

Anahid stared at her, at her knowing smile, at the card she held out. As the palanquin lurched into motion, she grabbed the card, and the Vidama gave her a little wave before tucking her hand into the Captain's elbow as they strolled away.

The card was perfectly plain, just one of the Vidama Selsan's calling cards. As though her name alone was enough to open doors Anahid hadn't even realised existed.

She tucked it carefully into her sash, held snug against her middle. It did nothing to still the turmoil in her stomach, a roil of anger and fear and guilt. She might never get the chance to come back. Nihath had been carried unconscious from the Summer Club by the inquisitors. Her beautiful night had been turned upside down, and possibly her life as well.

There's a thing on tonight, Zagiri had told her sister, like it was bravi business as usual. Not at all like Little Bracken were smuggling two dozen alchemists and family across the upper city, to a secret exit in the wall.

It was a good night for it. Out to sea, thunder grumbled like someone's maiden aunt, but over the city the sky was clear, beaded with stars, and the moon was nearing full. Enough light to see by. Enough light to be seen by.

They'd split the alchemists up into smaller groups—twos or threes or even fours if there were children. There were, in some of the groups, and those parties were staying on the ground, creeping through alleyways, guided by rooftop scouts keeping their whistled signals as low as possible.

Nervous business, this. On the ground, on the rooftops. Zagiri had never bothered before about how much noise she made racing from roof to roof. But now, none of them knew whether they'd earn the usual shouts about interrupted sleep, or someone calling for the inqs.

And that was before the two alchemists Zagiri was escorting had stumbled and slipped, nearly falling off the roof altogether before Zagiri had lunged forward and grabbed them, hauling them into the lee of a chimney.

The big guy—Ingermann—recovered first, shaking his shaggy blond head. He was pale as a ghost in the moonlight, but he'd started out that way, with his Northern white skin and grey eyes. He braced a hand against the chimney and pinched at the bridge of his nose.

"What the fuck was that?" Zagiri demanded, in what she thought was a very reasonable tone for the circumstances.

"Didn't you *feel* it?" Melis snapped.

She'd been short from the moment she arrived in the Chapel, and as much as Zagiri sympathised with the stress of having to leave your entire life behind and flee, she could do with a bit less directed at *her* when she was just trying to help.

"The planes," Ingermann said. A wince flickered across his face—both he and Melis swayed in unison.

The hair prickled at the back of Zagiri's neck. She couldn't feel a *thing*, and it was more than a little unnerving.

"It's steadying," Melis stated, pushing herself toward standing. "Let's keep moving."

"Let's wait one bloody moment," Zagiri countered. Maybe it was steadying, but Melis still looked wobbly in the knees. "I don't want to be halfway across a bridge when you pair come over all weird. Sit. Wait. We have time."

The lack of argument was all the confirmation Zagiri needed. The pair had seemed spry enough earlier, and they'd made good time from the Chapel to here. They did have time to wait.

Zagiri stepped out from behind the chimney to take a quick look around—the rooftops were clear. The bridge was still in place; a board hooked into this roof's gutter, spanning the street to the building opposite. Zagiri leaned over enough to see the street far below. It was entirely quiet. Now might be a good time to cross, if she could be sure they'd all make it.

Better to wait.

When she looked back, Melis had recovered enough to be frowning at her. "What are you even doing out here, za? Risking your neck for us?"

Ingermann responded before Zagiri could. "Didn't you hear, Mel? This one got Corbinus out in the first place. This was all her idea."

"Not all of it," Zagiri said. From there to here, she'd been running just fast enough to keep ahead of it all. "I'm trying to help."

Melis gave her a look, too brief for Zagiri to interpret before she turned to Ingermann. "Where are you going, anyway? Back north?"

"Doubt my name's off the cull list," he replied. "I thought maybe taking ship from one of the free cities, see if I can't find a place in the Republic needs a regular smith."

Melis snorted. "Boring work, with no alchemy."

"Boring's better than dead," Ingermann said. "What about you?"

Zagiri let their quiet words fade out of her attention as she frowned down at the street again. It was still absolutely empty. Where were the inqs? Sure, this was a quiet neighbourhood, tucked down between the university and the wall, but there had still been patrols when these routes were scouted last night.

A whistle floated over the rooftops behind them—*Runner incoming*—and Zagiri stepped up the roof's pitch to wave him in. He came bent low, down behind the spine of the roof, and paused only long enough to gasp his message.

"All clear on the ground," he panted. "Inqs raiding the Summer Club in force and not patrolling."

He turned away, but Zagiri gasped, "Wait! What? The Summer Club? But—"

The runner shook his head. "That's all I know."

He ran on, over the road bridge, whistling again as he went. Another figure popped up from a roof further on, waving for him.

Melis said, "So much for the dispensation of the Summer Club." She didn't sound smug so much as weary.

Zagiri's head was spinning, as it never did no matter how high off the street she was. Raiding the Summer Club in force. Nihath would be there—of course he would, he *always* was, always leaving her sister behind. Zagiri didn't like him, but she didn't want him dragged away to the Palace of Justice either.

"You think what we felt was something happening?" Ingermann asked.

"I think if they're there," Melis responded, "then they aren't here."

They weren't. *All clear on the ground*, the runner had said. Zagiri could leave this pair to follow the route by themselves. If she sprinted, cut through the university grounds, it wouldn't take her that long to get to the Summer Club and—

And do what?

Zagiri blinked the moonlight away. "Come on, let's move. Over the walkway, one at a time. Go carefully, just in case."

They went, Melis and then Ingermann edging along gingerly. Zagiri took them down the first easy way she could find, and did the rest of the trip on the ground, slinking through shadow for all they neither saw nor heard sign of anyone else out tonight.

Until they turned the corner to the little square, in the shadow of the looming city wall. The teahouse was nestled against the base of the wall, and another trio was just slipping in through the open front door, their bravi escort melting away into the night again.

Zagiri held them at the corner for a moment, in one last apparently unnecessary bout of caution. Her skin nearly itched with the anticlimax of this night's work, or perhaps with the need to be racing uselessly across the city.

"Twitchy, aren't you?" Melis remarked, and Zagiri stilled her fidgeting fingers on the basketwork of her sabre hilt.

"Know someone at the Summer Club?" Ingermann asked.

Zagiri shot him a look; his eyes were too sympathetic. Saw too much. "Nihath Joddani," she admitted.

"Oh." Both of them stilled; clearly they knew him. Of course they did. *Everyone* knew that Nihath Joddani was an alchemist.

Even if he wasn't at the club tonight—by some strange and

unlikely coincidence—he would surely be arrested regardless. If they were raiding the club again, closing the negotiated loophole that had allowed it to operate, then there would be no safety elsewhere.

If they raided the Joddani house as well, would they find Siyon this time?

Zagiri swallowed. "Turns out we're all at the mercy of the powerful."

Even if she could be one of those powerful, she wasn't yet. There was nothing she could do tonight. She couldn't save her brother-in-law.

But she could save this pair. She jerked her chin toward the teahouse. "Go on, get out of here."

Ingermann tipped her a nod and loped across the little square, a strange silver figure slipping between moonlight and shadow.

Melis hesitated, and said, "Thanks," before she followed him.

Zagiri waited a moment longer, making sure no one had seen them, no cry had gone up, no feet were running to fetch trouble down on all their heads.

But the night was still as the stars, save the rumble of thunder out over the sea. A storm far away, threatening ruin to others.

Zagiri turned on her heel, and ran.

She couldn't save her brother-in-law, but there was still Anahid, and Siyon, and other ways she could help. She would do what she could, try to help, until she couldn't anymore.

It wasn't a long way from the possibly former Summer Club to the Joddani townhouse. In the low, grey light of dawn, scuttling from one piece of cover to the next, it took Siyon a lot longer than it had going the other way, walking open and proud in a procession of azatani.

There were a lot of inquisitors out and about, but they were on business, rather than patrolling. They were even in the Avenues, hurrying beneath the hushed overhanging trees. The townhouses still had their curtains closed, silent and aghast as someone's scandalised aunt. No grey tunics in the alleyways, though, and Siyon slunk along them like a cat until he could let himself in through the back gate of the Joddani townhouse.

He sagged against the gate in relief until the shadows of the back door said, "Where is he?"

Siyon clapped a hand over his smothered yelp. Anahid stepped out of the shadows. She was tall and pale and grim in the silver light, still dressed in a plain gown, though her unscarved hair was braided down over one shoulder. Her face was hard as stone.

"Where *is* he?" she demanded. "What has happened?"

Siyon barely knew where to start. "The working failed. He didn't become the Alchemist—"

She gestured sharply, dismissively. "I don't *care* about your stupid *Art*." It was a horrible word in her mouth, callous and meaningless. "I came rushing home to find the house crawling with inquisitors, that Xhanari so *polite* as he went through everything..." She trailed off, her mouth a hard line. "What has *happened*?"

Siyon wished there was someone else to tell her this news. Guilt chewed at his stomach, which was stupid, because *he* hadn't made Nihath Joddani stand up and try to become the bloody Power of the Mundane. But he'd come here, wanted and dogged by the inquisitors, and Anahid Joddani had taken him in, protected him, sheltered him.

And now her shelter and protection had been torn down.

"They raided the Summer Club," Siyon told her. "A lot of arrests. Including Nihath." Maybe including Geryss, or maybe not.

"I know *that*." Anahid's jaw tightened. "Xhanari said something about massive planar shifts. Nihath's fault?"

Siyon could just nod, though there was something in there that plucked at his attention.

Anahid was still talking, as though she was forming plans even now. "But a lot of arrests...there'll be outcry. The prefect will—"

Siyon had to interrupt. "The prefect was there."

Anahid's breath caught. But a moment later, she drew herself up again. "Right," she declared, and marched into the house.

Siyon was pulled in her wake like a minnow shadowing a shark, his mind churning. There was something she'd said, about Xhanari...

The servants' hall was already bustling. When Anahid swept in, everyone paused to bob their courtesies, though the juniors all immediately went back to work.

Anahid beckoned, and the housekeeper and chief footman hurried over. "The master has been arrested for sorcery," she said, succinctly and quietly.

Not quietly enough; one of the kitchen girls squeaked and dropped a basin that shattered on the flags.

The footman didn't blink at the noise, too busy looking sour. "Suspected as much after the raid."

Anahid nodded. "Let's assume they'll be back. I want this house innocent as a lamb. Every book they didn't take gone from the library—" She turned to Nura. "Every herb not for common use gone from the still room. And we'll need to hide him somewhere too."

Siyon realised she meant him. "What? No. I'll clear out. You've risked enough." *Make your turn count*, Geryss had ordered him, but Siyon couldn't from a prison cell, and if the azatani were fair game now, he was no safer here than anywhere else. Maybe Daruj could still get him out of the city.

But where did that leave his promise to delve for Enkin?

"Nonsense," Anahid dropped into his thoughts. She was glaring at him; Nura looked like he'd said something uncouth. "You are our guest."

"I'm a liability," Siyon retorted; only the truth. "If Xhanari finds me here—wait." Xhanari. What Anahid had said earlier. Massive planar shifts. "How did they know what Nihath was doing?"

Siyon had assumed the timing was just unfortunate, that the inqs had been planning to raid the Summer Club anyway. But if they'd *felt* that juddering of the planes, the thing he'd thought only practitioners could feel...

"They have some way of sensing major acts of alchemy." Maybe another function of the dowsing rods, maybe something else they hadn't advertised. It made sense of so many things; how they'd shown up at the Club in the wake of Enkin's disappearance, or here after Siyon had caused the flare in the parlour.

Anahid's mouth was pressed thin; she'd put all that together as well.

Another voice called from the corridor, "Mistress!"

Her sigh was sharp as a kettle on the boil. "What *now*?"

Izmirlian Hisarani, standing just inside the back door, in full if somewhat disarranged evening dress. He looked like the most delicious distraction Siyon absolutely didn't need right now. He came down the hall, holding up the crisp white scrap of a calling card, of all things.

"Azatan Hisarani," Anahid said, exasperation biting into the edges of her politeness. "My compliments to your family, as always, but I cannot represent strongly enough that now is an inopportune time for visiting." She plucked the card from his hand, held it steady to read, and then spat a word that Siyon hadn't realised she knew. The look she turned on Siyon was out the other side of anger, into a weariness deep as the ravine beneath the Swanneck. "What have you done?"

Siyon took the card, so fine it had a satin sheen beneath his fingertips. Izmirlian's name and address on one side, and on the other, a handwritten message: *Voice gone. Thought I'd best come at once.*

Gone had been underlined.

"What do you mean—?" Siyon asked, but the moment he looked up, gaze meeting Izmirlian's, he realised. Voice gone. Not scratched away by illness or the excesses of a very long night. Gone by alchemy. Trapped in a bubble of hammer-rock and seagrass and ichor.

Siyon had done this. His alchemy had worked beyond his wildest imaginings.

Izmirlian was smiling. Just the slightest hook of the corner of his mouth, but it was there. His voice snatched by alchemy—gone. No more sly remarks, or biting comments, or his voice around Siyon's name. The first pang in Siyon's chest felt like horror; he hadn't expected this.

But Izmirlian was smiling. Because the alchemy was working. Siyon should be jubilant.

He started laughing, helplessly and bitterly. Izmirlian gave him a quizzical look. "They'd have to let me into the Summer Club," Siyon said, "if there were still a club to be admitted into. They've all been dragged off by the inquisitors."

Izmirlian's mouth fell open, but no sound of surprise came out. *Voice gone.*

"Fix it," Anahid said, urgent at Siyon's shoulder. She held up a hand to forestall an interruption Izmirlian could hardly make, though he shook his head vehemently. "No, I don't care. This is *not* the time. If we get through this you can scatter yourself to the planar winds, for all I care, but *not now.*"

She was right, she was so *very* right. Siyon turned over the card in his fingers, its quality just another reminder of the towering weight that the Hisarani family could bring down upon *him* if he sent their son back to them marred by alchemy. When the inquisitors were on a rampage already. When they wanted *him* already.

Because of Enkin Danelani.

Who Siyon had promised to delve for. Who Auntie Geryss thought *he* might be able to find. And if he could...

Save the boy, save the alchemists, save himself. Win the gratitude of the prefect, put the inquisitors back in their box, get Nihath back... and then *he* could figure out the rest of it.

Siyon looked up. "I might be able to find Enkin Danelani," he said, trying the words out loud.

"What?" Anahid snapped, and Izmirlian's blink of surprise echoed hers. "Where is he?"

"The Abyss, I think. Maybe. But I have his ring. And I should be able to—to delve for him..." Siyon didn't know *how*, but he could figure it out. Right?

"*Should.*" Anahid sounded on the verge of an explosion, a thin crack of something—anger, stress, outrage—running through her voice. "Now is hardly the time to be trying wild experiments."

Especially if the inquisitors might feel him doing it. "They're going to poison Nihath," he pointed out, even though it made her flinch. Like they'd already poisoned Othissa. "They're going to keep coming. Unless we can get Enkin back."

Not to mention the planar imbalance, but that seemed a problem for a future Siyon would consider himself lucky to see right now. Siyon glanced to Izmirlian—Izmirlian who was a walking, mute reminder that Siyon *could* achieve his alchemical ends, but also a reminder that there might be unexpected repercussions.

"One try," he said. "Let me have one attempt. Today, while you could still claim to the inquisitors you found something of Nihath's, if anything happens."

Anahid looked torn to pieces, on the verge of tears, and Siyon wished he could have saved her from all this somehow. But it was her life too, and when she took a sharp breath, it stiffened her spine again, and lifted her chin. "One try," she stated, lifting a stern finger. "Somewhere out of the way, up in the attics perhaps. Take him with you." The finger swung to Izmirlian, who looked startled by it. "Yes, you. Don't pretend like your mother will miss you for a day or three. It will hardly be the first time Izmirlian Hisarani has run off with a lover for a while."

Izmirlian just tilted his head in rueful acknowledgment even as Siyon coughed. "We're not—"

"I don't care," Anahid declared. "And, fortunately for you, neither will anyone else. Nura will show you the way."

The housekeeper was waiting, and Izmirlian gave her a little bow. But Siyon hesitated to say: "I'm so sorry about all this."

She gave him a tight and brittle smile. "You know where I was earlier? In the Flower district, at a carrick table, winning a small fortune at an absolutely thrilling game. Perhaps even..." She trailed off, laying a hand against the sash that bound her gown at the waist. "I've finally seen a life I might actually want, and it's all crashing down."

Siyon knew the feeling.

CHAPTER 18

The attics were reached by the staircase behind the portrait of the first prefect, where Siyon had hidden with Tehroun when the inquisitors came knocking after Siyon's Aethyreal flare. Izmirlian pulled a face at the painting, and Siyon remembered it was one of his ancestors. "They're following you," he quipped, and got a stern look from Nura, but a bright sidelong smile from Izmirlian, so that was all right.

The staircase was still dark and narrow, but it led to a perfectly normal corridor lined with perfectly normal doors. The rooms beyond were smaller than the others down lower in the house, and the few that were furnished had narrow beds, simple tables, plain dressers.

Siyon preferred them. Felt like places he could actually live, rather than just pass through at high speed and on sufferance.

All the material from the workroom needed bringing up, and the repetitive trudge gave Siyon ample time to think through how he might find Enkin. Bringing him back was the bigger problem, and he only had one shot.

He wished it wasn't the Abyss; he hated delving that plane at the best of times. He wished his last attempt at delving had actually *worked*. What if the Abyss was broken too? What if he had the ring, but couldn't even step through the gate?

He was more than a little edgy by the time Zagiri showed up, carrying the last of the equipment. She greeted him with, "Anahid says you're going to try something stupid."

Siyon fixed her with a glare. "And what were you doing last night? Smuggling more alchemists out of the city?"

With her eyes that wide and innocent, she looked like the ingénue in a lower-city burlesque. "If we were, wouldn't it have been convenient when all the inqs decided to go visit the Summer Club?"

Siyon snorted, then felt guilty about laughing in Nihath Joddani's house about his arrest. From her wince, Zagiri did too.

"Came up here, after I heard," Zagiri added, as they kept carrying. "Went to the Palace, but nobody would tell me anything, not even the clerk who usually flirts with me. And when I got here, the inqs wouldn't even let me in the house, though I could hear Ana shouting at them from the street. Never heard her that angry."

Siyon thought of how she'd greeted him in the back courtyard. Maybe anger. Maybe fear. Maybe two sides of the one coin.

He tugged Anahid aside as the last things were brought upstairs. "If there's something else you should be doing—" he started.

"There's nothing," she interjected, quick and clipped. Her hands kept clutching at the waist of her dress. "What, should I try to get support from people who wouldn't receive me anyway, and who could do nothing to save my husband when he called an audience to witness his sorcery?" She took a deep breath. "I need you to do this, Siyon. Let me help."

So she joined him and Zagiri in one of the attic rooms that now contained the bath Siyon had helped to bring up. Thankfully, he didn't need much water in it, and it certainly didn't need to be hot.

Izmirlian loitered with a notebook and pencil that Nura had given him so that he could convey information with something other than extremely expressive eyebrows. There hadn't been a chance to talk— well, communicate—with him privately. No chance since Siyon had left the Hisarani house the other night. Not that Siyon was entirely sure what he'd say. *That kiss was nice. That kiss was a mistake. Sorry about your voice. Sorry you're broken. Are you sure this is what you want?*

Probably best not to try. Better to concentrate on what he was trying to achieve *here*. Just a delve. Just a really special delve.

"If you're doing this," Zagiri declared, "I'm holding the tether. No getting my sister skewered by a flaming angel sword."

"I'm going to the Abyss, not Empyre," Siyon pointed out, trying to get his angles right. Triangles were easier than squares, but he was trying to draw this one *around* the bathtub, and that was challenging. "Can I borrow your pencil, Izmirlian?"

Zagiri snorted. "Yes, assault by demon will be so much less unsettling than assault by angel."

But she helped mark the points, and held the pot of fish-stinking ink as Siyon painted the triangle onto the floorboards. The Abyssal plane wasn't as strict as the Empyreal, but it liked a certain *feel* to the gateway. Siyon tried to make his brushstrokes free, careless, and confident all at once. The Abyss liked fakery almost more than sincerity.

Thinking about all that was easier than thinking about where he was going. It'd be bad enough without anticipating it.

Siyon was superstitiously reluctant to try the kitchen twine again as a tether, after the failed Empyreal delve. Nura produced an old bedsheet that she said was unwanted, though she still winced when Siyon tore it into strips. He tied them together firmly, giving himself lots of length to go . . . well, who knew how far.

Zagiri took the end of it with a resigned sigh. "Call and I'll haul, I guess."

"You're a peach," Siyon told her, and climbed carefully up onto the rim of the bathtub, straddling the few inches of cold, salted water. He fished the signet ring from his pocket and let it sit on his palm, heavy and square and, honestly, ugly.

A breath in. A breath out. Focus. Feel. He could do this. Geryss believed he could. Forget about the Abyss. Concentrate on Enkin Danelani. Gaudy, haughty, imperious, dropping this ring into Siyon's palm with a promise. A binding thing, a promise.

"Find your master," he suggested to the ring.

And was entirely unprepared when it *leapt* off his hand. Siyon yelped and lost his footing. Izmirlian lunged forward, reaching to catch the ring even as Siyon did. The world stretched for a moment—Zagiri swearing; Anahid starting forward from the door—and then Izmirlian's hand scooped under the falling ring just as Siyon's swooped down to close over it—and Izmirlian's fingers—from above.

Siyon kept falling, pulling Izmirlian with him, and landed *splash* in the bath.

Except he didn't land. He hit the water, and plunged in, Izmirlian with him, hands tangled together around the ring, as brackish sea closed over their heads and they sank like stones.

Panic snapped its jaws around Siyon. He twisted against rough sackcloth, clinging wet and choking to his face, thrashed against the rope binding his wrists—

But his hands were free, tangled up with other fingers. Izmirlian's grip tightened, yanked at his arm, pulled Siyon out of memory.

Just the Abyss, swallowing them whole. Like falling down a well. Like tangling with a new lover, salty and desperate. Like slogging through mangrove mud under a midday sun. They sank, into storm and sulphur, with reality sloshing around them. Siyon fought for a moment against the urge to breathe, the panic as to what would rush into his lungs. Willed himself calm.

Izmirlian clawed at his arm, hair billowing like ink in water as he shook his frantic head. Siyon grabbed for him, twisted and spun them both. "It's not real," he said, which wasn't quite true. Nor was, "It can't hurt you. Don't believe what you feel."

"Get me out of here!" Izmirlian demanded, and his eyes popped wide, his struggles stopping. "I can speak."

Siyon waved a hand; the movement was sluggish, and the atmosphere clung iridescent to his skin. He hated it here, but it *was* beautiful. "You aren't speaking, because this isn't air."

It had done the trick; curiosity was a far stronger pull on Izmirlian's attention. (Unsurprising; it was enough to pull him from his entire life.) Their feet touched down upon solid ground—or near enough—and he looked around, at the purpling grass wafting around their knees, at the massed spongy growth rising behind them, at the long fronds of kelp that swayed around it like a forest.

Izmirlian tilted back, looking straight up, and his mouth fell open. His grip on Siyon's arm loosened, and Siyon lunged forward, wrapped an arm around Izmirlian's waist, hauled him closer. "Don't look up," he ordered, and pulled Izmirlian's face into his neck.

Izmirlian shuddered. "There's no sky," he said, lips against Siyon's skin sending a shiver along his spine. "There's just—"

"The Abyss," Siyon provided, voice rough. Infinite black, ever deeper the longer you looked. You could fall forever. Perhaps you even would. "Don't look up, and don't let go of me. I'm the one who's tethered. You shouldn't be here at all. We should send you back."

But could they? Siyon would have to step back with him, and could they do this again? Did Siyon have enough paint, enough balance, enough time to make another delving? Would Anahid allow it? Would the inqs have felt this one, and already be on their way?

Get in, load up, get out. More true now than ever. He had one chance at this.

"Don't let go," Izmirlian repeated, rolling the words around his tongue, and then that tongue was flat against Siyon's throat. The stripe it left was both cold and hot in the not-air, and Siyon gasped— and Izmirlian *growled*—and all he could think of, crowded in his mind, was the twist of limbs and the press of hands, how soft the grass would be, how it would cling to sweat-slick skin like hair, how Izmirlian could make all the noise he wanted here, how they could—

"We have," Siyon gasped, getting a hand tangled in Izmirlian's curls, but only remembering after a moment that he wanted to pull him away. "We have work to do."

Izmirlian staggered back a step—Siyon kept hold of his wrist, nearly undone anew by the twist of the bones under his grip, by the glaze that Izmirlian had to blink—twice, thrice—to clear. His mouth quirked. "The poets are right. Natural habitat of vice and distraction."

"It's—" Siyon cleared his throat. "It's easy to get overly influenced."

He forced himself to look around. The sky pulsed blackest black above them. A reef of coral curved around the horizon, all pinks and oranges and the glimmer and dart of hidden little fish (or something, at least). Closer to hand, a school of silver fish-things flitted among a waving forest of red-edged kelp, twice as tall as Siyon or more.

"Oh." Siyon stepped closer, looking at the opalescent shine on the undulating fronds. "Infernal kelp. While we're here, perhaps I could—"

A shriek carved serrated through the gelatinous atmosphere, and the kelp thrashed; Siyon flinched back as a red-edged frond swiped at him, and that saved him.

Bursting out of the kelp forest came the kraken. A tentacle slammed past Siyon's nose, purple and blue and sheened with orange, each sucker on the underside edged in barbs. More tentacles coiled and curled against the fathomless shadow of the sky as the creature launched upward. A great eye like a moon opened. Swivelled. Fixed upon them.

It was impossible. They didn't hunt the nearer reaches of the Abyssal plane. None of the planar monsters came near the stable zone where passage from Bezim was possible.

Except the planes *weren't* stable right now, were they?

The kraken reared, tentacles flashing silver sparks across the maelstrom sky. It was the size of the opera house, tall as the clock tower. Its mouth yawned like a cave ringed in glittering diamond teeth.

Fuck this, they were getting out of here. Siyon tightened his grip on Izmirlian, reaching his other hand to the tether at his waist, but even as he opened his mouth to call to Zagiri, a tentacle came sweeping through the kelp and bowled them off their feet. They skidded across the sodden ground, sweeping the purple seagrass flat. There was no breath to be crushed out of him, and yet still Siyon lay winded, struggling to rise. He forced himself up on one elbow.

Just in time to see a bright figure leap from the top of the coral reef with a scream that buzzed like a tin can full of bees. A person in armour, except no person had wings that stretched saw-edged and ragged behind them. The wings flared in counterbalance to the swing of a massive gleaming blade. It sliced across a tentacle, quick as a darting fish, and thick orange blood spilled across the sky.

The kraken shrieked, shrill enough to rattle Siyon's teeth. Tentacles lashed, and the armoured fighter leapt over one, kicked off from another, hacked at a third with that mirror-bright sword. And all the while, there was a sound like pouring wine from a pitcher full of marbles. It took Siyon a moment to realise what it was.

Laughter. Their saviour was laughing. Was he *mad*?

A moment later, the battle was over. The kraken fled in a surge of bubbles and ink, leaving the twitching tip of a tentacle behind. From the slow-settling cloud of lingering blood, the figure strode, blade cocked over his shoulder.

No. *Her* shoulder.

Her hips rolled with her saunter, and her hooves dug into the churned-up sod. What had seemed to be armour was actually scales, slithering like the dull bronze petals of some jagged flower over her entire body. She was naked, save the shadows cast by those wings whose feathers rustled as they folded down against her back. The blade across her shoulders was long, strangely rippled, backed by a vicious hook.

Siyon realised he'd been edging backward when he ran into Izmirlian's shoulder. "Is that a—" Izmirlian whispered.

Siyon could only nod.

The harpy grinned; her teeth were pointed as a fish's. She looked just like in all the stories, except there was a difference between *terrifying* in word and in feeling. "Come on, then," she said, her voice all serration and rust. "Her Majesty doesn't like to be kept waiting."

Her Majesty the Demon Queen, Power of the Abyss, and absolutely, positively, not to be fucked with.

Her black-scaled body coiled around itself, belly red as the promise of blood. As Siyon and Izmirlian were led into the clearing by their saviour—or captor—the Queen's head lifted on her long neck, and she blinked eyes that were silver-pale and slit-pupilled. Arms sprouted from the length of her body—three pairs of them—and she carried a trident, a coiled whip, and one of those strange curved-and-hooked blades. Pearlescent horns curved away from her wine-dark forehead, and a forked tongue flickered between her serrated teeth. She was nothing like human, and still she was as beautiful as a summer storm over a reef. Glorious, powerful, terrifying.

Even more so when she smiled. "What an unexpected catch you have netted, Laxmi."

Their harpy escort made her bow with a flick of her barbed tail and a smirk on her lips. "All the better to gift to you, my Queen."

Izmirlian shifted at Siyon's shoulder. "Gift?" he murmured.

"Don't panic," Siyon muttered back. "She can't keep us here unless we choose to stay."

"Can't she?" Izmirlian looked past the Queen to the gathering behind her.

The demon court was a congregation of nightmare and menace, bristling with horns and talons and tusks, rustling with scales and weaponry and speculation. They were armed and armoured, smeared with ink and weed and gore. On the flattened purple seagrass around them lay greater monsters still—three-headed hounds with their otter-fur matted with blood; a smaller kraken, limp and bloating; things that Siyon didn't even have names for, like a massive glassy-eyed seal with a vivid orange-spined ruff and a scorpion's tail.

This was a hunting party. Out here hunting monsters where monsters should not have been, were the planes in balance.

Izmirlian's hand was still gripped tight in his own, and Siyon pressed their linked knuckles against the tether at his waist. "This is insanity. Let's get out of here."

But Izmirlian's other hand caught at Siyon's shoulder. "Wait. Look. Over there."

The crowded court shifted, a gap opening between the scaled and furred bodies, and through it Siyon caught a glimpse of a figure smaller, slighter, softer. Human.

Just a glimpse, and then the mass of armoured bodies closed between them again. Siyon might have discounted the possibility, if he hadn't come here precisely to find a human. "Was that—?"

And Izmirlian whispered back, "I think so."

Taloned fingers snapped in his vision, and Laxmi beckoned him

impatiently forward. Siyon went, tugging Izmirlian along with him.
The harpy, with her claws and hooves and massive hooked greatsword,
was the last person he wanted angry with him.

Or nearly the last, next to the Demon Queen herself. "Siyon Velo,"
she said, and her voice was honey poured over razor blades. "You've
violated our borders before. And without so much as asking."

Siyon felt a little dizzy, but beside him Izmirlian made an azatani
bow no less elegant for having only one hand free. Siyon managed a
clumsier bow without falling on his face. "Your Majesty, I thought
myself too far beneath your notice to trouble you with my petty needs.
I never dreamed you might know my name." How *did* she know his
name?

"This one—" The Queen waved one of her free hands; her fingers
were human, but her nails stretched long and pointed, blood red fading to black. "This one I don't know."

"Izmirlian Hisarani." To his credit, his voice only trembled
slightly.

That forked tongue flickered, as though the Queen could taste his
name on the not-air. The sheen of her eyes shifted. "How interesting.
Strange appetites are rather my area. Another time, I would love to
dig further." Her voice slithered and skewed, making *dig* sound simultaneously violent and appealing. She touched one of her trident's tines
beneath Siyon's chin. "But right now, things are a little too fraught,
wouldn't you agree?"

Siyon tried not to glance behind her, looking for a human in the
crowd. Looking for *the* human. "That's rather why we've come."

The Queen tilted her head and slithered a little closer. Hard to
read the inhuman planes of her face, but Siyon thought she looked
pleased. Maybe even…impressed? "Are you ready to take up your
responsibilities, then?"

Responsibilities? Was Siyon going to have to do something to
get Enkin back? Oh fuck, was he going to have to *fight* one of these
demons? He darted a sidelong look at Laxmi—taller than he was, and
an undulating riot of muscles and violence. She hefted that sword,
that massive shard of iron, and passed it into the hands of—

Of Enkin Danelani. He looked dramatic and handsome here; the thick underwater light glinted blue lights in his ink-dark hair and brought a sheen to his skin like some polished and exotic fruit. The slant to his mouth that Siyon had thought sullen seemed more sultry here, or maybe that was just for Laxmi. Beside her slick-scaled brawn, Enkin seemed a fragile and soft thing, beautiful and breakable, to be coveted and protected.

His eyes met Siyon's, and he scowled, turning a shoulder as he accepted Laxmi's sword. He needed both arms just to hold it up.

They'd found him. The ring had worked, had brought them right to him. But that was only half the battle; Geryss had managed that much, and then failed to bring him home. Something else, something more powerful, was holding him here. Something that needed to be overcome.

No time to think about it now, with the Queen saying, "I asked you a question, boy," and the point of the trident digging into Siyon's jaw.

"Um," he said magnificently, and tried harder. Was he ready to take up responsibilities? "If someone needs to? I guess?"

That hadn't been the right thing to say. "*If?*" The Queen's face curled into a snarl. "*Humans.* You act like you're all alone in the universe. Yes, someone needs to. Are you all this *useless?*"

Her anger was paralysing; Siyon felt frozen as a sparrow charmed by a snake. She wasn't talking about Enkin Danelani—she couldn't be—but his thoughts turned too sluggishly to grasp what she *did* mean.

It was Izmirlian who spoke up, cool and poised as ever. "Attempts have been made, but I understand they were insufficient."

When the Demon Queen turned her attention on Izmirlian, Siyon could think again. Realisation slid through him cold and sharp as though she'd stabbed him with the trident. "You mean the planar imbalance."

"What else could I mean?" she snapped. "You are *all* insufficient, but someone must take the reins, or your runaway kelpie of a plane will drag us all into oblivion. It cannot be allowed."

Siyon wondered dizzily how Nihath Joddani would feel, having his theory about the planar imbalance and the need for a Power of the Mundane confirmed by no less than the Demon Queen. *He* was more worried about that *cannot be allowed*.

There is a limit to how much support we can give you, Tehroun had said, *when you remain beyond our direct control*.

Siyon looked around at the power and violence of the mud-spattered demon court, and with a chill recognised one very direct way of exerting control. He could picture this host—scaled and clawed and gleefully armed to the over-sharp teeth—marauding down the Boulevard and carving its way through Tower Square.

Kolah Negedi would have said an invasion of demons was impossible. Kolah Negedi, it was becoming obvious, did not know everything about passage between the planes. Opera, on the other hand, loved the idea of invading demon hordes almost as much as the notion of fallen djinn.

Siyon couldn't fail. He needed to get Danelani back, fix this mess, get Joddani free so he could try again and perhaps—

At his shoulder, Izmirlian said, "Master Velo will of course take on the task."

"*What?*" Siyon yelped.

Izmirlian's calm gaze and faint smile remained fixed on the Demon Queen. "He has demonstrated a great capacity for innovation, and I am confident he will succeed where others have failed."

"Hang on," Siyon interjected, though Izmirlian's grip tightened enough to make him wince. "No, come on, I can't—I'm nothing like an alchemist of Joddani's calibre, I can't—"

"Joddani who *failed*," Izmirlian said, all crisp azatani consonants and confidence. *Ask for everything*, he'd said. *And be appalled if you don't get it*. "You have done the impossible. You are doing the impossible. However, he cannot bring his full attention to the matter in the current circumstances of the Mundane plane."

"Your little problems are hardly my concern," the Queen declared, but there was a considering tilt to her chin as she coiled her bulk more comfortably. She was listening.

Siyon realised where Izmirlian was going. "This one is, I'm afraid, Your Majesty. There is a human in your court, and while he is absent from his home, there is nothing that can be done."

Her gaze shifted back to him, like the weight of a summer storm, and a sneer curled her mouth. "You're holding the planes ransom for that pup?"

"Not me," Siyon objected. "He's important, back in the Mundane. His mother won't rest—won't let anyone rest—until she gets him back. So if you can let him go, I can—" Oh help; the last thing he wanted to do was lie to the Demon Queen. "I can help fix the balance."

The Demon Queen sighed, and lowered her trident. Another of her hands came up to cup Siyon's cheek. "There is no one else," she whispered. "And it is too late to start again." Whatever *that* meant, but before Siyon could even consider asking, her fingers closed on his ear, twisting like usury, and Siyon squeaked as she hauled him close enough to hiss in his ear, "You must do better than *help*."

Siyon grabbed at her wrist, which on second thought was a terrible idea. The scales flexed in his grip, the edges threatening sharpness like a thousand papercuts waiting to happen; he spoke fast. "I will, I'll pour everything into it, I'll make it happen, but you have to—"

"I don't *have to* do anything." She let him go, though her smirk was nothing like reassuring. "The boy is not here under *my* aegis. Talk to him, if you want him back."

She pointed the way with her trident, as though Siyon might have missed it.

The Demon Queen slithered away, the scrape of her scales just shrill enough to set the nerves on edge. The rest of the court came clamouring for her attention.

Siyon whirled around. "*Siyon can do it*—are you serious?"

Izmirlian shoved him away from the knot of courtiers, stumbling over the trampled seagrass. "What, you wanted to tell the damn Demon Queen that we can't help her? She was angling to invade the Mundane and take over, you know."

"I know," Siyon hissed back. And possibly not just her, if Tehroun's hints were to be believed. Would *all three* of the Powers invade the Mundane, divide it up between themselves, rather than let it fall out of balance? Shit, shit, *shit*. "But *me?*"

"Why not?" Izmirlian had that haughty azatan lift to his eyebrows. "And don't go on about Azatan Joddani. He told me my commission was impossible, and you—" Izmirlian lifted their joined hands, nudged a knuckle into Siyon's chest. "You have already stolen my voice. Perhaps even more, perhaps there's something from the first working that I'm missing and don't even realise. You are *doing it*, Siyon. You are doing the impossible. Of course you can do this too."

Siyon stared at him, hearing Auntie Geryss in the club library—*If you could reason your way into being Power, Negedi would have already done it, wouldn't he?* But remembering, also, the plummet of his stomach when Izmirlian had first shown up, with a handwritten card and no voice. Siyon hadn't *meant* to do that, hadn't known it would happen, and had felt—horrified.

Or did he just feel that way because now he'd never hear Izmirlian moan again the way he had when Siyon had bitten at his lip, tugged at his burnished hair?

Siyon shook his head, like he could rid himself of Abyssal influence when he was literally steeping in it. "One problem at a time," he declared.

Izmirlian pointed with their joined hands. "That problem."

Enkin Danelani loitered at Laxmi's side, the massive sword still cradled in his arms, and one of *her* arms curled around his waist. She was talking with another demon warrior, whose lower half was goat-bent, with blood and ichor matting the fur. Laxmi was hardly cleaner, though it didn't seem to bother Enkin as he tilted against her side. The harpy was certainly magnificent, all power and barely contained threat. If that was your thing, Siyon could see why you might jump planes for her, but surely there were easier dangerous thrills. Swimming the river, running the hippodrome, throwing yourself off the Scarp…

The other warrior strutted away, and Izmirlian nudged an elbow at his side. They stepped forward and made their bows.

Laxmi's smirk widened, and she pointed a talon over Siyon's shoulder. "He does it much more prettily. Perhaps he could teach you." The way she flicked the words between her pointed teeth made the suggestion salacious.

Danelani shifted beside her, but Siyon didn't look at him directly, not yet. "We wanted to thank you," he said. "For the rescue and the opportunity to meet Her Abyssal Majesty both."

Laxmi's grin was only mildly terrifying, too many teeth and too much feral delight. "I'll be honest, I didn't see you there until afterward. I just wanted the dance. But I accept your thanks, little human."

That would do for the polite forms; now Siyon let his gaze slide to the prefect's son. Danelani's curls were unruly and twisted with the damp, and his thin, leathery tunic sat skewed on his shoulders. Low on his throat was a dark bruise that Siyon didn't think was an injury.

But his mouth was still pulled awry by self-centred dissatisfaction, and as Siyon stared at him—not bowing, not to him—one of those thick black eyebrows lifted. "Yes, what?"

Honestly, Siyon had thought they'd have to break him out of a prison, snap some sort of alchemical chains. He hadn't expected this: that Danelani would simply be walking around. That there might be *no good reason* why he hadn't already come home and stopped all the fuckery his absence had engendered.

"You owe me," Siyon stated.

"What?" Danelani snapped.

Laxmi looked between them. "You two know each other? How cute! I thought there were more humans than that." She plucked her sword from Danelani's arms—with one hand—and added, "Take the chance to catch up, because we'll be heading back to Pandemonium very soon."

Indeed, all around them kelpies were being readied, the massive murderous horses shaking their weedy manes and snapping teeth in the thick atmosphere. The Queen slithered among them, congratulating her hunters and admiring their prizes. The spoils of the hunt were being rapidly processed, skinned and butchered and gone over for their useful parts.

Part of Siyon itched to be among them. Just the little discards he could snap up here and there would be worth plenty to Mundane purchasers. Not that there was anyone to buy them, right now. Or ever again, if he failed here.

No pressure. All the pressure.

Laxmi strode away to direct the skinning of one of those scorpion-tailed seal-creatures. She wiped the ink-smeared blade of her sword against her forearm as she went.

Danelani watched her go, before turning back to Siyon with a sigh. "I don't owe you," he said, petulant as ever. "I paid your price."

"Sure you did," Siyon agreed. "Bucket of money *and* this little trinket." He flashed the Danelani signet, before tucking it back into his pocket. "Fat lot of good it did me when you fucked off here. I didn't agree to give you the power to make this possible for an ugly ring. My price was *your name and influence.* Shelter from the inqs." He spread his hands, lifted his eyebrows, made a magnificent mime of: *And where is it?*

Danelani sneered. "It's hardly my fault if you go getting yourself in trouble."

"Actually," Izmirlian interjected, his words clipped curter than ever, "it very much is. Your mother has tipped the city upside down and doesn't care what she breaks trying to shake you out of the deepest corner. It is *entirely* your fault, and you must come back and fix it. Honour demands it."

Danelani glowered at them and drew himself up. It didn't have quite the same gravitas without all the trappings of azatani wealth and privilege, though, and Siyon was still taller than him. His teeth ground, and his mouth twisted, and he grumbled, "I don't know what you expect me to do."

Wasn't it obvious? "Come back," Siyon stated, in case it wasn't.

"I can't." Danelani looked even grumpier about that admission. "I've tried. It just—it slips away. I can't go back."

Siyon frowned, trying to make sense of that. If Danelani had come delving without a tether, perhaps he'd lack the presence in the plane to pull himself back. But he'd brought himself here bodily, expended significant power for the purpose. And there'd been no shortage of power used to try and get him back. Was this *falling*? It didn't seem to match what Tehroun had described. Tehroun had taken a Mundane form; Danelani looked no more a demon than he had before.

Auntie Geryss had thought there was some force holding him here. Something stronger than what she'd brought to bear. Danelani wasn't physically bound, and Siyon didn't think he was lying about having tried to get back. It seemed entirely in character for him to skip away from this love affair as callously as he'd skipped into it.

"You lot done yet?" Laxmi asked.

It said a lot about how hard Siyon had been thinking that he hadn't noticed her returning leading a massive bloody kelpie; from the tight twist of Izmirlian's grip in the small of his back, Izmirlian had certainly noticed.

Siyon had never been this close to an actual horse—they couldn't bear the city since the Sundering, and Siyon had never seen the point in trekking out to the hippodrome—but this was clearly something else. Its eyes glowed bloody beneath the ragged fall of its mane, and its teeth were as sharp and serrated as those of its mistress. It huffed a breath that blasted hot as a forge across Siyon's skin.

Laxmi grinned, clearly enjoying his unease. "Still catching up? Only we need to get going." Behind her, the rest of the court was starting to mount up, settling their weapons, shaking reins that rattled with coral and bones.

"He's here to take me back." Danelani lifted his chin like a challenge. "My mother wants me brought back home, apparently."

Laxmi laughed, sharp with mockery. "Oh, are you a *knight errant*?"

Siyon looked between her and Danelani. Was the harpy somehow keeping him here? Could he convince *her*?

"I'm not here doing Syrah Danelani's bidding," he said. "Though it would certainly make life easier if she called the hunt off. But you heard your Queen." He tilted his head, to where said Queen was coiling herself, massive and magnificent, into a verdigris-chased war chariot pulled by two massive lobsters. Because Siyon needed more nightmares. "We need a Power. We need to fix the imbalance. And it got worse when he came through. We all felt it."

Laxmi hooked a talon into Danelani's smock and pulled him close, tucking him beneath one muscled arm like a kitten. "Darling, you broke the planes." She sounded pleased and proud; Danelani tilted his chin with habitual ease to kiss her, just for a moment, before she turned back to Siyon. "Here's the thing: We're in love. It's why he's here. Why he *can* be here. So we're a package deal. You take him home, you take *me* home." She grinned, easy and serrated. "I'm up for it if you are."

Siyon couldn't possibly. This wasn't a little will-o'-the-wisp or an Empyreal spark like he'd heard the Margravine Othissa had once brazenly worn as a jewel. She was a *harpy*, and not even a grateful mother could fail to see a violation and crime in allowing her to manifest in the Mundane.

On the other hand, *Tehroun* claimed to be from another plane, didn't he? "I understand there are ways for a being to step across," Siyon started, still unsure whether he knew the truth in this matter.

But Laxmi pulled an immediate face. "Fall? Fuck that. I'm not losing the essence of who I really am, not even for you." That last she said to Danelani, touching his cheek with a ruthlessly taloned finger.

"I wouldn't ask you to," Danelani responded, but his smile twitched flat as she turned away again.

"So I guess we're staying here. Nice to meet you, though. Give his mother my love." Laxmi stepped around her kelpie, slapping its flank as though in warning before she hooked a hoof into the dangling stirrup to mount.

Siyon looked back at Danelani, feeling a tightening in his chest. Was that the tether, or just his own desperation? They needed him back. Siyon had to take him back. Or else it all fell apart—arrest might be the least of his concerns, if the Demon Queen was serious about her invasion hints.

Izmirlian ducked close to Danelani, a dart like a diving bird. "You want to come," Izmirlian hissed; Siyon could barely make it out, surely Laxmi wouldn't hear a word. "You said it yourself, that you'd tried."

Danelani glared at him, but he didn't step back. "And I failed."

"You failed alone." Izmirlian held out his other hand, a haughty demand rather than a desperate plea. "Now or never, Enkin. Now, or you're stuck here forever."

"Mudkin?" Laxmi called, rolling easily as the kelpie shifted its clawed feet. "Let's go, or we won't be home for dinner." Enkin looked up at her, and whatever she saw, it made her eyes widen and her face grow fierce. "No. Enkin, you can't."

But he'd already turned away. Determination on his face as he took Izmirlian's hand, and Siyon yelled, "*Zagiri!* Get us out!" even as he lunged forward to grab Danelani's other arm, getting a solid grip just above the elbow.

Many things happened at once.

The tether pulled tight around Siyon's waist. He hauled both Enkin and Izmirlian closer, wrapping arms around both of them; Izmirlian clung back, and though Enkin squirmed, he also grabbed hold of Siyon's shoulder.

The plane turned viscous around them, clinging like jelly that refused to give up its fruit. The tether slipped up his body, tightening until his ribs creaked. Slowly—far too slowly—Siyon felt himself pulled up. Away. Through.

It hurt. It hurt like it never had, like he was being ground against the edge of the plane. Izmirlian grunted; Enkin gasped in ragged pain. His face went pale, and his grip weakened, but Siyon's didn't.

Laxmi vaulted off the back of her kelpie, face contorted in feral desperation. She screamed, and Enkin screamed, and she lunged at them, one taloned hand stretching, so very near enough to touch.

Near enough for Siyon to see the pain in her golden eyes as the plane tore open and they snapped away.

CHAPTER 19

Zagiri could have laughed at the look on her sister's face as Anahid stared at the surface of the bath. It looked entirely placid, and not at all like two full-grown men had plunged into it—*through* it—a moment earlier.

"It's even weirder when he steps into solid stone like that," Zagiri remarked.

"From your lofty viewpoint of great experience?" Anahid snapped, but there was no real zing to it.

Zagiri couldn't blame her for being snappish. Her husband had been arrested, her house tossed by the inquisitors, and now…this. Hisarani hadn't been supposed to go as well. He didn't have a tether; what if they lost him? Siyon had mentioned being rescued, but Zagiri could hardly fetch Mistress Hanlun.

All she could do was hold on and wait for Siyon's call, so Zagiri wound the bedsheet more firmly around her fists and did just that.

Anahid folded her hands, over the sash at her waist, one way and then the other. As good as shouting that she was out of sorts. "I wish there was something I could be *doing*," she muttered, and pressed her fingers flat against her hips, obviously pulling herself together before she said brightly, "Mother mentioned the register is closing soon for sponsors to the Ball—"

"Don't," Zagiri interjected, tightening her grip on the tether, though it hadn't moved at all. "*Don't* bring up the Ball, not now." The last thing she wanted to think about right now was the future. She couldn't see how today was going to finish, let alone next season.

And yet, if she wanted to achieve anything—*change* anything—in that future, she needed to think about it. Make a decision. Step up.

"I was going to say," Anahid said quietly, "that you'll need Mother to help you with that. Whatever you decide. I don't know what my social standing will be like, even if this all goes well."

Zagiri stared at her. It hadn't even occurred to her... but of course, even if Siyon pulled Enkin out, what would happen to Nihath, arrested for sorcery? And what would happen to his wife? "Surely no one can blame *you* for what he's done?"

The look Anahid gave her was flat and tired, suggesting she should know better than that.

Zagiri did. As though azatani society had ever needed a reason for its capriciousness. She hadn't seen their parents at home; were they already scrambling to balance out the upheaval in their social and trade networks?

"We should—" Zagiri started.

Siyon's voice screamed from nowhere, "*Get us out!*"

Zagiri jumped, nearly fumbled the tether altogether, before she gripped it tight and heaved.

For a moment, nothing. She shook with effort, and pulled harder, and then she realised it wasn't *her* shaking, but the floor beneath her.

The tremble grew worse, the house shivering like a dog in a dream. Someone screamed in the street far below. A painting fell off the wall with a crash; two chairs clattered over; the bath juddered across the floorboards.

Zagiri sat down, hard, and braced her slippered foot against the bathtub, heaving on the tether. It gave grudgingly, in scant inches at a time. "Help," she croaked.

Anahid staggered across the room as though on the deck of a ship in a storm, and half fell over Zagiri before she also laid hands on the twisted and knotted bedsheet. With both of them pulling, it came a little easier, the bedsheet wet under Zagiri's grip now.

And then it came all in a rush, sending them sprawling backward in a heap on a floor suddenly still. The building creaked, and there was a thunderous splash from the bathtub, which cracked clean across. There were bodies in the tub, flailing limbs, a saltwater stench in the air and water all over the floor.

"Get them out!" Anahid shouted, and grabbed hold of the shoulder of Zagiri's dress, hauling her up.

There were *three* bodies in the bath. Siyon, hacking and coughing as he tried to sit up. Hisarani, elbow hooked over the bath's edge, grim and silent as he tried to hold up—

Enkin Danelani, wearing something outlandish and covered head to toe in muck.

Zagiri grabbed him under the arms. He was a dead weight, no help at all, and her feet skidded on the wet floor. "Salt and ashes," she spat.

"Get him out before he drowns." That was Anahid, clipped and curt and capable as the sergeant of a bravi tribe. "How is there so much *water* now?"

"Came with us," Siyon gasped, wiping brine from his face.

Anahid hauled Hisarani half out of the bath, left him draped over the edge like wrung-out linen, and came to help Zagiri with Danelani. They dragged him up until Anahid could wrap an arm around his chest and heave; he obligingly puked thick, oily liquid and croaked, "Stop."

Zagiri could see the shadow of her own panic in the wideness of Anahid's eyes. "What *was* that?" Zagiri asked.

"What was what?" Siyon tipped himself inelegantly onto the floor, and beamed at the ceiling. "We did it. We *did* it."

Anahid tried to brush down her dress—a useless gesture when everyone and everything in the room was sodden. "There was a tremor."

Zagiri snorted. *Tremor* hardly covered it. "Or there was another Sundering." Fuck, she hoped it hadn't been another Sundering.

Siyon exchanged a look with Hisarani. "He's back where he belongs," Siyon said, as though reassuring someone, possibly himself. "The imbalance will improve, and with his mother off our backs, we'll have time to figure it out. For someone to..."

He trailed off. Hisarani raised an eyebrow that Zagiri might have termed challenging in other circumstances.

Anahid planted her hands on her hips. "Well, we have to get him back to his mother in order for that to happen. And the longer we have him here, the greater the risk of—"

A hammering drifted up from below, distant but not distant enough. A voice shouted: "Open up! Inquisitors!"

"That," Anahid sighed, her eyes squeezing closed for a moment. "The greater the risk of that. Right!" She clapped her hands, and they all flinched. On the floor, Danelani groaned. "No good in hiding up here. You two, pick him up. Giri, you're clearing the path and opening doors. Get downstairs. We figure out the rest on the way."

Siyon staggered to his feet, far more unsteady than Hisarani, who was already hooking his hands beneath Danelani's armpits. Zagiri knew this—the eerie way Siyon was swaying. The way he had to pause in picking up Danelani's ankles. She'd seen it on the rooftop with Melis and Ingermann. The earth might have stopped shaking, but the planes hadn't.

"Are you—?" Zagiri started, but Siyon glared at her, and she shut up and shoved the bath aside to give them a clear path to the door. "We could just tell the inqs," she said instead. "They're looking for him, after all, and here he is."

"We can't let them say they found him here," Siyon huffed, as they shuffled out into the hallway. "They'll just as likely claim we've been hiding him all along."

"And then they get the credit for returning him," Anahid agreed, helping them around the corner. "This is your work, Velo. *You* claim this. You..." Her gaze went distant for a moment, and then hard and glinting as a blade. "Yes. You claim this, in front of witnesses. Azatan Hisarani can be the first."

"He can't—" Siyon started.

Anahid waved a hand. "Just nod. Look haughty and bored and *nod*. I'll do the rest. Zagiri, you need to go and get us more people. Whoever you can find, get them out on the street, right now. Can you do that?"

"Of course," Zagiri agreed, and took off down the back stairs. She had no idea how, but like Anahid said, she could figure it out on the way.

The run was exhilarating, like it always was. Even in a dress, she took the stairs in leaps. The slippers let her skid around the corners without coming to a dead halt.

And with every step, her mind ticked over, worrying at the task Anahid had given her like it had come from Voski Tolan herself. Get people out onto the street.

How?

It was still early in the morning, for the Avenues. Past breakfast for most, but morning calls were only paid for serious business. No one in society would be at home at this hour to a *Miss*, and certainly not one whose dress was pasted to her legs with Abyssal brine.

Zagiri sprinted through the servants' hall as another thunderous knock echoed through the corridors. That familiar frustration welled up inside her. If she were an azata, they'd receive her. Or she'd have her own calling cards, that she could trust to be conveyed straight to the family.

But she wasn't. So what could she *do*?

She was still azatani, though. She could use that. In her own way. The quick way, the clever way, the bravi way.

Out in the courtyard, Zagiri ignored the back gate, instead leaping for the massive copper laundry tub. As the laundress squawked, she pushed off the edge, grabbed for the top of the yard wall, and hauled herself up. Brick scraped against the beadwork on her gown, threads popping and tearing, but Zagiri ignored them, getting a foot atop the wall, and then the other.

Too unsteady in the slippers; she pulled them off and hurried barefoot along the back wall, looking up at the row of houses. Anahid's neighbours on one side were older and stuffy, but on this side were the Andanis, and Lucine's window was...that one.

Zagiri threw her slipper at the glass. It made a rather soggy clack, and fell down into the yard, but a moment later Lucine opened the window. "Zagiri?" She sounded riveted by scandal. "What are you *doing*?"

"Get your family out front," Zagiri shouted back. "Quick as you can."

"What?" Lucine gaped at her. "I'm hardly *dressed*!"

Zagiri strangled the urge to throw the other slipper at her. "Quickly." And then, as Lucine just kept staring, she added, "It's Enkin Danelani. He's back."

"Danelani!" The shout came from behind her. Zagiri whirled around, nearly tipping off the wall, to see a boy of perhaps eleven hanging out of *his* bedroom window on the other side of the laneway. "Are you serious? Out front over there! I gotta see this. Oi! Balian!" And he hammered against the wall of his room.

The window in the next house popped open, and another boy stuck his head out. "Yeah, what?"

When Zagiri whirled back, Lucine was gone from her window—gone from the room beyond, the door open.

Maybe this just might work.

She raced further along the wall, finding other windows she knew, calling the message as loud as possible. Other staff, out in the yard, scurried inside to tell their families. By the time Zagiri dropped down from the wall at the end of the laneway, she thought perhaps a dozen families had been roused. Would it be enough?

She tried her best to straighten her dress, but it was useless—it was snagged and smeared with dirt, hopelessly wrinkled and reeking like she'd rolled in a fisherman's catch. Nothing for it but to walk—bedraggled and barefoot—around to the front of the block.

There were people hurrying from all directions, and a small gathering forming in front of the Joddani house. Zagiri hurried to join them, as her proud smile grew wider.

A stern inquisitor stood on the Joddani doorstep. The woman behind him glared at the crowd like she could take an axe to the lot of them. Facing them down in the doorway, of course, was Anahid.

Anahid, who declared grandiosely, like she was playing to the audience twitching their lace curtains in the houses across the way: "By *that man*, do you mean the Azatan Danelani, or the man who rescued the latter from torment in the depths of the Abyss? Or perhaps our good friend the Azatan Hisarani, who witnessed the rescue—oh, where are my manners? Have you met Izmirlian Hisarani?"

Hisarani stepped forward and inclined his head.

As they played out this careful drama, more people were coming out of their houses, shrugging into coats, hurrying over to join the crowd.

"I say!" someone called from just behind Zagiri. "Did you say Danelani?"

"He's just there!" someone closer to the Joddani house shouted back. "Bring him out so we can see."

But the inquisitor drew himself up thunderously. "This man is a dangerous sorcerer," he stated. "And he is under arrest."

"This man," Anahid declared stridently, speaking less to him than to the whole street, "is a selfless hero who has ventured into the very depths of the Demon Queen's palace at Pandemonium to rescue our city's beloved son."

The crowd gasped and thrilled, and one azata even began to applaud. Zagiri glanced around the crowd—thoroughly enjoying Anahid's street theatre already. With just a little nudge...

So she shouted, "Huzzah!"

A moment later, they were *all* cheering and clapping, and shouting, "To the Palace!"

In the joyous tumult, Zagiri edged and dodged her way through the crowd to the steps. The inquisitor had withdrawn to the street to have a hurried and sullen conference with his squad. Siyon had taken a moment to put on that lurid old purple coat of Nihath's. He was carrying Danelani over one shoulder, and looking only a little likely to tip over or drop him.

Zagiri grinned at Anahid, who grinned right back at her. "Good work!" Anahid called, and pulled Zagiri up into a hug.

It was mildly astonishing; Zagiri struggled for a moment. "I'm all mucky!" she objected.

"Who isn't?" Anahid laughed—*laughed*—in her ear, and held her tighter. "You did well."

Zagiri relaxed into the hug, pressing her face into her sister's shoulder. She'd done well. Made it work. Used what she had, what she was, in her *own* way.

She pulled back, as people started moving around them, and smiled up at her sister. "When all this is done, will you come with me to sign the sponsor register?" she asked.

Absolutely not the time and place for that request, but Anahid just smiled. "I'd be honoured."

In the flurry of getting ready—both Xhanari and Anahid giving curt instructions—Siyon had to take a moment to steady himself, lest he actually drop Enkin Danelani right on top of the inquisitors.

He was going to have to carry him all the way to the Palace of Justice. At least it wasn't so far from the Avenues.

The inquisitors formed up into ranks around them, and something nudged at Siyon's side. Probably some annoying bit of Enkin Danelani, but when Siyon turned, it was Izmirlian, standing very close. "Oh." Siyon swallowed. He wasn't sure what he should say; he'd never been all that good at romantic relationships, even when they weren't tangled up with alchemical complications. "Look, I'm sorry about—"

Izmirlian frowned, and jabbed him again in the ribs with, it turned out, a many-folded page from his notebook. Siyon couldn't take it— had his hands a little bit full—but Izmirlian tucked it into the pocket of his coat. Gave him a pointed nod, and stalked back up the stairs into the Joddani townhouse.

"Hey," Siyon called, but the door closed behind him.

Anahid ducked in where he'd been, helping to steady Danelani on Siyon's shoulder. "He will wake up, won't he?"

"I hope so," Siyon replied. Maybe this was normal for being dragged bodily between the planes; how would Siyon know? But he'd better wake up, or the prefect's gratitude might be a bit less than full.

A few cheers broke out among the azatani, as more of them got a glimpse of the body over Siyon's shoulder. Vartan Xhanari glared at him. "This changes nothing," he warned balefully. "I'll see you done down, sorcerer."

It made Siyon's skin crawl to just talk with the man. The moment Anahid first swung open the door to show him there had been one of pure terror. Xhanari might have bowed to the pressure of the crowd, but given any gap, he'd pounce.

Siyon was putting all his hopes in the muck-smeared body over his shoulder.

The azatani came along, parading toward the Palace with morning hats and parasols lifted like sails over a regatta. They were cheerful and chattering, while unease gnawed in the pit of Siyon's stomach. He couldn't enjoy this, for all he'd earned it, until he knew whether it would *work*.

They marched down the Avenues until the shaded streets flowed into the sun-soaked lawn around the Palace of Justice. Siyon was lost in just trying to put one foot in front of the other, in *not* dropping Enkin Danelani, when the bloody boy woke up. He did it with the same subtlety he did everything: with a yell, and a wild kick.

Siyon staggered and went down on one knee. Even as he wrestled to get the flailing Danelani onto his own two feet, the world skewed around them. Siyon felt in two places at once, smeared between them, wrenched back as the planes snapped back together.

It left him panting and dizzy, holding on to the ground with one hand and Danelani with the other.

The inquisitors closed around them, Olenka shoving Anahid aside to help steady Danelani. But the moment she set hands on him, she hissed like a displeased cat and jerked away again. Siyon shook his head, after-images dancing across his vision.

"He has the Abyss *baked* into him." Olenka towered over him with the sun burning a halo into her curls. "What did you do, pull him out without taking proper leave?"

Siyon met Danelani's wide, bloodshot eyes with a wince. That was exactly what they'd done. "None of your business," Siyon muttered, and hauled Danelani's arm over his shoulder to help him up.

Olenka huffed and turned her back on them. "Form up! Let's keep moving."

Danelani winced and blinked in the sun, lifting a trembling hand to shade his eyes. If Siyon didn't know better, he'd have said the bloke had the worst hangover in the world. Siyon could sympathise.

"All these people." Danelani frowned at the crowd. "What's going on?"

"We told you." Siyon tried to nudge a little more of Danelani's weight back off himself. The leathery tunic stuck to his arm. "Your mother has turned the place upside down. Everyone's really excited that now she might bloody stop."

The crowd was starting to look like a festival. People were streaming up from the city, merchants and artisans, canny vendors wheeling carts carrying food or drink or trinkets—Siyon spied a knot of musicians in matching Flowerhouse livery.

Figures appeared on the front steps of the Palace of Justice, grey inquisitors and white-sashed functionaries and there, stepping into the arch of the massive double doorway, was Syrah Danelani herself, tall and stern as the statues that flanked the entrance. Her white surcoat of office blazed in the sun, and her ink-dark hair—same as her son's—was braided up atop her head like a crown.

The prefect of the city did not come rushing out in a panic, though Siyon saw the tension in her body change as she saw Enkin. She was in one moment transformed from a pillar of dread to an arrow set to the string, ready to fly.

Xhanari gestured, and his squad tightened their formation around Enkin—and Siyon with him. At the bottom of the stairs, they saluted, fist to candle-badged shoulder, and Xhanari bowed. "Your Excellence, your son is returned."

She came down slowly, no eyes for anything but her son. Siyon nudged at Enkin's shoulder, and the boy stumbled forward, tripped over the bottom step, and fell into his mother's arms.

She caught him; the crowd roared in exuberant approval, flinging hats and even a parasol or two into the air.

The hug was not allowed to linger. Syrah soon set her son back on his feet, seizing his chin in an iron grip and inspecting his face. "We are overjoyed at this turn of events," she declared grimly, and finally looked at the rest of them. Yes, that was the voice Siyon had heard in the Summer Club library, suggesting to Geryss that she flee. But he couldn't think of that now, when she was skewering him with her sharp gaze. "To whom is our gratitude owed?"

Xhanari opened his mouth, but the crowd shouted first. "That one!" they called, and, "There, in the purple coat!"

Siyon stepped forward, but Xhanari elbowed in front of him. "Your Excellency, this sorcerer Velo claims to have found your son."

Syrah Danelani considered Siyon, and never had he felt quite so efficiently weighed, itemised, and tallied. By the time he had finished his bow—taking even more care than he had with the Demon Queen—he was sure she knew every iota of his merit.

This plan, suddenly, seemed ridiculous. *His* merit couldn't warrant a reward. Not a muck-smeared, unshaven gutter brat. Far more likely that he had kidnapped the prefect's son in the first place than that he was somehow the hero of the hour.

But the cheers were still rising from the crowd, people calling, "The Sorcerer Velo!" with wild acclaim, as though Xhanari had bestowed a bladename.

Syrah Danelani's gaze flickered over the crowd and she turned on a smile, faint and professional. "You have lifted a shadow from my heart and from this city." She sounded joyful as stone, but it hardly mattered, when the next thing she said was: "Come, and we will discuss your rewards."

She turned on her heel, dragging Enkin up the stairs and into the building. The white-sashed civil servants filed in behind her. Siyon gaped after her.

He'd done it?

Anahid grabbed his elbow, hissed, "Keep your wits about you" in his ear.

And then Olenka was grabbing his *other* elbow, yanking him up the stairs as well. Siyon looked back at Anahid, standing tall and unconcerned in the midst of the inquisitors. A great cheer lifted from the jubilant crowd behind her. Music started up. The sun beamed down on them all.

Keep his wits about him. He'd done it, but he hadn't quite won. Not yet. Not until he faced off with the prefect herself.

He should have asked for Anahid to come, Siyon thought desperately, as the Palace of Justice closed around him, a cool and polished cavern of marble and procedure. The entry hall was massive, a forest of pillars and a calm ocean of floor mosaic. Siyon craned his neck at the dome overhead and nearly ran into the white-sashed clerk waiting for him.

"This way," she snipped, and Olenka hauled Siyon after her, into a room about the size of the Joddani formal dining room.

What was he *doing* here? Bravi alchemist, plane-raider, enthusiastic amateur. He didn't belong here, and everyone arrayed on the other side of the long, gleaming table knew it. The prefect and a dozen white-sashed dignitaries—where had they bundled Enkin off to? Siyon never thought he'd *miss* the brat, but at least he knew exactly what Siyon could do.

All of these people saw him just as he was.

Siyon smoothed down his coat, wincing at the pull of the sun-dried ichor against his palms. Something in his coat pocket crackled and prodded at him. Absently, Siyon pulled it out.

A much-folded sheet of notebook paper. He peeled apart a corner, and saw the now familiar curve of Izmirlian's handwriting. The first line on the page read: *Rewards that might be of use.*

Siyon took a deep breath for the first time all morning.

Syrah Danelani lifted an eyebrow thick as her son's, but twice as haughty with the certainty of her office. "It will be money, I assume? The amount listed on the latest notice was—"

"Actually," Siyon said, unfolding the notebook paper entirely. Quite a list Izmirlian had made, his writing whiplash-messy with haste.

The prefect's mouth tightened, and Siyon realised interruptions probably didn't happen to her a lot in this building. Whoops.

"Money's great, don't get me wrong. But there are some other pressing matters. People. Things." He took a breath, and if he was doing this—if he was being *this person*, the person that Izmirlian His-arani had suggested he be—he might as well enjoy it. So he pulled up a grin, wild around the edges, and said, "Shall we sit down and talk about it?"

CHAPTER 20

Nihath Joddani's cell was far nicer than any Siyon had ever slept off a hangover in. It was high up in the Palace, with a nice view out the barred window, and it was large and clean and more comfortable than some places Siyon had lived in the lower city.

But when the door swung open, Joddani's head jerked up with the sharp panic of a man waiting for the executioner. Confusion chased it quickly at the sight of Siyon—and no one else—in the doorway, and then he pulled up haughty disdain like shrugging into a coat. "Are you joining me?"

"Rescuing, actually." Siyon stepped back from the doorway and flourished a hand. "Come on, you're free to go."

Azatan Joddani had been wearing full evening dress when he was jailed, fresh from his intended ascension to Power at the Summer Club. The rest of his clothes and his miscellaneous effects had been dumped on a table in the anteroom; while he sorted it all out, Siyon filled him in on everything that had happened since then.

"In the Abyssal plane all this time, you say." Joddani fussed at the settle of his longvest across his shoulders. "I suppose that just shows that for all the flash and drama of Madame Hanlun's demonstration, there was little real power to her method. As I told her, time and again, emotional matters may *feel* very powerful, but they cannot translate across the planes."

"Except it was emotion keeping Danelani in the Abyss." Siyon perched on a corner of the table, the only one free from longvest and coat and hat and scarf and gloves and fob watch and rings and necklaces and eyeglasses. Had Siyon ever owned this many things in his life?

Siyon felt a bit like he'd been dragged in by a fishing boat, bounced and trounced in its nets. The negotiations had taken a long time, as Siyon worked down the list Izmirlian had shoved into his pocket. Satisfaction still glowed in his bones, but it was nestled alongside weariness, and an awareness of what he *hadn't* achieved. Othissa poisoned, and Talyar the textile practitioner as well, it turned out. How many others had already fled the city? This victory wasn't as sharp or clean as the thrill of winning a duel.

He'd also negotiated the release of the other alchemists taken at the Summer Club and earlier. The list hadn't included Geryss Hanlun. Siyon wondered where she was. He could really use her help.

Instead, he had Nihath Joddani, shrugging into his longvest and saying, "You should consider writing this whole escapade up for posterity. The club will be..." He trailed off, hands stilling on his collar. "Is the Summer Club—?"

"Reinstated in all particulars." Siyon waved a hand; *just another of my magical tricks! Now I'll pull a seagull out of this basket.* "Though the Prefecture will be making no recompense for damage sustained in the enforcement of law as it stood at the time. Or something like that." He fished in the purple coat and pulled out a sheaf of paper so thick he'd had trouble folding it up in the first place so it would fit in the pocket. "It's one of many details outlined in here. Amazing what you can get for effecting a dashing rescue." *And having a canny, if silent, negotiating partner.*

"Hm." Joddani fastened the longvest absently. "Does young Enkin show any ill effects from his forcible removal from one plane to another?"

Aside from having to be carried through the Avenues, being weak at the knees, squinting at the sun? Siyon had asked after him, suggested he make sure there were no lingering effects, and been told curtly that his services were no longer required. Well, fine. Good riddance to him. "Do you mean compared to all those people who spend weeks living in another plane and return voluntarily?"

Joddani snorted. "At least the boy is back now. We can put all this nonsense behind us and—"

The planes turned over beneath them like a drunkard in bed, lurching and grumbling. The table Siyon was perched on screeched against the floor as he tilted and staggered; Joddani fell to his knees, scattering his rings on the floor.

It stopped as quickly as it started, leaving Siyon's heart hammering.

Still kneeling, Nihath reached for his rings, slotting them onto his fingers. "At least this wasn't an *actual* tremor. But it would seem not all our problems have been magically solved."

Siyon's shoulders wanted to stay tense, anticipating more unsteadiness. "The Demon Queen outright stated that we need a Power of the Mundane to fix it. She's...very keen on it."

Joddani frowned as he climbed back to his feet, brushing off the knees of his trousers. "What's her interest in the matter?"

Siyon supposed that was justified, but all he could think of was her saying *Someone must take the reins.* A lewd promise and a threat, in her rich sword-blade rasp of a voice. "The other planes can't let us slip out of balance. They *won't* let us slip out of balance. They'll take forcible steps."

"What *are* you suggesting? They'll...invade?" Joddani seemed aghast, but more in surprise than concern.

"That was certainly the implication," Siyon said, made curt by the memory of the Demon Queen and her heavily armed hunting party.

Nihath just laughed. "My goodness, it's fanciful. *How?* Negedi, from all references, was always quite explicit about the transition of beings of higher intelligence."

"Could Negedi explain Enkin Danelani?" Siyon demanded. "Could he explain Tehroun?"

"An affinity is hardly an invasion." Though Nihath had a little frown between his eyebrows now. Siyon wondered if he were quite as sure as he seemed to be. "And nor are individual traverses. Really, Danelani's jaunt was just a different variety of what you do."

Siyon opened his mouth to point out that *he* should know, and it was nothing like—and closed it again. If he was right, they didn't have time for this argument, and if he was wrong, it hardly mattered. "Well, you're going to have plenty of time with your pal Negedi." He unfolded his sheaf of papers. "Turns out the notebooks and compiled correspondence of Kolah Negedi were *not* burnt by the inquisitors after the Sundering, but were in fact locked up in a special section of the university library to which I've now been given access. Look! It has a seal and everything."

By his face, Nihath Joddani no more knew how he felt about all of that than Siyon did. He plucked up his eyeglasses to inspect the seal as though by reflex. "What a privilege," he whispered; his lips twisted. "I hope my guidance has given you sufficient scholarship to get *something* out of it."

Siyon considered, very seriously, just walking out. But he'd made a promise to *do everything he could*. And whatever Izmirlian Hisarani thought, Siyon was nowhere near able to do it himself. If he practised assiduously for a year with an abundance of supplies, he still couldn't replicate the precision and calculation of Joddani's attempt to become the Power. He certainly couldn't surpass it.

No, Nihath Joddani needed to become the Power, if Siyon had to drag him to it kicking and screaming. And so Siyon gritted his teeth, pointed at the relevant paragraph in the document, and stressed, "And my associates. So finish getting dressed, and let's go."

"Me?" Nihath lifted an eyebrow. "What on earth—or indeed in all the planes—do you believe I can possibly do?"

Maybe Siyon could just put him back in his cell and trade him for something else. Anahid wouldn't be *that* unhappy not to have him back, surely. "We can check Negedi himself. We can fix your ritual and do it properly. You can become the Power and balance the planes."

Joddani shrugged into his coat, and into the full depth of his aza-tani arrogance along with it. "My ritual cannot be *fixed*; it was perfect to begin with."

"Clearly not." Siyon tried to parrot his diction. "Since it *didn't fucking work*. Is that the problem, are you embarrassed? I fuck up all the time."

"Of course you do," Joddani snapped. "You have no diligence, no concept of thorough preparation, barely a passing familiarity with the Negedic structure—for which I do not blame you. You have done remarkable things despite the burdens under which you labour."

Amazing; it sounded almost like a compliment, and yet Siyon wasn't sure he'd ever wanted to smack someone in the mouth so much in his life.

"But allow me to assure you," Joddani continued, "that I was *meticulous*. I left no gaps, no leaps of faith, no best attempts. I crossreferenced every step, I checked and rechecked, I completed the work Negedi left unfinished, and it *failed*."

The words hung in the air. Nihath Joddani smoothed his alreadytidy clothes again.

Siyon shrugged. "Maybe there's something you don't know. Maybe there's something in the actual notebooks that will explain what happened." Joddani opened his prickly, arrogant, azatan mouth, and Siyon kept talking. "No, shut up. I get that this is not a usual situation for you, and you have my sympathy, but you can *feel* the planes, the same as I can. They are going to tear themselves apart like rotting linen, even if the other Powers don't try to forcibly stop it. We *need* a fix, so you need to get over yourself and take this once-in-a-lifetime opportunity I am handing you to lay eyes on Kolah Negedi's actual fucking notebooks."

Joddani opened his mouth again, then closed it. He cleared his throat. "I have always wanted to fill in the blanks of my knowledge."

"Thank you," Siyon nearly shouted. "Angels help us."

A voice from the door said, "They won't." The inquisitor Olenka watched them like a lazy hawk. "Still here, little alchemists? We can tell them you'd like to go back to the cells after all."

"Thank you, ma'am, but unnecessary." Joddani snatched up the last of his things. "We will be leaving directly."

Olenka leaned flat against the door to allow him past, then swayed back again to block Siyon's exit, fixing him again with that ice-bright stare. Everything about her was unyielding, uncompromising, stern, and straight.

"Careful," he said. "Your boss thinks I'm a hero."

"My boss," Olenka replied, unhurried, "thinks you're a dangerous sorcerer who needs to be poisoned at the first opportunity lest you drag the rest of the city into the ocean. He's got quite a bee in his bonnet about it."

Xhanari, of course. But Xhanari couldn't touch him now, and it brought a smirk to Siyon's lips. "Well, *his* boss thinks I'm a hero, and there ain't a thing he can do about it."

She didn't shift as he stepped up to the doorway, fighting her strange vertigo. She was nearly the same height as him, and entirely unperturbed. "If you think that, you aren't paying attention," she said. "We'll be on you like alchemical glue. Watching every step of the way to make sure you don't put so much as the edge of a toe over the boundaries of that very vague license the prefect has given you in her overblown gratitude."

She made Siyon uncomfortable, like grit under his collar, like sun in his eyes, like something scratching at the edge of memory.

He remembered, from far away, Joddani talking about fallen beings as people with *affinities*. He'd wondered if an Empyreal affinity might incline the holder to the inquisitors.

Siyon blinked, hard, and really *looked* at Olenka.

"What?" she snapped.

"Where are you from?" he asked, breathless like he'd just fallen from a height into burning dunes.

Her lip curled. "Run along, little sorcerer," she snarled. "And hope you don't find out."

The city was still celebrating.

A jubilant atmosphere caught Siyon and Nihath up as soon as they stepped out of the Palace of Justice—the lawns were strewn with merry picnics and clumps of dancing, children running and shrieking, vendors touting food, drink, souvenirs. They passed one selling straw dolls barely the length of Siyon's finger, but wearing little purple coats. Siyon gaped until Nihath grabbed his arm and hauled him along.

The merriment clogged the streets with slow-moving good cheer. Down one street, dancers whirled in bright costumes Siyon could have sworn he'd seen at the opera with Izmirlian; down the next street, there was the unmistakable flash and clash of duelling sabres, a crowd packed tight around them, hissing and cheering.

Siyon hoped Bracken was somewhere getting riotously drunk. He hoped he could rejoin them one day soon, trade stories with Daruj, race the roof tiles and raise a ruckus. It seemed a strange and distant notion. But that's where he belonged, wasn't it? Once this was all done.

Amid the fizz of celebration, the university library was a serene hulk of sandstone, topped with a stained-glass dome that glowed in the afternoon sun. Siyon had been past it half a hundred times, cutting through the university on his way to somewhere else, and even once up on its roof, part of a dramatic all-blades betwixt Bracken and the Bleeding Dawn. Every single time, he'd known he would never step inside, let alone crack open one of the tomes of wisdom.

The clerk at the front desk nearly fainted at the sight of Siyon's letter from the prefect. He summoned his superior, who went pale and summoned *his* superior, who very gravely produced a heavy ring of keys and pronounced, "Please follow me."

Siyon had expected silence, but there was a low wash of noise, like the sea at midnight—dozens of students turning pages, scribbling notes, whispering gossip to each other. The place was cavernous, the central hall lined with balconies behind which shelves carved away into shadows. The grand-high-clerk led them up, on staircases that looped from one level to the next. Dust motes danced in light tinted by the stained glass.

The contraband knowledge of a bygone era languished in the circular gallery that ran around the neck of the dome, fenced off with an ornate gilded screen. It invoked planar enchantments with every symbol and curve of its carving, but when Siyon brushed his fingers against it, there was only a faint sting of wardings long faded. A plaque was affixed to the screen: *Sealed by order of the prefect, BY 376.*

"Stand back." The librarian shook out the ring of keys; the jangle echoed off the dome. "These locks have not been unfastened in more than two decades, and they may be temperamental."

A junior clerk brought up a cunning little portable desk filled with writing materials. "Pencils only," the librarian intoned. "The articles of storage were quite precise. No reagents or potential sympathetic links, which includes ink."

"Of course," Siyon said, because some response seemed warranted, and Nihath was too busy staring at a big black chest like a sailor making land after months adrift.

And then the planes twitched around them—three sharp jolts like an attack of cramps, gone the next moment. It left Nihath's eyes shut tight and Siyon clutching at the edge of the golden screen, the pinpricks of the wardings almost a comfort.

The librarian blinked at them. "Is everything all right?"

No, absolutely not. The planes weren't settling down. They could all be inches from ruin, and most of the city remained oblivious. *All right?*

"Cheers," Siyon managed. "We'll take it from here."

Shelves lined the outer wall, filled not just with bound books, but with sheaves of loose notes, stacks of copper bowls, trussed-up bundles of glass pipes, a hodge-podge of other equipment. Everything that was confiscated from the university's Department of Alchemy after the Sundering. At the end of the gallery was the trunk, over whose brass-bound lid Nihath now ran trembling hands. He had to take a deep breath before he could lift the lid.

Inside, a row of plain folios nestled inside ancient velvet, scattered with herbs desiccated with age. Siyon reached for one, and Joddani smacked the back of his wrist, holding out a pair of white cotton gloves.

Already gloved, Joddani extracted a notebook and laid it flat on a nearby table. It was bound in camel-pale leather, the pages brittle as he levered them delicately open. The writing was cramped and crabbed, marching across page after page in narrow lines as straight as truth, interspersed with careful diagrams and illustrations—the workings of a simple alembic, a sketch of a piece of seaweed, a chart of moon phases.

Joddani turned the pages with reverent fingers. "All my life," he murmured, "I have yearned toward this wisdom, like a flower turns toward the sun."

"Is that from an opera?" Siyon asked, and earned himself a filthy look. "Never mind. Tell me what you want, and I'll fish it out for you. Is there an index?"

Joddani sighed, but he pulled up a chair, and they got to work.

There was an index, big and bound in black leather and almost impenetrably coded. Subject entries were nested, contracted, abbreviated, referenced with strings of numbers. Just figuring out what they needed to look up took a long time, until Siyon started to get used to Negedi's convoluted terms. He'd never talk about *reaching the plane* if he could instead call it *a passive diagnostic for an extramundane field*, but Joddani knew exactly what he was looking for.

As he pored over three different folios, Siyon flicked further through the index. All the collected wisdom of Kolah Negedi—so *much* of it. The man seemed to have written down *everything*, from the moment he arrived at the city fresh from the Lyraec provinces, through his apprenticeship with a hedgewizard, and all the experiments he'd conducted for himself. At least two of these notebooks for every year of his life from seventeen onward, plus the voluminous correspondence he'd entered into with clever people around the world.

How had he found the time? No social life, obviously.

Surely the answers they needed must be here. Surely *all* answers were here.

Could Siyon find confirmation of his work with Izmirlian? Information that would set to rest his still-simmering misgivings about the eerie, uncanny loss of Izmirlian's voice?

Siyon picked up a notebook at random—one that Joddani had already checked and discarded. He turned pages, past exhaustive notes on every physical property of infernal kelp, past a half-dozen experiments with the boiling point of brines of various salinities, past a catalogue of the variations in pigeons observed on the rooftops of the city, past a rant about the inaccuracies of stellar navigation in a popular sea shanty. Words blurred and swam past his eyes, until a phrase leapt out—*dragon skull.*

A story told to Negedi by a Khanate sellsword who claimed to have become lost in a sandstorm and separated from his caravan— *Taking refuge in a small cave that was revealed, upon the rising of a clear morn following, to be in fact the ocular orbit of the skull of a massive creature. He described in lavish detail the teeth, the length, the trailing spine that he claimed to have excavated some portion of.*

I sent him away in a rage of which I am not proud. But the veracity or otherwise of this tale is irrelevant. The dragon is dead, if it ever lived; it is of the past, gone the way of myths and fairy tales.

We must put away these childish things. A modern alchemy must be more discerning. Eschew the ephemeral and the numinous, the things that cannot be proven. Let an alchemist define himself by this! We must look cold upon the world as it really exists.

It rang an echo in Siyon's memory: Auntie Geryss at the Summer Club, saying *We need to work with what we can see.* Not so different after all.

Except what someone saw wasn't always the same as what really existed. Siyon wasn't sure he agreed with Negedi—whether there *had been* dragons or not seemed interesting, at the very least. He wished he could see that skull in the desert.

Nihath was still working, his frown deepening, his pencil scratching. Siyon rose to prowl the rest of the room, all those other shelves of the fallen Department of Alchemy. There was a stack of at least two dozen of the same bowl; had it been standard equipment? And over here was a shelf of identical copies of a book entitled *An Introduction to Planar Theory.*

Siyon's fingers twitched. Could he smuggle one of those out?

He forced his attention to the next shelf along, stacks of handwritten notes tied up into bundles. This one read *Examination records, BY 368-9.* The next along seemed to be a pile of student essays. Another read: *Notes of the Committee for the Completion of the Master Work—In the year of our City 375.*

That date snagged at Siyon's memory. With cold unease knotting his stomach, Siyon stepped over to the gilded screen that had sealed all this knowledge away, by order of the prefect, after it had proven itself so dangerous it cracked the city and plunged half of it into the sea. He found the plaque.

In Bezim Year 376.

Seemed an unlikely coincidence. *Completion of the Master Work.* What were the chances that was something *other* than becoming the Power? Had they tried it, this committee? Had they broken the city in their failure?

The knot around the bundle of papers had fused with age, but Siyon flipped frantically through the top half of the pages. The handwriting was cramped, but legible—which didn't mean Siyon could *read* it. He understood barely half the words, and not at all the ways in which they were strung together. The product of a department that had progressed so far beyond Siyon's understanding of things.

"Right," Joddani stated, and Siyon flinched, dropping the bundle of papers. Nihath flipped his reference notebooks closed, one after another, stacking them neatly together. "As I thought." He carefully folded his eyeglasses up, and tucked them into his pocket.

"You should—" *read this*, Siyon started to say, but then the tone of Nihath's voice registered, his calm stretched tight as a drumskin. "What's wrong?"

"Nothing." Joddani gave him a smile, brittle as old paper. "All is just as I expected. As I worked from. As I calculated."

"What?" Siyon blinked. As he'd calculated. *I completed the work Negedi left unfinished*, he'd claimed, back at the Palace. *And it failed.* "There has to be a way to get it right."

"What, because the *Demon Queen* told you so?" Joddani lurched upright, tipping his chair over backward, slamming his hand down on the table next to his stack of notebooks. "This is Kolah Negedi! Father of the Art! He hasn't *missed something*. He made preparations himself, you know. He outlined every step. He weighed and balanced every consideration—just as I did! Our workings are entirely in parallel and I didn't even—" Another abrupt stop. Now Joddani just looked like he might cry, which was terrible. "He outlines it all, and then never mentions it again. There are another ten notebooks—more—and he never mentions it."

The Master Work. Siyon looked down at the stack of paper he'd dropped. The notes of a committee who'd also failed.

"He tried it," Joddani said, stark and sour. "He must have. He tried it, and it didn't work, and he didn't know why, and he never mentioned it again." He drew dignity around him, like an embroidered longvest. Picked up his chair, and put the notebooks back in the trunk, one by one. He peeled off his gloves, and declared: "It is not possible."

Without further comment, he stalked out of the gallery. Siyon didn't try to stop him. He knew when someone had lost the will for a fight.

Siyon stared around him, at all this knowledge, all the astounding wisdom of generations of alchemists who had *failed*. Negedi himself, the committee, and Nihath Joddani; none of them had made it work.

But it had to be possible. It *had to be*, or what else was there? The planes falling out of balance, the world falling into darkness, the other planes wresting control over them. The forcible intervention of harpies and demons and monsters.

Siyon closed the black trunk and pulled the gilded screen closed behind him, fingers lingering on the whorls.

Look cold upon the world as it really exists.

Maybe this had broken the city before. But it would *all* break if they just did nothing.

CHAPTER 21

The streets of Bezim overflowed with relief, the festival atmosphere only deepening as sunset fell over the city. Everyone seemed determined to make up for those curfewed nights and nervous days.

Zagiri ducked between revellers spilling from wineshops, staggering with purloined bottles through the purpling dusk, stopping on the corners where musicians played from overhanging balconies. Windows were open, lanterns hung from buildings, the streets rife with singing and dancing. The rooftop restaurants were full and raucous, spilling noise and laughter; scampering children climbed the fountain statues and set off firecrackers.

In her bravi leathers, Zagiri was spun through a dance, passed a bottle of cheap moonshine that she passed on without taking more than a sniff, and confronted by a trio of giggling women armed not with blades, but with an empty bottle, a long stick of bread, and a grilling fork.

"Dance with us, bravi!" the lady with the bottle declared. When Zagiri made a great show of yielding, her hands spread wide and empty, she gave a wild cry and lunged at one of her fellows instead.

Zagiri left them to it, brawling merrily, tipping each other into the fountain, as a cheering crowd started to gather.

The evening was warm, the heat of the sun lingering on the stones and in the crowd. The streets less ran with jubilation than they oozed like syrup. Zagiri waded through it, letting the last of her tension leach away.

It was over. The prefect's son was returned to his family, the inquisitors back on their leash, the paranoid nightmare woken from. The bravi could get back to their *own* business, instead of people-smuggling. Zagiri wouldn't miss it. It had been very satisfying, fixing just a few of the problems of the city, but she'd rather run free.

For now. While she could.

The crowds thickened the closer she came to Tower Square, until Zagiri was jostled from all sides, moving at a crawl, ducking beneath lifted arms, slipping around fervent embraces.

The teahouses were all full, crowds spilling and churning among the umbrellas. The tribes were all there in full splendour—Bower's Scythe frothing with lace, Awl Quarter glittering like a pirate's treasure haul. Haruspex had alchemical lanterns strung among their forest-green umbrellas, the light shifting from ruddy to gold to deep sea-green.

Little Bracken were raucous beneath the orange umbrellas of Café Regal. As Zagiri worked her way across the square, a youngster squared up to arm-wrestle Tein Geras—she didn't see that going well for him. But it was hard to get closer for the audience—shouting encouragement and exchanging bets on the outcome. Zagiri paused on the edges, laughing along as Tein slammed the youngster's knuckles into the table with little prevarication.

"Excuse me."

Zagiri barely heard the voice over the crowd, didn't realise it was for *her* until fingers caught at her sleeve.

She turned to see a woman—sharp features beneath a black kerchief wrapped around her hair almost like an azata's headscarf. No azata this, not with such a plain dress, or that desperation in her eyes. But she seemed familiar, though Zagiri couldn't think where from.

"Are you the one to talk to about leaving?" the woman asked, drawing close enough that she could speak quietly despite the tumult around them.

Zagiri stared at her, a surprised bubble of laughter in her throat. "It's over. You're safe."

The woman shook her head, drew closer still, her fingers digging in to Zagiri's wrist. "I don't trust this," she hissed, and nodded significantly across the square. "They're still watching."

When Zagiri looked, there seemed nothing but seething celebration. But then Zagiri saw, past a young girl being carried on her father's shoulders, a pair of inquisitors leaning against the fountain beneath the Last Duke.

She could see more then—around the edge of the square, loitering in the arcade beneath the Clock Tower, moving slowly amid the crowds that billowed uncaring around them.

Not doing anything. But there.

Zagiri turned back. "They haven't been *disbanded*," she said. "Things are just returned to normal."

"Normal." The woman grimaced. "The normal where alchemy is technically *illegal*."

Zagiri hadn't thought of it that way. She opened her mouth to argue—surely it would be fine, as it *had* been fine.

Daruj came crashing out of the crowd and swept her up in a hug. Zagiri teetered around on tiptoes with him, as Daruj hollered, "Brave the knife!" The cry was echoed from within the Bracken ranks, embroidered with cheers.

When he let Zagiri go, the woman was still there, though looking like she'd rather flee. When Daruj saw her, his jubilant grin collapsed into a scowl. "What are *you* doing here?"

The woman raised her hands, though she still stood her ground. "I just want—"

"You want bravi, you have brothers who are happy enough with their blades," Daruj interrupted. He loomed over her. "You want to cause Siyon more trouble, you'll need to go through me, Jaleh."

That was where Zagiri had seen this woman before—fixing the same glare she was giving Daruj now on Siyon, in the upper corridor of the Summer Club, as they traded barbed comments.

Zagiri stepped forward and tugged at Daruj's elbow. "She wants to leave."

"What?" Daruj frowned at the woman—Jaleh. "Why? I thought you had yourself a plush apprenticeship in the Summer Club."

Jaleh's face twisted, into a knot of emotion too tangled for Zagiri to unpick. "They *killed* my master." She snarled it, and would have said more, but she cut off abruptly, swaying on her feet.

Zagiri knew that stagger, that sudden queasy horror in her eyes. That look like the ground that was steady beneath Zagiri's feet had turned to water. "The planes are still shifting," she realised.

"Like they're on the boil," Jaleh spat, jerking her elbow away from Zagiri's steadying hand.

"What does that mean?" Daruj demanded.

"Ask your bladebrother." Jaleh tossed her head. "Siyon Velo, saviour of Bezim, the notorious sorcerer himself. Maybe he can fix it, but I'm not sticking around to find out. Not for a second Sundering, nor to be rounded up and poisoned in the aftermath. So can you help me or not?"

The crowd still surged and celebrated around them, but Zagiri felt stranded in an island of dread. The tension was back, knotting at the back of her neck. She looked at the inquisitors again, at the fountain, in the arcade. Were they just biding their time?

Waiting until Siyon fucked up? Zagiri believed in Siyon—he'd caught her; *saved* her—but she couldn't help also remembering the messes he'd made at Anahid's house. How helpless he'd looked amid an array of Nihath's books. His bitter expression as he admitted to not being a real alchemist.

The way the world seemed to be shaking, beyond anything she could feel.

Could Siyon fix this? Or had it been past fixing before he even got involved?

Zagiri looked at Daruj, who dragged a hand over his face and muttered, "Fuck."

"Yes," Zagiri told Jaleh. "We can help you."

The Avenues were quiet, when Siyon made it back, the promenade over, or maybe subsumed into the rest of the city's celebration. He wasn't clear on the time. Didn't know how long he'd spent wandering the streets, lost in thought, the purple coat turned inside out and slung over his arm.

Just one more body in streets teeming with them.

Anahid was in the entry hall, checking her beaded headscarf in the mirror, when Siyon climbed up from the servants' hall. She eyed him and said, "The front door is right here."

Siyon shook the purple coat out, and hung it on a hook. "I don't belong here. Why pretend?"

"Why not?" Anahid said lightly. "You should hear them in the drawing rooms. Sure you're already a member—an office-bearer—of the Summer Club. Everyone claims your acquaintance. It's been suggested you're an undeclared child of an upper-tier family."

"Fuck." Siyon felt weary beyond the ability to describe it. "Can't bear to have been saved by a Dockside brat, can they?"

"Seize this chance," Anahid told him, her eyes clear and intense. "Stand on the hands they'll hold out willingly. Get everything you can."

Siyon brandished the sheaf of paper, marked with the prefect's seal. "I got a fair bit."

"You got Nihath's freedom. Thank you." So he had made it home; good to know. Anahid raised an eyebrow. "And your... auntie?"

"Geryss wasn't arrested." Siyon didn't know where she was. He wished she was still here. Wished there was someone—anyone— other than just him to take on this burden.

My turn's done, she'd said. *Make your turn count.*

"Sorry," he said. "What?"

Light sparked in the elaborate beading of Anahid's evening gown. "I said, I *should* be going to the Azata Josepani's garden jubilee—in your honour, of course—but I think..." She picked up a calling card, and smiled at it with satisfaction before tucking it into the sash at her waist. "I think I might go and see just what sort of games are taking place in the private gaming rooms of the Flower district."

It made Siyon smile, despite everything, and he bowed with a flourish toward the door. "Take them for all they're worth, za."

"Oh," Anahid added, her hand upon the door. "Azatan Hisarani is still here, though the seclusion in the attic no longer seemed necessary." She flashed one last smile, and went out into the night.

Siyon discovered Izmirlian waiting upstairs, lying on Siyon's bed, surrounded by open alchemical books and pages of notes that Siyon recognised as his own. Something in his chest leapt at the sight—lantern light made the pages glow, sparked fire in Izmirlian's burnished curls, cast tempting shadows across his collarbones where his shirt was unlaced.

Izmirlian looked up, and smiled, and unearthed his battered notebook to hold up a page on which was written: *Congratulations. I hear you did well.*

"Thanks to you," Siyon replied. He tossed the papers down on the desk, the note from Izmirlian bundled up inside. All the things he'd asked for, even the ones marked, *She'll never give you this, but you can trade it off to get the others.* Not just a list, but a strategy. A map to a territory Siyon had no familiarity with, and would have been wildly lost in.

Izmirlian flipped through the pages of his notebook. He'd written the pages in advance, and now he was finding the right one. Held it up: *Just rewards for the hero of the city.*

Siyon snorted a laugh. He nudged a couple of books aside to sit on the bed. "I don't feel much like a hero. I feel like that old woodsman in the opera, dragging the kid back home after he ran away with his lover."

Izmirlian grinned widely, grabbing a pencil to add on the page: *I thought you'd fallen asleep for that bit.*

"And miss all that useful research?" The joke felt flat when so many wild, dramatic, grandiose things in that opera may just be real. The Demon Queen, the fallen angel, the Alchemist putting on his hat and riding off on a dragon.

If only it were that easy.

Look cold upon the world the way it really exists . . .

Long, manicured fingers snapped in front of Siyon's eyes; he focused again on Izmirlian's amused face. It wasn't like he could say Siyon's name to get his attention. Couldn't even make a noise clearing his throat. But he lifted an eyebrow, as eloquent a question as ever had passed his lips.

"I took Nihath to the locked archives of Kolah Negedi's work," Siyon told him. "I thought, if he could just figure out what went wrong, then that would—fix the problem." Siyon's problem, that he'd made a promise to the Demon Queen; everyone's problem, that she'd implicitly made one in return. Fix this, or she would. Get a Power to defend yourself, or she'd lay waste to the world. "He failed. Negedi failed. There's no one left but..." Siyon couldn't say it out loud. He shook his head. "And I'm pretty sure the last lot who tried caused the Sundering."

Izmirlian flipped to a new page in his notebook, pencil scribbling. *Then don't do it their way*, he wrote, and underlined *their*. Gave Siyon a pointed look before adding, *They didn't know how you caught Miss Savani under the tower. They could not even imagine getting this far with my commission.*

Siyon traced over the words, pencil smearing under his fingertip. "Have I got this far?" Once he let the doubt out, it came in a flood. "I've stolen your voice, Izmirlian. I didn't realise—it's unnatural, it's dangerous, it wasn't *planned*." He missed hearing it, clipped Avenue accent and haughty intonation and the faint wistful note when Izmirlian talked about his commission. "What if this isn't progress, what if I'm just—"

A finger laid across his lips stopped his words. Izmirlian smiled, and wrote again. *I trust you. I believe in you. You are more than them. You can do more. You can do this. You can become the Alchemist.* Izmirlian tilted the page toward Siyon, as though ensuring he got the message. And then he scribbled at the bottom: *Let me show you.*

Izmirlian scrabbled around on the bed, rifling through the books and pages. Came up with a page—Siyon's original diagram. His fanciful, hopeful, wildly optimistic plan. Izmirlian shuffled across the bed on his knees, jabbing a finger at the plan. The third quadrant, bottom left. The Abyssal working.

"You want to take the next step?" Siyon asked, and Izmirlian tilted his head, that way he did, in a single confirming nod. Siyon glanced at the paper, cleared his throat, a bit of heat climbing into his face. "Uh," he said, very suavely.

And Izmirlian laughed—no sound to it, but the toss of his head, the open grin, the puff of breath. He held up the page with a smile sly and knowing, and waved the other hand over the books spread over the bed. He'd been reading.

He knew exactly what the most appropriate bodily humour was for the Abyss, the plane of vice and lust and base delights.

Siyon cleared his throat. "If you want privacy, I can go and—"

But Izmirlian dropped the page, wrapped long fingers around Siyon's wrist. His touch was cool against Siyon's skin. Had to let go—alas—to pull back his notebook from where it had fallen amid his searching. *I do not want privacy.* He hesitated, then added, *Won't it be more powerful, the greater the context? The more emotion? The more physical?*

It would. It would, and that had nothing to do with how badly Siyon wanted to say yes. A terrible idea, all of this was terrible, and Siyon couldn't help the curve of his mouth, couldn't stop himself smiling even more when he brushed a thumb against the delicate bones in Izmirlian's wrist and the pencil trembled in his grip. "Are you propositioning me, Azatan Hisarani?"

Izmirlian looked up, eyes hot beneath those long azatani lashes, and Siyon grinned. Grinned wider still as Izmirlian glanced around the book-strewn bed, and his nose got a little wrinkle of regret. "What? Not quite the beautiful seduction you'd have liked?" Siyon laughed, so delighted by the embarrassed twitch of Izmirlian's chin. He leaned in, close to Izmirlian's ear. "No flower petals here, azatan. Just dirty sorcery. Sweat and—"

Izmirlian turned sharply, his kiss swallowing the last word. His fingers in Siyon's hair, pressing insistent into the back of his neck. His weight pulling them both down atop open books and crinkling pages. His teeth in Siyon's lip and breath coming harsh and his skin, hot and bare beneath Siyon's hands, beneath his lips, beneath his teeth in turn.

No flower petals here, just haste and want, tearing at clothes, smearing sweat across the open pages. Izmirlian sucked a gloriously painful bruise into Siyon's shoulder as Siyon got a hand down his trousers, and then Izmirlian's head knocked back, burnished hair curling around the edges of a treatise on planar correlations. His eyes closed, his mouth open.

No sound on his lips, no moan or cry, no breathy gasp of Siyon's name. It was untenable, it was awful, it made Siyon want to break everything. He wanted Izmirlian's voice back, wanted him all here, in Siyon's arms, in his bed. Wanted every little part of him.

Couldn't have him. Could only have this.

So Siyon kissed him, hard and deep and desperately. Kissed Izmirlian, licked the sweat from his neck, felt the rattle of breath in his throat as Siyon curled a hand around him.

Wrung the most power from this ritual. Wrung the most from this chance. Because it was all he could have.

CHAPTER 22

"Siyon?"

The touch on his arm was gentle as the voice, but Siyon still startled awake. The stool tilted beneath him, and the planes tilted beneath *that*, and for a moment he teetered, hardly knowing which way was down, only knowing he would fall.

Then Anahid caught his shoulders, holding him steady and upright as he flailed. Siyon slapped his hands down on the bench, held on as the world steadied around him. "What?" he croaked.

Anahid looked amused. "You were asleep on the workbench."

She glittered in the low light from the single lantern; Siyon had doused all the rest when darkness had seemed more appropriate to the work he was doing. She was still in her evening finery—headscarf and gown, her make-up faded and smeared in places, but her eyes merry.

He dragged a hand over his face. "What time is it?"

"Somewhere not too far from dawn." Anahid stopped, blinking at the workbench. "Is that—*it*? What you are making for Azatan Hisarani?"

Dark, clear liquid lurked in this little ceramic dish, with a whiff of burnt spice to it. The surface was still as a mirror.

An eerie glow had danced through it, as each drop plinked out of the apparatus into the dish. An eerie and potent glow, and Siyon had wondered what it was drawn from, what it was binding, what else might be gone from Izmirlian when this was done. He'd wondered, and he'd gone to stand on the other side of the room until the urge to bump the bench, spill the liquid, break the working was gone.

"Part of it." Siyon reached across to pull the other two dishes out of their box. They'd been taken up to the attics with all the other alchemical bits and bobs, and brought down again. One dish with a little rakia-soaked linen, another with the solid inken bubble. He set them next to this latest dish, like three corners of a square, and tapped the empty fourth space. "One more, and then...well, I don't know."

He didn't know, but he thought he could figure it out. This working had been...not *easy*. Complex. Very tedious, with the distillation process that he'd had to watch for what felt like years, carefully adjusting the flame, watching the condensed liquid darken with each drop.

But he'd done it all himself—no need for Tehroun's assistance, or anyone else's. The fine details had presented themselves clearly to him, without fudging and fine-tuning. One clear, smooth movement of work.

Maybe he was getting the hang of this. Maybe if he just let himself, *trusted* himself, he could do this.

Maybe he could do more. *I believe in you*, Izmirlian had written. *Let me show you*. (*Make your turn count*, Geryss had told him. *Someone must take the reins*, the Demon Queen had told him.)

Siyon touched the edge of the dish. The faintest tremors trembled the mirror-dark surface of the liquid. Power of the Mundane. Not just an alchemist, but *the* Alchemist. Too important for the likes of him. Too responsible. But the likes of him had no cause to be where he was *right now*. Hero of the city. Favourite of the Avenues. Doing the impossible.

Look cold upon the world as it really exists. Someone had to do it. Who was left, if not him?

He had to find a way. But he'd found a way to do *this*.

Maybe he could, after all.

Siyon took a breath, let it out, turned his back on the dishes. "How was *your* evening?"

Anahid's smile was one he hadn't seen on her before; not so much wide as deeply pleased, very nearly wicked. "Rather successful. I have won a not-inconsiderable sum of money *and* a share in a merchant venture to the Khanate due to return in autumn. And the play itself was remarkably invigorating."

Siyon grinned right back. "It's all due to my expert instruction, obviously."

"Obviously," Anahid echoed, with a buoyantly sardonic tilt to her mouth. It slipped for a moment toward something far sadder. "At least one of my instructors approves of my choice."

"What?" There was something he was missing here.

She shook her head. "It doesn't matter. I'm being made maudlin by the hour and fatigue. I will retire. To a proper bed. You may have heard of them."

Siyon thought of his proper bed, of how he'd left Izmirlian in it, most *im*proper, naked and tangled in the salt-damp sheets. An extremely tempting prospect. He could spend all day there, if he let himself. He could spend weeks.

How long did they have? Even now, he could feel the planes, not quite still against each other. Some massive beast, shifting its weight, liable to bolt at any moment.

Someone must take the reins.

Siyon sighed. "There's still work to be done."

Anahid turned away, smothering a yawn behind one slim, ring-laden hand. "As you will—oh!"

Siyon spun around at her cry of surprise. Tehroun was standing in the door of the still room, frowning at both of them—or perhaps neither. How long had he been there?

"Excuse me, sir," Anahid said, perfectly politely if somewhat stiffly. There was no response until she snapped, "Tehroun!"

Then he stepped aside to let her stalk past. He still frowned, not at Siyon, but at the working, in its little ceramic dish, on the bench.

"Is something wrong?" Siyon asked.

"I don't know," Tehroun whispered. For a moment his eyes reflected light much as the surface of the liquid did. After a blink, they were just pale and strange all on their own. "You did this one without any aid. It felt...supple."

Unusual word, but it felt right, just as the work had. The confirmation made Siyon stand a little straighter, for all there was still a puzzled notch of frown between Tehroun's pale brows. "I'm going to do it," he told Tehroun. He told *himself.* A statement of intent, binding himself to the work as surely as cutting a lock of hair. "The thing that's needed. The thing Nihath wasn't enough to do alone. So if you've any other advice, I would really appreciate it." Tehroun looked at him, head cocked like a quizzical little bird. "I believe you," Siyon told him. "And I'm listening."

Tehroun nodded. "I'd like you to succeed. This is not my home, but I like it here. I don't want it subsumed. I don't want it erased."

The words sent a chill down Siyon's neck. "That's what will happen, then?"

"I think it must." Tehroun's strange eyes went distant, as though he were looking at something Siyon couldn't quite see. "You have been so *long* without a Power, here in the Mundane. You have done so well to hold things together. But it cannot last. And if the other Powers do nothing, this destruction will spread."

So they'd breach the barriers instead. *Subsumed.* The Mundane pulled apart. Pick your death: immolated in Empyre, drowned in the Abyss, disintegrated in Aethyr.

There was no one left. Nihath had called it impossible. If *he* couldn't do it, no other Negedic alchemist would manage it.

But Siyon wasn't quite a Negedic alchemist, was he?

He took a deep breath, and asked: "How long do I have?"

Tehroun considered that. "Not long, I think. The planes are barely settling between spasms now. You feel it, yes?"

Siyon did. Near constant enough to grow accustomed to it, like getting your sea legs. Not violent, but always there.

Until the storm came and smashed it all apart. It was on the horizon right now. It was coming for them.

Siyon had to try. Not Nihath's way, not Negedi's way. *His* way. Cobbled together, more cunning than power, outside the lines and unexpected. An alchemy not of books but of the streets.

The streets...

"I've got an idea."

Tehroun watched Siyon snatch up his satchel, swing it over his head. All he said, mild as a suggestion, was: "Hurry."

Dawn was a funny, drawn-out thing in the city. The Scarp seemed to hinder the sun far more than it really should, leaving the light crawling along the upper city streets long after it had flooded the alley canals below. This morning it crept particularly sluggishly, loitering in glints and gleams on the shattered remnants of festivities cluttering up the gutters.

Siyon wasn't alone as he hurried along the Boulevard. Little knots of people trailed this way and that—quietly happy and on their way home, or still in raucous denial that the celebrations were over. There were inquisitors too; he'd counted four pairs on patrol, hands off but eyes on, watching everything.

Watching Siyon too. He wasn't wearing the purple coat, but had it stuffed in his satchel; he might need it later, the symbolism and grandeur. He had the prefect's dispensation in there as well, but Siyon still felt a prickle across his shoulders at every sight of a grey uniform.

At the grand intersection of the Boulevard and the Kellian Way, the last carts from the landward gate were trundling through, delayed by the newly free population's stubborn refusal to give up on last night. The street sweepers came behind the carts, rendering the cobblestones safe for the day's traffic. Essential, but mundane.

Instinct nudged Siyon forward, skirting around the rear of a cart piled high with melons, to scrape up a little ox dung squashed flat on the cobblestones. He coaxed it into a vial, corked and tucked away as he dodged out of the way of another cart piled high with barrels.

Mundane matter, heavy with the rhythms of mundane life. This was what he would build his attempt from. The things that the Mundane *was*, rather than what it was not.

Just one symbol wouldn't do—there were so many aspects to bring together and evoke. If Siyon gathered together as much of it as possible...would that be enough?

Probably not. Not enough alone. But he didn't have to be alone.

Down in Tower Square, dawn found the last dregs of the bravi scraping themselves together after a night on the tiles that had been even longer than usual. The last crumbs of warm pastries tossed to the waiting birds, the last sweet-spiced drams of coffee drained. Sergeants and quartermasters divvied up the night's spoils and warnings to distribute to the blades.

Beneath the orange umbrellas at Café Regal, Voski Tolan sat like a siren on a rock, the rest of the tribe washed up around her like the detritus of a shipwreck. Habit drew Siyon's steps in that direction, but he changed his path.

He wasn't a bravi, asking his tribe for aid. He was a client, and this was the whole city's business. *Ours*; all of ours.

The Last Duke had a raffia-wrapped bottle of rakia—presumably empty—balanced atop his head. Siyon hopped up onto the rim of the fountain bowl and turned to survey the square. The tribes were already watching; they knew him even without the purple coat. He took a deep breath, and wrapped a little Aethyr around his voice—then relented, and untwisted some, made it less likely to ring off the buildings when he called: "I have a commission for any and all tribes still capable of mustering a showing and willing to run a little more in daylight."

Chairs shifted and leathers creaked around the square. Siyon held out his arms—here he was.

Bracken came first, and the relief of it almost made Siyon sag. Daruj beamed at him, bright as the dawn; Zagiri half-slumped against his shoulder, still holding a pastry.

Siyon stayed up on the fountain bowl, as blades started to saunter out from the other tribes. A half-dozen in the plain black of Haruspex kept their distance, arms folded, but they came out to hear. Awl Quarter came plumed and swaggering, and the Bowerboys singing in harmony, arm in arm. Bleeding Dawn were last, five straggling out while the sixth drained his coffee and ran to catch up.

All five tribes—all five sergeants—waiting for Siyon's commission. This wasn't daunting *at all*.

Siyon hopped down from the fountain, cleared his throat, and then hurriedly untwisted the Aethyric amplification. "I need you to bring me the city," he told them all.

As a commission it hardly came cheap, even with just a six-squad from each tribe, but various azatani had paid Siyon quite a lot of money recently. He sent them out to all the places that mattered to them, whether good or bad or too important to categorise. Go forth, and bring him back a little piece of it. Something wood, or stone, or plant, or animal. Something ordinary, but meaningful. Something Mundane.

They took their rivna and scattered, save the Bracken wedge. Daruj was still grinning, but it was Voski Tolan who stepped forward. "Well met, Notorious Sorcerer."

Siyon blinked. "What?"

"They're singing songs about you all across the city, and that's what they name you." Voski lifted an eyebrow, a little amused, a little challenging. "Seems you've earned a name after all."

Not a bladename. Not a bravi name. He'd become something else. The realisation was a pang of regret in Siyon's chest, and yet it came wrapped in a sort of pride. "I was never that good a bravi anyway," he managed, through a suddenly thick throat.

Voski shook her head. "Once Bracken, always Bracken. We all put our blades aside sooner or later." She smiled. "We're proud of you."

As though that were that, she turned away and whistled sharply. The Bracken six scattered as well.

Save Daruj, no longer grinning, and Zagiri sagged against his shoulder, in the middle of a yawn that seemed likely to crack her jaw. She straightened as Siyon approached, getting in before he could make a joke about her tired state. "Siyon, we saw Jaleh Kurit."

Just the name twisted up Siyon's stomach. Jaleh, who'd sold him out to the inqs. Jaleh, who'd lost her alchemist master to poison. He didn't know what to feel; he couldn't deal with this right now.

He glanced at Daruj—who despite whatever he'd said since the break-up *had* always liked her. "She still wants to leave the city," was all Daruj said. "And she's not the only one."

Siyon couldn't blame her. Couldn't blame any of them. But he didn't think it would save them, if the planar barriers were breached and the universe rearranged.

It didn't change what he had to do.

"Thanks for letting me know," Siyon told Zagiri, and tried to conjure up a smile. "Now go get some sleep. You can't come where we're going, anyway."

"Why?" she demanded. "Where are you going?"

Over the Swanneck, down the switchback main road. Along the narrow, mud-grimed alleyways, under the cross-strung washing and over the dank drainage ditches. Into the heart of Dockside.

Into Siyon's past.

"You sure about this?" Daruj asked, as they took the lichen-scaled stairs into the depths of the Dockside stews.

"Yeah." But Siyon didn't meet his eyes. "Sure."

He knew he had to. He knew he desperately didn't want to.

It stank—of fish and muck and ocean rubbish, of blood and spilled liquor and yet more fish. Always more fish. The rank tang of it crawled up his nose and straight into his memories, painting familiarity over every step they took. Laborers and fishwives, darting sharp-eyed children and their older siblings loitering malevolently in the doorways, too old to play and too young yet to crew a boat.

It was a dangerous age, that. They eyed Siyon and Daruj; Daruj eyed them right back, his hand resting comfortably on the hilt of his sabre.

Siyon just wanted to get this done. Except now that he was here, he didn't know where to start. It was all vital, it was all where he'd come from; it was all what he'd run from, and kept running.

Then he looked down, at the mud caked between the cobblestones. In that mud, daisies sprang up, cheerful and uncaring. As a child, Siyon had plucked them, weaving them into limp, muddy crowns that he'd presented to his mother and sisters. Now he pulled one up, tucked it into his satchel.

Suddenly he saw options everywhere. He scraped lichen off the landward side of a leaning stone wall. He pinched up a little of the sawdust that they still scattered on the front step of the Sailor's Rest, covering over last night's spilled blood. He plunged down Scale Street, letting the calls and cackles of the fishwives roll over him. (They had a lot of blunt offers for a good-looking young man with a working sabre, and no Flowery delicacy.) On his third attempt, Siyon managed to get to a discarded fishtail before one of the alley cats.

And then they turned a corner and found the laneway blocked by a wall of muscle.

Not bravi muscle, lean and dramatic, nor the sculpted and intimidating heavies the crime barons preferred. This was solid shipside brawn, built by dragging against the sea from age fourteen, when the fisherclan boys first went out on the boats.

And Velo was a proud and potent fisherclan.

Only three of them. That was enough. Three of them, and no one else on the street. The one in the middle spat into the mud at his feet. "Heard you were wandering around with your pretty boy. Didn't believe it. But here you are."

"Prettier than you," Daruj shot back. That bright lilt to his voice, a bounce to his step; he knew a fight when one introduced itself politely.

Siyon set a bracing hand against Daruj's chest. Now that they were here, the dread fell away. He felt clear as the eye of a storm. "Nice to see you too, Mezin. Bayan. Hep." He nodded to each of them. "This is my bladebrother, Daruj. Daruj, these are my born brothers."

Daruj went still beneath his hand. Was he scanning the faces, looking for familiarities? They'd all changed, all grown—it had been nine years—but Siyon could still spot them. He and Bayan had their mother's eyes. He and Hep shared a father, had got the red in their hair from him. And he and Mezin...

Mezin—the biggest, the strongest, the oldest; the leader, always—sneered. "Thought you were dead, little brother. Or rather, we *hoped*."

He and Mezin had their mother's ability to hold a grudge.

Siyon smiled, and didn't bother to make it pleasant. "Should have tried harder, Zin. How's Ma?"

"She don't want to see *you*," Hep jumped in.

"You talk for her now?" Siyon shot back.

Mezin ignored them all, his big bass voice cutting through the squabbling. "And then we start hearing this name. Siyon Velo. The *Notorious Sorcerer*. Saved the city." His lip curled again. Bayan spat, this time. "You think you're something now? Come swanning back down here—is that it?"

Siyon's heart was beating fast, despite it all, and his breath was coming quick. Mezin had always had that effect. Had been out on the boats for all of Siyon's life that he could remember. Could probably still pick Siyon up with one hand like he was a kitten.

Didn't matter.

"I think I was always something," Siyon said. "That's how I ended up here. How I survived. Why you put me in the sack in the first place. Isn't it? I was something *different*." Memories closed over Siyon's head; he couldn't stop the words bubbling up, the crack in his voice. "I was your *brother*, and you threw me in the river to *die*."

"You weren't supposed to—" Bayan stopped with a grunt as Mezin's elbow hit his side.

Say this for Mezin: He didn't flinch from meeting Siyon's glare like the other two. Just folded his arms, thick and scarred, and glared right back. "Yeah, you're something different. You and your fancy dancing boy here. Entertaining the za. Just another of their pets. Saved the city, my arse—you saved *them*. *Their* problems, *their* nonsense, and we all suffer." He sneered, and waved a dismissive hand. "Run along, dance some more. One day soon, we'll put you all in sacks."

He shouldered between the other two, marching away down the alley as they scuttled after. Bayan glanced back. Siyon didn't bother to wave.

In the silence, Daruj released a great sigh. "I see why you haven't invited me home before now." Siyon huffed a breath—not nearly a laugh—and Daruj added, "You told me you swam across the river to escape your family. I thought you were being *dramatic*."

Siyon scrubbed a hand over his face. He felt strangely numb. He didn't know what he'd expected here. Catharsis? A reconciliation? An *apology*? All laughable. "I wasn't supposed to drown," he allowed. "It was making a point. We all have to pull together, or we sink. I'd been resisting my assigned role. It was supposed to convince me to mind my place."

"Throwing you into the river in a sack?" Daruj sounded aghast. "Like drowning kittens?"

Just like. Excess sons who wouldn't work for the clan were just a wasteful nuisance. "Come on," Siyon said, and strode down the alley without looking to see if Daruj was following.

Not far at all, if you went straight down to the water. That thick and familiar stench—salty as the Abyss, rife with rubbish and rot, laden with spice and tar and a hundred other possibilities. The view was a forest of bobbing masts. Memory swamped Siyon as he strode along the dock, bootheels echoing against the wood. Here he'd lost a tooth biting the hand of a man trying to haul him off to join a work gang. Down there he'd won big playing knucklebones only to spend the lot on violets to impress a girl who was never going to be impressed, not by him. And just down here, around the corner toward the estuary, where the piers were rotting and silted up...

This was where he'd gone into the water, trussed up like some sacrifice to a river spirit. He usually kept the memory twisted up and shoved into a corner, but now he let it rise like a bubble, burst open around him.

The snarl in his ear—*You swim with us or you swim alone*—and the smack of the surface and the murk of the thick water. It had been shockingly cold. The rough hemp they'd tied him with had snagged on something, too dark to tell what, not going to give as he pulled and heaved and thrashed. Lungs burning, vision flaring, heart thundering.

"I wasn't supposed to drown," Siyon repeated. "That part was an accident."

Daruj nudged close to his shoulder, one point of warmth against the chill of sea breeze and memory. "So what—they relented and saved you?"

"No." The memory was murky and deep, but that hadn't been it at all.

Help, he'd begged, a violent burning need in his chest. *Help, please.* He had reached—with everything he had, with every part that *could* reach when his hands couldn't.

He had *reached*. Siyon realised that now. The first time he'd felt that. Not the last.

And then—what? The impossible. The weight on his lungs had eased, like they'd found air from somewhere, and the rope had come undone just like that, like a mystery.

Siyon had flailed for the surface in a cloud of bubbles—where had they come from? Flailed and kept flailing, churning through the water, no thought but *away*, not stopping until his fingernails scraped scum from stone and he realised that he'd somehow swum the entire width of the river, pulling against its urging to slip away into the sea. He'd hauled himself out of the water into the lower city, and a whole new life.

I walked out of the water and into a human life. Tehroun had said that. The first thing he remembered was the docks. *There was need.*

And Siyon, saved by air, and a mystery.

Siyon clutched at the bulwark of the harbour, digging fingers into cold stone. Couldn't tell if the planes were shifting again, or if this giddiness was from realisation. It could be a coincidence. Siyon didn't think it was, though. What did it mean?

"Well," Daruj said beside him, clapping his hands together with forced jollity. "This is a fucking awful spot for it, so get a move on with your filthy sorcery so we can get gone before your murderous brother returns with your last brother and half a dozen cousins as well."

He grinned when Siyon looked at him, so Siyon laughed along with him.

Maybe it didn't mean anything. Maybe it didn't even matter what had saved him. He *had* survived. He was here.

He had always been something different.

CHAPTER 23

"You blessed and beautiful angel of the dawn,'" Daruj intoned as the waitress brought out a copper-burnished tray bearing a coffee pot and stack of thimble-shaped cups.

"It's evening," Siyon remarked.

"I am *quoting*. 'Thou multifarious and manifest—'" Daruj broke whatever nonsense might have come next with a yawn wide as a cat's. Siyon heard his jaw pop.

The waitress rolled her eyes, set the tray on the edge of the fountain, and headed back inside Café Regal.

"Thanks," Siyon called after her, pouring himself a thimble of coffee. Each sip was sharp and spiced, the liquid dark and glossy like the third of Izmirlian's workings.

Don't think about that now. Siyon had enough things to worry about.

Despite the coffee, Daruj sprawled against the fountain bowl like he could go to sleep right there. "You really don't have to do this now," he grumbled, and squinted up at Siyon. "How are you still so awake?"

Siyon shrugged. He *was* tired—bone-deep tired, an aching weariness behind his eyes—but he also felt strangely alert. As though he had sailed through the storm of fatigue into calm waters beyond. The

Square was gripped by evening bustle—water pattering in the fountain, crockery clattering in the teahouses, gossip and laughter and exhortations. Music floated from somewhere nearby, wafting strains of a zither, and a tambour, and the eerie wail of a flute.

Daruj was no doubt right. This was probably a terrible way to contemplate a major working, let alone...whatever category you might use for attempting to become the Power of the entire plane.

But how much time did he have left before the planes shook themselves thin enough for the Powers to breach?

So he shook out the purple coat and shrugged into it. If only he could become the Power of the Mundane as easily as he could become the Notorious Sorcerer. Put on the coat. Put on the hat.

Siyon tugged the collar straight, and picked up the sack. It was rough sackcloth, stamped with a blurred and indistinct brand. A tangled knot of scents wafted from it—the ghost of the coffee beans that it had once held, but also rich earth, dry brick, the tang of sawdust, a rank whiff of once-living things going bad. The contents shifted as Siyon picked it up, with a clink and rattle and slow, sliding rustle.

Daruj groaned, and refilled his coffee from the pot. "You want us to go shout the word? Auntie Geryss bade us tell anyone and everyone."

"Auntie Geryss wasn't doing *this*." Siyon peered inside the sack, at the muddle of wood and stone and other bits and pieces. A mess, really, jumbled together and stirred up.

Then again, just because bread was mixed and kneaded didn't make the individual ingredients any less important.

This wasn't just *his* city, in the sack. It was the city of all of them, high and low, wherever they were born, wherever they were heading. The true Bezim. A cross section of the city that the bravi provided, giving Siyon what mattered to them. Sand from the hippodrome and starflower from the rooftops of the Flower district and the thick, greenish mud that silted up the alley canals of the lower city. Those little, frilly leaves from the Avenue trees, one of the rushes they still scattered on the floor of the students' common hall at the university, even—"Bloody hell." Siyon pulled something cold and hard and gleaming out of the sack.

The candle badge of an inquisitor.

Daruj blinked. "I am not asking how they came by that."

Siyon neither, but he dropped it back into the sack. After all, the inqs were the city too, part of it by blood and life and love, even if they'd like to murder Siyon for even attempting this. He was still doing it for them as much as anyone else.

All the things Siyon himself had collected were in there too, along with the splinters and brick, stone and glass, fruit and seashells. No one thing more or less important than the rest.

"Right," he muttered, and looked around. The centre of the square would be most appropriate—it could stand in as the heart of a city that was, really, heartless. But the square was actually a complicated misshape, and the sprawl of teahouse tables made the centre more difficult still to reckon. The paving was more chaos than pattern, a whole history of the uses of the square and artistic movements of the city mingled with ad hoc repairs in different sorts of stone.

All of that made this the best place to do this. History, stone, endeavour, the constant stamp of passing traffic. So Siyon just stepped far enough from the fountain to give himself space, and figured here would do as well as anywhere.

Daruj shoved aside the coffee tray. "What do you want me to do, then?"

The night was properly settling into its swing around them. The bravi tribes had mostly trickled away into the alleyways, hiding their true paths and destinations. The other patrons of the teahouses were moving on to other evening entertainments.

More than a few were lingering, casting curious looks in Siyon's direction.

"Keep your distance, you and everyone else too." He hesitated a moment, then added, "And lend me your blade."

Daruj looked scandalised, but it was a show of the strength of their friendship that he drew his sabre all the same. Lantern light ran over the etchings on the blade, and caught in the basket hilt. His blade right now, but Daruj was hardly the first Diviner Prince to run with Little Bracken and carry this sabre. The way the bravi saw it, what

Daruj did—and now, by extension, what Siyon was about to do—would attach to the tale of the blade, and be carried on into history.

Siyon thought that all the more fitting.

He used it to draw the circle, shaking the salt down the blade. Useful stuff, salt. Altered the boiling point of liquids and helped things crystallise, but it was also of all planes and none, especially this sort, dried from the sea with sun and air into crystals. Cost more than Siyon could usually countenance, but nothing was *usual* right now. The salt made an excellent border, a demarcation line, dividing the specific area of his working from the rest of the universe.

Also made an obvious boundary to keep out the overly curious and foolhardy.

Speaking of—two bravi came sauntering around the fountain, with the blue-fringed leathers and many-pierced ears of the Awl Quarter. "Steady as she goes," one with a sea-green plume on her tricorn called.

"Brave the knife," Daruj responded, squaring up outside the salt circle. He held up empty hands. "This isn't business of the blade."

The other Awl Quarter, purple-plumed, pointed at Siyon. "Here, you're that alchemist what brung back the prefect's son, ain't you?"

"He never is. The Notorious Sorcerer?" Sea-Green squinted. "I thought he'd be... grander."

Siyon couldn't argue with the lack of grandeur; even with the purple coat stiff across his shoulder, his boots were scuffed by the day's travel, and his fingernails rimed in black Docks grime. But this was who he was. This was what the Mundane was. Not just grand, but also the dirt.

More people drifted over as Siyon hefted the sack. A giggling group in their theatre finery, an older couple hanging back, a trio of black-clad Haruspex bravi. There was even a pair of inquisitors, loitering back near the teahouse tables. Their regard still sent unease crawling over Siyon's skin, but he shrugged it off. Let them watch.

Gawking was as much a part of Bezim as anything in this sack.

Siyon tipped it all out in a heap inside the circle. The scent of it now reminded him of nothing so much as a building site—of things disturbed and things being put into order, creation and destruction in progress. He nudged his toes into the outer edge of his pile of detritus and considered what to do from here. Bury his hands in the mess? Paint it over his skin? He'd get filthy, but he'd been filthy before, and probably would be again.

But the thing he wanted wasn't *in* these things. Siyon climbed up atop the mound instead, balancing carefully. He looked up, past the buildings and the ponderous tick of the clock, up into the sky. The stars were faded, but scattered like seeds upon the earth. Like promises and potential.

He wished Izmirlian were here, could see this too. But he couldn't start delaying his life to make Izmirlian a part of it. Not when Izmirlian, if all went well, would be even more than gone soon.

Focus, Velo.

He drew a breath, and laid Daruj's sabre against his palm. "I am of this plane," he muttered. The words weren't for the gathered curious, shifting and shuffling and wondering what he was about. He was speaking to the universe. This wasn't about the mastery that Joddani had claimed, but something else. "I am of this plane, and this plane is of me. With this, I assert my belonging. I lay claim to the Power of the Mundane."

He turned the blade and let it cut into the meat of his palm, let it drag forth blood. It hurt—of course it did, of course it *should*. Siyon was binding himself to the working, making his intent manifest.

He tilted his hand and let the blood drip down. One drop, two, three, splashing down upon the city in symbol beneath his boots.

The clock ticked once, and then silence. The wind stopped. The gentle simmer of the crowd ceased. The universe turned to look upon him.

Siyon felt the weight of it. It settled gently, and kept settling—a blanket of the drowning deep, a smothering of dense fire, a crushing stone of nothing at all. It kept coming, more and more and more, too much wine in a too-small cup. The universe leaned upon his shoulders—no, not all of it, just a quarter, just this part that he had the temerity to lay claim to, but even that was far too much. Siyon gasped, but there was no air. He flexed his shoulders, and braced his feet against the shifting rubble, and—

Just for a moment, he held it. Bore it up, the city and the people and the *world*. He could feel the breadth and depth and intricacy of it all, he could *taste it*. It was pushing *up* through him even as the universe bore down.

For a moment.

And then it tilted in his grasp, too wide and deep and immense for him to balance. It slipped through his fingers and slid away in all directions at once, and there was nothing he could do, no way to catch it all. Might as well try to catch the rain.

The clock ticked again, and Siyon landed on his knees in a pile of mud and rubbish. Blood on his hand, tears on his face. The sabre rattled against the cobblestones.

The universe leered and veered around him. Stars burst across his vision. He held on to consciousness with fingernails and grim determination. The universe shook—

Not just the universe. The rattle of plates, the scrape of the café tables against the paving, shrieks and cries, as the entire city trembled, like a shudder passing down a spine.

Panic clutched Siyon's heart in its fist. He'd failed, like the Committee, and just like then the earth would shake, and shake, and fall into the sea.

But it settled, and stilled, and the night closed silent and shocked around them.

Silent only for a moment, before exploding into babble, cries, people rushing about.

Siyon couldn't take it in. That brief moment of relief—that he hadn't Sundered the city again—was drowning in a flood of bitter truth. He had still *failed*. It burned like the breath scraping at his lungs, pounded in his mind like the headache knocking its corners against his skull.

He'd thought he was *different*. He'd thought he could do the impossible. He'd felt it, for just a moment. But a moment wasn't enough.

"Siyon," Daruj was calling, outside the salt line. "Brother! Are you well?" An edge to his concern, and Siyon couldn't blame him.

He was not well. He was on his knees in the muck, and teetering at the edge of a cliff. He had *failed*, and he didn't know what to do. *I fuck up all the time*, he'd told Nihath, and he did, but this time *mattered*.

He'd failed, and now there was nothing between them and the storm.

Siyon tilted his head back, staring up at the night sky, and struggled to breathe against the weight of this.

Someone was shouting his name, and he didn't care. What did it matter? The crowd shifted and muttered and there were feet scuffing and—

"Siyon!" Zagiri shouted, grabbing his shoulder, looming in his vision, demanding his attention. She was panting, wild-eyed, hair blown back like she'd been sprinting. "You have to come. *Now.*"

Her urgency pricked at the thick blanket that smothered him, but Siyon could barely feel it. He shook his head. "I didn't—"

She cut him off. "It's Hisarani. Something's wrong."

Wrong was an understatement.

Hot on Zagiri's heels, Siyon took the front door of the Joddani townhouse—up the stairs, through the front hall, up again two at a time—without even thinking about it. The clock that stood in the front hall had crashed down on its face during the tremor, and Siyon leapt over it. The planes still twitched and shivered around him, and Siyon ignored them. Anahid stepped back on the landing to let him pass.

Siyon's door was open, his room unchanged. Curtains drawn, bed covers disarranged, Izmirlian Hisarani lying almost neatly in the midst of it, limbs quiet beneath the rumpled sheets. Still naked, from the bare shoulder visible.

When Siyon careened into the doorframe, Izmirlian's head turned, just a little, from his contemplation of the ceiling. His eyes glittered in the light of the lantern left on the table. But that was the only movement in his face. He didn't smile, or frown. He lay, and breathed, and watched with complete disinterest.

Siyon's skin crawled under that impassive stare. He didn't realise he was moving until his knees hit the carpet beside the bed. He reached out to lay a hand against Izmirlian's jaw, and turned his face away, up toward the ceiling again.

Izmirlian just let him do it. Didn't tilt away, or bat at Siyon's wrist, or even flinch from the icy touch of Siyon's night-chilled hands. Siyon's hand was still bleeding where he'd slashed his palm; he left smears of red against Izmirlian's cheek.

Siyon stared at the obliging tilt of Izmirlian's neck in horror.

Gone. He was just—*gone*. First his voice, and now this. Was this what Siyon was doing? Stripping away, piece by piece, everything that made Izmirlian beautiful, vibrant, alive. Everything that made him *himself*.

Siyon's breath laboured in his throat. His stomach twisted. He lurched backward, caught his heel in the carpet, sat down hard on the floor.

Izmirlian just lay there. No amusement, no concern, no caustic commentary.

There was a notebook on the floor near Siyon's foot, pages splayed to reveal familiar whiplash handwriting. The pencil had been smeared, but was still legible.

I trust you. I believe in you.

He shouldn't have. This was wrong. It was *terrible*.

Siyon skidded back out of his room, tearing past Anahid on the landing to leap down the stairs in dangerous bounds. A thundering noise followed him down, but even if Siyon had knocked something else over, he wasn't stopping to check.

But the noise came again—a hammering against the front door. A voice bellowed.

Siyon fled down the servants' stairs as well, through the still room, into the workroom.

He would find what had gone wrong. Something must have gone wrong, and he would fix it, would fix Izmirlian, would fix all of this—

The three workings still sat on the bench, in their careful incomplete square of ceramic dishes, as he'd shown them to Anahid.

This morning, they had seemed perfect. A display of Siyon's mastery, of the strength of his new style of working, of the balance and grace of his blend of instinct and Negedic structure. He had been inspired and enthused by his achievement. He had believed he could achieve anything. Could become the Power.

He couldn't. He hadn't. He'd nearly Sundered the city all over again. The planes were still echoing with it, ringing like a gong that wouldn't return to silence.

And now he stared at the workings and couldn't see anything wrong. Not here, in the alchemy. Only upstairs, in the results. He had no clue where to start fixing this. No idea what had gone wrong. He had *no idea*. What had he been thinking? Gutter brat, plane-raider, enthusiastic amateur. Just enough Negedic knowledge to get in trouble. Just enough to ruin someone's *life*.

Izmirlian had trusted him. Siyon was a fool and worse than a fool.

"Siyon Velo!" someone bellowed, powerful and stern and familiar.

Siyon started to laugh. Turned around as Vartan Xhanari loomed in the doorway to the still room. Those black eyes travelled swiftly over every incriminating inch—hanging herbs and stacked glassware and the benches and the vial of firesand Siyon had left out. Did it matter? "I have license from the prefect to practise the Art," Siyon pointed out, the irony curling bitter around his tongue. He had license to break everything.

Xhanari's smile was flat with satisfaction. "Your license has been revoked. Enkin Danelani has sickened of the foul magics that you worked upon him, *sorcerer*." He stepped inside the room, close enough now to lay hands on Siyon. "The truth will always come out. He will die, and so will you."

Siyon had to close his eyes against the shock of it, and yet he couldn't say he was surprised. Of *course*. Everything Siyon had wrought was broken. Was *wrong*.

He deserved to be dragged away for it. Deserved every vengeful and righteous piece of *justice* that Xhanari would delight in bringing to pass. Siyon had lived in such fear of Xhanari, and now he couldn't even argue. He'd earned the poison that awaited him.

But there was at least one thing that he *could* fix.

Xhanari grabbed his arm, just above the elbow, but Siyon threw him off. Nowhere he could go, of course, not with Olenka in the doorway, another pair of inqs behind her. All Siyon's resistance could buy him was a moment or three.

That was all he needed.

He snatched up that careless vial of firesand, whipped out the stopper—with his injured hand, blood smearing the glass—and flung the contents at his three *perfect* workings on the bench.

The firesand glimmered in the air, white and gold and diamond-bright. It ignited the rakia-soaked linen of the first working, sheared through the inken bubble of the second, turned the dark liquid of the third into instant, hissing steam. The ceramic dishes cracked.

And the workings exploded.

Scalding gold and harsh grey sparks fountained up toward the ceiling, sizzling and skittering across the bench. *Empyreal flare*, Siyon realised, with a wondrous satisfaction. The release of power from a broken working. He'd done it. He had freed Izmirlian.

Xhanari bellowed, and Anahid was shouting in the hall outside, but neither of them were audible over the excoriating noise of the flare. Olenka leapt forward, with her arms spread wide as wings and her hair a wild halo, dazzling with sparks. She screamed—like a raptor plummeting onto its prey.

Something heavy hit the side of Siyon's head, and darkness swallowed him whole.

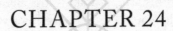

CHAPTER 24

Helplessness clawed at Anahid as Siyon was carried unconscious from her house. The hawk-faced woman closed the door firmly behind them all, and the house fell into silence.

Save for Zagiri, who shouted for the third time, "Let me *go!*"

The footman had her pinned in a corner, more successful at restraining her than Anahid had imagined possible when she'd given the desperate order. The last thing any of them needed was Zagiri getting taken in as well for assault upon an inquisitor. "Thank you," Anahid said now. "You may return to your duties."

He stepped away with such alacrity that Zagiri staggered, but only for a moment before she charged forward. "How could you just let them *take* him?"

"How could I have stopped them?" Anahid shouted back, like a release. "Inquisitors, Giri! He caused a flare right in front of them!"

Her face twisted up in anguish, and Anahid's heart twisted with it.

"We must do something, though," Nihath said from the parlour where he'd been cowering—or sensibly keeping out of the way—during the whole business.

Zagiri stared at him. "*You're* on my side?"

"I'm on *his* side," Nihath corrected. "Or maybe all our sides. There was a moment earlier—"

"When the world shook, yes, we all felt it." Anahid slumped down on the stairs, overcome by weariness.

But Nihath shook his head. "Before that. Before he lost his hold. He *had* a hold. And for that moment, the planes were as a sea becalmed."

Anahid wondered if that news made any more sense to Zagiri than it made to her.

Nihath huffed, but further explanation was interrupted by the rasp of a new voice from upstairs. "He means that Siyon nearly did it."

At the top of the stairs, Izmirlian Hisarani leaned heavily against the railing. His shirt was unlaced, and his eyes hollow, but he was upright, and speaking.

Or croaking, at least. "He nearly became the Power of the Mundane, didn't he?"

"I believe so, yes." Nihath drew himself up. "And he must be given the chance to try again. For all our sakes. You said it—" He pointed at Anahid. "You all felt that tremor. We need a balancing influence."

Zagiri snorted. "Well, I'm sure if you explain it to the inquisitors, they'll be *happy* to let him have another crack."

"The prefect might," Izmirlian rasped. He took a step down, blanched, and sat down hard on the stairs. "If she could be applied to."

"She might," Anahid agreed, "save that her son is sickening fit to perish. You missed that part." It seemed insensitive to bring up, even before Izmirlian winced; how did one refer delicately to the time an acquaintance had spent apparently absent from his body?

"And it's not like we could get to her." Zagiri kicked at a rucked-up fold of the rug.

The others nodded glumly, but Anahid hesitated. "Perhaps I could," she said, considering her options. She knew the prefect's sister-in-law, after all. Knew her well enough to know her secrets.

But would Tahera even receive her? Nihath had been pardoned for his arrest, but now another sorcerer had been dragged from their house by the inquisitors.

If she went *now*, the news may not have spread so far.

The others watched her expectantly. "If I can get him a chance with the prefect, whether to fix Enkin or have another go at"—Anahid

waved a hand toward Nihath, and all his alchemical accoutrement—
"he'll need to make best use of it. He'll need help. What can be mustered, right now?"

Nihath frowned deeper still. "I don't know that the practitioners
will come to his aid. Yesterday, without a doubt, but today…"

Today, Siyon had fallen from grace.

"Would they come for *you*?" Anahid demanded.

If Siyon's victory was coming undone, that cast a cloud over
Nihath's pardon as well. From the uneasiness on her husband's face,
the thought had occurred to him too. But what he said was: "I won't
know until I ask."

Anahid nodded. "Then let's ask." Quickly. Before the news spread.

"I'll carry the notes," Izmirlian said, a little more power to his
voice now. "Let me put my name behind this as well."

And Zagiri piped up. "We still have a lot of alchemists at the
Chapel. Their knowledge might not be so fancy—"

"But it may be even more appropriate, in the circumstances,"
Nihath agreed, to Anahid's surprise.

"We'll meet tomorrow, here, with as many as will come." Anahid stood, and brushed down her dress. She'd still not changed for
evening, with all the hullabaloo, but she couldn't delay now. "And in
the meantime, I will pay a call, and see whether the prefect cannot be
influenced in our direction."

If the Danelani footman was perplexed by Anahid's plain dress,
he hid it behind an impassive mask, though the parlour he showed her
into was small and simple. She had just long enough to wait that she
started to rethink this entire business. Maybe she should have written
instead? But her last letter to Tahera had not gained the reaction she'd
hoped. This time, Anahid wanted to see Tahera's face.

She wanted, she realised, to judge the comparative strengths of
both their hands. Like this was cards, and she was playing to win.

Like she had against Vartan Xhanari, before a crowd on the steps
of her house. She'd been terrified, and yet…it hadn't been entirely
unpleasant. Not just the winning, but the contest. Matching her will
against another's.

But that had been an inquisitor, and this—here and now—was someone Anahid had thought a friend.

Tahera finally swept in with a smile nearly as dazzling as her evening gown, the beading on her headscarf glittering like her laughter. "Ana, *darling*, what a surprise! You only just caught me, we're on the way out—my goodness, *look* at you, is there an emergency?"

Perhaps Anahid should have stayed sitting to start this conversation with a semblance of casual ease. But nervous energy popped her to her feet. "There rather is," she admitted. "A dear friend of mine has been arrested."

Tahera gasped. "Oh, how terrible! Come, sit, do you need tea? Perhaps rakia would be better." She reached for the bell.

But Anahid stopped her, left her hand on Tahera's wrist as she said, "I need your intervention."

"My—?" Tahera blinked at her, and a shadow came over her eyes. As she learned that this visit was not about friendship, but influence. She stayed as she was, but a distance slid between them nonetheless.

Anahid regretted that, but not nearly as much as she would Siyon's execution.

"I fear you overestimate my influence with my sister-in-law," Tahera said, all composure now. "Perhaps if the matter is minor..." She trailed off, lifted a questioning brow.

Of course Anahid would not be here, in desperation, for a *minor* matter. "It is sorcery."

With helplessly spread hands, Tahera shook her head. "I wish there was more I could do, but the law is the law, and Syrah is a woman of great strength of will."

Anahid's heart thundered. "Please," she begged. "I know you cannot set him free, but just a word to her might help. For the friendship growing between us, that I treasure beyond the telling of it, please won't you—"

"Anahid," Tahera interjected firmly. Almost disapprovingly. Like the tone of the note she'd sent. Like Anahid was being *inappropriate* again.

Anahid drew herself up. She released Tahera's arm and clasped her hands together. She could almost feel Tahera's secret between her palms, like the winning card waiting to be played.

She hadn't wanted to play it. But Tahera had left her no choice.

"Syrah Danelani *is* a woman of great strength of will," Anahid said, in echo of Tahera's earlier words. "But I know she has some flexibility when it comes to her family. After all, if she'll whisk you overseas to avoid a few little debts, surely she'll listen on other matters."

Tahera went suddenly, entirely still. She'd had excellent control at the carrick table, as well. Over her face, at least. Not so much over her losses. "What are you talking about?" she said, voice like ice.

Anahid hated it. Would give almost anything to have the warmth back in Tahera's voice. To not be seeing the last budding shoot of their friendship dying in the frost. Tahera had been a breath of fresh air when Anahid had not even realised she was suffocating.

She would give almost anything, but she wouldn't give Siyon's life.

"I met some interesting people in the district," Anahid said. "Who told me some positively scurrilous rumours that of *course* I won't be repeating to anyone else. Not when we're such good friends."

She didn't smile. She couldn't. There was too much on the table, to be won and lost.

Tahera turned stiffly away and threw open the parlour door. Anahid felt faint, sure she was about to be ordered out. Sure she had lost everything.

But Tahera shouted up the stairs, "Darling, I'll see you at the party. I need to pop over and chat with Syrah about something." She turned back and glared at Anahid. "Get out."

Relief flooded Anahid, making her knees wobble even as she slipped past Tahera in the doorway. "Good evening to you, and compliments to your family," she managed.

She left the house, and made it to the first of the avenue's tall trees before her knees gave way entirely. Anahid pressed a hand against the trunk, careful not to snag her net gloves, and drew a shaky breath.

The door of the Danelani townhouse opened behind her, and Anahid slipped around the tree, peeking out of the shadows to watch

Tahera, now swathed in a shawl, march down the stairs and off toward the Palace of Justice.

Anahid wanted to laugh. She wanted to cry. She had no idea if the hand would be worth anything at all—if Syrah would listen, or if Siyon could do anything with the chance—but she had played and won.

And it had only cost her the first true friend she'd made in years.

Zagiri hadn't expected to find Voski Tolan in the Chapel, not at this late evening hour. And from the surprised once-over, Voski certainly hadn't expected to see Zagiri in a gown rather than bravi leathers.

"Shouldn't you be out on the tiles?" Zagiri asked.

The Bracken sergeant snorted. "Telling me how to do my business now, za?"

Most of the tribe *were* out, the space of the Chapel echoing around only the skeleton double-six always in residence to meet any opportunistic incursion. They sparred, or played carrick, or tended their kit.

When Voski whistled, one of them popped to his feet and came jogging over, carrying something slung over one shoulder. Siyon's satchel, Zagiri realised.

"This got left behind," Voski said, "when you and Velo went haring off from the square. Figured he'd want it back."

He would. If he ever got out, if he ever got his chance, he would need it. "There's a problem with that," Zagiri admitted. "The inqs took him."

Voski swore. "Then that lot in the crypt were right to be worried."

That lot. "There's more?" Zagiri slung the satchel across her body, the way Siyon wore it. It hung low on her, and looked stupid with her dress, but she had other things to worry about. "They're actually why I'm here."

The crypt had been fitted out with bunks, with other furniture, with alchemical lanterns. It was no less comfortable than the Bracken dormitory upstairs now, but like the dorm, it wasn't really a place to live.

When Zagiri descended the stairs, her slippers barely whispering on the stone floor, heads popped out of the niches. A family of four over here, the children fast asleep; a pair of older women; a trio of what looked to be brothers; more up the back.

The place was half full again, and none of them even knew yet that their fears were entirely justified.

Jaleh Kurit stepped out of a niche. "I'm guessing it's no good news that you're here so soon after that earthquake." Her eyes snagged on the satchel strap across Zagiri's body, and she frowned deeper still.

She'd known Siyon well, at one point, and he'd had this satchel a long time.

"Siyon's been arrested," Zagiri confirmed. "He tried something, and it—didn't work. And the prefect's son has taken sick, and the rewards and protections have been revoked."

Consternation rippled through the listening practitioners, but none of them looked particularly surprised. They would be entirely justified in saying *I told you so*.

"Then we need to get out tonight," one of the brothers said.

Voski spoke up from behind Zagiri. "Plans are underway. Rushing won't get you nothing but caught. Be patient, and you'll be got out."

Zagiri took a deep breath. "Or you could stay and help." They looked at her, concerned and uneasy. "Siyon needs help, and I have no faith that he will get it from my lot." An understatement, and Zagiri sighed, standing there in her azatani gown. "We say the city is ours, that we manage things for the good of everyone, but we'll only fight for the parts that we like. When it gets hard and inconvenient, it's people like Siyon who take the risk, and get the blame. People like Geryss Hanlun. People like you."

She met Jaleh's challenging gaze. The woman had her arms folded, but she was listening. They all were.

"I won't blame you at all if you choose to go," Zagiri said. "That's only fair. You can feel how bad it's got in ways I can't. And you've already fought every day just to have a life here. I don't know how to fix that, though I'd like to try. But we need to fix this first. Get the city properly back in balance. And Siyon can, if we can get him a chance, and the support he needs."

Jaleh's mouth twisted thoughtfully. "You believe in him that much?"

Zagiri wasn't sure if she sounded more sceptical or challenging. It didn't matter. She'd doubted Siyon before—when Jaleh first came to her—because he'd not quite matched what she thought an alchemist should be.

But he was using what he had in different ways, to get things done.

"I do believe in him," Zagiri declared. "He caught me in the Tower Square, when I fell from the clock." The memory still made her throat close in panic; Zagiri forced the words through. "And he found the prefect's son in the first place."

"Fucked it up, by the sounds of it," one of the older women pointed out.

"But he did it," one of the brothers shot back.

Zagiri kept going: "Nihath said he was nearly successful in whatever he was doing in the square earlier this evening. He said it could be felt, a moment of stillness in the planes."

Some of them exchanged looks, and Zagiri's heart leapt a little. Yes, they *had* felt it.

"Nihath Joddani?" someone asked. "Is he on board with this?"

"You still want azatani approval?" Jaleh Kurit snapped. "After everything that brought you here?" There was a belligerent jut to her jaw. "Look, I like Siyon. I always did. Anyone can pull off some audacious gullshit, it's him. But he's not an alchemist."

"He's not," Zagiri agreed, and squared her shoulders, the strap of his satchel shifting on her shoulder. "He wouldn't disagree with you. But the alchemists have failed already. We need something else now. Siyon has done the impossible. But he can't do it alone."

Zagiri didn't know what she saw in their faces, as she looked desperately from one to another. Uncertainty, distrust, concern, speculation.

The practitioners turned to each other, and whispers sizzled around the stone crypt.

Voski Tolan laid a hand on Zagiri's shoulder, tugging her attention around. "For what it's worth," the sergeant said, "*we're* with you."

Zagiri shook her head. "This is defying the inqs direct," she pointed out. "It's too big a risk for the tribe—for all the bravi. I didn't wear my leathers for a reason."

Voski smiled, like she did fronting an all-blades, like she did waiting in ambush. Above everything else, she hated to be bored; and she loved a glorious challenge. "Once Bracken, always Bracken," she stated. "Both you and him. This is our city too. And you, who talked the other tribes into being a part of this—" She flicked her fingers toward the furiously arguing knots of alchemists. "You think they won't want in on this? You'll need runners and distractions aplenty, before this is done."

They would, they surely would, and Zagiri felt brimful of gratitude, worried it might spill over in tears.

But before she could thank Voski, Jaleh's strident voice cut through the murmurs. "Right. You lot can make your own choices, but I've made mine."

Zagiri's heart sank. Surely the woman—Siyon's vehement former lover, who had raised such pointed objections, whose master had been poisoned—would choose to flee. How many others would follow her lead? "Please," Zagiri said, stepping forward.

But Jaleh interrupted. "I'm in." Zagiri blinked at her, and one corner of Jaleh's mouth twitched up in a humourless smirk. "I owe him one anyway. What's your plan?"

"We—" *don't really have one.* Zagiri couldn't say that. "Are still working it out."

That was hardly any better, but Jaleh's snort sounded amused. "Typical for Velo. You said something about the Danelani kid sickening? We might as well start there. See if we can figure out some breathing room. But let's wait for them." She jerked her chin toward the rest of the crypt.

"You think they'll come too?" Zagiri asked.

Jaleh was definitely smiling now, though it was a grim expression.

"This is our city too. Our *alchemy* too. None of us *want* to leave. If we have a real choice."

In the end, she was right. They all asked to stay, though the family of four elected to remain in the crypt, working on brewing up alchemical surprises to be scattered over the city by the bravi as distractions to draw inq attention.

Zagiri watched them all, eagerly arguing over ways to make a bigger bang, and hoped fervently that she hadn't just invited them all to their deaths.

Siyon clawed his way out of unconsciousness with pain thumping in his head, throbbing counterpoint in his hand. He pressed hand to head—both were padded with bandages—and groaned. Memory came back in shards. Racing through the city with Zagiri; his brother's sneer; Izmirlian's blank gaze; the slipping weight of the universe; the fountaining of Empyreal sparks.

The world heaved around him, and he didn't know if it was the planes, or just the pain in his head. With gentle fingers, Siyon skirted the edges of the bandage over the lump on his head. Blood matted his hair. What had they hit him with?

"Dowsing rod," Olenka said.

Siyon jerked upright, eyes flying open in a surge of panic. The room veered and skewed sickeningly around him. He caught one wild glimpse of a stern silhouette in eye-gouging sunlight, before he slumped back onto the soft sheets.

Where *was* he? He'd expected the holding cells, a hard wooden bench, no sympathy as they dragged him before a perfunctory magistrate. It wouldn't have surprised him to not wake up at all; they could have just poured the executioner's poison down his unconscious throat.

Instead, when Siyon took brief and dizzy peeks around a spacious room, he saw a bed, and windows, and a heavy table with heavier chairs, in one of which sat a grey-uniformed woman with her wild hair pulled back severely.

Siyon had last seen Olenka limned in Empyreal sparks like they loved her. The leap, the scream, the righteous focus of her face.

So familiar. Why hadn't he realised sooner? Not just *an* angel.

"You attacked me," Siyon croaked. "In Empyre. Tried to sever my tether."

It was still too bright in the room, but if Siyon opened his eyes only a sliver, he could just about see her. She cocked her head like a hawk. "You have often," she said, "deserved attacking."

Not even slightly a denial. How had she Fallen? Why was she working with the inquisitors? What had she done with that massive flaming broadsword?

But even as Siyon opened his mouth, Olenka said, "You have far bigger problems than me, little sorcerer. Were you paying attention at all, at your arrest, or just keen to indulge in mayhem?" She leaned forward, her eyes keen as a blade. "The prefect's son is dying."

That mayhem hadn't been an indulgence, and now Siyon was burning with other questions—had it worked? Was Izmirlian whole again? Was it *enough*?

Would Izmirlian ever forgive him for breaking his trust? Or would it be breaking the working—the thing he wanted most—that would do the damage?

He'd never find out, of course. They were going to kill him. Or maybe the planes would rupture first. Just like it was pointless to worry about the mess he'd left at Anahid's house, but still Siyon asked: "Did you contain the flare?"

Olenka snorted. "Lucky for you I was there. You are a walking disaster, Velo. Appalling that you are the best chance we have." She stood, and the scrape of the chair legs carved through Siyon's head. By the time he could see again, she was standing over him, holding a glass of water. "Sit up," she ordered. "Drink. You need to be functional."

She made a better sentinel than nursemaid, but with her none-too-gentle assistance Siyon managed to slump a little more upright. The water was bliss, cool and soothing down his throat. He drank a little more. He needed to be functional. "Then you shouldn't have hit me with a—" He blinked. "A dowsing rod, seriously?"

"What Xhanari had to hand."

Solid star-iron, or so the story went. No wonder Siyon's head felt half-cracked. But with the water, and Olenka blocking the worst of the light, Siyon could summon enough reason to wonder... "Why do I need to be functional to be executed for sorcery?"

She cocked her head. "So eager to die? I thought you'd made promises. I thought you had *plans*."

A spark of curiosity—how did she know all of that?—was smothered under a rising tide of despair. "Promises I can't keep. Plans that don't work. Surely you felt it too—I nearly broke the city again."

"Nearly," Olenka echoed. "It's been a long time since anyone else managed that sort of grasp, and then it was eight of them."

Siyon thought of that sheaf of notes in the locked annex of the library: *The Committee for the Completion of the Master Work*. Had there been eight names on the list?

Wait a moment. "How do you know that?"

She looked down at him with blank judgment. "I watched them try. Fools all. How would being Power by committee have worked?"

"You *watched* them?" Siyon gaped at her. "That was a century and a half ago."

Olenka looked mildly surprised about that, then shrugged. "I was young. So are you. There's time to try again."

Siyon dropped his head into his hands; it ached worse than ever, the pain throbbing along spiderweb cracks with every thud of his heart. He just wanted to give up, but desperate scrambling was a habit carved on his bones. He *hadn't* broken the city. And it had nearly worked. *Could* he try again?

Not from here, he couldn't. Not in what he now recognised as the cell he'd sprung Joddani from. Ironic. As quick as it had kindled, the trembling light of possibility was snuffed out. "Sure. Plenty of time before they kill me."

Olenka reached down and grabbed the front of his shirt with fingers sharp enough to be talons. Her smile was stern and unyielding as she said, "Maybe not."

She hauled him out of bed—one-handed, easy as you please—and set Siyon on shaky legs. He had to grab at her arm just to stay upright, but she held him there until he was steady and the room stopped whirling around him. Had the door been open all this time? There were two armed men out there, in the white of the Prefecture, rather than the grey of the inquisitors.

Olenka said, "The prefect wants to see you."

Siyon grabbed at the back of a chair. "What?"

"One last chance to plead your case." Olenka considered him, and Siyon felt more like the mouse to her hawk than ever.

"I don't have any pleas," he admitted. "I fucked it all up. And Enkin Danelani is *dying*, and the Demon Queen will bite a chunk out of us like a ripe peach, maybe duel your old boss in Tower Square for who gets the shark's share of reality, and all of this is *my fault*." The last words were more like a wail than Siyon liked.

But Olenka just shrugged, and laid a hand on his shoulder to steer him out into the corridor. "You might want to think of something, between here and there. Because someone's pulled a lot of strings to get you this chance. *Someone* believes in you, Siyon Velo." She shoved something into his arms—that stupid purple coat. "Try not to let them down."

CHAPTER 25

For someone who apparently wanted to see him, the prefect glared poisonously enough to execute Siyon right then and there, beside her son's sickbed.

No, she wasn't wearing her robes of office, was stripped back to bloodshot eyes, twisted-up hair, plain dress, and plainer desperation. Not the prefect, but Syrah Danelani who snapped, "Well, what do you have to say for yourself?"

The white-sashed Palace guard escorting Siyon had no compunction about putting pressure on Siyon's already injured hand. Siyon barely had the strength to stand, let alone fight his way out of the armlock.

Someone had bought him this chance, and Siyon wondered who, and what it had cost. *Try not to let them down*, Olenka had said, and all Siyon could think was that he already had. He let everyone down— his family, Little Bracken, all those who'd taken him in and given him a chance.

Think of something, Olenka had said, and Siyon couldn't. He'd tried everything. Was this how Nihath had felt, closing Negedi's notebooks? *It is not possible*. Nothing to be done but walk away.

Siyon couldn't walk away. Could go nowhere but where the guard dragged him, and that was forward, to the bedside of Enkin Danelani.

The prefect's son was a terrible sight. Sweat spiked his hair, plastered it to clammy skin that looked yellow where it wasn't almost green. Shadows clustered around his closed eyes, hollows sunk beneath his cheeks. Fever-gripped, he lacked the energy to toss or writhe, though his head tipped sluggishly back and forth, and one hand spasmed occasionally against the coverlet. The other was caught in his mother's white-knuckled grip.

As though her grasp could be tighter than death's.

Siyon looked up, and met her gaze. Haughty, sure, but also desperate. A mother watching her son die, with nothing she could do.

What did Siyon have to say for himself? Not a lot. They'd all be better off if he didn't even try—and he opened his mouth to tell her so. He'd broken everything—Izmirlian's commission, Enkin's retrieval, becoming the Power. He'd thought he could do all of it, and he'd been wrong. The only thing that *had* worked was...catching Zagiri.

The one thing he'd done without any Negedic structure at all.

Siyon closed his mouth again, thinking fast.

Syrah Danelani's face grew stormy. "If you can't even—"

"I fucked up," Siyon said quickly. "I admit it. I got your son back, but I did it wrong. I did a lot of things wrong. Please let me try to fix it. Let me try to find the right way."

She didn't sneer at him. Instead, despair carved lines down her face, which was almost worse. "I think you've done enough, don't you?"

Siyon couldn't even call it unfair.

But a new voice spoke from the corner. "He can hardly do more harm."

Siyon hadn't realised anyone else was in the room. The slender, quiet man faded into the background, just generic azatani—dark hair going to grey, good tailoring, that bone structure the Avenues stamped on a man. But there was something familiar about the line of his jaw, the cant of his head.

Oh, of course. Enkin had a father as well as a mother.

Syrah closed her eyes, and her mouth tightened further, but she said, "Fine. Let him come."

The guard let Siyon go, but with every step closer to the bedside, Siyon's hopes—never high—fell further. He could feel the heat rising from Enkin's skin. A smell wafted with it, salty and ammonia-sharp and barbed with rank promise. The planes shifted and tilted, like they were uneasy as well, and Siyon barely noticed it for all the other wrongness.

What *was* this, that had Enkin in its grips? Xhanari had said he was *sickening of foul magics*. Was this some sort of withdrawal from being yanked out of the Abyss? Or was it something more specific? Siyon found himself wishing for Negedi's notebooks, and shoved that thought away.

Negedi knew no more than Siyon did. It was time to step away from that crutch, and see the world as it *was*.

Siyon picked up Enkin's wrist to check his heartbeat, and nearly dropped it again; the boy was hot as a full glass of tea. His pulse fluttered like a bird in Siyon's hand. Enkin's breath came harsh and rasping and yet somehow still damp as a swamp.

It all *felt* Abyssal, thick and fetid and tacky. Was there a chance this was just... Enkin sweating the planar influence out? Once he was rid of it, would he be fine?

A slender hope to balance his life upon.

Not to mention that it seemed impossible Enkin could ever be anything like fine. He was wrung out like a washcloth, churned by a storm and cast up on a desolate beach. His bones grated as he writhed.

This would kill him.

Try something, Siyon. *Think.* Something had been keeping Enkin in the Abyss—but he knew what that was. He remembered the harpy Laxmi, her serrated grin, her assertion that *You take him home, you take me home.*

Siyon hadn't. But Enkin had come along, and he'd thought no more of it.

He couldn't trust her, of course. She was a harpy, a demon, a creature of the Abyss. But she might know more. She might help. She'd said they were in love.

He couldn't believe he was even considering this, but Siyon didn't have many other options.

"Well?" Syrah Danelani snapped. A woman used to instant obedience.

Best to just say it. "I need to delve the Abyssal plane."

"More *sorcery*." She twisted the word like a victim on the rack. Siyon had thought he'd saved alchemy in the city; she seemed likely to kill them all after this.

Enkin's father spoke again, barely a sigh. "Syrah."

Her face crumpled like a clenched fist, along tangled lines of age and grief and desperation. She didn't look azatani, like this. She could be a fishwife whose sons had sailed into a storm.

"What do you need?" she demanded, without opening her eyes again.

"I need ink to draw the boundary, and rope to tether my return."

"I'll see to it." Enkin's father let himself out through a discreet inner door.

Syrah pinned Siyon with a red-rimmed stare. "Anything else?"

There was, inescapably, and Siyon could see no option but to tell her. "I need someone to hold the tether. To pull me back when needed." He glanced over his shoulder at the guard, who'd returned to his post beside the door. "Perhaps he could—"

"I'll do it." Syrah looked like she'd rather stand on his fingers than save him from drowning, but she leaned forward across the fever-wracked body of her son and grated, "I will haul you back to face what you've done whether you like it or not, Velo. You will never escape from me, not through all the planes of the universe."

Siyon swallowed. "I'm sorry. About all this. I didn't mean—"

"I don't care." Syrah sat back again. "Save him or die."

The rope was something expensive and silky with tassels smooth as water. It looked like it was intended to summon servants, or hold back equally luxurious drapery, but Siyon supposed it should work just as well as salt-stained, tar-smeared dock rope.

Honestly, the tether was the least of his worries. If this didn't work, he might as well stay stranded in the Abyss as come back to die.

The prefect sat on the side of her son's bed—his deathbed, unless Siyon changed something—with one hand holding Enkin's and one hand wrapped around the silken tether. Siyon didn't doubt that her grip would prove sufficient. Her face was stone, her eyes flint; he'd back her against the Demon Queen herself.

"If I tug on the tether, pull me back," Siyon reminded her.

"Get on with it," she reminded him.

This was a terrible idea. His hand throbbed, his head pounded, he felt unsteady on his feet. He had no other options.

Siyon looked at Enkin, and thought of how they'd found him in the Abyss, standing by the side of the warrior Laxmi. How she'd looked at him, golden eyes shining. How she'd stretched to try and stop him leaving.

The power of her love, binding them together.

The planes skewed as Siyon stepped into the triangle, and for a panicked moment he thought he'd be left on his knees on the carpet, closed out yet again, left to die.

But he plunged into the Abyss—faster than ever, whisked past coalescing spires and the shadow-impression of roofs, caught in the grip of a vicious current. Darkness lurched and smeared in a fast-firming hallucination. Siyon slammed down on a floor of overlapping shells. The edges clawed at his fingers, scraped at his knees as he scrambled to his feet.

The looming walls were encrusted with barnacles and verdigris, draped with banners in virulent greens and caustic oranges. Coral-crusted pillars thrust up to a ceiling vaulted with the rib cages of whales. The dangling chandeliers were twisted from the barbs of kraken and dripping with pearls.

No human had ever been here—not and lived to tell about it—but this could only be one place: the throne room of Pandemonium. The salt-and-poison heart of the Abyss.

Steps rose like sea cliffs to the needle-tall throne, with the Queen wrapped around it in heavy loops of black-scaled might and power.

Even lounging, she was terrifying and potent, her eyes heavy-lidded, her horns glinting in the low light. "Well well," she said, and her forked tongue flickered. A smile, Siyon realised.

A roar rattled the bones of the roof. Siyon's spine curled by primal instinct, and he whirled around—turned his back on the Demon Queen, he was that affrighted. There was no time to duck as Laxmi the harpy descended upon him, her wings flared behind her, claws glinting on the open hand she swung at him.

Better than poison, he thought.

Her swipe caught him on the shoulder, and Siyon slammed into a pillar, coral crunching and clawing at him. He gasped—stupid reflex; there was no *air* here—and Laxmi was on him again, clawed fist tearing at his shirt as she hauled him up, feet dangling, face to her beautiful, horrifying face.

Her bared teeth were serrated in rows like ranks of pikemen. "I should tear your face off and wear it in the nightmares of your nearest and dearest." She slammed him back against the pillar, and Siyon saw stars, felt the coral bite into his coat. Tearing at it, save it wasn't really here.

He didn't reach for the silken tether knotted at his waist. Maybe she'd kill him, but if he fled without something to save Enkin, he'd *definitely* die.

And he wasn't dead yet. Siyon remembered the massive barbed monstrosity of her greatsword, the almost gleeful violence with which she'd dispatched the kraken. If Laxmi wanted him dead, he'd be dead already.

Or perhaps it was a matter of whether she was *allowed* to kill him...

Nothing to lose, Siyon turned his head and croaked, "Your Majesty."

Laxmi shook him like a shark with a fish. "She doesn't want to talk to *you*, Velo." Siyon could feel the hot trickle of his own blood, where her claws sliced his shoulder, where the coral chewed at his back. "You," Laxmi sneered luxuriantly, "are a *disappointment*. Our best hope for a Power of the Mundane—what a joke. Was that paltry attempt the best you could manage?"

Just the truth. Not something he could spend time on, right now. Siyon wrapped his hand around her scaled wrist. It was like grabbing a solid steel bar. "I'm here about Enkin." His voice was a gasp. "He's dying."

"Of course he is." Laxmi let Siyon go, and his knees buckled; when he caught himself against the pillar, the coral snagged at his bandaged hand. Laxmi's wings folded behind her with a skittering hiss. "You dragged him across the planes. You can't even take up the Power, but you think you can solve all your problems with brute force. You're pathetic."

It stung, worse than all the coral cuts. "It wasn't brute force," Siyon snapped, before he could think better of it. "He *chose* to leave."

A harsh truth, one he knew would hurt.

He ducked as she swung, and her claws ripped through the pillar above his head. A fist-sized chunk of volcanic stone bounced away across the hall, bowling through a gathered audience of imps that Siyon hadn't noticed until now.

Not just the imps. The whole court seemed to be here, lining the walls, flitting like fish behind the pillars, hissing with speculation and baring their fangs in anticipation.

He couldn't afford the moment of distraction; Laxmi's kick caught the back of his leg and sent him sprawling. He rolled aside, as her hoof smashed through a seashell tile where he'd been.

Her wings spread like rustling nightfall, and her roar rattled Siyon's ears. "And is *his* the only choice that matters? Is love a bridge with only one end?"

Pain streaked the rage in her voice. Siyon gaped up at her. "*You're* doing this to him."

She shifted, wings drooping a little. "Not by choice. No more than I chose to love a human in the first place. But love I did."

"And love you still do," Siyon realised. That was how Enkin had stepped across in the first place—Siyon had sold him significant power, but it would never have been enough without the bridge already built between them. (He wondered *how*, but it hardly mattered now.) That bridge—that love—still bound Enkin. Was hauling against him, grinding him against the barrier between the planes.

"Let him go." Siyon scrambled up to a half-crouch. "You have to, this will kill him."

Laxmi sneered. "So easy, is it? Simply *let go* of someone you love."

Was it the way she said it, or simply Siyon's own guilty conscience that made him think of Izmirlian? Let him go. Let him turn into a husk. Let him slip away entirely. *Let him go.*

Siyon couldn't. Had broken the working instead, let it flare wild and destructive, rather than face that helplessness.

No, it was nothing like simple to let go of someone you loved.

Laxmi snarled her barbed grin at him. "Exactly."

Siyon reached for excuses, for justifications, for arguments—and something yanked at him, sending him staggering sideways. Not Laxmi's impatience, this time, but Syrah's; the tether pressed at Siyon's ribs. He grabbed at it, as though he could hold himself here longer. "Listen," he insisted. "Sometimes you *have* to let go. Enkin is failing, and fast. He is going to *die*, don't you care?"

He was looking straight into her face, bold with desperation, and so he saw the flicker of feeling, the sideways slant of her golden eyes, the twitch of her lips. Yes, she cared. She *loved him*, so deeply that it was shredding Enkin's soul an entire plane away. But—

But the audience, Siyon realised. The imps, scampering and jeering, and the fanged and horned and vicious of the Demon Queen's court. They stamped their hooves and cried for blood, for pain, for murder.

Not a bunch who did things for love, Siyon guessed. But they all answered to a higher Power here, didn't they?

Before he could think it through—before Laxmi could stop him—he scrambled around her, sprinting down the hall to skid to his knees again (*ouch*) in front of the throne. "Your Majesty!" he gasped. "I am only human, and I have failed you, but I beg another chance. I will do it, I swear, but I can only try if Enkin Danelani survives."

Laxmi grabbed the back of his skull, claws pricking through the bandage into skin, but the Demon Queen lifted one of her many hands, and the hold eased, just a little.

The looped coils of the Queen's long body shifted as she swayed forward. Her long neck dipped down until she was close enough to brush her tongue across his forehead. Where it grazed him, the skin burned.

She laughed as though this were all good entertainment, however it turned out. "Such promises. Can you make them, little alchemist? What is it that you will do differently than you have?"

Siyon had *no idea*. Why did people keep asking him questions to which he had no answer?

"Something different," he said, and looked up. The Queen's snake-slit eyes were piercing; Siyon swallowed, licked lips that couldn't possibly be dry. "Negedi is wrong. His methods are wrong. They keep it all at arm's length. You can't *live* it, not like that. You can't be what is needed. I thought I was breaking away, but I didn't do enough. Go far enough."

The Queen hummed, consideration wrapped in threat, like a drowsy hive of bees. She tilted her head the other way, as though waiting for prey to bolt. When he stood firm, she gave a little huff of laughter. "It's something, I suppose. Laxmi!"

The claws pricked again at Siyon's scalp as Laxmi said, "My Queen?"

"You will go with this little sorcerer and assist him as though he were me. And if he fails—" The Queen grinned, her fangs glinting. "*When* he fails, you may eat his heart. Do you agree, Siyon Velo?"

Out of the boat and into the deep sea, but Siyon already knew he could swim. "I agree, Your Majesty. Thank you."

Her grin stretched nauseatingly and impossibly wide. "Don't thank me yet. If you succeed, you will owe me for this, and I always collect. If you fail—" Her tongue flickered along her sharp and hungry teeth. "Either way, I'll be seeing you very soon."

Siyon's stomach lurched, but perhaps that was Laxmi hauling him to his feet, wrapping herself around him, wings and talons and tail. Perhaps it was just the grip of the tether, as Syrah Danelani hauled him back.

Hauled them both back.

The universe screamed like it was being torn asunder.

Or maybe it was Siyon screaming. The passage between planes usually took barely a blink, but this dragged—like a net through the water, like a jagged blade through flesh. Every instant of between-plane nothing scraped at Siyon.

No, that was Laxmi, claws sunk into his upper arms, tail coiled like a snake around his knee. Her wings flared, sheen and sparks skittering over their span, glinting off her horns, dancing between her bared teeth. Siyon had time for a moment of doubt—

What is he bringing back with him?

—before the Mundane crushed him with reality. He slammed into the floor, ink smearing beneath his cheek, no air in his lungs to be lost. He lay in a brackish and gritty puddle, brine soaking into the purple coat; weight shifted on his back and dug an elbow into his kidneys. He grunted.

Someone *else* screamed. "Demon!"

Well spotted.

Laxmi shoved him down again as she pushed herself upright—comedy if not for the circumstances. Siyon lurched unsteadily up to hands and knees, tilted his head to get a drunken view of the room.

The guard yanked open the door and shrieked for help; he was smarter than he looked.

Laxmi snatched something off a nearby table—a heavy Northern clock—and hurled it across the room to smash the door shut. The guard flinched in a shower of cogs and splinters.

Laxmi leapt.

The low light sparked off the edges of her dark scales, outlining in gold the power of her shoulders cocked to strike, the balancing stretch of her wings, the ragged and violent future of her splayed talons. She seemed immense and impossible, here in the Mundane. There could be no more glorious way to die.

The guard screamed again, rolled frantically aside, and Laxmi plunged her hand through an armchair instead. She ripped out a handful of upholstery and kicked the chair out of her way; the guard was already scrambling backward.

Siyon made it to standing and felt unreasonably proud of that achievement. The planes lurched and skittered, like a school of fish put to fright. Laxmi's wings flared with it, but a moment later the room shook as well, chandelier chiming and drapery shimmying. The guard steadied himself, but he had no fear to spare from the harpy dancing toward him.

Every part of Siyon ached. The bandage on his hand was sodden, the wound beneath stinging with salt water. He turned around, and Syrah Danelani slapped him with the other end of the tether.

"This is how you repay me?" she bellowed. "I hope you choke on the poison!"

This looked bad; Siyon couldn't deny that. He raised warding hands, though she had nothing left to throw but Enkin, still held white-knuckled tight. "This is your son's cure!" Siyon shouted back.

That cure vaulted over a sofa, prowling with sinuous hips and the light of a hunter in her eyes. Laxmi danced the guard backward one panicked step at a time, feinting this way, then that; her tail lashed, eager.

The guard snatched the tasselled spear from the antique suit of armour beside the fireplace and jabbed at Laxmi. She snarled, then laughed as he flinched; hooking a hoof beneath an overstuffed footstool, she kicked it up into the air, caught and flung it. The guard ducked, and the stool smashed through the drawn drapes and the window beyond.

The curtains billowed apart on a gentle breeze, and sunlight slashed across the room. Across the bed. Across the occupant, who turned his head away, and said—or croaked, at least—quite clearly: "No."

Syrah froze, eyes wide, and looked down at her son. He writhed against the sweat-damp sheets now, limbs moving with more energy than he'd had when Siyon first came into the room. Enkin's face twisted up in a grimace, and there was colour in his skin again, a hectic flush.

"Enkin!" Syrah curled herself around him, taut with desperation.

"Wait!" Siyon shouted—at Laxmi, at the guard, at everything.

But no one was listening. Laxmi slid forward, a cat after a mouse. But the mouse found strength of will in its panicked corner. The guard lunged forward, and though Laxmi lifted a hand to turn the spear aside, it stabbed hard, and fast, and straight through her shoulder.

She screamed—like metal tearing, like bones grinding—and snatched the guard up by the front of his jerkin. Flung him to smash into the wall above the fireplace; he fell limp and broken on the hearth, leaving the wall spiderwebbed with cracked plaster.

"No!" Siyon shouted, in the sudden silence. He dashed forward to catch Laxmi's wrist; he couldn't even close his fingers around it. "No," he repeated. "Do not hurt anyone."

The sheer stupidity of what he'd done caught up a moment later, and Siyon braced to be the next one bouncing off a wall. But Laxmi's golden eyes turned his way and for all her glower, she didn't so much as yank her hand out of his grip. "Not anyone?" she snarled.

Like the precise details of what he said mattered. "Do not hurt people," Siyon repeated, in any case. "Unless I tell you otherwise."

Her lip curled and her eyes rolled. "You're so *boring*."

But she lowered her hand. Relief surged dizzy within Siyon; perhaps this situation could be salvaged.

The door burst open, scattering smashed clock cogs, and the inquisitors came rushing in.

Xhanari, of course, in the lead. He had the standard-issue shortsword in one hand—no style, no grace, the bravi called them pig-stickers—but in the other he held a dowsing rod, a short truncheon of star-forged iron that made Siyon's head twinge with the memory of its brutal weight.

Laxmi's gaze fixed upon it, and she shifted uneasily at Siyon's side. "What is *that*?"

"Trouble," Siyon replied.

Olenka was at her master's shoulder, glaring righteous ire, and four other inquisitors behind them. Six all told, though Siyon wasn't sure Laxmi couldn't dispatch them. But if the harpy killed half a dozen inquisitors, would it even matter why Siyon had brought her back?

"Hold!"

A voice accustomed to being obeyed, for all it was scratched with grief and cracked with fatigue. Syrah Danelani still sat on the edge of her son's bed, but now that son was sitting up, holding on to her in his turn, and his eyes were open. Open, and wide, and staring.

"Laxmi?" Enkin breathed, audible only because a hush had fallen over the room.

The harpy stared back, her face gone soft—horribly open, and vulnerable, and her eyes shining with something entirely unlike her usual gleeful bloodlust.

Siyon looked away. It was all the privacy he could give her.

"Cease this violence," Syrah Danelani ordered. "The alchemist has acted in good faith—"

"With all due respect, Madam Prefect," Xhanari interrupted, and pointed his dowsing rod at Laxmi. "That is a harpy demon in full manifest, in direct contravention of all the laws of this city and of nature. In the face of grievous threat, my duty is clear and beyond your authority. Inquisitors! Kill the demon and apprehend the sorcerer."

Say this for Vartan Xhanari: He didn't send his men to any doom he wasn't prepared to meet as well. He strode forward, weapons at the ready. Olenka came with him, and the rest a little slower.

Laxmi shoved Siyon aside and snatched up the long, low table. She swung it wild with one hand, stopping the inquisitors at the limit of her range. They paused, eyed her warily.

She could have swatted them as easily as she had the guard. But she didn't. She was following Siyon's instruction.

Which meant he needed to find a way out of here.

Siyon ran to the window she'd smashed, hauling the heavy velvet drapery aside. The frame of the window hung shattered amid vicious shards of fine glass. Outside, the wall fell away, not so much as a ledge between here and the ground, four floors away. Siyon shoved gingerly at the frame, peering up instead. Could they reach the roof?

"Sheathe your weapons!" Syrah Danelani was still shouting, bless the woman's stubbornness. "Guards!"

No time to wait for rescue. Laxmi kicked at one of the sofas, sent it bowling into three of the inquisitors. But Xhanari lunged forward, slamming his dowsing rod down on the scaled knuckles holding the table.

Laxmi howled, and there was briefly a sharp scent of sulphur. She dropped the table and fell back a step, shaking out her injured hand.

Olenka stalked forward, lifting her pig-sticker in both hands, like it was twice as long and three times as heavy. Sunlight ran along the length of the blade, and Olenka swung it in an arc of fire.

Laxmi caught it, blade in her palm with no sign that she was bothered by the sharpness of the edge. She lifted a leg and kicked Olenka, hard, in the stomach.

Olenka flew backward, much as the guard had—the guard who still hadn't moved from where he'd fallen. She slammed into the door-frame, and the wood cracked behind her. But though she clutched her ribs as she forced herself upright, the vengeful gleam never left her eye. She strode forward again, snatching up in one hand the spear that the guard had dropped, hefting it like a javelin.

Of course. Not quite human.

"Let's all just—" Siyon managed, before Laxmi turned and grabbed him.

Tackled him, really, hefting him effortlessly as she bounded across the room, her hooves thudding against the carpet. The velvet drapes billowed around them, and glass shattered further, as Laxmi launched through the already-smashed window.

"There's no way down!" Siyon howled. Already too late; they were out, into clear air, into the sunshine. The spear came whistling past them, heavy point grazing Siyon's elbow before it spiralled away, succumbing to gravity.

Oh shit, gravity.

CHAPTER 26

Zagiri paced beneath a plane tree in the gardens surrounding the Palace of Justice, trying to enjoy the dappled sunshine and not scream with frustrated impatience. She'd wanted to be *doing* something—had been going entirely out of her mind back at Anahid's, amid the arguments between the Bracken-rescued practitioners and the scant few azatani who'd responded to Nihath and Izmirlian's request. She couldn't follow their theories on the cause of Enkin Danelani's problems, so she'd left them to it and come to keep an eye on the inquisitors. They'd need to know what was going on, if they ever figured out a way to help Siyon.

A runner had come in, not long ago, and a squad of inqs marched out shortly thereafter. Zagiri sent her own runner down into the city, where a strange assortment of bravi were making chaotically merry with the alchemical distractions that had been cooked up in the crypt of the Chapel. Weird and wild, to have the tribes working together on something this big, but Zagiri felt a surge of satisfaction watching the inqs hurry off to deal with it. Bezim was not going to be intimidated or tamed into good behaviour. It had never been that sort of city. Ask the fallen Lyraec Empire. Ask the Last Duke.

Shortly afterward, Zagiri's renewed pacing had been interrupted by a tremble of the ground that set the plane leaves rustling. This one was brief, barely worth noticing; Zagiri was a little worried that such things were becoming almost too common to trouble her. Siyon could fix it, if they could get him out. That *if* itched in her veins.

Maybe she should go down and help with the mayhem. Maybe she should go back to Anahid's to check on things. Maybe she—

With a crash, a window high on the Palace exploded outward in a shower of glass and splintered wooden frame as something came smashing out. Zagiri hurried closer to where that something had fallen to the grass. It was...a footstool?

She looked up at the broken window. Could she hear shouting, faint on the breeze?

And then she flinched as something bigger came barrelling out through the broken window, scattering more glass with its dark bulk.

An animal? But then a pair of massive wings unfurled in a metallic rasp of feathers, and Zagiri couldn't make sense of it—too big for a bird, too many limbs, too dark and scaled and—

A distant, delighted, *terrified* corner of her mind whispered: *A dragon?*

But no, it was person-shaped, if glimmering like a demon fish, and that person was holding another, who was wearing a purple—

Zagiri ran out onto open grass, waving her arms. "Siyon!" she shouted. "Hey, Siyon!" She couldn't tell if they could even hear her, Siyon's limbs flailing and the—what *was* that thing carrying him? It looked like a harpy from some luridly illustrated adventure novel, but surely it couldn't be. Disbelief could wait; Zagiri lifted a hand to her mouth and whistled, short and sharp and designed to carry over rooftops, the Bracken signal for *pay attention*.

Siyon twisted, and pointed, and possibly waved, or possibly just flailed. The harpy's wings clawed at the air, less soaring like a gull than scrambling like a first-night bravi sliding down a roof.

Behind them, in the wreckage of the window, other people were pointing, shouting, disappearing back inside. Zagiri didn't think them friendly.

Time to not be here.

She whistled again—*follow*—and took off, sprinting across the park, dodging around a walking couple who'd stopped to gawk. Zagiri ran—down the path, cutting across the grass toward the grotto, heading for the Avenues—with a heavy shadow skimming in her wake, and then overtaking her. Graceless the harpy might be, but flying was *fast*.

Zagiri craned her neck, envying the rush and freedom of it, and nearly tripped on a tussock of grass. She kept her head down after that, and pushed faster still.

As they cut into the Avenues, the winged shape cut between tall townhouses, swooping down toward a roof. Then it skewed away abruptly, wings lurching and Siyon's dangling legs kicking, and Zagiri ducked after it, down the back of Anahid's row of townhouses. The harpy was lurching down into the chasm, weirdly oversized, like a crow landing on a child's playset.

Curtains twitched at windows. No way to keep this quiet. Zagiri skidded into the Joddani courtyard as the harpy flared her—definitely her—wings, the feathers black as night and sharp as the consequences of sin, and came down with a slithering thump.

Zagiri leaned against the gate, catching her breath; Siyon hauled himself creakily to his feet. She wanted to rush forward and grab Siyon, make sure he was all right, whoop her exhilaration right into his ear. But every instinct screamed to get *away* from the bloody *demon*.

She was massive, even taller than Siyon, and twice as hefty, with muscle beneath scales that faded from black to a dark gold. Her wings scratched at each other like a handful of knives as she folded them at her back. Her golden eyes flashed, and her serrated teeth glinted as she grinned at Zagiri.

"Hello, little morsel," she purred.

"Laxmi," Siyon croaked, tugging his coat straight. "Behave yourself."

Laxmi grumbled and followed him across the courtyard, her hooves—*hooves*—sounding dull and flat on the paving.

"You—" Zagiri started, and then everything that came next

seemed ridiculous. *Have escaped*; well yes, obviously. *Have a bloody great harpy-demon-thing with you*; as though he might not have noticed? So in the end, she simply said, "Let's go in. Everyone's going to be keen to see you."

"Everyone?" Siyon repeated, but he followed along readily enough.

Laxmi, though, hesitated on the threshold. "Is the house warded?"

Siyon looked at Zagiri, who shrugged—how would she know? "Is that why you didn't want to land on the roof?" Siyon asked.

In the end, Laxmi curled herself up very tight and stepped inside like a cat through a puddle, dainty with disgust. She kept her wings close-furled and her tail tucked close to her legs, like she didn't want to brush against anything.

Something shattered in the kitchen, though when Zagiri looked, the staff had all vanished. She could hardly blame them. She turned back to Siyon and his harpy, who hunched to keep her horns from striking sparks off the ceiling. "Clearly a lot's happened since we last saw you. But come upstairs so you only have to tell it once."

Siyon shook his head. "No time for tea. The prefect—well, I don't know how she feels about me right now. But the inquisitors are over-reacting a bit."

Laxmi snorted. "You could have just let me kill them."

"Let!" Siyon rounded on her. "You had a damn good go at it. I thought I told you not to hurt anyone."

"Any people," Laxmi corrected. "And I didn't."

Siyon's eyes narrowed. "How did you know Olenka wasn't a person?"

"Olenka's not a person?" Zagiri felt out of her depth, but she'd never let that stop her before. "Actually, that explains a few things. Come on."

Siyon came, saying, "No, the inqs will be right on my heels, that was hardly a discreet exit, and I have to try again, with the whole Power thing. I need to—I don't even know." He dragged a hand through his hair, following along absently in his distraction. "Do something totally different. There was a moment, up there, when I looked down on the city…"

"We can maybe help with all that." Zagiri reached for the door to the back parlour.

"We." Siyon turned back with a frown. "You said *everyone* before..."

She opened the parlour door, and showed him just who *everyone* was.

Another time, Izmirlian might have enjoyed the alchemical debate, especially as it reached the point of raised voices and reference works, the practitioners of all stripes strewing the parlour with books, pages of notes, empty teaglasses, and pushed-aside furniture. The knotting and untangling of theories and factions of knowledge was fascinating, in its own way.

But his eyes kept straying to the clock on the mantel, and to the window. Time was passing, without a sure way of helping Siyon, and there was nothing Izmirlian could *do*.

A shadow flitted over the window—too large to be a bird, surely—and he leapt out of his armchair to investigate. It landed in the courtyard, but the view was occluded by a wrought-iron railing. Izmirlian let the lace curtain fall back into place and turned back to the argument.

"At least the situation would be stabilised." A woman called Jaleh Kurit was holding forth. Her hair-kerchief had come adrift half a bell ago, but she'd been disinclined to pause to fix it. "Putting Danelani into stasis would give us all time to—"

"The prefect will *not* be mollified by a son in stasis!" one of the azatani alchemists shouted.

Izmirlian shuddered at the word. *Stasis.* The swaddling of numb distance, the muffled and frozen drift of it, the inability to keep grip on thought or feeling, even the terror of it fleeting.

It had been the exact opposite of the freedom and discovery Izmirlian wanted. Waking had been such a *relief.*

The door of the parlour was thrown open suddenly, and the argument skidded to an abrupt halt.

There was a harpy in the doorway.

She looked familiar, which was not a thought Izmirlian had ever expected he'd have outside an opera house. Something in her wide, scaled shoulders, the cant of her hip, the smirk as she shook out her hair. That hair should billow more, like ink in water, the way it had—

In the Abyss.

Enkin Danelani's paramour, Laxmi, ducked her horned head to step into the parlour behind Zagiri and Siyon.

The room erupted in uproar—questions and greetings and exclamations. The alchemists from the Bracken safe house and the half-dozen azatani practitioners all shoved forward, mobbing the doorway.

Izmirlian hung back, tilting to see through the clamour. *There* was Siyon, looking a mess as always. His head was bandaged and his hair grey with dust, but he was grinning as he was swept up in a vehement hug by that bravi from the Archipelago, the one with the beaded hair who'd looked Izmirlian up and down and said, "*You're* the one, then," before introducing himself as Daruj. The Diviner Prince himself.

Now Siyon was gaping at Miss Kurit, like seeing her here was astonishing. For her part, the woman shrugged. Her words were largely lost in the din, but Izmirlian heard, "—owe you one."

And then Siyon looked up, and saw Izmirlian. His eyes widened, and his face went still, and Izmirlian didn't know what he saw there. Surprise? Relief? Dread?

Siyon shoved through the pack, and behind him, Zagiri clapped her hands, lifting her voice like an azata never would, but possibly bravi did all the time. "Right, give him a moment or six, let me bring you up to speed. First up, this here is Laxmi, do *not* pull her tail."

Izmirlian was grinning. Couldn't help it. Sure, there was a planar emergency, and no doubt the inquisitors were on the way to deal with the *demoness*, but here was Siyon, striding toward him. And here was Izmirlian, watching him do it.

"What happened to you?" he asked, nearly laughing despite his concern as he lifted a hand toward Siyon's bandaged head.

But Siyon caught his wrist and tugged him further back, into the window embrasure. As close to a private corner as they could get in this room. There were salty stains daubing the sleeves of that purple coat, and dried blood in the whorls of Siyon's ear, and a shadow in his eyes when he looked at Izmirlian.

"Listen," Siyon said, solid and serious. "I'm sorry. That I broke your working." Then he grimaced, and leaned back against the window frame. "And not sorry at all. I know it seemed like it was working, but I think—I was wrong. *It* was wrong. And I thought that might be my only chance to fix it, but it wasn't my choice to make, and—"

The words were running out of him like sand, so Izmirlian simply interrupted. "You were right."

Siyon blinked at him. "What?"

Stasis. Just thinking about it made Izmirlian's face feel tight, though he tried to keep his smile. It seemed like Siyon could use the reassurance. "You know, now that I look back at it all, I think I hadn't been dreaming since the first working. Since you took my tears. And then the voice, of course, and I—I've been so used to thinking this could never work, that I never stopped to think it might not work *correctly*. I trusted you—"

Siyon flinched, and Izmirlian grabbed his hand—the one wrapped in a salt-stained bandage. "You shouldn't have," Siyon snapped.

"I *should*," Izmirlian countered. "Even when I was cut off, I knew—as much as I knew anything—that you would find one way or another to fix it. And you did." No need to force the smile now. "My unexpected alchemist."

Siyon closed his eyes. "I'm not an alchemist. I'm nothing like one. I have no idea about...anything."

But his hand shifted in Izmirlian's, their fingers winding together. Izmirlian eased closer. "Maybe that's why you're the only one who could do it."

Siyon went still, even his breath catching. Had something strange happened with the plane again? But then his eyes opened, his gaze sharp. "Nothing like an alchemist," he muttered. "It was still too Negedic. I need something different. Something—" Siyon waved his free hand—unbandaged, but with ink under the fingernails. "Intangible. What was the word Geryss used? *Numinous*."

Izmirlian couldn't help swaying toward Siyon when he was like this; a walking wonder that Izmirlian wanted to discover all the details of. "You're trying again, then? Not *an* alchemist at all."

"*The* Alchemist." Siyon's laugh scraped in his throat. "Someone has to. Maybe I'm the only one who can. Right?"

"Right," Izmirlian echoed.

"And then." Siyon squeezed Izmirlian's fingers, and his smile got a strange slant. "And then I'll figure out how to do your thing. Properly, this time."

Izmirlian felt just the way Siyon looked—happiness and regret and hope all in an impossible tangle. "I still want to go," he confirmed, and as Siyon's smile twitched, Izmirlian touched his cheek, the rasp of stubble and the stickiness of drying salt. "You," Izmirlian said with emphasis, "are a delicious wonder in a world full of them. I have enjoyed every moment we've had together, and I am so pleased to have had the chance to know you. But we both have so many more wonders to discover."

Siyon leant down and kissed him, warm and gentle and all too brief. Izmirlian might describe their entire relationship that way, except little of it had been gentle. Vibrant, outrageous, pell-mell. Unexpected.

Perfect.

Izmirlian opened eyes he didn't remember closing. "I wish I'd met you years ago."

Siyon chuckled. "Don't. I was a brat."

"So was I," Izmirlian returned.

He was easing back when something beyond the lace curtain caught his eye. Movement in the laneway outside. Izmirlian twitched the curtain a little aside, and Siyon shifted to look as well.

A grey-cloaked figure slipped down the laneway, ducking into the shadowed recess of a gate three houses down. He looked up at the Joddani house.

"Fuck," Siyon spat.

◄─────────── ┤├ ◇ ┤├ ───────────►

There were inquisitors out the front as well, though Anahid spotted them lurking near gateposts and behind trees only when Nura pointed them out to her.

"Keeping an eye on us while they gather in force," Daruj diagnosed, his ever-ready smile smothered now.

One of the azatani alchemists gave a little whimper. "So much for distractions."

"It's not too late." Anahid looked around at the gathered alchemists—a paltry collection, but she was grateful that they'd shown up at all. Keeping them here to be trapped by the inquisitors would be poor repayment.

Zagiri nodded. "Scatter now, if they follow you all it will buy us some time. Bravi do it all the time."

Most of the assembly were happy to flee, already edging toward the door. But Jaleh Kurit planted her hands on her hips, her frown ferocious as she turned on Siyon. "We came to help you. I'm not running away." It was more a challenge than a support, though as Siyon lifted an eyebrow back at her, her cheeks grew a little pink. "Not this time," she added.

"You can help me by running away," Siyon replied.

That was all the encouragement the others needed, streaming away down the hall. Daruj hurried along with them, calling out advice—some go out the back, split groups at intersections, arrange further meeting points.

To the still-steadfast Jaleh, Siyon said, "You've helped me by being here. You've all reminded me that I'm not alone. I think I know what to do." He drew in a great breath. "I just need the time to figure out how precisely to do it."

Jaleh sniffed and cast a sidelong glance at Izmirlian, who was close against Siyon's shoulder. "Fine," she stated. "But I'm not coming to your trial if they catch you."

As she left, the rest of them gathered close in the parlour. Not very many—Siyon and Izmirlian, Anahid and her sister, Nihath and Tehroun, Daruj and, rather difficult to overlook, the harpy Laxmi, stretching her wings out along the mantelpiece. Just them, against whatever the inquisitors brought to bear.

"I bolstered the house's wardings against uninvited ingress yesterday," Nihath noted. He was fidgeting with his spectacles, opening and closing them, setting them on his nose only to tug them off and set to polishing with the tail of his shirt. "The doors should hold against Mundane force."

"Should I try to get through again to the prefect?" Anahid wasn't sure that she could; Tahera would surely never be at home to her again. The pang that gave her was hardly useful in the circumstances, so Anahid shoved it aside.

"Again?" Siyon glanced at her, amusement tugging at the corner of his mouth. "Seems I owe you more thanks than ever. But it's too late now. Xhanari will be coming, with or without the prefect's permission. And he'll be bringing his dowsing rod."

Laxmi shifted, her wings scraping, and Tehroun sighed: "Which nothing can ward against."

From beside Siyon, Izmirlian said, "So you're doing it here and now."

Anahid blinked. "In the parlour?"

She wasn't really sure why that was surprising. From the moment Siyon Velo had entered her house, carrying her alchemy-struck—and alchemy-saved—sister, he'd been turning it upside down. With Nihath, everything had been very shut away. *His* things. *His* purposes. *His* business. Everything careful, considered, in its place.

Siyon left alchemy in his wake like footprints.

In the parlour, then. Anahid said, "Well, roll up the carpet first. I've seen what you do to floors."

The laughter helped kick them all into action, Izmirlian and Nihath starting to move furniture. Daruj and Zagiri heaved at a larger sofa until Siyon waved at Laxmi, who just shrugged.

Siyon said, "Get over here and help," and the harpy rolled her eyes, but slouched away from the fireplace. She shifted the sofa with one hand and bad grace. Siyon, on the other hand, looked *delighted*. "You have to do as I say, don't you? Obey me like I was her."

Laxmi's grin was feral, her teeth serrated in ranks. "Only if I want to eat your heart when you fail."

"I'm not going to fail," Siyon told her. Told himself, perhaps. He frowned around the room, as the clearing continued. "But I need..."

Nihath finished shoving aside an armchair. "My stores have been significantly depleted by the inquisitorial attention, but the others brought what they thought might be useful."

Siyon's frown deepened. "I wish I had my own things."

Daruj snapped his fingers. "Zagiri, where did we—?"

She'd already leaned down beneath a side table and pulled out a battered leather satchel and a filthy, coarse sack.

Siyon's eyes lit up, as though the sudden fall of a card had opened a dozen paths to victory. He took the sack, a cloud of complicated scents drifting to Anahid from the sackcloth—new building and old furniture and flowers left too long in the vase. "The city," he murmured. "The Mundane. Don't *draw* the border. Just claim it. Defend it."

The carpet—a genuine Khanate piece—was rolled up, and Laxmi leaned it in the corner. Siyon looked around at the exposed floor, the intricate parquetry tessellations that had been so fashionable last century.

"Does anyone have a knife?" Siyon asked, and turned to Anahid, with a little apologetic twitch to his nose. "I'm going to ruin another of your floors, sorry. I need to carve a symbol. Or maybe three."

"In that case," Anahid said, "I'll have Nura fetch a proper knife from the kitchen, shall I?"

He looked surprised at that, as though Anahid were going to get precious about it at a time like this.

Nura brought the entire block of knives and a crock of salt, and then turned her back resolutely on Siyon as he set the point of the largest carving knife to the parquetry. Precious or not, Anahid felt a twinge of regret watching him cut into the pristine lacquered surface.

Then Nura turned to her and murmured, "A significant squad of inquisitors is forming up at the end of the avenue."

This was it. Captain Xhanari was coming. Anahid nodded. "Anyone downstairs who wishes to leave may do so, with no recriminations."

Nura inclined her head. "I'll let them know. But we've just started cleaning out the laundry tub. We've had to move it, and it's blocking the gate. I hope that won't be a problem."

Anahid beamed at her. "Not for me."

With a tight answering smile, Nura went to stand near the front door, keeping an eye on the street.

Meanwhile, Siyon had carved a triangle into the parquetry, more than large enough for a person to stand inside, and now he lay a square over the top. With a low muttering, and a shuffle of his knees, he started curving a circle atop the whole mess. He cut without hesitation, without any of the measuring or consideration he'd used when setting out to fetch Enkin Danelani.

"It's a symbol. An idea." He sat back on his heels to consider the shapes. They fit over each other with surprising regularity for something he'd done freehand.

"And this." Siyon hefted the sack. "This is an idea. Not just mine, but everyone's." He tossed the sack into the centre of the shapes and then grabbed the crock of salt to scatter it into the carved lines.

They all gathered around. Daruj said, "So the circle for Aethyr, the triangle for the Abyss, the square for Empyre. All the planes at once?"

"All the Powers at once," Siyon said, a correction or an agreement, Anahid wasn't sure which. He nudged the last of the salt into place with his toe. "And me. I'm the Mundane. And the sack. And—" He looked up, at the circle of them. "And all of you, as well. Supporting me. Sending me, maybe."

"Is this going to help with the inquisitors waiting outside?" Zagiri sounded decidedly sceptical.

Quick and hurried steps heralded Nura's return. "Not waiting. That Xhanari fellow and his cross lieutenant are leading a squad down the street right now."

Daruj and Nihath rushed out with her, thundering back down the corridor to the front door.

Siyon called after them, "Does Xhanari have his dowsing rod?" but he was still frowning at the floor, as though he was trying to figure out what part he was missing.

"He's got a big damn crossbow," Daruj called back. "Aren't those only legal aboard a trading vessel?"

"Can't feel a negation rod," Laxmi said, over the top of him. From the other corner, Tehroun shook his head in a swish of pale hair.

"Then I don't care. The locks should hold." Siyon's frown deepened. "I am nearly there. I know it. There's just...*something*. What am I missing?"

Feet on the front steps, and Nihath came rushing back into the parlour. "They're here!" he yelped, even as a fist hammered on the front door.

Anahid could say it along with him, by now. *Inquisitors. Open up.*

She stepped up beside Siyon at the edge of the symbol mutilating her floor. "You said something about our support?" She beckoned to the others. "Come on! Step up. Make a circle. And let's—oh, I don't know. Focus? Channel our energy?"

"Hold hands and sing the old hymn of Bezim?" Zagiri suggested caustically.

Anahid ignored her. "Siyon, what do you need?"

It was like chivvying a row of recalcitrant debutantes into their dancing lines, but Anahid had done *that*, the second year she was a sponsor, and she wasn't going to let this fail because no one wanted to be first. Izmirlian came readily to stand on Siyon's other side, and despite her snide remarks, Zagiri nudged the toes of her boots against the salt-etched line.

Anahid reached for Laxmi—who was closest—and ignored how strange her scaled wrist felt to tug her away from the fireplace. "Come on." The harpy rolled her eyes, but she slouched forward, stepping up between Zagiri and Izmirlian to set her hooves near one point of the triangle.

Siyon said, "Oh," the noise small and almost involuntary, falling from his lips. He seemed almost shocked.

Laxmi blinked her golden eyes. "I suppose that makes sense," she said.

"What are you *talking* about?" Anahid demanded.

But Siyon whirled to point across the room. "Tehroun! Get over here!"

Anahid watched her husband's lover—her husband's alchemical assistant, who he had described once as having *a great affinity for the Aethyreal*—step across the floor to take up a spot on the opposite side of the circle from Siyon.

The harpy for the Abyss. Tehroun for the Aethyr. Siyon for the Mundane.

Anahid looked around the room. "Who should be the Empyreal?" None of them seemed appropriate, not to be righteous and sternly just and burningly upright. Not Daruj, or Zagiri, or Nihath...Anahid pulled a face. "Not *me*."

The thundering at the front door had been going on so long, the sudden cessation was noticeable. Daruj called, "That woman is going to try."

Siyon's eyes widened. "Open the door!"

"What?" Anahid gasped.

Daruj shouted back, "Xhanari's still got that bloody crossbow!"

Siyon's face twisted through any number of unpleasant considerations in the moment before he shouted, "Stop him, if you can, but I need Olenka."

"Olenka," Zagiri repeated, as though something was coming together for her. At Anahid's glance, she said, "She's not a person."

"She's an angel," Siyon confirmed, and glanced at Tehroun. "Or something."

The Empyreal. What they needed. But still..."I hope you know what you're doing," Anahid muttered.

"So do I," Siyon breathed.

On his other side, Izmirlian took his hand, gave him a bright smile that Siyon seemed helpless not to return.

Anahid rolled her eyes and stepped away from the circle, heading toward the door. Unlikely *she* could provide any more hindrance, should Xhanari get past Daruj at the front door. But this was her house too, and she wouldn't just let him come barging in.

Daruj threw back the bolt on the door, the clang far too loud in the tense house. The door opened, and the shouting started. Xhanari's booming voice, of course—*Inquisitors, stand aside*—and Daruj also bellowing—*The woman only, keep back.*

Nura was out there as well, half-blocking the narrow gap, speaking too steadily to be heard, while Daruj held his shoulder against the door that Xhanari was trying to shove open.

Olenka slid past them all, striding down the hall. She looked human—a hawk-faced woman in an inquisitor's tunic—and yet also not quite. Her eyes were bright with a cold fire, and she gripped her truncheon in one hand, and everything about her bearing made that weapon feel longer, heftier, heavier. A burning blade of justice.

She filled the corridor, blocking the ongoing struggle at the front door. Anahid fell back as Olenka swept into the parlour like a wildfire come to consume; she marched forward and slammed her boot down at the corner of the square Siyon had carved into the floor.

Siyon grunted and stiffened, like something had prodded him in the spine.

The front door slammed, Daruj shouting, *Nura* shouting.

And Vartan Xhanari came charging into the parlour. If Olenka had been sternly furious, he was irate, wild-eyed and grim-jawed. He swept one quick glance over the parlour—over the symbol and the ritual launching into being—and bellowed, "Cease at once!"

With both hands, he lifted a crossbow, just as Daruj had said, big and blackened and gleaming with oil. The sort traders used to defend the ship in foreign ports, and seeing it here dragged horror at Anahid's heels for just one moment before she stepped forward. "How dare you?" she demanded. Another step, and she could shove the weapon aside, could get in his face, could let out this rage—How dare he keep bursting in like this, how dare he upend her entire *life*?

But she was too late. In the corner of her eye she saw movement at the circle, Siyon lifting an arm, reaching into the centre of the shapes.

Xhanari shouted, "I said stop!"

Anahid saw his finger jerk on the trigger of the crossbow. Something small and dark whisked past her cheek; she registered it in the same moment she heard a small sound behind her.

Zagiri screamed; Anahid whipped around. Izmirlian staggered against Siyon's side, even as Siyon swayed as though his feet were stuck to the symbol. He caught Izmirlian, who sagged against him, and there was—there was so much—

Blood. Slicking down Izmirlian's shoulder from the bolt jutting from the side of his neck. Covering Siyon's hands and bubbling on Izmirlian's lips as he tried to speak. In the horrified hush, his choking was loud as thunder.

Izmirlian's knees had given way, his fingers twisting in Siyon's shirtsleeves. Siyon teetered, dragged down by this, body and heart. He pulled Izmirlian tighter, his face twisting, and the pair of them tipped forward.

Into the middle of the symbol carved on the floor.

They fell, far further than there was to fall. Down, down—

And gone.

CHAPTER 27

Between the planes was the void, and the void was perfect. The ultimate nothing that bounded all somethings, and a barrier that only will and intent could penetrate.

It was not something Siyon had ever really paid attention to, any more than he did the walls while stepping through a doorway. The void had been a blip on the way to somewhere else—right up until he'd stepped into it briefly and catastrophically with Izmirlian.

Here they were again, and there was still nothing to see, or hear, or feel. But Siyon's eyes and ears and mind were doing their utmost, so he supposed he'd better play along.

The void looked blank, and sounded like the piercing whistle of hearing strained to its limits, but it *felt*. Siyon was wracked by howling wind and scalded by dancing fire and churned by violent seas, none of which actually existed.

He clutched tighter to Izmirlian, curling around him, holding him closer against the forces here that would tear them apart and dash them both into insignificance. He couldn't even see Izmirlian, but he could feel the blood warm and sluggish over his clutching knuckles. Couldn't hear the bubble of his breath, but he could feel the shudder of his body.

Couldn't rid himself of that last sight of Izmirlian, shocked and bleeding and slumped in Siyon's arms.

He wasn't dying, not here. They were in a moment between moments, within an unreality.

But they couldn't stay forever.

An echo of serrated laughter scraped down his spine. It was familiar—but Laxmi was still standing outside the circle, wings flared as she hissed at Olenka. So this was someone else.

Siyon lifted his face and said, "Hello again, Your Majesty."

The void churned around him. Siyon could feel his mind twisting, his senses scrambling to produce something that made sense. They colluded, brain and body, and played pretend. Let's imagine we can actually see. Let's imagine we see...

A coalescing. Direction sprang into existence, and in front of Siyon a looming man appeared, the colour of sky and lightning, stalking on padded cat's feet and bound by glittering bands. A flicker to his right became a giant figure the hue of desert mirages and the dancing air above a fire. Its eyes were flame in a sharp and feathered face, and its wings were the billowing of a phoenix's flight; it gripped a dire broadsword in scarred and human hands. And to the left, a figure Siyon recognised from prior acquaintance. The Demon Queen looped her lithe snake's body, her horns glinting on her wine-dark forehead. She held her trident in one taloned hand, a wickedly barbed dagger in a second hand, and a goblet half-full of midnight wine in a third.

"Siyon Velo." She rolled his name around her mouth like something luscious. "Fucking finally."

They were here. *He* was here. He had brought all the Powers together, so that he might join them.

The Djinn Sultan stood across from Siyon where Tehroun had been; he crossed arms like heavy weather systems over his chest. The Arch Dominion, as forbidding as Olenka, propped a sword the length of cities across his shoulders.

How on earth did Siyon think he could stand among these beings of power and majesty?

Well, that was the point. He couldn't, *on earth*, and so here they all were.

He needed to stand. He needed to take his place. He needed to do what he had worked for, the only thing that could save them all. And yet there was a heavy and motionless weight in his arms, there was *Izmirlian* bleeding and gasping (not really, not here, but he *was* and Siyon couldn't forget it). What did any of it matter, how could he even *think* of anything else?

The Demon Queen made a sharp *tsk* between her fangs and snapped her fingers; the weight was gone from Siyon's arms. He cried out, reached out wildly—*reached* out—and hauled Izmirlian back to him.

The Queen frowned. "Don't get distracted."

"Don't tell me what to do," Siyon snapped back.

At the Demon Queen. At the Power of the Abyss.

Before he could start to panic, the Arch Dominion chuckled—like the crackle of an open fire—and shot a proud look at the Queen. "The Mundane Is No Longer Your Playground, Harlot-In-Chief."

The Demon Queen stuck out a long and forked tongue at him.

Between them, the Djinn Sultan tilted a thunderous head. *To care and to cling is very human.* He didn't actually speak, but the voice coiled inside Siyon's ear regardless, more known than heard. *We are glad to see you, Alchemist.*

Siyon looked up at these looming manifestations of the power and magic and presence of their planes. "What, just like that?"

The Arch Dominion looked at him down a long nose—or perhaps it was a raptor's beak. "Has This Path Been Too Easy?"

Easy? If Siyon had been holding his sabre, instead of his bleeding lover, he might have drawn on the Arch Dominion, never mind that that Empyreal sword was longer than Siyon's entire life. But if he hadn't been weighed down with Izmirlian, maybe this conversation would be going very differently. Somewhere in the back of Siyon's mind was a sense of what he might have been feeling—a jubilation of achievement, of vindication, of visceral discovery. An appreciation of this unique experience unfolding for him, at his behest.

He stood up—had he been on his knees? Or was he less standing and more growing, swelling up until he matched the others in stature. Until he could look them in the eyes, nacreous silver and thunder-bruised and white fire.

"Save him," Siyon demanded.

The Queen wrinkled up her nose. "The little mortal?" She flicked her tail at the body in Siyon's arms. "Why? He wants to abandon you anyway."

"Save him," Siyon repeated. "That's my price."

The Arch Dominion's tufted eyebrows went up; he looked astonished. "Your *price?*"

"You want a Power of the Mundane." Siyon should have been aquiver with his own audacity, bargaining with these beings. He merely felt hollow. "You need one, or—well, I don't know what. You all invade us, probably, but it won't be enough, will it? There's *balance* in four planes, like there wouldn't be if you carved us up between you, to buy a little more time. So you need me. I'm your only shot, and that's my price. Save him, or get fucked."

The Demon Queen snarled, scraping her dagger and trident together in a slow shower of sparks. The Arch Dominion swung his broadsword ponderously down from his shoulder, planted the point between his armoured feet.

The Djinn Sultan clapped his palms together; lightning flashed, dancing in afterimage across Siyon's vision. *Enough. Alchemist, I cannot say I understand your pain, but I can taste your resolve. In this, however, there can be no deal. What you ask is impossible.*

Despair stuck a claw into Siyon's heart; he tore it out again. "Then forget about—"

The Djinn Sultan raised a hand. *What you* ask *is impossible. We cannot return him to a Mundane life. He has lost too much of it, even before this frozen moment. We have no leverage upon your plane to return it to him, and even in all your newfound Power, you cannot step back to before you gained it. What we do have is sway upon our own domains.*

The Demon Queen grimaced as though the Sultan had suggested a sexual practice even she found distasteful. "You want me to take another little human into my plane? Bad enough when my warriors are collecting them like helpless chicks."

The Arch Dominion looked similarly troubled by the idea, and less pleased by agreeing with the Queen about anything.

But Siyon didn't think that was what the Sultan was suggesting at all. He hauled at his mind, sluggish with grief and reeling disorientation. "'Sway upon our own domains,'" he repeated. "Each of us. But what about all together?"

Impossible for a thundercloud to smile, but the Djinn Sultan managed it. *Though it has been some time since we could try, surely together, we have sway over the universe entire.*

"What?" the Queen snarled, and "What?" the Arch Dominion barked.

Siyon shifted Izmirlian in his arms, curling him close again. Not holding a body, holding his lover. He brushed his cheek against Izmirlian's forehead—not cold, but still living; *Believe it*—and tilted his lips close to Izmirlian's ear.

He had no idea what he was doing. He did it anyway. *Reached*—into Izmirlian, across the barrier back into the Mundane—and whispered: "Come with me. It's going to be all right. Trust me."

He whispered, and he coaxed, and Izmirlian opened his eyes and said, "Enough, for the love of—" He blinked, and blinked again, harder. "Where on earth are we?"

No blood on his lips, no clammy pallor to his skin. Those were not welcome here. Siyon smiled at him; found it easy and natural to do so. "Nowhere on earth. You're getting your wish a bit sooner than planned."

Izmirlian found his own feet—planted them on solid nothing, and stood up, still clutching at Siyon's shoulders. His wide eyes raked over their surroundings—the void, the Powers, however they looked to his scrambling mind—and to his credit he merely swallowed hard and said, "I see."

Joy filled Siyon at being able to share this with Izmirlian. Not unmitigated joy; he wished, more fervently than ever, that they could share all the rest of whatever came next as well. This was only the beginning, he knew it like he'd known how to get here—clearly, if incompletely. And all the mysteries and possibilities of those missing details would be a fascination to untangle.

He wanted to have Izmirlian there. But if he couldn't, he'd be damned if he let death have him.

"Are you ready?" Siyon asked.

"What?" Izmirlian whirled back to him. His eyes widened further. "Now?"

Siyon couldn't keep the sadness out of his voice. "There's no more time."

Izmirlian set a hand to his neck—where there was no crossbow bolt, no gush of blood, not here in the void. "Ah." His hand fell away, and he smiled, bright and nearly wild. "In that case, there is one last thing."

"One last—" Siyon repeated, and then Izmirlian was back in his arms, kissing him with depth and fervour and all the promise of his smile.

They wrapped around each other, and Siyon could have kissed him forever. Perhaps, here, really *could* have kissed him forever. But what came next would not get any easier, no matter how long he put it off.

It was not easy to let go of someone you loved. But sometimes, it was necessary.

So they eased slowly, but inexorably, apart. Izmirlian slid out of his embrace, and then out to arm's reach. He lingered there, their fingers entwined, and a smile curved trembling and complicated across Izmirlian's face. "I wish you could come with me."

Siyon almost did too. But that *almost* was the hindrance, the hat too wide to fit through the doorway, the hat he couldn't quite bring himself to take off just yet. There were so many things to do *here*. So much more to discover and unravel. They rooted him to the Mundane, even if he thought flying sounded magnificent.

In Izmirlian's eyes he saw an echo—that Izmirlian knew all the wonders of staying, but was so passionately eager to fly.

And Siyon loved him for it. That he dared to think of it, and having thought of it, burned to achieve it.

Siyon brushed his thumb across Izmirlian's knuckles, and smiled. "Maybe I can follow you. One day. When I'm done here."

Izmirlian's smile bloomed into a grin, bright to the point of blinding, enough to light the universe. "I'll hold you to that," he declared.

They let each other go, fingers sliding easily apart, and Izmirlian stepped away. Into the centre of the void between the Powers, who were now arrayed around him in a circle, Siyon one among four.

A perfect reflection of the circle Siyon had made in Anahid's parlour. Across from Siyon, the Djinn Sultan lifted his galeforce arms. *Shall we?*

"How do I—?" Siyon asked.

The Queen shot him a scathing look. "We can't tell you how to use your Power, nitwit."

His Power, now. A thing he used. A thing he was. A thing he did.

Siyon *reached* again, through himself this time. Back into the Mundane, through his own body and out into the world.

He saw the whole grisly and panicked tableau—Izmirlian punctured and bleeding out in his arms, the room frozen in chaos, Anahid screaming, Zagiri and Daruj and even Nihath lunging at Xhanari. Saw it and moved on, *reached* wider. The house, in all its constructed and mundane strength, and the inquisitors on the doorstep, the servants blockading the back courtyard. The whole Avenue, a regimented line of constructed expectations, and all the curious neighbours avid at their windows. The city that surrounded it, piles of brick and wood and lives. The headland it stood upon, the deep roots of the bluff, the stony hills, and beyond, beyond, to the rich fields of Lyraea, the grasslands and deserts of the Khanate, the snowbound forests of the North, the dotting Archipelago in the glittering sea, the intricate patchwork of the New Republic, the strange lands beyond, the world, the world, the whole wide Mundane and amazing world...

You don't claim it. It claims you.

Siyon felt the weight come down on him again—the whole world, a quarter of the universe, laying itself on his shoulders.

But not just his shoulders. Izmirlian was with him, standing strong even while slumped in his arms, eyes shining and full of trust. Laxmi and Olenka and Tehroun were with him, shadows and echoes, binding the edges of his domain with the whispers of their own natures. Anahid and Zagiri and Daruj and Nihath and even Nura were with him, coming together in his aid without knowing what it might mean.

All the alchemists and the bravi, sent out into the streets, working to his assistance in tiny actions that built a scaffold for him to stand upon.

A quarter of the universe was too much for any man to hold alone. But he *was not alone.*

So Siyon let them lift him up, and he lifted the world, and held it in his soul, and let its Power flow to his purpose.

He held out his hand toward Izmirlian—and Izmirlian lifted his in return, their fingers not quite touching. Siyon whispered: "Be free."

The others spoke too, but Siyon didn't hear it. Didn't need to. He was focused on Izmirlian's lips, on the words lingering there even as Izmirlian sublimed in a shimmer of *something.* "I love you. See you soon."

Siyon let his arm fall, and the power fell with it, and he fell, and fell, and fell.

He fell—forever—with a promise on his lips.

A sound followed him down; a rasping snicker, and another promise. "This is far from over, little Alchemist," the Demon Queen whispered.

Her voice scraped against his skin and reminded Siyon that he was still here.

Between the planes was the void, and the void was perfect. The ultimate nothing that bounded all somethings, and a barrier that only will and intent could penetrate.

But now Siyon was inside it, and *he had no tether.*

He'd come through with Izmirlian tying him back to the world, but now Izmirlian was gone—more gone than gone—and Siyon was alone and lost in the featureless void. A Power come adrift from his plane, with nowhere to stand to apply leverage, and nothing to apply it to, if he had.

He could die laughing from the bitter irony of it. He'd done the impossible three times over, and would be trapped here forever for want of the most basic plane-raider's safety leash.

How had the others done it? More sensibly, presumably. Maybe they hadn't really been there, just…projecting, somehow. It didn't matter. *Siyon* was here, really and truly, and there was no way he could—

Something tapped at his hand.

He spun around, but where was *around* when there was only more nothingness in every non-direction? He stretched out—he *reached*— but it was like drowning all over again. No use, no use at all…

Something *grabbed* his hand.

And a voice, so very far away, shouting his name. It existed, it created direction; he turned *toward* it, and the hold on his hand grew stronger. He could feel someone else's hand now, small and slim and soft with care, save for the familiar calluses a sabre wore into the palm of a bravi.

Zagiri shouted, "Now *pull*."

And the world crashed through him.

Pain was the first thing to return—the thud of Siyon's heart, the scrape of breath in his raw throat, and the agony of a knee pressed too hard, too long (barely a moment; enough time to shift the universe) into rough sackcloth over the carved-up floor of the parlour. Zagiri hauled at his arm, and Siyon tipped over sideways, salt grinding beneath him. A thump as Zagiri landed beside him, and behind her Nihath teetered. They'd pulled him back, making a tether where none had been.

When the whirling sparks cleared from Siyon's vision, there was no one else on the floor with them. Just a few spots of blood, dark on the empty sack.

Sound came back next, in cacophony. Everyone was shouting, except those who were screaming. —*killed him!* and *Stand back!* and *Get the crossbow!*

Crossbow.

Siyon tried to push upright, but his hand skidded on the salted floor, and he tipped over again, landing on his shoulder in an inelegant sprawl up against someone's legs.

Some Power of the Mundane he was. He couldn't even stand up.

The room veered around him, smears of colour and swooping shadow. Siyon had to force himself to make sense of it. This shadow, limned in golden light like a halo, looming above him like consequences: That must be Olenka. She snarled across him, which made that shadow—sinuous and sinister as the ghost of a shark in deep water—Laxmi. A faint, whispering suggestion of a figure over there: Tehroun.

The planes lay quiescent around him, and Siyon grabbed them, gripped them tight, forced them to align into sense.

The parlour sprang into sharp and vivid reality around Siyon. The air rushed into his lungs.

Anahid stood, arms outstretched, in front of Vartan Xhanari, as though she would bar his way physically. The string of the crossbow in Xhanari's hands still buzzed with released tension. He had, of course and impossibly, loosed the bolt only a moment and a half ago. Surprise was starting to bloom on his face, the realisation of what he'd just done. In another moment, it would harden into the resolve of the determined righteous.

Before it could, Daruj came lunging in from the corridor and wrapped an arm around him, yanking the crossbow away to send it skittering into the corner. His movements were silver starbursts in Siyon's vision, shimmering over the hard facts.

Anahid drew herself up, limned in scarlet fury and golden resolve. "How *dare* you!" she thundered. "This trespass, this outrage—you have *murdered* a son of the Hisarani house!" She pointed like a veiled Doom in an opera, to the centre of the circle.

Where Izmirlian wasn't. All eyes swung to Siyon alone.

There was still blood on his hands, tacky on his skin as he pushed himself upright. He needed to lean on the planes to make it; they held him up, yielding to his grip, though the moment he released them, they skittered away again.

There was blood all down his front as well, sticking Siyon's shirt to his skin. He tried to speak and only coughed, hacking like the space between the planes was still coating his lungs in nothingness anathema to the Mundane.

"Where—?" Zagiri said, up on her knees now and looking around the room like Izmirlian had somehow ended up behind one of the sofas.

"How—?" Nihath echoed, actually speechless for once.

For a moment, it was a tableau of astonishment. Then Olenka stepped back from the circle—Siyon felt something snap, but it was gentle and distant, a thing used up and ready to break. Her boots echoed on the floorboards as she stalked across the room to pick up the crossbow and return to stand beside her boss. He could feel the planes twitch with her footsteps. He could feel so much. It went deeper and deeper still—

Movement pulled Siyon's attention back, as Xhanari shook off Daruj's restraining arm. "A sorcerous ritual has been performed here, in violation of the laws of the city. You will all accompany me to the Palace for questioning regarding—" He ran out of steam, flailed for a moment. His voice cracked as he added, "There is a harpy *right there*."

Laxmi laid a clawed hand over her scaled breast and performed a parody of surprised innocence. Siyon could feel the flex of her wings in the planes.

"Nonsense," Anahid declared. The look she shot Siyon was wild and demanding, as full of questions as any of the others, but her words were crisp and prim. "Really, Inquisitor, you are getting quite hysterical and making appalling accusations. That is my *cousin*, and her flair for the dramatic and costuming might be a trial to the patience of the entire family, but it's hardly any of *your* concern."

Xhanari stared at her like he couldn't believe what he was hearing. Siyon couldn't help but laugh, though it came out as more of a weak wheeze. The inquisitor's glare fixed on him, and he stabbed a finger at him. "Izmirlian Hisarani," he said, like an accusation.

The name was a pang; Siyon winced, and felt the planes shiver, and wondered how on earth he could explain this to another azatani mother whose son had fled the plane.

But here and now, Anahid stepped smoothly in the middle again. "Does not appear to be here." She lifted a questioning eyebrow. "Which is it, Captain Xhanari? Is he not here at all, or did you just shoot and kill the Councillor Hisarani's middle son with a weapon for which inquisitors require special dispensation?"

Olenka, dangling the crossbow from one casual hand, gave her a flat look, but that didn't seem to bother Anahid either. With the other hand, Olenka grabbed her boss by the elbow. "Let's go."

Xhanari hesitated a moment longer, mouth pressed thin, but he didn't throw off her hand. "I will return, with warrant and reinforcements and—"

"Return with panoply and fanfare," Anahid interrupted, "but for now: Go."

He slunk out of the room, nursing injuries and shattered dignity. Olenka paused for a moment, her gaze lingering on Siyon, cool and sharp as a blade. "I guess you had it in you after all. Try not to ruin it. This is far from over."

Siyon's chin jerked up at the echo of the Demon Queen's last words, but Olenka was already gone, marching away down the corridor with eddies of Empyre and the Abyss at her heels.

Anahid let out a wavering breath, pressing a hand to her chest. Nihath touched an uncertain hand to her elbow, not quite support. "You, er. That was impressive."

"I know." She gave her husband a thin fragment of a smile, already turning a heavy look upon Siyon. "Tell me that I have bent the truth to good purpose."

"Bent the truth?" Zagiri repeated, an incredulous grin unfurling on her face. "Sister, you *lied your arse off.*" She bounded forward to catch Anahid up in an enormous hug. They gleamed and glittered, spinning in a circle together.

The world was so *thick*. Like a soup made of hallucinations and hangover. Siyon pressed the heels of his hands to his eyes, but the constant shifting—echoing, gilding, embellishing—made him queasy.

"Goodness," Nihath breathed beside him. "Can you feel that?"

"Yeah," Siyon croaked, but when he blinked away shadow and dazzle, Nihath was looking...wondering. Almost beatific.

He beamed at Siyon. "You did it. The planes are...I've never felt them this peaceful."

Siyon stared at him. Stared at the shivers of all kinds spinning out from Nihath, as he turned to grip the hands of Tehroun, who billowed in a cloud of eggshell-pale Aethyr. Siyon looked down at his own hands, and there might have been blood—Izmirlian's blood, don't think about that—drying brown in the creases, but at least there were no sparks and whorls.

Siyon reached out his senses—and *reached*. He seemed to stretch a lot further now, wider and deeper and yet never extending beyond the Mundane. Feel the weight and the warmth and the winter bite and the whirl among the stars. That helped; helped give him a solid base from which to consider the endless seething gyre of everything else atop the Mundane.

He didn't think it was supposed to be like that. He didn't know what it *was* supposed to be like.

He had no one to ask, when no one else could see it.

He reached further still. Felt the pinprick shimmer of life and the dusty waiting where once things had been and, perhaps, could be again. Felt the slow sway of the world, so much less unbalanced than it had been, and as he stretched just a little further, pushing at the edges, he heard—

Breathing in the dark, slow as ages, so heavy it bent the world.

Something seized him, and Siyon startled, shoved so hard that Daruj went teetering back on one foot. "Brother," he laughed, half merry, half chiding, as he righted himself. "I said, you have *done it*." His grin glinted with bright sparks in Siyon's sight, even as that grin faltered. "But where is—?"

His gaze dropped to Siyon's empty but blood-sticky hands.

Where is Izmirlian?

The breath Siyon took stabbed in his chest, like he'd broken a rib. "Where he wants to be," he replied. The truth, and that sweetened the pain a little. Siyon managed a smile. "I did it."

He'd done what Izmirlian wanted. But more than that. He'd become the Power of the Mundane.

"Huh," Zagiri said, as the moment stretched, no one sure what to say. "Funny, because you still look like you got scraped off someone's boot."

"Zagiri," Anahid scolded.

And then Daruj was laughing again, and Siyon as well. Bubbling up from inside him. He *had* done it. Done it, and the city was still whole.

Daruj pulled him into a hug, and Zagiri hit them from the side, with Anahid muttering about what a filthy mess they all were, and it was true, it was all true...

Siyon had gained something impossible, and he'd lost Izmirlian, and he had never wanted *any* of this, but here he was.

He refused to cry. Held on grimly, and was held, and let their warmth hold him up. Whatever came next, whatever still had to be done, Siyon could deal with it.

He wasn't alone.

EPILOGUE

"I saved the world," Zagiri said, lifting two jagged shards of mirror glass to make a frame, "and all I got was this stupid reputation."

She centred the frame on Siyon, where he was sitting on the floor of Geryss Hanlun's old apartment, trying to put all the drawers back into an intricate piece of cabinetry. As far as Zagiri could tell, the inquisitors had ripped every single one out and thrown it in a different direction, like they were more interested in making a mess than actually finding anything useful.

"You didn't save shit," Siyon pointed out absently.

"I saved *you*," Zagiri shot back, lowering the mirror shards again. She'd woken up in a cold sweat this morning from another dream that she was back there, leaning into whatever strange portal Siyon had carved, with only Nihath's grip holding her to reality.

Siyon had once told her that she—anyone—could delve the planes, but Zagiri was more convinced than ever that the reckless suppliers could *keep it*.

She took a deep breath and went back to picking up the mirror glass. The frame was massive and beautifully carved—she thought it had once been a genuine Khanate luck-mirror, with the etching and everything, but now it was just a hundred cuts waiting to happen.

"I'm just saying," Zagiri carried on, "that the prefect could show

a little more gratitude. Throw you a parade. Give you an official title.
Decree that you could live at the Summer Club."

"I'm not living in that museum," Siyon snorted. "Some piece of
taxidermy would eat me in the night." He slotted in another drawer,
and picked up the next, narrow but deep. The cabinet seemed to have
five dozen of them. He'd been at it for half a bell, but he was nearly
done. "She's leaving me alone. She's not demanding reparations for
the state Laxmi left the Palace in. She's not even asking where Laxmi
is. And we haven't seen Xhanari since he stormed out of your sister's
place ranting about coming back with a big stick. So I consider it all
a win, frankly. The less I have to do with—" He waved a hand in the
general direction of the Avenues, and then stopped.

"My lot?" Zagiri suggested. She sounded bitter, and she didn't
know how to explain that it wasn't at *him*.

She was angry with the prefect for letting Siyon solve all her problems, even the ones she hadn't known about, and not giving him a thing
beyond *graciously* letting him keep this apartment that Geryss Hanlun
had apparently gifted to him. (Their first time here, Siyon had sat down
beside a drooping rubber fig in a cracked pot, and it had been nearly a
quarter bell of Zagiri noisily rummaging through things before he got
himself together enough to scold her for making more mess.)

She was angry with her parents' cronies, carrying on over dinner
about the *tremendous disruption* of the past few weeks, as though *they*
had been creeping through the streets at midnight, carrying their
lives, like the alchemists the Little Bracken bravi had been smuggling
out of the city. (When she'd told Siyon about that, he'd just snorted
and said, "Like any other day.")

She was angry with herself, for being angry about all of this and
still putting her name down in the ivory- and gilt-bound Register,
announcing her intention of making her presentation at next season's
Ball. Her mother had called it *the proudest moment in any mother's life*,
though Anahid had warned her it would be a carnival of nonsense
from start to finish.

It was what she had to do. She could use being an azata in her own
way. But she had to parade for the harbour master first. So she would.

Zagiri dumped the last of the shattered glass into their waste barrel. Beside it, sprawling out on the floor in a spill of sunshine, was a shadowed creature. In periphery, the mind could just about accept it as a cat. But looked at directly, it was obviously too large, too dark, and somehow seemed to glint and gleam rather more than a furry animal really should.

"You could help, you know," Zagiri told her, not for the first time.

Laxmi yawned a too-wide yawn populated with too many teeth and rolled over with a flick of her forked tail.

Zagiri turned back to Siyon. "So now what?"

Siyon didn't even look up, busy trying his drawer in one after another of the remaining gaps. "I was thinking probably sorting out the shelves, but can you reach?"

"Not that." Zagiri planted her hands on her hips. "I mean *you*. The Power of the Mundane. You faced off with the other Powers and balanced the planes. You've got a pet harpy—"

Behind her, Laxmi growled. "If you try to make me trot around at your heels like a familiar, I'll eat your heart in your sleep."

"Can't." Siyon smirked. "Not until I fail."

"Which will happen sooner or later," Laxmi promised.

Zagiri grabbed at that. "Fail at *what*?" she asked.

Siyon set down the drawer, leaning an elbow on it, and looked up at her. His gaze had that strange quality, skittering over her, the way it had been doing since that day at Anahid's house. It made Zagiri's skin prickle, like she was standing in a cloud of insects only he could see. But they were all dealing with what had happened in their own way, she guessed.

"I don't know," he admitted. "But there's more to do. It's like..." He frowned, and waved a hand through the air. "Like a *tangle*, or perhaps more like the caulking that you do on a ship."

Like *what*? But before she could ask, a new voice came up the staircase. "Hello?"

Siyon came to his feet, and in a flit of shadow, Laxmi was cat-crouched on the edge of the barrel, golden eyes fixed on the doorway.

But the woman who stepped into it was familiar, with a plain blue kerchief restraining her dark curls, a match for the sash around her simple grey dress. "Hello, Jaleh," Zagiri said.

"Miss Savani," Jaleh Kurit returned, and ignored the face that Zagiri pulled. She nodded at Siyon. "I'd heard that you were tidying this place up, so I volunteered to carry the Summer Club's invitation to—"

"Nope," Siyon interrupted. "Like I told the last three messengers."

"Siyon, you can't—" Jaleh started forward with a tight look of frustration, then shrank back again so sharply she knocked the open door against the wall. "That is *not* a cat."

Laxmi grinned at her in a way that cats certainly didn't.

"Look," Siyon said. "You don't have to run their errands just because your mistress is dead. We could—"

"Think on your own problems," Jaleh snapped, interrupting him. "You can't keep the club at arm's length forever, Velo."

Siyon snorted. "Are they interested in listening to me?"

Jaleh ignored that. "Whatever you've done alchemically, there are realities in this plane. In this city. Social, and political, and powerful realities. You need to compromise."

"Well, you're the queen of—" Siyon started, and then stopped, pressing his mouth tight. Jaleh glared at him, like daring him to finish that. But all he said was, "I'll bear it in mind."

"Fine." Jaleh gave Laxmi one last wary look as she sidled back out, down the stairs again.

"I *like* her," Laxmi declared, now perched on the barrel in her own form, one scaled leg daintily crossed over the other.

"You would," Siyon sighed, and slotted his drawer into its place. "Come on. That's enough of this for one day. Let's head back." His mouth twitched toward a smirk, and he slapped at his thigh. "Here kitty, kitty."

Laxmi snapped her teeth at him.

Anahid closed the sitting room door behind her, shutting out the noise of sawing and the plasterer's assistants swearing at each other in Lyraec. "I do apologise for the tumult," she told her guest. "We're in the middle of some unfortunately essential redecorations, and not really receiving many visitors."

But of course she could not refuse the card of the woman peeling off her net gloves on the other side of the low table. Anahid marked the gesture; Azata Minej Hisarani, wife of a councillor and mother to Izmirlian, intended to take refreshments. Just as well Anahid had ordered them already.

She was a woman just as handsome as her sons. Anahid had tended to associate Minej's keen dark eyes and lusciously burnished hair with her eldest son, Avarair, but now she couldn't glance at the woman without seeing Izmirlian. It was a more pleasant association, but also potentially a dangerous one.

Little point in playing coy when any of the cards in this hand could get her into trouble, so Anahid smiled blandly, and said, "I did not think I would ever have the pleasure of entertaining you directly, azata, given how our previous association concluded."

By which she meant her slapping Avarair at the Regatta, after he'd listed off all the faults of Anahid's that he felt prevented the marriage both their mothers were considering. It wasn't as though any of them had come as a *surprise* to Anahid, but...well, it had been a very long day. A long week. A long *season*.

Azata Hisarani shrugged an elegant shoulder. "I dare say all my sons can do with chastisement now and then. Today," she continued, as the door opened again—hammering now, and laughter—and Nura brought in the teaglasses, and a little plate of almond pastries, "I find myself vexed by the second of them."

Anahid smiled politely as she took up her teaglass, allowing Minej to take the first sip of her own. She drew calm around her—it wouldn't do to give a glimmer of nervousness, not sitting at this game—and asked, "Oh, has Izmirlian done something?"

Izmirlian, staggering on the very floor that was being re-laid right now in the back parlour. Izmirlian, bleeding in Siyon's arms. Izmirlian, vanished into thin air.

"It seems the last time he was seen was here, on the day there was that...unfortunate misunderstanding with the inquisitors."

That seemed to be the official story. A misunderstanding, so sorry, the offending captain has of course been chastised, demoted, banished to paperwork, will never bother you again. So sorry, azata, azatan.

Anahid sipped at her tea, mint unfurling across her tongue. "With all the other excitement, I'd forgotten he was there. He had some alchemical business, I never quite understood the details. He left, of course."

Azata Hisarani set her teaglass down, still mostly full. "Do you know where he went?" she asked. So blunt, so focused, it was very nearly a demand.

"I'm afraid I haven't the slightest idea," Anahid told her.

Only the truth.

Minej Hisarani watched her for a long moment, but Anahid was learning how to make of her face a bland mask, in which an opponent at the table could see whatever it was she most feared or desired. With a sniff, the azata tugged her net gloves back over her fingers. "I hear your younger sister has signed the Register. I do hope her presentation is a sparkling one. I take a keen interest in the success of my friends."

And she rose. Anahid showed her out, of course, but they said not another word that was not merely a step in the intricate dance of etiquette.

She rested her forehead against the door, once it was closed behind the departed guest, and nearly yelped when a voice said from behind her, "What did she want?"

Siyon was sitting on the stairs, tucked into the shadowed lee of the banister. Anahid pressed a hand against the sash of her dress, letting her heart slow down again. Not his fault she'd been already wound tight. Or at least, only indirectly his fault. "What do you think she wanted?"

Siyon—who Anahid knew from Nura slept with a notebook under his pillow, the pages filled with handwriting not his own—smiled grimly in the shadows. "Are we in trouble?"

"I don't know," Anahid admitted. She started to climb the stairs toward him. "She suggested that she'd support Zagiri's forthcoming season if I helped find him. If the lure fails, there may yet be a net."

"I'm sorry," Siyon said, guilt sliding his gaze across her face and away again.

Not the first time he'd apologised—for the mess in the parlour that was being remodeled, for the flurry of gossip the whole business had caused, for the fact that Nihath had barely emerged for meals from his wild burst of new alchemical theorising.

Not for the first time, Anahid said, "Don't be."

She sat beside him on the stairs. A strange vantage. Not one she'd had before. This was not the sort of place a proper azata sat. But it was her staircase. She'd sit on it if she wanted to.

Maybe she was starting to live in her own life, after all.

It wasn't all heedless freedom. She'd been out last night, at the house of Azata Malkasani, necessary socialising for putting out the embers of gossip before they could bloom into wildfires. Among other entertainments—other conversations Anahid had felt she needed to have—there had been a table set up for cards. Not carrick, merely tapers. Anahid had approached the table anyway, for the familiar face among the players.

But when Anahid had laid a hand on an empty chair, Tahera Danelani had stood abruptly from her own, and declared herself quite bored with the game and determined to find other entertainment.

Nothing less than Anahid had expected. Possibly nothing less than she deserved, for what she had done. It still stung.

However, Tahera was not the only new friend she'd made this season. Anahid did not regret the choice she had made.

"I'll miss you when you go," she said, here and now, on the stairs.

Siyon nudged his shoulder against hers, and she caught the edge of his smile at the corner of her eye. "I won't be far. It's almost on the way from here to the Flowerhouses." She looked at him, a little embarrassed before she could help herself. He was *grinning* now. "You've been again, haven't you?"

Anahid had, playing in the surprisingly elegant private back room of a Flowerhouse called the Banked Ember, with the Vidama Selsan, the Captain, and a variety of other intriguing players.

They weren't friends. But she was having far more fun than she'd had since…since she'd made her presentation to the harbour master for the first time.

"Here we are," Anahid said, looking at her life from a whole new angle. "Not quite what we are supposed to be. At least you've solved your problem. Saved the world." She looked at Siyon, next to her on the steps. He had shadows beneath his eyes—had done since that day in the parlour. Had shadows *in* those eyes, questions and ghosts. It made her suddenly uncertain. "Haven't you?"

"I don't know," he admitted.

"Nihath thinks you have," Anahid pointed out. "I've not seen him for a full bell together in the past four days, and for all that time he's been volubly excited about the things that are apparently possible now that the planes are balanced."

"He does say that, doesn't he." Siyon leaned back on the stairs and grimaced at nothing—or at nothing that Anahid could see. "Maybe I have. But it's still not…right."

"What sort of not right?"

He looked at her, with a wry smile. "If I knew *that*, maybe I'd have the faintest clue what I should be doing about it."

Anahid knew how it felt, to have no idea how to step forward. She still felt that way, more than a little, but she *had* taken some steps. Thanks, in part, to him. "In that case," she said, "we simply keep going, and we see what we see."

"Find out what's in the unknown space over the horizon," Siyon murmured, his gaze distant, and perhaps a touch melancholy.

Anahid laid a hand over his, on the step between them. "Well, you know what they say at the edges of the maps."

He looked at her, blank and querying. Of course, he probably hadn't seen that many azatani maps; families tended to guard such things. Anahid's smile widened as she told him: "Here be dragons."

Later, when Anahid had gone off to dress for family dinner—celebration of Zagiri finally signing herself up to do the harbour master's whatnot—and the decorators had all trooped away, Siyon went into the back parlour, silent as a ghost in the dusk.

Everything was half torn apart, half put back together. The air was tacky with fresh plaster, and the room looked enormous with no curtains or furniture.

The floor had been torn up from the corners, but the centre—and the overlapping symbols Siyon had carved there—remained for now. There had been arguments, he understood, about the potential of replicating the symbol, tessellated in the new parquetry. The sort of brazen gullshit the azatani got away with. But it was none of his business. As soon as he had Auntie Geryss's old apartment livable, he'd be gone.

The next stage of his life. New challenges. New problems to solve. But also new wonders to discover.

Siyon crouched down to touch the rough edges of the carving. There was a bloodstain still on one splinter, old and brown. He smiled; he blinked away tears. "See you soon," he whispered.

And he would. He knew it.

But this was far from over.

The story continues in . . .

Book TWO of The Burnished City

Coming in 2023!

ACKNOWLEDGMENTS

This book was written on the traditional lands of the Wurundjeri Woi Wurrung peoples of the Kulin Nation.

Huge thanks to all the publishing professionals who've made this book a reality. My wonderful agent, Kurestin Armada, never stopped believing in Siyon, no matter how long it took. Nivia Evans, Nadia Saward, and Tiana Coven just *got it*, and helped me make it so much better. The entire talented and enthusiastic team at Orbit, on both sides of the Atlantic, caused me to squeal like a Beatles fangirl over and over with their amazing work on bookifying my pile of words. Plus Laura Blackwell's patient and thoughtful copyediting made the process of translating from my original Australian a joyous rather than painful one.

But I also owe a massive debt to every friend and colleague who helped me get here—not just with this book, but all the false starts that came before.

First and foremost, to Jennifer Rimmer, thank you for twenty years and counting of rolling around in gleeful words, for one very important roadtrip, and for being the perfect recipient for an indulgent collection of so many of our favourite things. This one's always been for you, dearest. Thanks for agreeing to share.

Ginger Stampley has helped in a hundred different ways, but also waited patiently, again and again, until I finished working and could come and play. (And also Michael. Hi, Michael!) My husband, Anthony Massaro, got confused every time I changed the story (so... a *lot*) but still offered unflagging support and suggestions that were anarchic, puntastic, and whimsical, but also helpful more often than not. Jess Howard and Dorian Hadgraft have been *essential* over many years of excellent feedback cocktails (just the perfect mix of rigorous interrogation and squealing enthusiasm).

Thanks to the Armada, the best bunch to be sailing these seas with. To the 22 Debuts, full of excellent advice and excited emojis. To the Fantasy-Faction forum crowd, for the discussions, the enthusiasm, and the running jokes. And to everyone else who's read one of the *many* different versions of this book over the last, oh, *nine* years—Katrina, Stephanie, Heather, Elizabeth, Catherine, Anita, Claire, Renate, Marissa, everyone I am no doubt still missing... Every single comment helped, and I'm so grateful.

Thanks—always and fundamentally—to my mother and father, for teaching me to love books and storytelling (respectively). And also to my grade nine English teacher, Mr. Chambers (I said I'd do it!), whose wild and creative approach struck a spark that grew into the fire that forged this novel.

Last but never least, thanks to Gabe Saporta, without whom I literally could not have done it. Fangs up.

extras

orbit

meet the author

Photo Credit: Gray Tham

DAVINIA EVANS was born in the tropics and raised on British comedy. With a lifelong fantasy-reading habit and an honors thesis in political strategy, it was perhaps inevitable that she turn to a life of crafting stories full of sneaky ratbags tangling with magic. She lives in Melbourne, Australia, with two humans (one large and one small), a neurotic cat, and a cellar full of craft beer. Dee talks more about all of that on Twitter as @cupiscent.

Find out more about Davinia Evans and other Orbit authors by registering for the free monthly newsletter at orbitbooks.net.

interview

What was the first book that made you fall in love with the fantasy genre?

I have a very vivid memory of encountering a particular cover of J. R. R. Tolkien's *The Hobbit* when I was about twelve. A computer game asked a riddle involving the book, and I, having never heard of it, asked the school librarian. She pulled out this book that had a magnificent dragon on the cover, perched on a mountain and spewing poisonous flames into a foreboding and bloody sky. I was immediately and totally hooked. I went on to enjoy the book so much I read it out loud to my mother over a period of weeks. Later, I asked another librarian for "books like that one" and she showed me there was a whole *genre* of this stuff. (The moral of this story is: Librarians *rock*.)

Where did the initial idea for Notorious Sorcerer *come from and how did the story begin to take shape?*

The very first kernel of the story was actually a fanfic, a fantasy alternate-universe story I wrote for a friend's birthday, featuring some characters we both loved. It was an exercise in self-indulgence, cramming as many favourite things into the setting and story as I could—melodramatic street gangs, exotic (at least to me) liquor, decaying grandeur, rock star opera singers, elegant houses of disrepute, a murder-kitten succubus on a leash, and a pair of outrageous young men daring each other into the impossible. I couldn't stop thinking about the setting, and eventually I set to work turning it into a proper novel, braiding in even more things I love—like various flavours of badass women, ridiculous society fashions, ladylike skills turned to outrageous purposes, posh social clubs, and terribly complicated card games.

What was the most challenging moment of writing* Notorious Sorcerer*?

Getting Izmirlian just right—in his goal and his arc and his personality—was a delicate and tricky process. In the first version of the story he was much more fey, more a poet in search of wonder beyond these earthly shadows, but that wasn't quite what the novel version needed. Then I read a profile piece on a woman who was a candidate for the never-realised Mars One concept. She talked about the problem with dating in that position; at what point in a burgeoning relationship should she tell a person, "Oh, by the way, in ten years, I might leave the Earth and go to Mars *forever*"? But she both wanted to go and couldn't stop living while waiting to see if it happened! That clicked for me—that was Izmirlian. Conveying that properly in the story—especially before I included his point of view—was another challenge altogether, but Izmirlian himself would probably suggest that if it were easy, it wouldn't be worth striving to achieve...

Bezim is vibrant and broken and feels incredibly lived-in. What was your approach to creating this setting? Did you do any specific research to build the world?

Bezim is a love letter to so many magnificent fantasy cities that have lit my imagination on fire. Biggest debt is probably owed to M. John Harrison's *Viriconium Knights*, for first helping me realise that a city could be far more modern than most fantasy I'd read at the time but still absolutely brimming with wonder and danger (and also elegant but violent duelling gangs). But I should also mention K. J. Bishop's *The Etched City*, Ellen Kushner's *Swordspoint*, KJ Parker's Perimadeia in *Colours in the Steel*, and Scott Lynch's *The Lies of Locke Lamora*.

In terms of research, I settled very early on a Byzantine/Caucasus vibe, at first for the tremendously flimsy reason of including that area's liquor in the story's earliest iteration—not just rakia, but also retsina and arak. I read quite a bit about Constantinople, in various forms, because the feeling of a grand city enduring through ebbs and flows in history and empire was particularly what I wanted for Bezim. As I worked more on azatani history and society, I also found myself reading about Venice, with all its strong independence, patrician merchants, flawed egalitarian notions, and ability to put on a show.

The characters in Notorious Sorcerer *are fun and have compelling voices. If you had to pick, who would you say is your favorite? Who did you find the most difficult to write?*

I love everyone in this bar! I enjoy Zagiri's youthful exuberance, and Izmirlian's self-possession, and Anahid's measured observation. But I do particularly love writing Siyon (fortunately for me!) because he's a perfect outlet for my own irreverence (and tendency toward salty language...).

I found Anahid the most challenging point of view to write, partly because of her reserve. There's so much she's unwilling to admit, even to herself, that it was a delicate dance to tease out enough to hint at her truths but not so much that it felt unrealistically candid. For just this reason, opening her up further in the sequel is something I'm very much looking forward to!

Siyon is striving to find his place in the world where the rules are shifting due to his actions. What was it like writing this character?

In my first version of this story, Siyon was older, with his daring rescue of the prefect's son in his past, and he'd left behind some of his delinquency to find a certain insouciant stability. (I mean, #goals!) When I decided it would be far more fun to make him deal with everything all at once, I threw him back into the wild uncertainties of his tumultuous youth, when he had zero clues about anything, and honestly I loved doing it. (Sorry not sorry, Siyon!) In the process, I thought a lot about the frustrations of reaching for a thing that turns out to be a bit hollow, and the need to fix the things that we can, because others can't necessarily be relied upon for it. Sometimes it's less about finding a place than making your own, but it's wonderful to share the burden with other people.

So I think the short version here is: Writing Siyon ended up being a whole lot more thoughtful and thought-provoking than I really expected writing about a mouthy, disreputable brat to be!

Finally, without giving too much away, could you give us a hint of what happens in the next novel?

Siyon gets an apprentice (or two), Zagiri gets a job and a date to her presentation ball, and Anahid gets tangled up with the city's shady criminal barons. Meanwhile, Izmirlian will never really be gone while his family is making everyone's life hell looking for him...

if you enjoyed
NOTORIOUS SORCERER

look out for

THE UNDERTAKING OF HART AND MERCY

by

Megan Bannen

Hart Ralston is a marshal, tasked with patrolling the wasteland of Tanria, hunting for drudges. It's an unforgiving job, and Hart's got nothing but time to ponder his loneliness.

Mercy Birdsall never has a moment to herself. She's been single-handedly keeping Birdsall & Son, Undertakers, afloat—despite definitely not being a son—in defiance of sullen jerks like Hart Ralston, the man with a knack for showing up right when her patience is thinnest.

*After yet another exasperating run-in with Mercy, Hart
finds himself penning a letter addressed simply to
"a friend." Much to his surprise, an anonymous
letter comes back in return, and a tentative friendship is born.*

*If only Hart knew he's been baring his soul to the person
who infuriates him most—Mercy. As the unlikely pen pals grow
closer, so does the danger posed by the drudges. And suddenly their
old animosity seems so small compared to what they might be
able to do: end the drudges forever. But can their blossoming
romance survive the fated discovery that their pen pals are
their worst nightmares—each other?*

CHAPTER ONE

It was always a gamble, dropping off a body at Birdsall & Son,
Undertakers, but this morning, the Bride of Fortune favored
Hart Ralston.

Out of habit, he ducked his head as he stepped into the
lobby so that he wouldn't smack his forehead on the doorframe. Bold-colored paintings of the death gods—the Salt Sea,
the Warden, and Grandfather Bones—decorated the walls in
gold frames. Two green velvet armchairs sat in front of a wal-
nut coffee table, their whimsical lines imbuing the room with an
upbeat charm. Vintage coffee bean tins served as homes for pens
and candy on a counter that was polished to a sheen. This was
not the somber, staid lobby of a respectable place like Cunningham's Funeral Services. This was the appalling warmth of an
undertaker who welcomed other people's deaths with open arms.

It was also blessedly empty, save for the dog draped over one of the chairs. The mutt was scratching so furiously at his ribs he didn't notice that his favorite Tanrian Marshal had walked through the front door. Hart watched in delight as the mongrel's back paw sent a cyclone of dog hair whirling through a shaft of sunlight before the bristly fur settled on the velvet upholstery.

"Good boy, Leonard," said Hart, knowing full well that Mercy Birdsall did not want her dog wallowing on the furniture.

At the sound of his name, Leonard perked up and wagged his nubbin tail. He leaped off the chair and hurled himself at Hart, who petted him with equal enthusiasm.

Leonard was an ugly beast—half boxer, half the gods knew what, brindle-coated, eyes bugging and veined, jowls hanging loose. In any other case, this would be a face only his owner could love, but there was a reason Hart continued to patronize his least favorite undertaker in all the border towns that clung to the hem of the Tanrian Marshals' West Station like beggar children. After a thorough round of petting and a game of fetch with the tennis ball Leonard unearthed from underneath his chair, Hart pulled his watch out of his vest pocket and, seeing that it was already late in the afternoon, resigned himself to getting on with his job.

He took a moment to doff his hat and brush back his overgrown blond hair with his fingers. Not that he cared how he looked. Not at Birdsall & Son, at any rate. As a matter of fact, if he had been a praying man, he would have begged the Mother of Sorrows to have mercy on him, no pun intended. But he was not entirely a man—not by half—much less one of the praying variety, so he left religion to the dog.

"Pray for me, Leonard," he said before he pinged the counter bell.

"Pop, can you get that?" Mercy's voice called from somewhere in the bowels of Birdsall & Son, loudly enough so that her father should be able to hear her but softly enough that she wouldn't sound like a hoyden shouting across the building.

Hart waited.

And waited.

"I swear," he muttered as he rang the bell again.

This time, Mercy threw caution to the wind and hollered, "Pop! The bell!" But silence met this request, and Hart remained standing at the counter, his impatience expanding by the second. He shook his head at the dog. "Salt fucking Sea, how does your owner manage to stay in business?"

Leonard's nubbin started up again, and Hart bent down to pet the ever-loving snot out of the boxer mix.

"I'm so sorry," Mercy said, winded, as she rushed from the back to take her place behind the counter. "Welcome to Birdsall & Son. How can I help you?"

Hart stood up—and up and up—towering over Mercy as her stomach (hopefully) sank down and down.

"Oh. It's you," she said, the words and the unenthusiastic tone that went with them dropping off her tongue like a lead weight. Hart resisted the urge to grind his molars into a fine powder.

"Most people start with *hello*."

"Hello, Hart-ache," she sighed.

"Hello, Merciless." He gave her a thin, venomous smile as he took in her oddly disheveled appearance. Whatever else he might say about her, she was usually neat as a pin, her bright-colored dresses flattering her tall, buxom frame, and her equally bright lipstick meticulously applied to her full lips. Today, however, she wore overalls, and her olive skin was dewy with sweat, making her red horn-rimmed glasses slide down her nose. A couple of dark curls had come loose from the floral scarf that bound up her hair, as if she'd stuck her head out the window while driving full speed across a waterway.

"I guess you're still alive, then," she said flatly.

"I am. Try to contain your joy."

Leonard, who could not contain his joy, jumped up to paw Hart's stomach, and Hart couldn't help but squeeze those sweet jowls in his hands. What a shame that such a great dog belonged to the worst of all undertaking office managers.

"Are you here to pet my dog, or do you actually have a body to drop off?"

A shot of cold humiliation zinged through Hart's veins, but he'd never let her see it. He held up his hands as if Mercy were leveling a pistol crossbow at his head, and declared with mock innocence, "I stopped by for a cup of tea. Is this a bad time?"

Bereft of adoration, Leonard leaped up higher, mauling Hart's ribs.

"Leonard, get down." Mercy nabbed her dog by the collar to drag him upstairs to her apartment. Hart could hear him scratching at the door and whining piteously behind the wood. It was monstrous of Mercy to deprive both Hart and her dog of each other's company. Typical.

"Now then, where were we?" she said when she returned, propping her fists on her hips, which made the bib of her overalls stretch over the swell of her breasts. The square of denim seemed to scream, *Hey, look at these! Aren't they fucking magnificent?* It was so unfair of Mercy to have magnificent breasts.

"You're dropping off a body, I assume?" she asked.

"Yep. No key."

"Another one? This is our third indigent this week."

"More bodies mean more money for you. I'd think you'd be jumping for joy."

427

"I'm not going to dignify that with a response. I'll meet you at the dock. You do know there's a bell back there, right?"

"I prefer the formality of checking in at the front desk."

"Sure you do." She rolled her eyes, and Hart wished they'd roll right out of her unforgivably pretty face.

"Does no one else work here? Why can't your father do it?"

Like a gift from the Bride of Fortune, one of Roy Birdsall's legendary snores galloped through the lobby from behind the thin wall separating it from the office. Hart smirked at Mercy, whose face darkened in embarrassment.

"I'll meet you at the dock," she repeated through gritted teeth.

Hart's smirk came with him as he put on his hat, sauntered out to his autoduck, and backed it up to the dock.

"Are you sure you're up for this?" he asked Mercy as he swung open the door of his duck's cargo hold, knowing full well that she would find the question unbearably condescending.

As if to prove that she didn't need anyone's help, least of all his, she snatched the dolly from its pegs on the wall, strode past him into the hold, and strapped the sailcloth-wrapped body to the rods with the practiced moves of an expert. Unfortunately, this particular corpse was extremely leaky, even through the thick canvas. Despite the fact that he had kept it on ice, the liquid rot wasn't completely frozen over, and Mercy wound up smearing it all over her hands and arms and the front of her overalls. Relishing her horror as it registered on her face, Hart sidled up to her, his tongue poking into the corner of his cheek. "I don't want to say I told you so, but—"

She wheeled the corpse past him, forcing him to step out of the autoduck to make room for her. "Hart-ache, if you don't want my help, maybe you should finally find yourself a partner."

The insinuation lit his Mercy Fuse, which was admittedly short. As if he would have any trouble finding a partner if he wanted one. Which he didn't.

"I didn't ask for your help," he shot back. "And look who's talking, by the way."

She halted the dolly and pulled out the kickstand with the toe of her sneaker. "What's that supposed to mean?"

"It means I don't see anyone helping you either." He fished inside his black vest for the paperwork she would need to complete in order to receive her government stipend for processing the body, and he held it out to her. He had long since learned to have his end all filled out ahead of time so that he didn't have to spend a second longer in her presence than was necessary.

She wiped one hand on the clean fabric over her ass before snatching the papers out of his hand. Without the consent of his reason, Hart's own hands itched with curiosity, wondering exactly how the round curves of her backside would feel in his grasp. His brain was trying to shove aside the unwanted lust when Mercy stepped into him and stood on her tiptoes. Most women couldn't get anywhere near Hart's head without the assistance of a ladder, but Mercy was tall enough to put her into kissing range when she stood on the tips of her red canvas shoes. Her big brown eyes blazed behind the lenses of her glasses, and the unexpected proximity of her whole body felt bizarrely intimate as she fired the next words into his face.

"Do you know what I think, Hart-ache?"

He swallowed his unease and kept his voice cool. "Do tell, Merciless."

"You must be a pathetically friendless loser to be this much of a jerk." On the word *jerk*, she poked him in the chest with the emphatic pointer finger of her filthy hand, dotting his vest with brown rot and making him stumble onto the edge of the dock. Then she pulled down the gate before he could utter another word, letting it slam shut between them with a resounding *clang*.

Hart stood teetering on the lip of the dock in stunned silence. Slowly, insidiously, as he regained his balance, her words seeped beneath his skin and slithered into his veins.

I will never come here again unless I absolutely have to, he promised himself for the hundredth time. Birdsall & Son was not the only official drop-off site for bodies recovered in Tanria without ID tags. From now on, he would take his keyless cadavers to Cunningham's. But as he thought the words, he knew they constituted a lie. Every time he slayed an indigent drudge in Tanria, he brought the corpse to Birdsall & Son, Undertakers.

For a dog.

Because he was a pathetically friendless loser.

He already knew this about himself, but the fact that Mercy knew it, too, made his spine bunch up. He got into his auto-duck and drove to the station, his hands white-knuckling the wheel as he berated himself for letting Mercy get to him.

Mercy, with her snotty *Oh. It's you.* As if a dumpster rat had waltzed into her lobby instead of Hart.

Mercy, whose every word was a thumbtack spat in his face, pointy end first.

The first time he'd met her, four years ago, she had walked into the lobby, wearing a bright yellow dress, like a jolt of sunlight bursting through glowering clouds on a gloomy day. The large brown eyes behind her glasses had met his and widened, and he could see the word form in her mind as she took in the color of his irises, as pale and colorlessly gray as the morning sky on a cloudy day.

Demigod.

Now he found himself wondering which was worse: a pretty young woman seeing him as nothing more than the offspring of a divine parent, or Merciless Mercy loathing him for the man he was.

Any hope he'd cherished of skulking back to his post in Sector W-38 unremarked vanished when he heard Chief Maguire's voice call to him from the front door of the West Station, as if she had been standing at the blinds in her office, waiting to pounce.

"Marshal Ralston."

His whole body wanted to sag at the sound of Alma's voice, but he forced himself to keep his shoulders straight as he took his pack out of the passenger seat and shut the door with a metallic *clunk*. "Hey, Chief."

"Where you been?"

"Eternity. I took out a drudge in Sector W-38, but it didn't have a key. Decomp was so bad, I decided to bring him in early. Poor pitiful bastard."

Alma scrutinized him over the steaming rim of her ever-present coffee mug, her aquamarine demigod eyes glinting in her wide brown face.

Hart's lips thinned. "Are you implying that *I'm* a poor pitiful bastard?"

"It's not so much an implication as a stone-cold statement of fact."

"Hardly."

"You have no social life. You work all the time. You don't even have a place to hang your hat. You might put up in a hotel for a few nights, but then you come right back here." She jerked her thumb toward the Mist, the cocoon of churning fog that formed the border of Tanria beyond the West Station. "This shithole is your home. How sad is that?"

Hart shrugged. "It's not so bad."

"Says you. I assume you took the body to Cunningham's?"

"No."

She raised an *I take no bullshit from you* eyebrow at him before leaning on the hood of his duck, and Hart frowned when she spilled a few drops of coffee onto the chipped blue paint. It was rusty enough as it was; she didn't need to go making it worse.

"Look, Ralston, we rely on the undertakers. We need them to do their jobs so that we can do ours."

Great. A lecture from his boss. Who used to be his partner and his friend. Who called him Ralston now.

"I know."

"You are aware of the fact that Roy Birdsall almost died a few months ago, right?"

Hart shifted his weight, the soles of his boots grinding into the gravel of the parking lot. "No."

"Well, he did. Heart attack or something. In theory, he's running the office, but Mercy's the one taking care of everything at Birdsall & Son—boatmaking, body prep, all of it."

"So?" His tone was petulant, but the memory of a disheveled Mercy with corpse rot smeared over her front made a frond of guilt unfurl in his gut.

"So if you're going to patronize Birdsall's, cut Mercy some slack and play nice. If you can't do that, go to Cunningham's. All right?"

"Yep, fine. Can I go now?" He adjusted his hat on his head, a clear signal that he was preparing to exit the conversation and get on with his job, but Alma held up her free hand.

"Hold on. I've been meaning to talk to you about something."

Hart grunted. He knew what was coming.

"Don't give me that. You've gone through three partners in four years, and you've been working solo for months. It's too dangerous to keep going it alone. For any of us." She added that last bit as if this conversation were about marshals in general rather than him specifically, but Hart knew better.

"I don't need a partner."

She gave him a look of pure exasperation, and for a fraction of a second, Hart could see the old Alma, the friend who'd been there for him when his mentor, Bill, died. She dismissed him with a jerk of her head. "Go on. But this conversation isn't finished."

He'd walked a few paces toward the stables when Alma called after him, "Come over for dinner one of these days, will you? Diane misses you."

This peace offering was almost certainly Diane's doing, and he could tell that it was as hard for Alma to deliver her wife's invitation as it was for Hart to hear it.

"Yep," he answered and continued on his way to the stables, but they both knew he wouldn't be standing on Alma and Diane's doorstep anytime soon. Although he and Alma had long since made peace on the surface of things, the old grudge hung in the air, as if Bill's ghost had taken up permanent residence in the space between them. Hart had no idea how to get past it, or if he wanted to, but it was painfully awkward to miss a friend when she was standing right behind him. It was worse to miss Diane. He almost never saw her anymore.

The stables were dark compared to the brutal sunlight of Bushong, and blessedly cooler, too. He went to the stalls to see which mounts were available. He knew it would be slim pickings at this time of day, but he was unprepared for how bad the pickings were: a gelding so young, Hart didn't trust it not to

433

bolt at the first whiff of a drudge; an older mare he'd taken in a few times and found too slow and plodding for his liking; and Saltlicker.

Saltlicker was one of those equimares that bolted for water every chance he got and maintained a constant, embittered opposition to anyone who dared to ride him. Some marshals liked him for his high-spiritedness; Hart loathed the beast, but of the three options, Saltlicker was, sadly, the best choice.

"Wonderful," Hart griped at him.

Saltlicker snorted, shook out his kelp-like mane, and dipped lower in his trough, blowing sulky bubbles in the water, as if to say, *The feeling's mutual, dickhead.*

All at once, an oppressive sadness overtook Hart. It was one thing to dislike an equimaris; it was another to have the equimaris hate him back. And honestly, who did genuinely like Hart these days? Mercy's barbed insult, which had followed him all the way from Eternity, surfaced in his mind once more.

You must be a pathetically friendless loser to be this much of a jerk.

She had a point. Only a pathetically friendless loser would face his nemesis time and again to pet her dog for five minutes.

Maybe I should suck it up and get another dog, he thought, but the second he entertained the idea, he knew he could never replace Gracie. And that left him with nothing but the occasional visit to Leonard.

Hart knew that he needed to get to his post, but he wound up sitting against the stable wall, shrouded in shadows. As if it had a mind of its own—call it ancient muscle memory—his hand snaked into his pack and pulled out his old notebook and a pen.

When he had first joined the Tanrian Marshals after his mother died, he used to write letters to her and slide them into nimkilim boxes whenever he and his mentor, Bill, made their way to the station or to a town. Then, after Bill was killed, Hart wrote to him, too, mostly letters full of remorse. But he hadn't written to either of them in years, because at the end of the day, it wasn't like they could write back. And that was what he wanted, wasn't it? For someone—anyone—to answer?

Poor pitiful bastard, the blank page splayed across his thighs seemed to say to him now. He clicked open the pen and wrote *Dear,* hesitated, and then added the word *friend.*

He had no idea how much time passed before he tore out the page, folded it into fourths, and got to his feet, relieving his aching knees. There was a similar relief in his aching chest, as if he'd managed to pour some of that loneliness from his heart onto the paper. Glancing about him to make sure he was unobserved as he crossed the stable yard, he walked to the station's nimkilim box and slid the note inside, even though he was certain that a letter addressed to no one would never be delivered to anyone.

Follow us:

f **/orbitbooksUS**

🐦 **/orbitbooks**

▶ **/orbitbooks**

Join our mailing list
to receive alerts on our
latest releases and deals.

orbitbooks.net

Enter our monthly
giveaway for the chance
to win some epic prizes.

orbitloot.com